Sir Ranulph Fiennes,  The Guinness Book of living explorer'. A former member of the SAS and the Army of the Sultan of Oman, he became the first man to reach both Poles by surface travel in 1982 and to cross the Antarctic landmass unsupported in 1993. He is the author of two previous bestselling books, *The Feather Men* and *The Sett*, as well as numerous works of expedition biography.

Also by Ranulph Fiennes

THE
SECRET
HUNTERS

Ranulph Fiennes

timewarner
paperbacks

A *Time Warner* Paperback

First published in Great Britain in 2001
by Little, Brown and Company

This edition published by Time Warner Paperbacks in 2002

*This is a work of fiction, portions of which are
based on actual events and real people.*

A CIP catalogue record for this book
is available from the British Library.

ISBN 0 7515 3193 6

Typeset in Imprint by M Rules
Printed and bound in Great Britain
by Clays Ltd, St Ives plc

Time Warner Paperbacks
An imprint of
Time Warner Books UK
Brettenham House
Lancaster Place
London WC2E 7EN

www.TimeWarnerBooks.co.uk

ACKNOWLEDGEMENTS

I am especially grateful to Mike Kobold of Frankfurt for his support, intelligence and patience in tracing the SS guards; for obtaining, despite considerable procrastination from the German and Austrian authorities, the relevant war criminal records and translating them; and for accompanying me on our many interviews with survivors and witnesses in Sudetenland.

My thanks to: Frances Pajović and Gina Rawle for all their hard work on the text; to Graeme Atkinson, Ben Barkow, Charles Petrie and Alan Carroll for their expertise and their time; to my wife Ginny for her patience; to the survivors for checking the accuracy of Ruth Jacobs' memory of the death march; and to Yurka Galitzine for his inspiration to the Secret Hunters. And of course, my thanks to Derek Jacobs, should he ever read this book.

For the many ways in which they have helped me, I am also grateful to: Bill Berry; Tamsyn Berryman; Peter Booth; Richard Boylan; Ray Brown; Alan

Carroll; Mitchell Coen; Steve Colwell; Gerry
Nicholson and Joanna Rae of the British Antarctic
Survey; Sue Young and Geoff Armitage at the
British Library Map Room; Norman Cobley; Neal
Davidge; Günther Degen; Renate Dindova-Silbiger;
Alwyn and Soo Dixon; Gudrun Döllner; Eva Erben;
John Bruno and Janet Baldwin of The Explorers
Club, New York; James Findlay; Lothar Fleischer;
Julian Freeman-Attwood; Gernot Freyer; Pete Goss;
Hilary Hale; John Heap; Greville Janner; Terry
Jesudason; David and Andrea Juleff; Cordula
Kappner; Rudy Kellar; Tony Kemp; Jadzia Kichler
and her son Harry; Halina Kleiner; Arnd Kluge;
William Knight; Robin Knox-Johnston; Minia
Kohn; Chana Kotlizki and her daughter Yona Kobo;
Lola Krispow; Liane Kümmerl; Kevin Lambe;
Trude Levi; Martyn Lewis; Megan Lewis; Charlie
Loader; Allan Hopton at Marine Instruments;
Marion Margies and Ludwig Mertel; Dick de Mildt;
Paul Cook at the National Maritime Museum; Skip
Novak; Heather and James O'Brien; Leon Paget;
Ken Pawson; Klaus Rauh; Geoff Renner; John
Reynolds; Martina Röber; Judith Reifen-Ronen;
Karl-Georg Rössler; Shirley Sawtell of the Scott
Polar Research Institute; Lilli Silbiger; Waltraud
Schmidt; Helen Stafford; Pamela Stevenson; Gordon
'Sockeye' Thomas; Sasha Treuherz; Steffen Unger;
Ruth Vered; Ed Victor; Jana, Svatopluk and Samuel
Vokurka; Reg Warkentin; Simon Wiesenthal; Gerda
Weissman-Klein and Kurt Klein; Reinhard Wentz;
Shaul Ferrero and Nomi Halpern at Yad Vashem.

THE
SECRET
HUNTERS

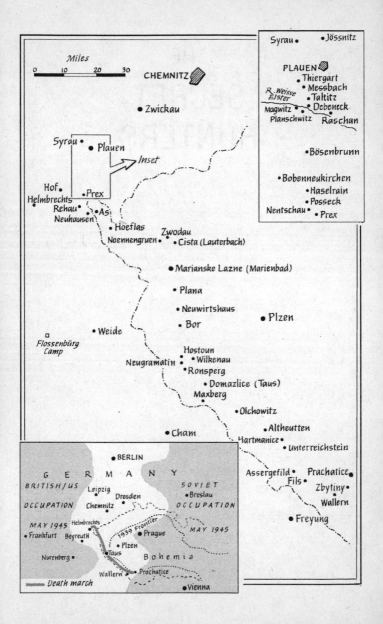

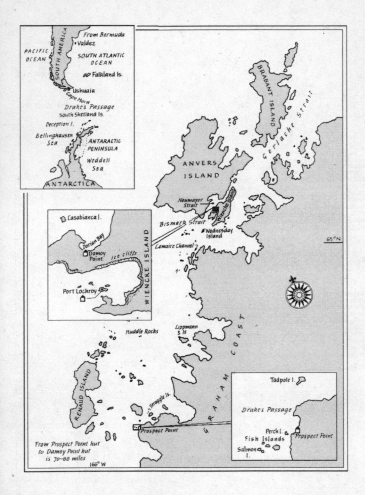

PROLOGUE

In 1995, I was paid by Abercrombie and Kent to lecture to 100 American and British passengers during a journey to the rugged coastline of Antarctica on their expedition ship, the MS *Explorer*.

Due to loose ice conditions, the ship managed to visit a deserted hut where scientists had worked in the 1950s. The senior British lecturer on board was Dr John Reynolds, one of Britain's most experienced polar geologists. He and I were dispatched in a rubber boat to check the safety of the hut before the passengers were allowed to land. Erected on a rocky spit, a stone's throw from the sea, the squat wooden shack sported six cramped bunks, a cosy eating space and a well-equipped kitchen.

Although the hut was still in surprisingly good condition, the roof was leaking and many of the scientific record books stashed on the kitchen shelves were damp, rotting and stuck together. We decided to remove them and, from the ship, cabled Dr John Heap, the Director of Britain's Scott Polar Research Institute. He suggested we take the records to the British Antarctic Survey in Cambridge for conservation.

Back at the Royal Geographical Society in London, I found that one of the books, which was bound differently from the rest, was not a scientific record at all, but the logbook of a yacht. Intrigued, I retained it, and informed the Polar Institute accordingly. I intended to unstick the pages but an expedition project got in the way, and it was not until early in the year 2000, while incapacitated by frostbite injuries, that I finally began to slit the pages apart with partial success.

The text was riveting, and I took a summary of its contents to my London publishers who commissioned me to reproduce it as a book. From those pages that I managed to salvage, the story appeared to be that of a fifty-five-year-old Canadian stranded at the hut in early 1994.

I sometimes spent a full working day unsticking just two badly pulped-together pages; others defeated me wholly, and some passages were only intermittently clear between blotches. I still cannot be one hundred per cent certain that every last detail of Derek Jacobs' remarkable story is as he wrote it, but I have done my best to fill in the gaps with my own careful research.

Where deciphering the text was impossible, I met up with Antarctic experts, death march survivors, members of the French secret services and German monitors of neo-nazism. I followed the nightmare route of the march through Sudetenland and spoke with witnesses in Prague.

I am aware that Derek Jacobs may at some point resurface and claim this book as his intellectual property, but I think it is more likely that he is dead. His story is a terrible indictment of man's inhumanity to man, of unimaginable cruelty by civilised people in our enlightened times. It is also a story of courage, love and endurance against great odds and great evil.

I feel no moral unease at presenting Derek Jacobs' account as my own book, for he wrote about himself and his family with the express intention of the pages being published one day. He wanted the world to know his story, his accusation.

Is what he wrote fact or fiction? I believe it to be true, but I was not there and I have not met him. So I have called the book fiction, and for this I apologise to him, to his family and to the survivors, especially those I have named. As for Michael Weingärtner, and those of his evil colleagues who still feel no remorse, I wonder how even God will find a way to forgive them. For those who join the Secret Hunters, forgiving is not the chosen option.

CHAPTER ONE

14 December 1993. We are stuck here on this remote and ice-girded coastline with plenty of food and a reasonable hope that, when summer comes, a yacht or tourist ship will visit and rescue us. We must stay mentally active to keep our spirits up. Thuy is so good-natured and easy. She has encouraged me to write this; my life story. When we are rescued I will check out the names and details, and find a publisher. I have always meant to bear witness to my family's time of terror and to my quest for justice, as nobody else can. I think I had best start back in 1975 – the turning point.

I was born in war-torn Germany in 1939, and grew up with the belief that RAF fire-bombs had killed all my family save my Aunt Ruth, who emigrated to Canada with me in 1946. I passed a happy childhood in a suburb of Ottawa and became a freelance welfare worker, specialising in the care of refugee children, often in trouble spots.

During my first working visit to Cambodia, I lived

in a small village near Phnom Penh. We treated poor people at a simple surgery set up by the French mission who paid my expenses. The Cambodians were gentle, lovely folk, and I fell for Sinoy Yan, whose black hair shone like the Mekong in moonlight. She was married to a major in the Cambodian Army, which for three years had fought a bitter civil war with the Communist Khmer Rouge.

On free afternoons, I would meet Sinoy by an old coconut tree near the river. The water was clear where we swam, and the sand warm. In the twilight, when a fresh breeze kept the insects away, we lay naked together and listened to the mango and banana trees outside the village whispering in the wind.

Some months later, on New Year's Day 1975, I met up with Sinoy at a karaoke bar in Phnom Penh. She had telephoned out of the blue demanding to see me urgently but giving no explanation. I was surprised as she had tearfully decided to end our relationship the previous month when her husband had come back from the front missing a leg.

She was wearing a fashionable blue mini-skirt which reminded me of the wonders of her body. Sinoy, however, was definitely not thinking of sex. She loved me, she said, and this was her only chance to warn me to leave Cambodia at once as Phnom Penh would be overrun by the Khmer Rouge by the end of the week. Her twin brother, Hong, was a Khmer Rouge leader, and he had arrived at her house the previous night to warn her to save herself while she still could. He had told her that, like all families of civil servants, she was on the death list of *Angka*.

'Who is *Angka*?' I asked her.

'The faceless group who control the PCK, the *Parti Communiste Khmer*.'

'And who are the PCK?'

She shook her head. 'They are extreme Communists who have eliminated most rival leadership factions. Their tactics are death and their strategy is murder. Even my brother fears them for he is an urban Communist.'

'What's wrong with that?' I was confused. 'Marx, Stalin and Lenin were all urbanists.'

'The PCK believe only in peasant power. They will kill all civil servants, intellectuals and city-dwellers. Outside Phnom Penh the process is already underway.'

A sprig of hibiscus nestled by Sinoy's ear where her hair snaked back. Its fragrance made me think of our days of blue skies and white sand by the Mekong. The PCK were just Cambodians, I reflected, and I knew Cambodians as gentle, lovely folk.

Sinoy's delicate fingers reached across the table for my arm. 'I will tell you something you must not pass on or my brother will die. I tell you only so that you will *know* you must go now. Tomorrow may be too late. I would come too, but my place is beside my husband and he will not leave.'

She leaned closer across the table, and I felt a twinge of regret at the memory of her dark-nippled breasts.

'Hong has come to Phnom Penh to warn the army, through my husband, of the major Communist offensive that will start tomorrow. He is disillusioned with the PCK because of what he has witnessed in the regions they already control. They divide people into "old" or "new". All "new" people are to be wiped out through death or slave labour. Only "old" people – peasants, villagers and uneducated farmers – are "correct". These are the types they make into leaders and managers. They teach them to hunt and destroy "new" people. They train them to suspect each other too, to hate and to cheat, to betray relatives and friends.

'Hong's men wear black uniforms with red *kramas* on their heads like the Apache warriors in John Wayne movies. They boast about their killings. Hong says *Angka* has a list of who to suspect and who to kill. Babies and children and women are to be treated like grown men. PCK cadres are to kill people from any town: merchants, police, poets, clever people, students, tailors, monks, doctors, teachers, people wearing spectacles or carrying books. Also businessmen, traders, rich farmers, landowners and people who speak a foreign language.'

Sinoy laughed, a bitter sound. 'That means you and me and everyone we know. All of us are on the list to die. Hong says *Angka* warn their cadres that these enemies will try to hide, so the PCK must watch for behaviour signs which will give away the guilty. These include people who are too popular, lazy, troublesome, clever, bold, individualistic, soft-fingered, considerate or loving.'

I knew Sinoy was incapable of lying to me or to anyone else. She was telling me all this purely to persuade me to flee Cambodia, and had no ulterior motive. But the PCK were just people like Sinoy's brother. They were country folk who lived in a beautiful paradise where the pace of life was slow and courteous, as it had been for centuries.

Sinoy must have seen my doubtful frown. '*Angka*,' she pressed me, 'teaches not to kill with bullets, as those must be saved for battle. They favour the old way of *vay choul* whereby their soldiers beat in the "new" person's skull and vertebrae with a field hoe. All peasants have hoes.'

She paused to sip her drink, and to check that her words were sinking in. They were.

'Hong says he has seen great cruelties but that *Angka* executes those who show repulsion at such acts. People to be butchered must first dig churn-sized holes then kneel by them. When they finish their pits, soldiers will come to crack their skulls and kick them into the holes. Others come and stomp them down. These *vay choul* victims are blessed with luck. The less lucky are tied up and thrown into deep mud, hanged slowly, boiled in pots, or raped and burned. Babies are used for football or knife practice. Children must kill parents. This is the way of *Angka*, the monster that will be here tomorrow. I love you Derek, and you *must* go today.'

'How can I go, knowing that you will stay and be killed? Surely you can come too. There is nothing to stop you. You have cousins in New York—'

Sinoy put her hand over my mouth. 'You go now. If I can change my husband's mind, we will come soon. I promise. You cannot help me by staying here.'

I did leave Phnom Penh with help from my charity

employers, for there was a general exodus, and Sinoy's prediction did prove partly correct. A major attack *was* launched by 50,000 Khmer Rouge on 8 January, but somehow the army held on for a year before finally yielding. Sinoy and many others did escape the killing fields of *Angka*, but a million Cambodians were not so lucky. They perished at the hands of their fellow countrymen and for five long years the paradise that I remembered became a living hell.

At the time, I felt sure that the horror of *Angka* was a one-off, an aberration. In Ottawa, where my loving Aunt Ruth had brought me up, I had known only kindness and charity, tolerance and understanding. Since leaving school in 1957 and training at college for a year to be a social worker, my innate faith in the goodness of humanity had taken only a few minor knocks, especially on postings to Africa. I was thirty-five at the time of Sinoy's revelations about *Angka* in the karaoke bar, and her words served as a warning of what was to come.

The polar wind cut knife-like through our Ottawa suburb of Nepean that January of 1975. The cosy little apartment I shared with Aunt Ruth was the only home I knew.

'I always thought that one day,' my aunt admonished, 'you would be a big man in business, like your grandfather. But no, *Traume sind Schaume*, dreams are bubbles. You're too keen on helping others to make good for yourself.' Aunt Ruth loved to scold me. At 65 her mind was razor-sharp, honed by her avid reading of anything and everything to do with history which she ordered through the local library.

'What I do is *your* fault, Auntie. You fixed my morals and my leanings long before I was old enough to think straight.'

She chuckled as she limped across the spotless but threadbare carpet. All the toes on one of her feet and three on the other were missing. I had long since given up asking her about her toes. Her stock response was, 'Don't look at the past. It is usually sad. Only memories and shadows.'

We had come from Germany, the Communist bit; that much I knew. A handsome Canadian truck driver, whom I had always known as Uncle Pete, had brought us both to Ottawa in 1946 when he was demobbed from the US Army. My first clear memory was as a six-year-old being held high by Uncle Pete as our ship berthed at Halifax.

Aunt Ruth was in remission from breast cancer, and for the past 18 months she had stayed well. It was clear she remembered Germany with both longing and pain. She would tell me how beautiful she and my mother had been in their youth. Her own beauty had never quite faded, but she had always smoked heavily which, along with the deep reservoir of grief and fear never far from the surface, had lined her face and buried her sparkle.

There were other clues to our past if you looked hard enough. Aunt Ruth never slept well. For as long as I could remember she had suffered from night-mares, calling out from her nocturnal terrors and needing sleeping pills to rest her weary mind. She very rarely talked about our past, her schooldays, where she had travelled, the escapades of her friends or even of her own sister, my mother. If ever I tried to prompt her she would retreat into silence and the pain in her eyes would hurt me, so I learned not to ask questions.

When I told her about Sinoy and her horror stories about the *Angka*, my aunt showed a familiar reluctance to talk on such a subject or even to listen. 'Where do you go next?' she asked, to close the topic.

'I have a three-week project in the North West Territories starting on Monday.'

She flinched imperceptibly, as was always the case when I announced I was soon to leave home.

'But you have only just got back from those *schreckliche* Khmers,' she murmured.

The next week, when the cab arrived to take me to the airport, Aunt Ruth gave me a pair of knee-high, white woolly socks with the red outline of a maple leaf on each turn-over. 'To keep you warm.' She hugged me, her head just reaching my chest. 'And you watch out for yourself with all those Eskimit *Menschen*.'

'Inuit,' I corrected her. 'And don't worry. It'll be a cinch after Cambodia. I'll write when I've settled in. I'll be back in three weeks.'

The cab driver was from Ghana so we talked about Africa. We passed along Foxhill Way and out of Nepean. My home town had been just a village when Uncle Pete, with help from Wartime Housing and Veterans' Affairs, had taken a rather poky little soap-box house just off Merivale Road in 1949. The

previous three years we had squatted, as had many
other returned vets, in one of the tourist cabins along
the Prescott Highway. Uncle Pete had found good
work at the McClelland door factory and later with
Canada Post, while my aunt's life had revolved
around my schooling and forcing the past from her
mind.

In the mid-1950s we bought our house from the
Crown. I progressed to Nepean High from Merivale
School, and finally, largely thanks to Uncle Pete's vet-
eran status, I graduated to Carleton University.
Academia did not enthuse me but, for a while, I was
among the top dozen cross-country skiers in Ontario.

After finishing college in 1958, I had spent a year
settling Aunt Ruth into a well-appointed apartment
in a more suitable part of Nepean which had grown
by then into a suburb of the capital. Just before the
move, Uncle Pete had died unexpectedly of a heart
attack, so I had taken a fill-in job at the local Pepsi
bottling plant. Preferring to make use of my social
work skills however, I had quickly switched to a part-
time paid job caring for children at a Catholic-run
orphanage. I stuck at this on and off until the late
'60s, when the government-sponsored Children's Aid
Society took over and the policy of child placement
with foster families closed down the orphanages
throughout Ontario.

To supplement my aunt's state pension, I always
sent a part of my wages back to her bank account.
This seldom amounted to much since many of the
jobs I took paid expenses only, but then I had no children and no expensive habits to service, and all my

travel, food and accommodation were provided by the charities or welfare agencies.

Until 1974, I could see no reason to change my way of life. I considered myself to be as lucky, happy and fulfilled as any man anywhere and a lot better off than most. As for marriage and children, there was plenty of time for that. I had enjoyed a long succession of pretty girls in many countries; usually married ones who had not been on the lookout for a permanent lover, and whose tears at our inevitable parting had been brief enough to ensure no mascara smudges were evident when they returned home to cook their husbands' dinner.

At the airport, I tipped the cabby well and he wished me 'a good time when you next go to my Africa'. As Air Canada wafted me at 600 miles per hour over the huge tundra of the North West Territories, I glanced at a copy of *The Ottawa Citizen*. Phnom Penh was under siege and America was reeling from the Watergate scandal. I ordered the chicken and rice menu option and settled back with the newspaper.

The Aerobar Club on Montreal's Cote Deliass Street gyrated. Aurora-like violet and green rays pulsed from ceiling strobes and caressed the writhing human carpet on the dance floor. Spilt beer and body odour doubtless neutralised any hovering pheromones, but the universal aim of most Aerobar clients was clearly sex. For the less ambitious, a dance with one of the girls cost five dollars, as did a drink or a hamburger with fries.

At the club, the local girls from Ontario and Quebec were outnumbered by professional strippers from South America and Asia. Table-dancing was in its infancy and the bar rules were not firmly established. Some girls slapped any male fingers inserted under their sequinned G-strings, but permitted the placing of dollar notes in their cleavage. And some, while rotating their buttocks over the straining laps of their seated customers, allowed their nipples to be kissed or even nibbled. Others restricted their activities to erotic sequences of table-top squirms with frequent off-putting admonishments of 'Don't touch me!'

A sudden scattering of chairs in the far corner of the table bar went unseen by the main mass of dancers but interrupted all nearby activities. A vicious fist fight had started between a German client and an in-house bouncer. The latter was young, bald and massive, but his middle-aged opponent, though frail-looking, moved fast and skilfully. Within seconds the bouncer fell to his knees clutching at his eyes, blood gushing from under his hands. 'My eyes,' he screamed. 'I'm blind.' Another bouncer appeared and pinioned the German. Two well-dressed men from his table, their hands outstretched in the international gesture of 'I surrender', assured the bouncer that there would be no more trouble. A large cash bribe was proffered, accepted and pocketed in the blink of an eye, and calm returned to the bar. The bleeding bouncer was led backstage; the naked table-girls meanwhile, had noticed nothing.

The three Germans left the club immediately and

the following evening, when a Royal Canadian Mounted Police (RCMP) Special Branch officer called at the Aerobar, neither the bouncers nor the habitual clients he questioned could recall what the three foreigners had looked like. The injured bouncer, who later lost the sight of one eye, had merely been doing his job trying to eject the customer, who according to one of the girls, had 'put his finger up my ass'. The German had then started the fight.

The RCMP file on the Aerobar incident back in 1975, formed part of a report which I saw for the first time 18 years later in 1993. The full report, as pieced together by the authorities, covered the three Germans' activities over a two-day period in Montreal as well as their subsequent three-week stay at a top-secret Canadian military base called Alert. A taxi had taken them from the Aerobar back to their hotel, the Dorval Hilton at Montreal Airport, and the cab driver had remembered the foreigners well due to the furious, but unintelligible tongue-lashing one of them had received from the other two. The RCMP officer who had compiled the file had included a comment for 7 February 1975: *Tango One (Bendl) was presumably reprimanding Tango Three (no identity yet) for risking their whole operation by his behaviour in the club.*

The report revealed that one or more of the staff at the Dorval Hilton's reception desk was salaried by Special Branch to place certain guests in certain suites. These suites were pre-bugged on a permanent basis and RCMP-monitored. Although nothing was stated, it seemed clear to me that the RCMP knew the Bendl group's Stasi identity from the outset. I could not tell, and presumably neither could the RCMP, whether Bendl was a real name or an alias.

On returning in a foul mood from the Aerobar outing, Bendl had placed a call from his room to a private Ottawa number which Special Branch had identified as a rented apartment used by a German diplomat who was a known agent of the *Staats-Sicherheit* (the Stasi), the East German intelligence network. The content of the call consisted exclusively of a supermarket shopping list; a code system unknown to the RCMP.

Their antennae quivering, the Canadians checked with the airlines and found that all three Germans were booked to fly out of Montreal on 8 February, bound for the Inuit settlement of Resolute Bay on remote Cornwallis Island, a mere 750 miles south of the North Pole. This in itself was of no consequence, but Resolute Bay was also a key airport for flights heading further north to the most isolated base in North America, Canadian Forces Station Alert. The Canadians then investigated every possible passage out of Resolute and soon found that the Germans had chartered a direct flight to Alert on a de Havilland Twin Otter from Bradley Air Services.

A hundred of Canada's top snoopers under the command of Major R. V. Brown were manning Alert that Cold-War winter of 1974/75. They called themselves the Chosen Frozen. Only closely vetted workers were otherwise allowed to land at the base;

men needed to work either on the military installations or on the Atmospheric Environmental Services station, then known as DOE, just outside the camp perimeter. The Security Branch of the RCMP screened each and every worker before giving security clearance, but Bendl and company had somehow managed to sail right through. Heads would roll.

At the time, Canada was smarting from various insensitive and protective trade moves by the USA and so was co-operating more closely with the UK's MI6. The MI6 representative at the British High Commission in Ottawa was therefore called to a spur-of-the-moment meeting with several top-level Canadian spooks, and they offered him Bendl as a potential Stasi double agent. While he was at Alert, the Canadians would try to lure the German into turning traitor by offering him attractive financial rewards. His exact rank in the Stasi was unknown but, to be tasked with infiltrating Alert, he must be at least a senior field agent.

The MI6 man jumped at the offer, but was let down by his fellow countrymen at GCHQ Cheltenham who meanwhile had been asked by the RCMP to decipher the shopping-list code used by Bendl the previous day. GCHQ, for reasons of their own, had said they would love to help but had not yet broken that particular Stasi code system. Since the RCMP knew full well that they had, Canadian noses were put firmly out of joint and MI6 lost their unique chance of handling Bendl. All this was clear from the report, which included records of correspondence with Major Brown at Alert.

On 8 February, a duty officer at the Supplementary Radio System or 'Suprad' Headquarters in Tunney's Pasture, Ottawa, sent a coded message to Alert and copies to its satellite stations at Whitehorse in the Yukon, nearby Leitrim in suburban Ottawa and way down south in sunny Bermuda. All these stations were classified top secret and hid under the title 'direction finding units'. They passed on the information they gleaned from Soviet bloc communications to the Canadian Security Establishment in Ottawa, the UK and the National Security Agency in Virginia, USA.

That evening, Major Brown was watching a boxing match. Inside the warm and comfortable environment of the Alert officers' mess, he and a group of young, bearded captains hooted with laughter at the antics of two great Arctic hares boxing one another on a patch of snow immediately outside the window. The mess cook daily left scraps there for the hares, and somebody had fixed up a small floodlight to illuminate the boxing ring, as Alert was still sunless for twenty-four hours a day. The hares danced about on their hind legs, more agile even than Muhammad Ali, flinging uppercuts and sharp jabs with skill and aggression.

Suprad Ops Officer Bruce Gemmil called Major Brown away to the Ops Room where he scanned the message from Tunney's Pasture: a warning that one of three electricians scheduled to fly from Montreal to Alert via Resolute later that night was a suspected Stasi agent. Major Brown was instructed to do nothing that might alarm or tip off the German but to ensure that he would learn nothing that might be useful to the Stasi.

I had devoured the contents of the RCMP file,
eager to know what had happened to Bendl all those
years ago, but Major Brown's subsequent reports had
apparently been transcribed onto broadband tape and
shipped south by air. High Frequency radio had not
been trusted except for routine administrative communications. When I tried to trace the reports, an
RCMP archivist told me they had 'got lost'. Two
years later the Canadians had installed a microwave
link between Alert and the equally remote weather
station of Eureka where a satellite terminal rendered
broadband tape communications a thing of the past.
The Brown tapes seemed to have been a casualty of
technological progress.

So, in 1993, I learned that in February 1975, Bendl
and his two companions had flown from Montreal to
Alert via Resolute Bay, but not what subsequently
happened to them nor whether Bendl became a
double agent.

On 8 February 1975, I jogged from my well-heated
hut down the long, straight track to Resolute Bay's
garbage dump; a half hour's return trip was quite
enough for my first post-Cambodia outing. Phnom
Penh had provided few safe jogging zones away from
traffic pollution and I had grown seriously unfit. My
lungs objected to the −48°C air temperature so I
moved at the pace of a geriatric. I had completed
brief work periods in these northern settlements
twice before and had grown to respect the tough,
good-humoured Inuit.

The Resolute Bay Inuit had been shipped here in

the 1950s after some heavy-handed persuasion by the government. In 1953 our prime minister had been worried that a vast tract of our barren northland was in danger of being claimed by the United States. To stake a foolproof claim of sovereignty over our Arctic lands, we had needed not just the odd RCMP outpost administering great chunks of tundra but a few Canadian citizens actually living there. 'This northland of ours,' Prime Minister St Laurent had noted, 'lies between the two great Cold War powers of the USA and USSR. We must leave no doubt about our active occupation right up to the North Pole.'

It soon became obvious to all concerned, that the only Canadians capable of living self-sufficiently in such hostile terrain were the Inuit. And so a dozen families, from two separate settlements many hundreds of miles to the south of Resolute Bay, were shipped north and dumped there with little ceremony. Still less concern was given to keeping the government's initial promise to take these heroic 'volunteers' back home if they didn't like it.

Government officials later claimed that the Inuit had been advised in advance what the conditions in the High Arctic would be like. But in the summer of 1953, when an icebreaker left them here with no prospect of return, it must have seemed as though they had been landed in hell. One of them subsequently told me that Resolute's months of darkness had come as a dreadful shock. 'The first two years were terrible for all of us. We had assumed the sun would behave as it always had where we came from. But no, it got darker and darker, and each November it disappeared entirely. We called Resolute *Qausuittuq*, the place of darkness. Back home there had been plentiful game to hunt on land and in the ocean, but not at Resolute. Our diet had to change and so did our traditional hunting skills. Everything was new. We were very hungry for long periods. There was no available water to drink except from the sea-ice floating in the sea which we had to collect.'

There was no love lost either between the two original Inuit clans which were settled in Resolute, and there was still some evidence of this more than twenty years later when I came to know several of them quite well. There were murders and ostracism. Teenagers were not encouraged to socialise outside their own clan, but the only other choice led more often than not to incest and a good deal of child abuse. This happens all over the world, even in well-populated cities, but as the exception rather than the rule. In Resolute, it was commonplace.

By 1975, things had improved a great deal but there was still much to be done by visiting social workers like me and, I felt, a lot of guilt to assuage, since it was my own government that had caused all the hardship in hoodwinking the families to locate here in the first place. In Africa and Asia, I had never held myself personally responsible for the plight of my temporary charges. Here it was different.

As I drew near to the garbage zone, I kept a wary eye out for the polar bears that often raided the dump when game was scarce. They could be difficult to spot even when the sky was brilliant with stars and the snowscape lit by moonlight. The moving shadows of scudding clouds added animation and menace to the stark beauty of the island.

I heard the drone of an aircraft circling above as I reached the end of the dump track. The arrival of the twice-weekly Nordair flight from Montreal, regular as clockwork when the weather allowed, was a main source of entertainment for both the Inuit from the village a mile south of the airport, and the whites, mostly civil servants, who worked in an assortment of huts clustered about the airstrip. We went to watch new arrivals or to see off departing colleagues, and also to catch up with local gossip, especially about who was sharing a bed with whom in the largely unmarried white community. In Resolute, the term 'unmarried' often meant that the person's spouse was not in Resolute at the time.

I speeded up a touch on the run back and headed straight for the airport building. A light breeze made my eyes water and the tips of my ears tingle under my thin, silk face mask, but I felt good, and proud in a macho sort of way, of the frost lining on my newly grown 'polar' moustache.

I reached the squat green hut of the airport just as the roar of the arriving Nordair Boeing 737's reverse thrust powered through the Arctic air, forming a dense fog all over the airstrip as the different temperatures met and moisturised the atmosphere.

In the friendly warmth of the airport lounge, a Hudson Bay Company worker who was a part-timer like me, bought me a Coke and we parked our backsides against a luggage bench.

'The word is that the Polar Shelf people have

taken on a blonde glaciologist from Toronto who goes like a racoon. She should be on this flight.'

'You said that last week,' I responded, but kept a sharp lookout for blonde hair as arrivals in the hall stomped snow off their feet and lowered their parka hoods.

'Finders keepers,' said my friend. 'The first to speak to her gets the first date.'

'I'll go for the first of us that *she* speaks to.' The Hudson Bay man had thick-lensed spectacles and a nose like Pierre Trudeau's so I fancied my chances if the blonde turned up.

Three men in blue parkas and white plastic moon-boots approached the coffee machine. I scanned the growing throng in the hall as the last of the new arrivals gathered by the baggage zone. No blonde. But a plump girl, looking self-conscious and vulner-able, was standing by herself. Very nice eyes, I noticed. Knowing that I was but one of at least a dozen predatorial airport vultures and that every second counted, I lurched forward from the bench, intent only on the girl with nice eyes. Pushing through a mêlée of Inuits hugging other Inuits with the happy laughter of old friends reunited, I bumped into one of the parka-and-moonboot trio, a big man.

'Watch it!' he snapped. As I apologised, he glanced at me.

Whether it was the sound of his slightly accented voice or the sight of his face, I will never know, but in that instant I *knew* that I feared him. More than fear, I felt the terror of a rabbit trapped by a snake. And an emotion very rare for me, hatred. Had I suddenly come face to face with the Devil himself, I could not have experienced a greater sense of menace than that which emanated from this unknown, yet somehow familiar, face in the crowd.

Acting entirely from instinct, I lunged out, my still gloved fist striking his mouth.

After that, I can remember only the local RCMP officer, Neal Davidge, enquiring if I felt okay. I did not. I had been simultaneously kneed in the groin and headbutted. As I recovered my senses, and realised that I was on a bench in the local RCMP prison cell, Constable Davidge warned me that I was lucky the transitee, an electrician apparently, had not pressed charges against me for unprovoked assault. Within an hour he had caught a Bradley Air charter flight north to Alert, no doubt wondering who I was and why I had assaulted him.

'You can go home now,' the officer told me, 'but make sure this doesn't get to be a habit.'

Back in my room, close by the Hudson Bay Company store, I took a hot shower and tried to work out the reason for my behaviour at the airport. I was certain that I *knew* the man. I was not suffering from 'winteritis', the term old hands used to describe the erratic behaviour of those who had been up north too long. I was clear-headed and sober. Why then, had I behaved so out of character? I was not normally aggressive; I avoided trouble. But somehow I knew the man had *not* been a stranger, and that could only mean one thing. He came from the blank time in my life, from my 'life before', which was the term Aunt Ruth used on those rare occasions when someone unwittingly broached the topic of that period.

Now, however much it upset her, my aunt must tell me everything. I must peel back the scar tissue that covered my childhood years and identify the face at the airport. Aunt Ruth was in remission, but I knew she could die any day if the cancer came back. Then there would be nobody left to tell me the secrets of my past.

When my tour in Resolute was over, Aunt Ruth welcomed me home in the same way she always had, as though I was the prodigal son. After the fatted calf, a small roast chicken, had been reduced to a carcass, she took to her chintz armchair by the oil stove and lit an untipped Camel with a wax taper. Matches were uneconomical.

'Come on now, boy.'

'Come on?'

'What is on your mind, little D? I read you like a book.' She peered at me above her bifocals through the wreaths of blue smoke. 'Since you came back you have been like a dog that wants a bone.'

I told her about the man at the airport, but not that I had hit him, for she hated violence. I tried to describe him. 'Maybe fifty. Powerful and tall. A face like Kirk Douglas, but cold eyes and a cold voice. Receding hair which I think had grey in it.'

She shook her head, then shrugged.

'His eyes were cold,' I repeated. 'The all-seeing, no-caring eyes of a shark and his voice was harsh . . . ugly. I *know* that I have seen his eyes and heard his

voice somewhere, sometime. I have wracked my brain
for a week now and I always end up suspecting it
came from the time before. Aunt Ruth, quite simply,
you must *please* tell me everything.'

She was quiet but, for the first time that I could
remember, the familiar pained look was absent. Her
expression was shrewd rather than sad, appraising
me.

'*Ach, neh,*' she sighed, her own particular version
of 'Oh, well.' 'I knew the time would have to come
and you are old enough. I had thought to wait for
your fortieth birthday but I may not last that long.
The memories of our family must not die with me.'

She moved to put the kettle on the hob and began
to talk about my mother. 'She was my friend as much
as my sister, was Anna. She never hurt anyone, but
nobody was ever more sinned against. For years I
wanted to see her killers crushed, to hear them
scream for mercy—' Realising what she had said, her
hands flew to her mouth. I rose and held her tightly.

'Aunt, I am ready for whatever you tell me.
However my parents died, we cannot bring them
back. It is worse for you as I have no memories of
them, Mother or Father. Take your time, there is no
hurry. I have waited this long.'

'You wonder why? Why I have never told you? It
was for your own good . . . and for my sanity.' She sat
down again and started to knit; something she always
did if she was not reading, sleeping or smoking. 'But
first' – again that shrewd look – 'can *you* not remember anything?'

I smiled. 'Only what I learned from you. Even my

"memory" of Mother is an amalgam of your own stories about her. Father, you once told me, was young and handsome. I sometimes think there was a dark garden, overgrown and exciting. There may have been some kind of funny uncle-type of person who I played with. Then there were terrible things on the edge of my dreams. There still are, even now, but they never materialise into recognisable images. They are just, I heard an apt phrase on the radio lately, chimeras of dread.'

I looked at my aunt. Her needles moved furiously as she nodded. She knew about such dreams.

'I think my first *clear* memory is of the ship. You held one of my hands, and Uncle Pete held the other and knelt down so I could see how grey and kind his eyes were. "This is Canada," he said. "Our home." There were cranes and people waving and foghorns.'

Aunt Ruth gave a little smile. 'Yes, Halifax. 6 August 1946, a year after the bombing of Hiroshima. We arrived in heaven that day.' She paused a while then added, 'My friends here still ask me how I feel about Germans. It is so many years now and I believe in forgiving. I forgive everyone else. But not the Germans. There is too much, things too terrible, to forgive or forget. No, I will never buy a German shoe or listen to a German composer. I *am* German and I grew up knowing that we were the greatest culture in the world, the embodiment of the word "civilised". So how come these same Germans became the most sadistic torturers in history? I saw it, I heard it, I felt it, I lived and smelled it through all those interminable years of hell. So, . . . forgive? I must leave that to you to decide once you know what they did to us.' She looked at me sharply. I nodded: I could see her point.

'We were chosen to survive, you and I,' she continued, 'just the two of us. One by one the rest of the family were taken. So why did God select us? Surely we are obliged to pay Him back, do something worthy with our lives? I have always believed my mission was to bring you up as your mother would have wanted. But a voice keeps asking me even today, what is the mission I should have been training you for? Should you find those who are guilty or should you leave them to God's own justice? That age-old conundrum of whether to turn the other cheek, or demand an eye for an eye.

'But my dear, you don't know what I am talking about. Blathering away, you are thinking. The old woman has finally taken leave of her senses.'

I smiled at her and shook my head. 'Enough of the old, Aunt Ruth. You are in your prime.'

She ignored me. 'For all these years I have kept the darkness in here.' She tapped her forehead. 'Memories never fade when you want them to. They are my inner life. Whatever I do, whoever I meet, the smell of fear, the feel of suspicion, hovers in the room. Tomorrow is something to be afraid of, for it will bring betrayal and terror. Of course, in gentle Ottawa that is so much *Quatsch*, rubbish, but try teaching my mind that.'

My aunt seemed so tiny in her big chair, shrivelled under burdens at which I could only guess.

'I am a survivor, Dieter,' she said, 'and survivors

are never the same people they were before the events
that nearly destroyed them. I go into Woolworths in
Nepean and I see the security guard. I feel again the
old fear. It is the same with soldiers and policemen,
any uniforms. A sudden knock on our door, the snarl
of a dog or a whistle blast. I cannot bear a blanket to
be grey . . .'

My aunt called me Dieter very rarely. When we
came to Canada, she had changed my name to Derek
as part of her break with all things German.

'Did you love Uncle Pete?' Her question came out
of the blue.

'Of course. I remember him as a gentle and funny
man. A natural Father Christmas who took on the
job of being my father and always made both of us
happy.'

My aunt smiled. 'That's the way I remember him
too. Amazing to think it's nearly seventeen years ago
now since he went. One day life was normal and I was
cooking his dinner. The next he was gone. That's the
way with heart problems.'

I held my aunt to me. We had both loved him.
Uncle Pete, my patron saint, my hero figure, who had
helped me with my homework, taught me to ski and
play handball, who in every way was the perfect
father to me from the age of six until I was nineteen.

'I have got over it,' said Aunt Ruth. 'I had always
prepared for the worst because as a truck driver, out
in all weathers and all over North America, you never
knew if he'd come back. But he was so strong. I never
thought his heart would go.' Her voice faltered.

Realising that my aunt was tired and upset, I

turned the conversation to lighter subjects and no more mention was made of the past that afternoon.

The following day, slowly and in her own round-about way, she began to tell me her life story. Aware that Aunt Ruth's health was fragile, and that this might be the only account of my family's history I would have, I had decided to tape her as she spoke. I placed my recorder on the table between us, switched it on and sat back.

For the past three and a half decades, I had believed I was a war orphan from a family of German Protestants killed in the great Dresden firestorms. My widowed aunt had met Uncle Pete, a truck driver with the US Army when the Allies liberated Germany, fallen in love with him and emigrated to Canada.

I had never questioned this version of my personal history. I was in for a shock.

CHAPTER TWO

'Our family had lived in eastern Germany for over nine hundred years, having arrived at the time of the Roman legions. We were Jews, but only after we were Germans.'

'Jews!' I interrupted. 'We were Jews? How come we are Christians now if we were always Jews?'

'*Halt die Klappe*, Dieter,' said my aunt. 'Don't interrupt. I was born in 1910, and by then the family was a higgledy-piggledy muddle of liberal Jews, reluctant Jews, purely nominal Jews and a few like my father who was *konfessionslos*, agnostic. When he married my Protestant mother, their wedding was merely a visit to the townhall to do their bit in the book of signatures. We never went to the synagogue but I occasionally accompanied Mother to her church in Plauen, our local town.

'On Jewish High Holidays, two dozen members of my father's extended family would eat in our living room and none bothered with Kosher food. Religious tolerance was the number one rule and we grew up

thinking of ourselves purely as middle-class
Germans. The Jewish connection was incidental and
unimportant to us, but settled in the Plauen area were
Jews from many countries and cultures. The Jewish
community, though small, was riven with contradic-
tions, but old Manny Heimann, a fair man, was for
thirty years the preacher, advisor and friend to
Orthodox and liberal Jews alike. He welded the community together from a makeshift synagogue in a
little room in Plauen's Schiller Street.

'Every Jewish family had its own rules, for they've
always been an individualistic lot. Look at the trouble
poor Moses had, and Israel today is riven with sec-
tarian schisms. I can remember Grandpa Eli saying
how common our Orthodox cousins were when they
weren't around. Most of them came from Poland and
spoke Yiddish, which to Grandpa was just an ugly
jargon. He, of course, was a cultured German and a
poet in the land of poets. He spouted Goethe to us at
the drop of a hat.

'Nowadays, I gather, Jösnitz is growing into a
suburb of Plauen, but back then we were quite isolated. We talked about the "lower village" in a
snobbish way rather than geographically, for there
were many hills and dales all around us, especially
off towards the village of Trieb, my favourite place.'

'Was Grandpa Eli very rich?' I asked.

'Ah, yes. Or so he'd have us believe. Always very
rich.' My aunt chuckled. 'But then before the first
great war the Plauen textiles trade made over a hundred millionaires, many of whom commuted out of
town to and from Jösnitz. Grandpa Elimelich, 'Eli'

for short, moved to Jösnitz in the 1860s because of the opportunities opened up by the textile industry. About ten years earlier, *Spitze*, embroidery, had become the big thing with manual machines sprouting like mushrooms.

'Soon after Father was born, Plauen experienced its very own miracle. One of the machines was left untended one day and went on working without the intermediate fabric layer. Somehow it spun an almost transparent lace, similar to French tulle, and the town's fortune was assured. Business was what mattered then. Not religion. Just about everyone was Protestant because Plauen is the heart of *Vogtland* and Luther's Reformation. A few Catholics were scattered about like us Jews but, as I say, money was what mattered, not the way you worshipped God. Some of the Jews had Yiddish-sounding surnames while others were non-biblical and ultra-Teutonic like "Siegfried".

'I remember some of our distant Orthodox cousins wore fur hats and black frock-coats. They looked like billy goats and talked of the importance of marital dowries. There had initially been a major rift with this part of the family when Father had "married out", but time and common sense had prevailed. My parents found them very old-fashioned but loved them nonetheless. For our part we dressed, ate, worked and thought like any fairly lax folk in that part of the *Vogtland* whether Protestant, Catholic or Jew.

'Most summers, we packed our commodious leather trunks, which looked like baby rhinos, and groomed and hushed by our maid, took the exciting train ride to Norderney, one of the Fresian islands. We loved the seaside cafes with their wondrous arrays of cream cakes, macaroons and fizzy-drinks. We would play along the seafront while the grown-ups played their favourite card game of skat.

'If my father felt any lingering Jewishness when away from his cousins, he certainly never showed it. I think he craved complete acceptance by the German bourgeoisie.

'There were those in the village that my father warned me about. He did not mention any Jewish problems *per se*. I would not have understood him if he had, but he told me the tale of a cousin of his – a dark tale that spoke of envy and hatred from a clan of ill repute at the village smithy, and a brutal beating. "Keep away from the lower village, little Ruth," my father said. And I did. For how long that hatred had simmered there who can tell, but . . .' Aunt Ruth tapped her head. 'It is still alive today, and when I have finished you will understand why, for you are a part of it.

'My father followed Grandpa Eli into the textile industry in Plauen. He would come home early on Wednesdays when we had a grand family tea, and he always brought us goodies. We owned the biggest, finest grandfather clock you've ever seen, and when it chimed four o'clock, all we children would scream with joy and rush to the kitchen. We had plump and noisy geese in our field, and Marianne Seidler, our maid from the village, killed one every so often. She made thick schmaltz paste from the fat which was delicious on toast. Alfred, the gardener, grew apples and pears from which Grandma Tilla bottled fruit and jellies. Ah, we grew even tubbier than the geese.

'The Kaiser told us on the wireless that Germany was the most powerful nation on Earth. Our navy, not Britain's, would soon rule the oceans. Grandpa Eli thumped the table and raised his mug. Father, who was eligible for conscription, kept quiet.

'Our main drawing room was quite pretentious – classical-revival in style with Biedermeier furnishings. A great many tasselled cushions littered the various sofas and armchairs and we children were forbidden to play with them.

'Also out of bounds was the larder, a dark and fascinating room stashed with nuts, *Zimmt*, wine racks, sultanas, sugar, flour, and smoked meats on hooks.

'I once saw Marianne stealing cakes from the larder. Her family was poor and lived in the lower village. I told my little brother Kurt, but neither of us sneaked to Mother for we were scared of Marianne. I had once seen her stick her tongue out at Grandma's back and her eyes had been black with venom.

'When not busy in the garden, Alfred took me, Kurt, and whichever young cousins were about, in the pony trap for outings. Sometimes he even took us to Plauen to watch jugglers, stilts-men and clowns in the square. My favourite was the *Kasperle* booth where Punch and Judy puppets squawked and squabbled.

'Alfred was also the keeper of our winter sleigh, complete with bells that tinkled and heavy fur rugs. Each December, on the night of Chanukah, the

Jewish Festival of Lights, we rode the sleigh through the forest trails. Alfred told us how wolf packs had chased his sleigh many years ago, but nobody believed him.

'My favourite cousin, Alma, was from Mother's side of the family. She and I grew up together and shared a love of dancing, especially the group numbers. In our early teens we adored the tango and showed off our prowess at the village dances. Marianne would be sent to chaperone us, but her eyes were mostly busy elsewhere and we learned about kissing far earlier than our other cousins who did not dance.

'In the summer, Father took Kurt and me over the Kaltenbach stream to the forest to pick berries and mushrooms, and he showed us how the most beautiful were often the most deadly. In 1917, when I was seven and Kurt five, Father's important job in textiles no longer barred him from military service. For eighteen months we never saw him, and then we heard he was in Plauen Hospital with shrapnel wounds. He nearly died from gas gangrene, but by my ninth birthday he was back in good health and took me to my first concert.'

'Can I interrupt?' I asked Aunt Ruth.

'Why, am I boring you already?'

'No, no. I am fascinated, but who were your non-family friends? Were they all Jews too?'

'No, we didn't really classify each other as Jews or non-Jews. There were Orthodox Jews in Plauen, many of whom were recent immigrants from Eastern Europe, especially Poland. I remember how we used to tease them and laugh behind their backs at their silly ways and clothes. They took themselves very seriously. Outside our school, which was run by Protestants, and at the cafés where we stopped for soft drinks and cakes, the others in my group were seldom Jews. All of us were proud Germans, first and foremost. Once, I danced with a dashing blond Catholic boy, and as I was also blonde then, I felt very much a Gentile.'

'So, you never experienced ethnic hostility?'

At first my aunt shook her head. 'Not until I was sixteen. Never.' Then she hesitated. 'Not anyway what I thought of as hostility. But twice there were times of . . . bewilderment. When I was twelve, I had my first period. I blossomed. Boys began to stare at me. My mother explained things and bought me suitable clothes. I owned a bodice before any of my school contemporaries. In a nearby village, west of Plauen, one of my schoolteachers entered four of us at the annual *Schützenfest* in the summer of 1923. I was voted *Schützenkönigin,* the youngest beauty queen on record. I was very proud and probably quite unbearable for a while, but two weeks later at the annual Jahrmarkt Fair, Kurt and I were watching the freak show in a tent when two big youths from our own village came up behind us. One twisted Kurt's arm behind his back. The other pulled my head back by my pigtail and whispered in my ear, "You people have too much money. You think you are too good for us." He spat in my ear, and when I screamed they quickly left the tent. Kurt told me that one of them was the brother of Marianne and came from the

lower village. We told nobody. It was an isolated incident. Overall our childhood was carefree. We were
lucky.'

'And the other occasion?'

'What other?'

'You said two incidents . . .'

'Oh, yes. I was about fifteen or sixteen I think, and
my mother, blonde like me, took me with your
mother, who was twelve years my junior, to a Passion
play in Bavaria. Many German villages, not just
Oberammergau, still staged them at the time. The
actors playing Jews were made to look oriental in
black cloaks with devil-horn hats, but what has always
remained stamped on my memory was a comment at
the play's end made by a smartly dressed neighbour
to her husband. "Why on earth," she complained
loudly, "do we allow these Christ-killers into our
country, never mind let them run the law and the
economy?"'

'I don't believe it.' I found myself gripping my
aunt's shoulder. 'Can you remember how you reacted
to such open bigotry? If someone said that today in
an Ottawan playhouse, most people would be dis-
gusted.'

'I hope you're right,' my aunt agreed, 'but remember, although German anti-Semitism was rife during
my youth, your mother and I, with our parochial
upbringing, were entirely sheltered from its ugliness.
Apart from those two little instances, the hatred
passed us by. For you to even begin to understand the
horrors that I must shortly describe, you must first get
an idea of how Germans generally viewed the Jews.

'Germany is at the centre of Europe, and Europe is a mainly Christian place. Not long after Christ's death, his disciples converted the Roman Empire to Christianity, which was a major feat. But remember, Christ was himself just an ordinary Jew until he started calling himself the son of God. The Jews did not and do not believe in Christ's revelations, and were seen as an ongoing threat to Christianity since they challenged its whole basis. So, of course Christians preached against Jews, even detested them. They shared the same Jewish Bible and the same God, but Christians believed that all Jews should move forwards, listen to Christ and metamorphose as they had.

'However, the Jews insisted that Christ himself was not a Christian; he was born a Jew and died as one. He did not go to Mass on Sundays – he went to synagogue on the Sabbath. No one called him Father or Reverend, they called him Rabbi, and he only read the Jewish Bible. He blasphemed in a way dangerous to the Roman rulers and so the Roman Pontius Pilate agreed he should be done away with. His death was at the hands of the Romans not the Jews.

'Every leading Christian *after* Christ's death fought this Jewish version of Roman guilt. The disciples, like Matthew, left behind gospels which stamped a blood curse onto the Jews by putting into their mouths the words, "*Sein Blut über uns, nicht minder, auch über unser Kinder Kinder.*" His blood be upon us and on our children's children. This Christian concept of Jews as the killers of Christ led them to promulgate hatred and destruction of Jews over the next eighteen centuries.

'I read recently that archaeologists had found a nine-hundred-year-old silver salver in a German convent engraved with a tableau of soldiers driving Jews into a furnace. The wording on the plate was, "Because they reject Christ, Jews deserve Hell." In 1543, during the Reformation, Martin Luther preached the words, "Their synagogues shall be put to the fire and they shall be covered with dirt."

'In the Middle Ages, a time of great cruelty and violence when witches were being burned to death all over Europe, Jews were a favourite target, especially during the Christian Holy Week. During such pogroms they cowered in their blazing ghettos and hid from screaming mobs of hate-filled Christians. This bitterness against Jews was so intense and illogical that every misfortune was thought to derive from them. They were even blamed for the killer plagues of the fifteenth and sixteenth centuries which meant they were either murdered or expelled from much of Europe.

'Anti-Semitism remained in Germany even after the mediaeval exterminations left a mere scattering of Jews there, certainly less than one per cent of the population, but for seventy years in the nineteenth century the level of hatred dropped to a mere background simmer. That was the time of my Grandpa Eli, who proudly fought for Prussia in two great wars.

'In 1871, only one hundred years ago, Emperor William I was crowned Emperor, or Kaizer, of Prussia and modern Germany was created. Back then, Jews were fleeing to Germany from vicious pogroms in Poland and Romania. In Russia, Czarist

Cossacks would target Jewish villages where they would murder and rape at will. Germany seemed a safe haven by comparison until the concept of a new German nation – the Imperial Reich – began to spread. Its advocates decreed that true Germans shared the sacred blood of the Aryan race which must never be tainted by people from Semitic tribes such as the Jews. With race as well as religion now fuelling German prejudice, the word "anti-Semitic" first entered European dictionaries.

'During the seventy years prior to the Reich's formation, Jews like Grandpa Eli had worked hard and done well, especially in finance. Now they were feared as a group planning to dominate Germany economically, as well as being Christ-killers and non-Aryans. The wildly celebrated German composer Richard Wagner saw Jewish plotters in every nook and cranny, and proposed their extermination as far back as 1870. Popular foreign literature, like Shakespeare's *The Merchant of Venice*, also villainised the Jews and helped fuel anti-Semitism.

'When we lost the First World War, the Kaiser was given the boot and the democratic Weimar Republic was forced to kowtow to the French and British victors. We had to pay huge crippling reparations which worsened the Depression. Our nationalists and war veterans seethed with humiliation and vented their fury against the Jews, most of whom were ardent supporters of the Weimar Republic.

'At the time, Marxism was the great expanding ideology of Europe and its most influential leaders, including Marx himself, were Jews. Fear of the Red

menace, resentment at recent defeat, and rage at
poverty from unemployment were all taken out on
the Jews by most of the German population.'

'What about the rest of Europe? How did they feel
about their own Jews when you were growing up?'

'By 1930, when I was twenty and had begun to
show an interest in the world outside Plauen, Jews
were universally unpopular but not hated. In places
like America, Britain and France, Jews went about
their normal business, but always with a background
of hostility due to the worldwide economic crisis, ten
years of unemployment and the growing threat of
Bolshevism. Anti-Semitism was used by a number of
governments to deflect the anger of the unemployed
and underpaid at the system that was exploiting them
onto the Jews.

'Over thirty per cent of Germans were out of
work, but a far lesser ratio of Jews due to the nature
of the professions they had chosen. In any country,
that sort of difference causes envy.'

'But you weren't really a Jew, Aunt Ruth. You certainly aren't one now. You could never have looked
like a typical Jew.'

'And what is the look of a typical Jew?'

'Well, hooked nose, black hair, black eyes, and long,
lumpy features like the Greeks.'

'If that was truly so, no Jewish woman would ever
have received a marriage proposal from a Gentile! Yet
in my teens, over a quarter of all German Jews were
marrying non-Jews. Children of my age from mixed
marriages were often blond, blue-eyed and utterly
un-Jewish-looking. Father, on the other hand, had a

definite Jewish air about him. "Distinguished and fine," Mother always called him. Although he only fought for the Fatherland for a year or so, he received the Honour Cross of Front Fighters and was promoted to corporal. After the war he was always proud of his wounds. Again, I must stress to you, Dieter, we were in our hearts and in our minds proud Germans who loved our Fatherland, and our liberal Jewishness meant no more to us then than your very rare attendance at church does to you today!'

'Sure, Aunt Ruth, I can see what you're saying. *I'm* a Canadian, and a Protestant, and one of my grandfathers was a German, non-practising Jew. *You* are a German and a Protestant, and your German father, a non-practising Jew, had liberal German Jewish parents. All in all, I'd say we were both pretty un-Jewish. You emphasise how German we are but that we have good reason for not being too proud of our German heritage. None of this has given me a bad time, Auntie, because I'm a Canadian in here.' I pointed a finger at my forehead. 'And here,' I placed my hand over my heart. 'So my lack of any contact with Germans or with Jews *macht nichts*. I'm not fussed. But so far, I still have no clue about the man in Resolute.'

'Patience, Dieter.' My aunt sighed. 'Your mother was the most patient person in the world. I sometimes wonder where on earth some of your more irksome characteristics come from.'

'It's because you jump all over the place. With all due respect, you're difficult to follow.'

'Okay, okay.' My aunt's eyebrows indicated long-sufferance. 'I will try to be chronological. By the end of the First Great War, when my father was back from hospital, there were four of us children – me, my brother Kurt and the twins, who were born in 1916. They were frail from birth, Tomi and Toni, and this convinced Mother she should bear no more children.'

'So *my* mother was a mistake?'

'Don't be silly,' my aunt crooned. 'Of course Anna was not a mistake. She just came along four years after the war to lighten up our lives. Mother must have had a brief change of family policy. Thank the Lord she did or you, my dear, would not be here.

'But you interrupt again. When we lost the First World War, we had a revolution, threw out the Kaiser and the Weimar Republic began; a time of weak democracy which saw bloody unrest between Communists and Conservatives. The latter were mainly anti-Semitic and began to raise the temperature against the Jews all over Germany. If only the Weimar leaders had possessed an iota of prescience and constancy, but no, they were so liberal they gave the fanatics full rein to destroy all liberty for a long while in our homeland.

'One of those fanatics, an Austrian army lance-corporal named Adolf Hitler, while wounded and in hospital on the Western Front in 1918, had a 'vision' that Germany's Jews were responsible for the Fatherland's humiliating defeat. So he resolved to exterminate them. Within a year, for he was a spellbinding street orator, he had attracted a band of talented disciples and, unimpeded by our weak government, formed his serpents' nest in Munich with a mission of mass murder.

'Even in 1921, anyone with their eyes and ears half open could see sinister writing on Jewish walls, to use the words of the German Jew, Albert Einstein. At that time my ears were wide open, but not for Einstein's warnings. I was an avid reader and did well at school – one teacher called me brilliant. I was also popular and strong-willed. I called a spade a spade.'

'Some things never change,' I couldn't help butting in.

'Watch your mouth, *Junge*.' My aunt's strong, bony finger prodded me playfully. She was enjoying herself. There was nothing here to upset her, nothing she could not have told me many years ago. Perhaps sensing my impatience, my aunt settled into her chair and began to reveal the darker secrets of our past.

In 1922, your mother was born and, as the eldest sister, I spent a great deal of time with her, for our maid was then fully occupied with my poor brothers Tomi and Toni. Kurt also doted on the new arrival. *Ach, neh!* It's a wonder she turned out such a truly sweet person, the way we spoiled her.

The following year I was the *Schützenkönigin*, the most precocious beauty queen in German history in all probability, and two months later the extremist Hitler party failed in its attempt to overthrow the Bavarian state government. State troops fortunately gunned down Hitler's mob in Munich and slung him into prison, but the fools stupidly released him only a year later. He called his party the National Socialist German Workers Party – the Nazis. He led them with the mixture of pent-up fury and cold calculation that would later mesmerise millions. Our family should have felt a small cold wind raise the hairs on our necks on the day they let the unknown Hitler loose onto the streets of Munich.

Of course, I neither knew nor cared about Hitler. How many pretty young girls the world over waste their precious teenage days with thoughts of politics? And I was truly beautiful, though I say it myself. All the boys in the village climbed over each other to dance with me, and it wasn't just the tango they had in mind. I could have done with six pairs of hands to keep their fingers from wandering. And I won't say I didn't enjoy it.

My first kiss came from a handsome Thüringen gypsy boy underneath the bridge over our local stream. But his breath smelled of goat's cheese and his stubble raked my skin like a grinding stone. There were many others too, but I'll not embarrass you with intimate details. My first real taste of hate came shortly afterwards.

I was sixteen in the beautiful summer of 1926, and Alfred, our gardener, had long since shown me his favourite secret place, the glade of the *Schattenlosen*, the folk without shadows. This fairy glade, between two streams, lay hidden deep within an old, proud forest as yet untouched by Plauen's tentacles. No sounds from distant traffic, nor even farms, disturbed my dreaming there and youths from the village kept away because of peasant stories and superstitions. A narrow path, part overgrown, first showed its tread at the southern limits of our land and then entered the birch woods. After reaching the *ödes* land of scrub grazed by stock from local farms, the path swung around the village and down to the stream. Had Alfred not first been my guide, I would have missed this perfect place, where beds of soft lichen and the rock walls of miniature waterfalls framed dells of wild flowers and berry bushes.

For many months I kept Alfred's secret all to myself, but when summer came, I felt it was a sin not to let close family and friends share such a paradise. So, on a lovely June morning, five of us left home furnished with picnic hampers and a chequered rug from Grandma Tilla. We must be back well before dark, Mother had scolded, and I must be sure to remember the twins' medicine. The twins, ten years old at the time, were still frail and sometimes had fits. They had private tutoring at home and spoke animatedly only to each other. Like Kurt and cousin Alma, I had sworn the twins to secrecy as to the very existence of our destination. Mother knew only that the picnic would be well away from the village.

As we passed through the gorse thickets of the common land about the village, a flock of silly sheep blocked our route. We waited while a foul-mouthed farm boy cursed the animals on their way. I saw him staring back at us as we moved on but thought no more of it.

I basked in the wonderment of the others when we reached Alfred's glade or, as I called it, my glade. All agreed that no better place for a picnic could exist anywhere on earth. Tomi and Toni took off their shoes and socks, and paddled in the cool stream. Then they sat holding hands in a mossy nook and chattered away like monkeys, pale but content. Kurt, always self-conscious in Alma's presence, read a book and tried not to look at her low-cut blouse.

Arm-in-arm, Alma and I went for little walks, made daisychains for each other and tittered at shared gossip of current school romances. Oh, but it was a happy time, a flawless day. We stayed too long, and my ever-worrying mother back home asked Alfred to keep an eye open for us on his own way back to the village.

When the last magic rays of sunlight no longer caressed our glade and the twins grew cold, the idyll came to an end and we left.

The way home looked different in the evening light, for the morning's shadows had reversed, disguising outward landmarks. I pressed on with caution and was rewarded soon enough with cooking smells coming from the lower village. In that place of low scrub, where the sheep had earlier delayed us, a figure suddenly loomed ahead and I screamed in shock. It was the same farmer's boy as before but now joined, I soon saw, by four of his village friends. They moved about us, hemming us in between bushes of thorny gorse. Kurt moved close to the twins who were hugging each other in fear, but it occurred to me that he would have preferred to be offering his manly protection to Alma.

I greeted the village boys in as even a voice as I could manage, but there was no reply and no movement to give us room to pass. My thoughts ran riot and I could hear my heart pounding. I saw the elder of the blacksmith's sons, for it was they, staring, or I should say, leering, at Alma's breasts. Kurt must have seen this too for he lurched forward and addressed the shepherd, a youth of about his own age.

'I know you. You are from the Kleiner farm. Your father sells us lamb. Please let us pass. We are late.'

'Not so quick, rich boy. We are in no hurry. We've been waiting for you. It's time to teach you manners. Your family thinks you own the likes of us just because you have money, a big flashy road-car, fancy clothes and talk with potatoes under your tongues.'

'That's not true—' Alma interrupted, but the largest of the tanner's boys closed on her.

'Your big lips are not for talking,' he slurred and caught her in a bear grip. With one hand he ripped at her blouse.

Kurt hit out, enraged. 'Leave her, you bastard!' he shouted.

The twins were terrified and I pulled them away from the fight. I watched helpless as the shepherd and three of the blacksmith's boys closed in on Kurt. The other concentrated on Alma.

'You *Kränzchen* bitch,' he spat at her as he tore off her bodice. 'I bet you don't do this at your smart cake-and-chocolate parties.' Alma's breasts came loose and the blacksmith's son rolled her to the ground.

I heard Kurt groan as the shepherd hit him in the stomach. He doubled over with pain and was set upon by the pack of them. The brutes kicked and punched him as though he represented all that they hated and envied. Then one moved behind him imprisoning his arms and his neck so the others could kick his groin.

In a while, they let him slump to the ground, but then the shepherd grabbed Kurt's hair and began to beat his head against the rocky ground.

I left the twins, and screaming furiously, kicked at the boy who was having trouble with the complex fastenings of Alma's underwear.

How much time passed during that nightmare I can't tell, but my screams brought Alfred running and he had with him his field sickle. He knew the blacksmith's boys, the shepherd and their parents, and in seconds had them disappearing into the gathering gloom.

Kurt was badly cut and bruised, Alma unscathed, and the twins in shock. Alfred accompanied us home and my father complained to the Plauen police. I do not remember if anything came of it, but we never again ventured anywhere near the lower village. We had been served notice that the world beyond our happy family circle was not to be trusted.

Our other cousin Hans, known to us by the diminutive Hänschen, was slight of stature but extremely handsome. He swore vengeance on the perpetrators of the picnic attack, as he called it. 'If only I had been there,' he growled.

Like the rest of us, Hänschen did not consider himself a Jew in any sense of the word, but whereas we had never had reason to bother with our identity, he was fiercely proud of his membership of the German University League, a university fraternity open only to pure Aryans. Somehow at Heidelberg University, Hänschen's popularity had allowed the Jewish taint to his background to be overlooked. He sported a textbook sword scar on one cheek and proudly wore his beribboned student's cap at a jaunty angle. Not long after the picnic attack, some of his student group, all motor-bicycle owners, burned down a Jewish store in Heidelberg and beat up the owner. Hänschen for the first time saw the true nature of his elitist associates and withdrew from their company – a brave thing to do at that time on a close-knit German campus. He left the university once his exams were over and joined the prestigious *Munich Post*, working under the tutelage of the controversial anti-Fascist journalist, Edmund Goldschagg.

Hänschen often visited us, and while I had previously shown little or no interest in the intense political conversations my father held with many of our guests, I used every excuse to sit and watch the gorgeous Hänschen as he briefed Father and others on the latest news 'hot off the press' from the *Post*. Despite myself, I began to absorb the alarming reality of what was going on outside my own coddled existence. The name 'Hitler' arose with increasing frequency.

That December, Hänschen said that Hitler's killer thugs, known as Cell G, had assaulted the *Munich Post*'s office, beaten him and everybody else in the building with clubs, and smashed costly printing gear. The self-styled *Führer* had then made a public Christmas speech including the words, 'Christ was the greatest fighter who ever lived. His teaching is fundamental in *our* ongoing fight against the Jew, the enemy of humanity.'

Hitler, Hänschen warned us, would not stop at pure Jews; he would relentlessly persecute 'hidden Jews' masquerading as Christians. People like us. Apart from his main hatred of the Jews, this maniac had also set his deadly sights on Democrats, Socialists and Communists.

Millions of Germans were flocking to vote – for voting was still an option until Hitler finished off democracy – for this clearly evil man. Factors such as the raging inflation of 1923, and the crushing economic depression of 1929, helped the Nazis gain an ever increasing percentage of the suffrage. Because the weak government of the Weimar Republic had led to such civil strife and misery, Hitler's promise to abolish democracy encouraged many Germans to back him in the hope that any change of system would be an improvement. Of course, they were wrong, but it took another 10 years for them to realise it, if they survived that long.

My father began to cluck like a protective cockerel even then in 1926. 'Baptism is the only answer,' he cried. Our grandparents shook their heads in disapproval. My mother was delighted, the twins nonplussed, and Kurt as annoyed as I was at the wasting of valuable free time learning how to be good little Protestants at the local *evangelische Kirche*.

The conversion was purely expedient, but looking back, I feel sure that the good Lord would have done exactly the same thing if he had been in our shoes at the time. He would have understood the instinct of self-preservation. Our rector, Emil Gunsteig, was earnest and very thorough in our preparation, and

Kurt and I were impressed by his sincerity. After our baptism we never again referred to our new religious status at home, lest we offend our grandparents or visiting cousins who still trod the true paths of Jewish righteousness.

By the end of 1928, a great many Jews were suffering from the anti-Semitic propaganda of the ever more influential Nazis, but in our region some things were slow to change. That winter, my father was one of many local heroes of the last war to be honoured by the local veterans' association. He was truly a decorated and proud pillar of the Fatherland. The textile industry was going strong and our standard of living had altered hardly at all, even at the nadir of the economic depression.

One night, as we came out of the cinema in Plauen, we witnessed a torchlight parade in the town centre in support of Hitler. The atmosphere was electric, even hypnotic, as the red flags swirled and a thousand voices sang to the rhythm of the march. A passer-by with shining eyes grabbed me and yelled in my ear above the clamour, 'He will make us strong again . . . give us back our pride.' I almost felt like running out to join the parade and the massed ranks of singing marchers. But I didn't.

Although I loved Hänschen to distraction, he continued to treat me as he always had, as a young cousin to be humoured and, despite a number of blatantly flirtatious forays, I could not get through to his heart. My ardour eventually began to evaporate helped by the appearance of Bruno from the nearby village of Oelsnitz. A raconteur with a silver tongue and a face to die for, Bruno was a rich Catholic student sadly afflicted by leukaemia.

We went to many dances together in the company of Alma and our friends. Every year our village elders organised a major charity barn dance and in the summer of 1929, Bruno had agreed to partner me there. On the very morning of the great event, his illness confined him to bed, so I went unaccompanied but for Kurt and some friends. Later in the evening a special dance was to be given in my honour as a past *Schützenkönigin*.

Stupidly, I drank too much *Glühwein* during the evening and my inhibitions fled. Many men were keen to dance with me, unattended as I was by my absent beau, and I adored all the attention. Two senior members of the local Hitler Youth vied with one another for my attentions which was an exciting experience, since both were tall and ruggedly hand-some. Somehow, I ended up being escorted by these two young gods – and that, I assure you, is how they saw themselves – out onto the veranda.

It may have been the way the fairylights played on his cheekbones, or just the fact that his uniform really did give him Olympian airs, but either way I really *looked* at one of these youths for the first time that evening, and I recognised him as the blacksmith's son who had assaulted Alma three years before. He did not see my sudden concern for he was addressing his friend.

'You know what the mayor is doing after the toast to our *Führer*?'

The other youth shrugged. 'Tell me, Ernst, I know

you know the answer. You know everything.' He lifted his beer mug to show he meant no offence.

'Well,' the blacksmith's son said, adjusting his deep-shine black belt and straightening his wide shoulders, 'Fräulein Ruth here will be honoured by the mayor as the youngest and prettiest *Schützenkönigin* in memory.'

I glanced at his thinly smiling mouth. There was no hint of irony. I was sure he did not connect me with the incident involving Kurt and Alma. Indeed, he had probably forgotten it. Now that the village world of his youth lay at his feet, he had no need to ponder on past resentments. This brownshirt cockerel, a prototype bully boy, could have what he wanted, thanks to Germany's new evolving order where the bully ruled in all things.

'And when she is wearing the mayoral coronet of flowers' – the smile became a smirk – 'she will get to choose from all those who line up on the stage as her suitors.' His smirk widened into a cocksure grin, and holding my shoulders to ensure I registered his whole handsome being, he added, 'I will be there, of course, to worship your beauty, and I feel sure when you choose your ideal man of the village, that your choice will be me. Then we will dance for them all. Never again will they see such a perfect couple . . . so . . .' His smile vanished and I have never seen so cruel a face. 'Fräulein Ruth, I am sure you will not disappoint me?'

In the silence that followed, my straightforward nature for once deserted me. I merely gave him a polite smile and turned back towards the hall. We

returned to the gay waltzing, the uproar of happy villagers, and I sought out Alma to warn her of the
Hitler Youth's identity. But, before I could find her,
the dance organisers rang the handbell for attention.

There was immediate stillness and silence; it was
amazing how our people were so ready to respond to
discipline. The good mayor, his chest bedecked with
the chains of office, beamed at his assembled flock
and told us that in our province National Socialism
was achieving unheard-of voting figures. Our sav-
iour-to-be, Adolf Hitler, was unstoppable. If only he
could be with us all on this happy night to witness our
enormous support and, yes, our love for him. He
waved at the forest of red Nazi flags and swastika
banners that sprouted from the walls of the hall. We
all cheered and cheered until he raised his hands for
silence and resumed his soliloquy with an account of
all that he, in his humility, had already done for the
parish, and what was to be done over the next year.
He read out a list of prominent parishioners who had
achieved local greatness in the name and cause of our
Hitler, whether through voluntary teaching of our
young as to the true history of our glorious Reich, or
merely through leading village cleanliness patrols of
Hitler Youth and their female equivalent, the *Bund
deutsch Mädschen* (BDM) – the League of German
Girls – of which I was a member. Fulsome praise of
each named individual prompted more cheers from
the audience and they were especially loud, it seemed
to me, for the blacksmith's boy. His name, I noted,
was Ernst Seidler, presumably one of our servant
Marianne's brothers.

At the end of his speech, the mayor announced the custom of honouring a past *Schützenkönigin* with the Dance of Romance, and said that the committee had selected an especially comely parish girl, whose father and grandfather held fine war records. He then read out details of donations that our family had made towards the restoration of the Protestant church over the past two decades.

The music struck up and, to the rhythmic clap of the assembled village, eight of our finest youths marched up the steps and onto the stage where they stood to attention in the spotlight. The last to arrive was Smitty Zend, a friend of Alma's, who often came to our house. He was a studious lad who loved to play chess and wore the thickest spectacles in all Thüringen. I had no idea that he fancied me but I was flattered, and when a section of the village youth started to boo his ascent to the stage, that decided me.

Each suitor was required to say a few lines of German poetry and strike a few classic Greek poses. The loudest cheers, led by his brothers, were of course for the blacksmith's boy Ernst Seidler, who was taller than the other seven suitors and resplendent in his uniform. His poem was in reality the latest catchline quote from Hitler, delivered with many a manly flourish and gesture. The lower village crowd went mad with applause.

When I stepped up to the stage, I did as bidden by the organiser and stood before each suitor for a few seconds to 'gaze into their eyes' while the megaphone purred to the silent crowd. You could have heard a

Wurst drop in a *Fleischerei*. I spent a few seconds longer in front of Seidler, remembering his treatment of Alma. Then, to the astonishment of all, and the humiliation of Seidler, I selected Smitty.

You may think later that all the long horror that was to befall us was surely my fault. To humiliate such a man in public was to ask for trouble. Of course, I see that now, but it is always easy to be wise after the event.

CHAPTER THREE

Three years later in the autumn of 1932, they tried to assassinate Hänschen. His *Munich Post* senior colleague, Erhard Auer, arrived at our house in a newspaper van in the early hours of the morning and rang our bell until my father let him in.

'Max,' he said, urgency written all over him. 'Things are bad in Munich. Two of our staff have been assaulted and I'm afraid Hänschen is one of them. He is no longer safe in the city, and he indicated that you would be prepared to look after him.'

'Of course, of course. Where is he?'

The noise woke us all, and we met in the hall as Father and Herr Auer helped Hänschen up the steps and into the sitting room. His shirt glistened with blood and his eyes were so swollen he could see nothing. One of his ears hung from a single bridge of flesh, and blood still streamed from his head wounds.

'Who did this?' we all seemed to ask at once.

It transpired that Hänschen and another *Munich Post* reporter were in the process of uncovering a plot by the Hitler party's death squad, Cell G, to assassinate President Hindenburg. Both reporters had subsequently been targeted for immediate murder at their homes, but Herr Auer had fortuitously interrupted the Cell G thugs when he called to collect a script from Hänschen.

'Hänschen was lucky,' he told us. 'The Nazis wanted to make it look like a simple beating that went too far after Hänschen had interrupted some burglars.'

We took Hänschen straight to bed, and Herr Auer left to check with his boss about their other threatened reporter.

In the morning after a brave but covert visit by our doctor to stitch his ear back in place, Hänschen told us his story, and for the first time the true precariousness of our own situation washed over me like ice-cold water.

For 10 years Hänschen's paper, the *Post*, had fought to warn Munich, Germany and the world of the evil incubus hatching in their city. They had seen Hitler's true colours and his enormous capacity for evil as early as 1921. They had spared no effort to expose him and his cohorts and, of course, they had suffered the consequences. Back in 1923, Hitler's thugs had ransacked their office and smashed their printing machinery. Their staff were constantly threatened, harried, and often badly beaten.

'Does Hitler himself know what's going on?' my father asked.

Hänschen's laugh was bitter. 'We will be using one of his quotes in our coming exposure. At a recent party meeting he screamed, "*Nothing* happens in the movement without my knowledge and without my wish." Hitler himself ordered my murder, of that I have no doubt.'

For nine years, the *Post* had relied on courageous individuals on the edge of the Hitler group to obtain Nazi memos and internal correspondence linking Cell G with political assassinations, sexual blackmail and financial fraud on a huge scale. One by one, all opponents to the Nazi Party were blackened with innuendo or scandal. When that failed they were murdered. Four hundred of Germany's bravest and best politicians vanished, or were gunned down, drowned, strangled, or knifed.

Hänschen told me, 'We catalogued this slaughter in the paper but nothing and nobody can stop this man. He has hypnotised Germany with his anti-Semitism, his propaganda and his feverish, hate-filled rhetoric. Unless we can somehow block him very, very soon, he will take over our country and, mark my words, he and his Nazis will redefine the word 'inhumanity'. Our reporter Goldschagg got it right last week when he described the Nazi machine as a homicidal enterprise in the clothing of a political party.'

'Surely, with your new disclosures, people will begin to see through him?' suggested my father.

Hänschen shrugged. 'I hope so, Max, and I am doing all I can to that end, but I cannot say that I am hopeful. Hundreds of thousands of Germans will follow *anyone* who looks like they can sort out the economy. Since the Wall Street crash three years back, the situation has spiralled downwards, banks have closed, big businesses have folded, and our middle-ground government is being squeezed into impotence between the Communists and the Nazis.'

'Luckily, in last month's vote, despite Nazi coercion at the ballots, they won less than thirty per cent of the vote,' my mother asserted hopefully. 'Maybe the tide is turning.'

Hänschen nodded. 'You would indeed think so since we are after all meant to be a democracy. But, if you had read some of the Nazi secret memos, as I have, you would fear for all our lives. Hitler will *force* Hindenburg out by intrigue if he does not murder him first. He will be the unchangeable dictator of all Germany within a few months, and my advice to you, Max, is to get out, emigrate immediately. Next month may be too late.'

'But why?' I blurted out. 'What possible danger are we to Hitler? We have never done anything to block the Nazis.'

Hänschen shook his bandaged head slowly and sadly. 'I have seen Hitler's plan set out clearly in a memorandum to his SA Nazi paramilitaries. He has a detailed programme to rid all Germany of Jews and' – he held up one hand – 'I know we do not think of ourselves as Jews any more but, should his embryonic plans become the law, we would need to be "Jew clean" for at least three generations. I fear you will all be classified as Jews. Hitler calls his ultimate plan for Jews the "final solution". This is not yet public knowledge but, in our big exposé on 9 December last year, we did reveal that this was the euphemism Hitler uses to describe his planned fate for all Jews.'

'At the *Post* we know more about Hitler than anybody alive. A secret plan of his was sent to us by an insider in the SA which reveals his longterm strategy. Hitler has forbidden any discussion of it in public for fear of the reaction from foreign governments, but let me give you the gist of it.

'If the Nazis sense their popularity with the voters is beginning to wane and they fail to gain power legally, they will seize it. When that happens woe betide any of us on Hitler's hate list. The few hundred assassinations of these past years will become a flood overnight. All members of the Socialist, Democratic and Catholic central parties will be arrested and sent to labour camps. Trade unionists, homosexuals, cripples and gypsies, to mention just a few of Hitler's pet hates, will join all Jews and Communists as non-desirables to be eradicated. Already, no opposition politician can openly address the voters, and all papers except ours are afraid to denounce Hitler due to illegal Nazi terror tactics which are ignored by our democratic government. Imagine how it will be when the Nazis *are* the government. We at the *Post* are doing our utmost to make the public see sense and realise that terrible events may follow if they continue to vote for Hitler.'

'That's why you must hide, Hänschen.' My father gripped his wrist and shook it. 'You can stay here as long as you want. We will look after all your needs.'

'You are kind.' Hänschen's pale lips shaped a smile. 'But if ever there was a time the *Post* needed all hands on deck, it is now.'

He left us after a few days when he was mostly

recovered, although he still resembled a prize boxer
on a losing streak. He would not tell us his new lodgings and we knew not to ask him. Those were days of
mistrust in Germany. You never knew who would
hear you, for the walls had ears. The Gestapo paid the
most unlikely people to inform so the fewer people
who knew Hänschen's whereabouts the better. He
continued to visit us every month but by night and
haphazardly.

The winter of 1932 passed slowly in those times of
menace and apprehension and none of us was exactly
happy with life, but little Anna, your mother, suffered the most for she was the gentlest, most sensitive
of children. And 10 can be a difficult age even in the
best of times, for children are natural bullies, cruel to
weaker classmates. Anna was vulnerable for she wore
her heart on her sleeve.

Mother made sure that our family's Jewish connections remained hidden from the school staff as
well as the kids. When she took Anna to school or
collected her she stressed at every opportunity her
own solid Lutheran ancestry. Brother Kurt, 10 years
Anna's senior, was still remembered as a popular captain of the school *Völkerball* team and superb soloist
in the school choir. Anna always wore a pretty, silver
cross round her neck and went to church with many
of her schoolfriends. The fact that Sandor and Heidi,
two of the tiny minority of local Jewish children,
were also good friends of Anna's had never been an
issue.

But things began to change, especially with the
arrival of a new history teacher who held radical Nazi

beliefs. He encouraged the children to participate in supporting our great *Führer*, and to join the Hitler Youth or the BDM if they had not already done so. Since free, very smart brown uniforms were available on joining, the children flocked to sign up. The anti-Semitic message soon spread among them like a hideous virus, and I quickly withdrew my membership on some health pretext.

Heidi and Sandor, being Jews, could not of course enrol, and Anna watched from the sidelines as her two Jewish friends, both amicable, bubbly children, and previously popular with everyone, began a slow and painful descent into a state of anguish.

'Ruthie' – Anna approached me one evening on returning home from school – 'can I ask you about the Jews?'

'Of course, Annie, but Father would know more. After all, he's meant to be one. I'm just your big sister and you often say I know nothing.'

She swatted the air near me. 'Of course I don't, silly. Or I don't mean it anyway.' She went very serious then and told me how badly her Jewish friends were being treated by her Protestant friends. One of her teachers that day had actually berated her for playing with Heidi during the morning break.

'The teacher told me, "People will think *you* are a Jew." I saw a newspaper in town last week, *Der Stürmer*, and it had a big cartoon of a Jew eating a child in BDM uniform. I compared the Jew with my face in the mirror. My hair is blonde and plaited and my nose is straight, not at all like the cartoon. And, why shouldn't I play with Sandor and Heidi?

They've done *nothing* wrong. People are horrid to them. I would hate it if they start being like that to me.'

I assured Anna that we were Christians not Jews. We were baptised, after all.

'Yes, I know.' She was on the verge of weeping. 'But last month Frau Lehner, the maths teacher, asked who in the class was Jewish. At first nobody put their hand up but then Renata Strauss said, "Please, ma'am, I'm not Jewish but my grandpa is." On Friday she was crying because they'd made her leave the BDM. They took her uniform away and said she *was* a Jew. And she had been baptised, just like me. Oh dear, Ruthie, I am so frightened!'

Then it all poured out. Everything she had seen and heard happening to the two Jewish children who had been her friends since she was a toddler. They were pushed about and called *Saujude*, Jew-filth, by erstwhile school chums. The Nazi history teacher had made Heidi stand in front of the class and compared her features with the official Nazi outline of a typical Jewish type which he had pinned to the board. She had stood there, tears pouring down her cheeks, as his cane prodded her nose, her ears, and her slightly frizzy black hair.

Renata's favourite schoolmistress, whom she greatly respected, no longer addressed her, or even looked at her in class, and one by one her best friends had begun to cold-shoulder her. 'What have I done wrong?' Renata had asked Anna after class. 'I've always paid attention, never broken the rules or whispered or cheated, but she's started to hate me. What's wrong with being a Jew all of a sudden? Tell me, Anna.'

'I couldn't tell her anything,' Anna said tearfully. 'I hate the way she's treated. But I did suggest she try to look as German as possible, and so she turned up in a richly embroidered *völkisch* peasant blouse the next day. It only made things worse though because the new history teacher mocked her and said in front of us all that nobody could be a Jew and a true Aryan German. He says that word "Aryan" the whole time.

'Renata has now been put at the back of the class next to Heidi and many of her best friends have started being horrid to her. She told me she blamed her stupid grandparents for being Jews.'

Anna was of course only witnessing the ordeal that Jewish children were suffering all over Germany. She was very lucky that, at the time, nobody questioned her own Christian status because in small towns in Germany, everybody usually knew everybody else's business and everyone's relationship to each other. Of course, Anna was well aware that our grandparents were liberal Jews. She knew all about our Orthodox cousins, and furthermore, she knew that Father was a lapsed Jew. I had often told her never ever to reveal this to anyone. I reminded her what had happened to her friend Renata when she'd innocently admitted to having Jewish grandparents, and Anna realised how serious the situation was. I think that the *Ostjuden*, the Jews recently arrived in Germany from eastern Europe, coped with the bullying a lot better because they knew what to expect. After all, they or their parents had already suffered anti-Jewish pogroms in Russia and Poland. It was worse for us German Jews to be rejected by people we had trusted and grown up with; by close neighbours and friends. And it was worst of all for those children who had had no inkling of their Jewish connections.

Imagine, at six or ten years old, your whole world turning upside down – the cold stares, the pointing fingers, the whispers and giggling, the birthday parties where *nobody* turns up, ostracism in the playground, dog dirt left in your locker or smeared on your games shirt, ink spilled on your homework. And the boys forced to use communal washrooms where everyone sneers at their circumcision, so that they wish they had been born girls.

Anna's friend Renata was a Protestant child of Lutheran parents, a Christian in every sense, but the persecution she suffered over the next three years, due to her new Nazi classification as a mongrel, eventually drove her from school an emotional wreck, and her parents had no choice but to enrol her at an Orthodox Jewish school. The persecution stopped but she was still cold-shouldered at her new school. The reality for children of mixed heritage was non-acceptance by *any* group.

And on the other side of the coin, there were many Jewish children who took their suffering out on their parents. They desperately wanted to join the Hitler Youth or the BDM, to be able to conform, to be Nazis, and to march with the swastika banners and sing the martial songs like the other kids did.

The strain of subterfuge slowly gnawed at little Anna for she was a naturally honest person. She found that very honesty increasingly at odds with her fear of discovery. Each time she went out on a limb to be friendly to Sandor, Heidi and Renata, she risked discovery and denunciation. One day a group of girls, Anna's friends, formed a circle around Heidi in the playground and began to kick her. Anna screamed at her schoolfriends to stop and when they didn't, she rushed to find a teacher. Nobody reacted but, in her helplessness and fear for Heidi's fate, Anna must have said something rash to one of the teachers.

By very good fortune, the teacher in question was an old family friend and secretly anti-Nazi. She warned Mother that Anna was on the edge and might soon reveal our family's mixed status to somebody less sympathetic.

That put the cat among the pigeons with our parents. The importance of keeping up our non-Jewish status was by then very clear to all our family. Hänschen had stressed to Father what Hitler had in store for anybody of mixed race, so poor Anna was taken away from the school where your Uncle Kurt and I had also been educated, and joined the twins in having lessons at home.

Hänschen came to us that Christmas in a high state of tension. Hitler, he said, was hatching secret plans to take over Germany within a month. He showed us the text he had brought from the *Post* of a recent Nazi Party speech made by Hitler, which clearly outlined his intentions. 'The extermination of all Jews and half-Jews in Germany,' Hänschen told us '*will* take place and that will include all your family if you don't emigrate now, before this madman takes over.'

We believed Hänschen was right; he had never advised us wrongly before. Only Grandpa Eli was adamant we should stay right where we were. And Grandma Tilla was always loyal to him. *We* could all go abroad, Grandpa grumbled, but we would be making an enormous mistake. He and Tilla would never leave the *Heimat*, the homeland of Goethe, for which he had fought and been wounded, the fairest and most cultured country in the world. This Hitler trouble would soon blow over. Hänschen had got it all wrong. We would see.

Father, who had also fought and been wounded for the Fatherland, was equally convinced that we should get out while the going was good. He told Hänschen this, and he agreed to explore the best way to set about it. They said nothing to Grandpa so as not to rock the boat. After all, emigration might not prove possible.

We decided to go anywhere that would have us with the least possible delay. Hänschen had really put the wind up my parents.

I was married in the New Year and even the Nazis could not ruin the bliss of discovering what love was all about. Bruno was so gentle and caring. But three weeks after our wedding, on 30 January, our fate was sealed.

Hänschen called us to let us know that President Hindenburg would be making a speech of national importance and that he, Hänschen, was on his way to join us. The whole family sat in the dining room with the box radio tuned in to the news. And what news it was. Hindenburg was resigning in favour of Hitler.

The openly professed Jew-killer now had absolute power over us.

My mother wept quietly, her arms around the twins. They were seventeen by then but still too frail, and still tutored at home. I think everyone was too stunned for a while to make any comment. It felt as though a tidal wave was about to engulf us and there was *no* high ground to run for.

'*Quatsch und Unsinn*,' Grandpa spluttered at the wireless. 'Utter rubbish. This bastard Hitler, this Austrian psycho, has hoodwinked the voters until now, but mark my words, once he shows his true colours in power, they'll vote him right back out again. We Germans aren't stupid.'

Hänschen's normally gentle voice was strident. 'Eli, you are fooling yourself, and with all respect, your attitude is dangerous to yourself and all your family. Hitler is not some passing political fad. He is here to stay. As of today we are living in, indeed trapped in, a dictatorship. Yesterday's republic is already a dream that has passed.'

'In Hitler's mind,' he continued, 'all of us in this room, whatever our sex, age and religion, are Jews. Thirteen years ago, he swore an oath to avenge Germany's defeat at, in his eyes, the hands of the Jews. Even back then, mass murder of German Jewry was his dream. As of today, he is free to indulge in that dream and we are his prey.'

'How can sane Germans have voted for this maniac?' My father's hands were tightly clasped as though in prayer.

Nobody answered him. Each of us sat silently

around the table with our own thoughts and fears. All over Germany, hundreds of thousands of Jews and other enemies of the Nazis were equally shocked.

Hänschen finally responded to my father's question. 'No sane German did vote for him, Max, for Hitler's own insanity, his murderous rage, has blinded them. His open hatred is compelling to a people desperately wanting an end to their national humiliation, to the political and economic chaos of the last decade, the violence, inflation and poverty. They want order, solidarity and the restoration of Germany as a great world power. Only Hitler has promised them all these things and they love him for it.

'When he came back to Munich after the war he took over a tiny right-wing party of ten extremists and manipulated it to gain power, step by murderous step, over the most powerful nation on earth. That party, the Nazis, is now merely an instrument of his will. He will kill millions. He has said as much, and we at the *Post* have warned our readers against him for over ten years. Now it is too late to block him and it may be too late to escape his killers.'

'But our emigration plans . . . ?'

'Yes, of course, Max. I am doing my best, but it is a long, painstaking process as I warned you.'

'What do you suggest we do now?' my mother asked.

'Above all, you must work to keep clear of suspicion. I am a known trouble-maker and, as a reporter of the *Post*, I am on the Nazi death list, but you may yet avoid classification as Jews. There *are* things you can do . . . with money and caution. But for the moment, keep your heads down and, though it hurts me to say this, keep away from anybody or anything Jewish.'

On the sofa, Grandpa and Grandma glanced at each other and held hands.

The road to the end came with many a twist and turn. At that time, the Nazis' first targets were Hitler's political opponents, mainly the Communists. The hunt was swift and thorough. Within two months 25,000 were arrested and slung into concentration camps such as the newly created Dachau.

In May 1933, with the Communists obliterated, Hitler focused his regime of oppression elsewhere. He took away all power from the individual German states, especially proud Bavaria, imprisoning or killing many popular statesmen. He abolished all trade unions and all political parties. Then he removed all civil liberties and any legal mechanism that might have served to depose him.

With regard to the Jewish question, the paramilitary wing of the Nazis, the SA, responded to each new Hitler order in every town and village throughout Germany. At first, he tried to frighten rich Jews into emigrating, leaving the bulk of their wealth, a huge fortune, to the Nazis. But this was an unattractive option to some Jews and they would need 'encouragement'. So, along with the Communists, all left-wing Jews were sent to the camps. Then all Jewish businesses were boycotted. Local newspapers warned Germans not to buy from any Jewish shop nor to use Jewish doctors, lawyers or other services.

Anti-Jew signs proliferated, warning Jews to stay away from restaurants, cinemas, swimming pools, parks and even their own gardens.

Whatever the Nazis wished to do to Jews they did with impunity. Jews had nowhere to hide and nobody in authority was prepared to protect them.

A Jew in Germany was worse off than a rat, for at least rats can hide. They have the sewers all to themselves. There was *no* hiding place for a Jew. As enemies of the state anybody could steal from them, rape them and beat their children to death, without fear of the law.

If you catch a cockroach and crush it under your heel, there is nothing that roach can do to protect itself. It has nobody to appeal to. It is utterly vulnerable. That is how it was for a Jew in Germany through the Hitler years.

I remember the feeling of real fear which ran through our dining room on that dreadful spring day when the coarse rant of Adolf Hitler's voice followed that of the radio announcer. His new Enabling Law gave his government complete freedom of action with *no* constitutional limitations. To think that this megalomaniac now held each and every one of us in the palm of his hand. To think that he inspired love, yes *love*, in the hearts of many millions of Germans. All over Germany, houses were hung with great red flags and swastika pennants; village and town bands blared and oompah'd their pride and joy. Men in brown, green or black uniforms goose-stepped in threatening columns and cheering crowds lined the pavements.

In response to Hitler's spellbinding oratory of

hatred, German citizens in schools, universities, factories, hospitals and even prisons, rose to their feet, their hands upraised in the Nazi salute and their voices united in a deafening cry of adulation, '*Sieg Heil! Sieg Heil!*'

Our own band of Hitler Youth boys marched proudly through Plauen and on to the outlying houses like ours. The stamp of their boots and their martial songs was a menacing sound. As required, we lined the verge of the lane as they passed, raised our hands and shouted, '*Heil Hitler!*' at the red Hitler Youth banner flying in their vanguard. Tomi and Toni shouted, '*Drei Liter!*' instead of '*Heil Hitler!*' but, fortunately, none of the marchers could hear.

Although Father had given many handsome donations to our local church over the years, Grandpa Eli's largesse had always been anonymously funnelled into the Plauen synagogue. There were some 900 Jews in the community and, at the turn of the decade, they had pooled their resources to build a magnificent, new synagogue on Senefelder Street; consecrated in April 1930, it was one of the last synagogues to be built in Germany before the war.

Our local Jösnitz friend, Alex Löwenthal, had long been a senior figure in the Jewish community and he also had good contacts in Berlin. He came to visit us soon after Hitler's accession.

'Listen, Max,' he warned my father. 'The Gestapo have copies of all our congregational lists from the synagogue, and all of us on those lists are at risk. They intend to start arresting us anytime now. But your family is not listed. Not even Eli and Tilla, who though staunch supporters, have not worshipped with us these last fifty years. The point I am making is this. Be as Protestant as you possibly can. Destroy any reference, even in your most personal papers, of any Jewish relations.'

'We have baptised the children.'

'I know, and that is good, but it is not enough. You must be three full generations clear on both sides of the family, and that you are not. If the Gestapo dig deep into records they will find your own and Eli's Jewish origins and label your children *Mischlinge*, half-breeds. My friends in Berlin predict the worst possible fate for all Jews including *Mischlinge*. If you cannot emigrate then at least do your utmost to bury your Jewish connections.'

Following Alex Löwenthal's warning, and knowing that emigration, if it proved at all possible, was a long way off, Father began systematically erasing all records revealing our Jewish background. Money or expensive gifts passed to officials and to old acquaintances.

Father visited a genealogist in Munich who produced an impressive family tree going back 15 generations, which demonstrated that our Jewish ancestors had married into Lutheran stock in the mid-nineteenth century, and clearly 'proved' that Eli and Tilla were Christians. The cost of all this was exorbitant, but our lives were at stake. Documentary proof of our Aryan lineage might soon prove crucial. Father had no doubt that if he did not provide the authorities with such evidence of our clean roots, then the Gestapo would direct their 'bloodhound' researchers at the birth and parish records. He sent our beautiful doctored family tree to the Vital Statistics Office, which eventually sent us a certificate acknowledging our Aryan status.

Had we lived in the Frankfurt area, even these measures might not have been enough, for all residents there were individually investigated by the Ministry of Health for 'Jewish blood or any other genetic disease'. One scientist claimed to have discovered a chemical test which could identify Jewish blood. He boasted, 'Now with a test tube I can catch all non-Aryans. No longer can they escape the net through deception, baptism, name change or nasal surgery, for they cannot change their blood.'

A new law demanded all state employees, students, doctors, lawyers and many other professionals provide proof of their Aryan ancestry, or face immediate sacking. The police did not need to carry out such investigations as the Nazis involved, and therefore implicated, tens of thousands of non-Nazis in their snooping. Town clerks, librarians, priests and hospital archivists were all made to join the racial hunt whether they liked it or not.

Father made sure that copies of our 'new' family tree were placed with all relevant authorities in the Plauen bureaucratic machine and, sensibly, with key individuals such as active Jösnitz gossips, suspected Gestapo informers in Plauen textile circles, and any older folk in the village who might vaguely remember that our grandparents were Jews, however non-practising and liberal they might have been over the past half century. And for a while, all this intrigue, subterfuge and corruption on Father's part certainly paid dividends. While all around us Jews and half-Jews disappeared, or were hounded into ghettos, we kept our heads down and the Gestapo stayed away.

In the spring of 1934, I gave birth to my beloved little Uschi. She was our pride and delight through so many difficult times.

Our doctor in Plauen, Heinrich Meyburg from Windmühlen Street, was an old non-Jewish friend, and he warned us in 1936 that the Gestapo had asked him if Father was circumcised. This was apparently just a routine enquiry. Doctor Meyburg read between the lines and bravely lied to the Gestapo, stating that he had carried out the cut purely because of a local infection. This served as a warning to us not to become complacent, a warning that was reinforced from an unexpected quarter in the summer of 1937.

Alfred had worked for the family since long before we children had been born, and was a wizard with vegetables and fruit. He could be bad-tempered when we trampled a flower or messed up the lawn, but that said, you could not find a better example of that rare quality, loyalty. Cap in hand, he approached my father one evening on his return from the Plauen factory. Father was an expert at translating Alfred's virtually unintelligible *Vogtländer* patois, the gist of which on this occasion was an urgent warning.

'He's been plucking up his courage for a week,' Father told us, 'to advise me of what's going on in the village. He won't name names, but he says old hatreds never die in Jösnitz. Apparently, back at the turn of the century, there was great rivalry between a number of blacksmiths in this area and when Grandpa switched all our business from one smith to another he encouraged a number of his friends to do likewise. This, completely unbeknownst to us, caused the first smithy family a long period of great poverty and even drove one member to suicide, which they blamed entirely on our family. They still do, and according to Alfred, they have documents *stolen from my desk* proving that your grandparents and I are Jews. They have given them to the local Gestapo and are bragging about it in the local inn.'

'Stolen from your desk?' My mother was incredulous. 'How on earth—?'

Father held up his hand. 'Alfred says Marianne's family is involved, that she stole the papers at her father's bidding and that we must not trust her. Of course I thanked Alfred from all of us and assured him nobody would ever know that he had warned us.'

'Will you sack her?' my mother asked.

'Of course I would like to, but with things as they are, diplomacy must come before my natural reaction. I have gone through all my desk drawers and the only missing papers are old newspaper cuttings reporting our marriage. A Munich reporter, a troublemaker, wrote at the time that ours was yet another of the Jew–Protestant weddings that were so diluting the purity of the German race. I subsequently spoke to the senior editor, an old acquaintance, and he printed a retraction which I still have and which Marianne failed to locate.'

'But the inn gossip factory will tell all the village that we are Jews.'

Father nodded. 'Of course they will, but he who laughs last laughs longest. I will get our friendly church verger to spread the news of the retraction. There's no love lost between his family and the blacksmith's. He'll be only too happy to brand them as false rumourmongers and restore our reputation.'

'I hope you're right, Max.' My mother did not look convinced.

'Well, if I'm not, let me know. Don't forget what happened to the poor Spiers, denounced to the Gestapo by their own chauffeur merely because they had ruffled his feathers with some well-deserved reprimand. It's a sorry state of affairs when we are frightened of our own maid, but in this topsy-turvy Nazi world, self-preservation must come before all else, including pride.'

All over Germany, former class hierarchies were being overturned as far as rich Jews were concerned. Domestic staff broke house rules, were openly rude and anti-Semitic, and stole from their employers. Of course, they got away with it even without uttering explicit blackmail threats. So, none of us ever mentioned the stolen cuttings to Marianne, nor was her employment with us terminated.

Father's rearguard action with the retraction must have worked, for we didn't hear from the Gestapo, but it was surely a very near miss.

We tried to live through those years as though there was no tomorrow because, of course, we could never be sure that there would be a tomorrow. For *all* the Jews and most of the *Mischlinge* in Plauen, the dreaded knock on the door came sooner or later. Out of the 900 Jews in Plauen, only 11 would survive, and that number includes you and me.

I have an abiding memory of one lovely day in the early summer of 1938 before the Nazis destroyed our family. Mother announced that we were to have a picnic. We had all loved picnics since as far back as I can recall. Usually Alfred would take us in the pony trap, and it would be piled high with laughing children and heavy hampers, but in 1938 we stayed at home, as that was the only place we considered safe in an increasingly dangerous world.

'Alfred's garden', as we called the two acres of lawn and ponds, birch clumps and shrubs, was our refuge and delight. A place where you could slowly wander, watch the ducks dabble and ponder the loveliness of the surrounding hills, all green behind the outline of our house. A light breeze kept the flies away but not the honey bees and butterflies. Our old dog, Günther, lolled in the shade of Grandpa's wheelchair. Grandma Tilla suffered gently from dementia and seldom left her bedroom. From time to time one of us would visit and sit by her bedside, and she always looked happy.

Doves cooed and the charcoal smells of sausage emanated from Alfred's stone stove by the lower pond. Tomi, Toni, and my own little Uschi, four years old but very active, played croquet with a deal of friendly shouting and many accusations of 'cheat'. I watched her proudly, for I had brought her up by myself since my dear Bruno had passed away the previous winter. With leukaemia in those days, his early death had been inevitable. I loved him dearly and love him still. I kept his family name and gave it to you when we came to Canada – something I have never told you before.

Alma and I helped Mother with the picnic for we had given Marianne the day off. We never felt entirely at ease when she was there. Nowadays we'd say it was like having a KGB agent in residence. Alma's husband was away with the *Wehrmacht*, the armed forces. Like my brother Kurt, who was training to be a submariner, he was expecting a European war sooner rather than later. Hänschen had been murdered by then, but more of that later. Once our picnic tea was in full swing, Father held his hand high for silence. He had an announcement.

'For once we will *not* switch the wireless on, although for us Germans the news is always full of excitement. Unemployment is down. Our forces have become the most powerful on Earth. The street violence of the Weimar years is a distant memory and our beloved *Führer* is leading us back to world greatness.' He paused and looked around at each of us before continuing. No doubt he registered our surprise.

'Throughout Germany, millions of honest patriots, including men like Grandpa here and me, who fought in wars for the Fatherland, are thinking these things and hoping for them. *We*, of course, are not because we know only too well of Hitler's other, despicable policy, an agenda of murder which a European war will doubtless accelerate. So, today, since we intend to be happy, we will cut ourselves off from outside news and banish the wireless. Instead, I am proud to announce the engagement of our beloved Anna to Erich. He and his parents sadly cannot join us today, but they are holding a similar celebration in Frankfurt at this time.'

We all raised our glasses of fine Rüdesheim hock and drank to Anna. She was too shy to speak, but her face was dimpled with pride and she sang a beautiful version of '*Ich bin ein Jägersmann*' for us, which was followed by much clapping, kissing, congratulations and wishes for a long, happy married life. Most of us present understood why her childhood sweetheart Erich, only three years her senior, had proposed now despite her tender age of 16. As the Reich's racist inquisitions delved ever deeper, our two families had agreed that Anna's safety would be much enhanced by early marriage into an Aryan family.

We toasted absent friends including Bruno and Hänschen, and Kurt and Alma's husband. Then each of us, in turn or in groups, sang our favourite tunes. Tomi and Toni produced a painfully discordant duet to which Uschi danced. The twins, at 22, were sadly as delicate as ever and Doctor Meyburg had twice sent them for spells in a specialist Munich clinic. Both had holes in their hearts, but so long as they stayed home under Mother's loving care, they were happy and carefree.

Mother's elder brother Ludwig, and his wife Rais, clapped especially hard at the twins' effort. Uncle Ludwig then turned to Father. 'We must talk later about the twins.'

Father nodded and said, 'Before you young ones go back to your games and us seniors to our siesta, one more thing. As you know, we intend to leave our beloved Jösnitz for a few years and go abroad. It will be exciting and much safer than Germany. Quite soon, I believe, Hitler will be voted out of power, Germany will go back to normal and we will return home. I had hoped today to announce the actual destination and date of our emigration, but alas, there has been yet another hitch. Don't worry about this for we are applying again. We have several options and I am sure, quite soon, we will be off.'

A sudden wild yelping sounded from under Grandpa Eli's chair. He slept on, snoring gently, but Günther shot up quicker than I had seen him move in years and belted off down the garden, his tail tucked fast between his legs. A wasp, we assumed, had stung him somewhere sensitive. A chorus of 'Poor Günther', mingled with a good deal of laughter at the dog's expense, faded away to silence. Even at such homely moments our overall predicament sat heavily on our minds and in the pit of our stomachs; a steady lingering fear that would often surface as a sharp panic, when you'd feel your mouth go dry and your heart thud fast against your ribs.

Uncle Ludwig's message to my parents was not a happy one. He and Rais were about to move their home and Ludwig's private psychiatry clinic to a new address not far away, that would have to remain confidential even from close relatives. He had that very week received a personal visit, in great secrecy, from two high-ranking Gestapo officers from Berlin, and they had told him he was to head up a specialist clinic on behalf of the government to carry out vital work on child schizophrenia. Looking grave, he said, 'For some time I have been worried about the twins, and once I start my new job, I will not be able to visit any more. So I felt it best to acquaint you now of a new Nazi threat and, if you wish, I will try to help find a way of avoiding it before I "disappear" to do this new job.'

Ludwig then outlined to Father the as yet unannounced Nazi policy of ridding Germany of any individual they considered to be a burden on the state. Every citizen would have to prove they were *lebenswertig*, socially worthy, and those who could not must be prevented from passing on their genes to the next generation of the Reich. To this end they would be sterilised. The proposed new law would demand sterilisation for 'the mentally and physically defective including alcoholics, sexual deviants, promiscuous women, anti-socials, prostitutes, backward students, and the habitually unemployed'.

'The Ministry of Health,' Ludwig warned us, 'will soon start to comb the records of all psychiatric departments of regular hospitals including the Munich hospital where Doctor Meyburg twice sent your twins. Once that happens you will receive an order to have them both sterilised. That in itself may not be disastrous, but I have learned of further Nazi plans, part of their step-by-step policy to eventually murder by injection or gas, all those previously sterilised. The Nazis estimate approximately three million "invalids" in Germany will have to be gassed.'

'Unbelievable,' my father whispered. The rest of us sat there in shock. I glanced at the twins playing so happily with Uschi and Günther.

'Yes,' Ludwig agreed. 'But then much of what the Nazis plan is utterly incredible by normal human standards. My suggestion to you is this: as soon as possible, I will enrol the twins with false identities into a gender-segregated "closed" institution in Bavaria, where they should be safe from government attention. It will be expensive, of course, very expensive . . .'

Father waved his hands at Ludwig. 'The cost doesn't matter, we must do it, Ludwig. Please arrange it as soon as you can.'

After the delicious picnic, Father called Alfred over from his toolshed and presented him with a custom-made forester's jacket along with a superbly embroidered tablecloth from the textile factory for his wife. 'For all that you do for us, Alfred, a small token of this family's great gratitude.'

I swear that, for the first time, I saw tears glint in Alfred's eyes and his lips twitching as he fought to control his emotions.

When the day was over and the sun had sunk behind the wooded hills of Jösnitz, I stayed with my father and uncle as their talk turned to world events.

That morning the English and German football teams had played a great match in Berlin. Germany had lost 3–6 to England, but the latter's team, Ludwig noted with distaste, had given the Nazi salute at the start of the game. The previous week, Hitler and Mussolini had come to an alliance agreement and, soon after, Britain's peace-seeking Chamberlain had sold out to the Fascists with a new Anglo-Italian agreement. However, Father remarked, Britain, France and Czechoslovakia had all accelerated their own preparations for war; Hitler would not have things entirely his own way.

Years later, in the times of horror, I clung to my memory of that happy family day and I prayed to God that such occasions would once again become possible.

As for dear Hänschen, so handsome and kind; they finally murdered him as he had so often predicted. After he went underground, the *Munich Post* attached him to another anti-Nazi newspaper *Der Gerade Weg*, where he did research for the editor, Fritz Gerlich. They had prepared an exposé, utterly damaging to Hitler personally, and including the revelation that the *Führer* had murdered his own niece after their incestuous relationship had turned sour. Gerlich's intent was to publish full details of this scandal a month after Hitler's accession to power, but before he'd had time to consolidate his dictatorship. Their hope at the time was that President Hindenburg would depose the new Chancellor before it was too late.

The Gestapo learned of Gerlich's plan, and in March 1933 burst into his office, beat him almost to death, destroyed all traces of the exposé and dragged him off to Dachau. A year later they shot him and posted his blood-spattered spectacles to his wife to inform her she had become a widow. Hänschen was at work in the *Munich Post*'s offices when the Hitler thugs arrived to destroy the place and arrest the staff. After two days of torture he died in agony suspended from a meat hook in a Munich cellar. Following the *Post*'s elimination and right up until 1945, every German newspaper was *gleichgeschaltet*, or brought into line.

Apart from that picnic, there was one other joyous event in 1938 before the dark blanket of war fell over us – Anna's marriage to Erich. They married in Frankfurt by the agreement of both families. We had to be certain never to take a false step, and we feared that if they married in our Plauen parish, it might somehow stir up memories of our grandparents' Jewishness.

All marriages were being closely inspected to check for racial impurity on either side, and the law for the Protection of German Blood was rigidly enforced. One Catholic priest in Berlin was imprisoned for abetting 'racial defilement' after merely officiating at a *Mischling* marriage. And many German Aryans were flung into prison just for flirting with Jews, Negroes or gypsies. The 'aliens' involved were sent to concentration camps. The law's interpretation of intercourse included any act which 'satisfied a person's sex drive'. Mutual masturbation or kissing led many to prison, and in one case an Aryan thera-peutic masseuse was arrested for massaging a Jew who 'might have achieved sexual gratification whether she was aware of it or not'. On that occasion the masseuse was betrayed to the Gestapo by her long-time secretary.

If a priest from the Church tried to remonstrate, he would invariably be denounced by one of his congregation. There was a brave Lutheran priest, Pastor Umfried, who complained that the beating and murder of two Jews in his parish by SA thugs was unjust. Umfried was sacked, and fearful that he and his wife would be sent to Dachau, he committed suicide. Throughout the country, the majority of faithful churchgoers, both Catholic and Protestant, expelled from their congregations fellow Christians they had worshipped with for 25 years and more, purely because of some real or imagined Jewish connection. And a great many Christian parishioners, thus betrayed by neighbours, died in the camps. Conversion to Christianity, or even having Christian parents when you were baptised, was not enough to transform a Jew into a German, any more than a black could ever be made white. In Berlin, Göring boasted, '*I* decide who is a Jew and who is not.'

After Anna and Erich's wedding came an episode of my life which, along with much that came after it, I would prefer never to think about, nor talk of, nor suffer in nightmares. The only warning of what was to happen, which at the time we failed to recognise as such, was a visit one night from a weasel-like master plumber from Oelsnitz, a village near Plauen where Father rented out two small houses. The plumber, a long-time tenant, had somehow heard a rumour that Father had been born a Jew, and so when Father sent him a polite reminder requesting his long-overdue rent payment, the plumber responded with blackmail, brazenly demanding a receipt for the full amount that he owed without offering a *Pfennig* of payment. Otherwise, he threatened, he would denounce our whole family to the Gestapo as Jews and enemies of the state. Perhaps unwisely, Father refused to yield to this threat, stating emphatically that he was as Christian as the plumber, and ordering him to leave the cottage with all his belongings by the end of the week.

Ten days later Father drove to Oelsnitz and never returned. That night, considerably alarmed lest there had been some sort of accident, Mother called Doctor Meyburg in Plauen, who went at once to the Oelsnitz property. The plumber's family had left, but Father's body lay sprawled in the backyard in a pool of dried blood: his skull had been smashed by a heavy steel bar which lay beside him.

Neither Doctor Meyburg nor any of our other Aryan friends and relatives could afford to be seen trying to help us, for it quickly became apparent that we were now labelled as dangerous *Mischlinge* in the Plauen Gestapo files. The plumber's denouncement had triggered an immediate investigation into our family's status. Time would tell whether all Father's hard work to Aryanise us and our records would hold out against the Gestapo bloodhounds.

We grieved for Father, but I will not dwell on such terrible memories. The funeral was held in Plauen and, despite the rumours, many of Father's colleagues from the company turned up. During the war, however, his gravestone was smashed to pieces. I found that out soon after the war ended, so I paid for a brass plaque here in the park. I never told you about it, but now I have. When I am gone you can polish it, although you never knew him. He was the finest and best of men. I am sure God forgave his lack of belief and accepted him into heaven.

Our father's murder meant that the word of our 'suspected' status spread like wildfire. We were descended from Jews. We *were* Jews. As though overnight we had broken out in plague spots, neighbours began to avoid us. Friends we had loved for years shunned us. Suddenly we were different from them. Fear took away all memories of friendship and old times. The long years of Nazi-inspired anti-Semitic terror had been largely successful, but many non-Jews were still being arrested for having maintained close friendships with Jews. Goebbels kept up an intense five-year propaganda barrage against Aryans who still showed signs of sympathy against the beating and murder of Jews. 'I attack,' he ranted, 'all those mindless or deluded Germans who still shamelessly think that Jews are in fact human beings.'

Very few Germans were brave enough to maintain even covert friendships with Jews. Painfully, more often the reverse was true, and they joined the Jews' tormentors. And, now that *we* were labelled as Jews, we tasted a tiny sample of what most German Jews had already suffered for five long years. The very Sunday after Father's death, one of my mother's fellow communicants at the Jösnitz church complained to the priest that he should be ashamed to give communion to the consort of a Jew, and that if he did so again, she would denounce him.

Shopping in the village became a trial of cold hard stares, theatrical behind-your-back whispers, and aggressive shoves off the pavement, often by folk who had been acquaintances or even friends since childhood. People who had lived, worked, buried relatives and shared festive holidays alongside my parents for decades, now treated us like dirt.

It was as though life as I had known it had ceased. I was on another planet where everybody hated and despised me. If somebody could only have told me that I was *not a Jew*, the relief would have been intense.

Early in October, a bank cheque that Mother had written bounced, and when she called her once-obsequious bank manager, she was rudely informed that the account had been closed by the government. No explanation was given and further attempts to call the man were blocked by secretaries.

A friend of our wonderful Ludwig called after dark later that month and the twins went with him to the relative safety of the clinic in Bavaria. When the clinic's director had originally demanded funds for a minimum of four full years, Father had paid up grudgingly for there had been no alternative. Now, with our bank funds seized, we were only too pleased with the arrangement. The twins went off arm in arm and as happy as ever, in blissful ignorance of the evil that swirled all about them. Mother wept bitterly as the car lurched away up the gravel darkness of our drive. If only the nightmare had stopped then, but no, God deserted us entirely at that point and the Devil took over.

At this point in her story, Aunt Ruth looked up at me, her face pallid, and sweat on her brow. 'I am not sure I can continue,' she said. 'I do not feel at all well.'

CHAPTER FOUR

My aunt spent a week in hospital and the doctor's diagnosis was bad. He had found a couple of small cancerous tumours in her groin and the treatment was to begin at once.

Alone in our flat, I began to brood. It took a while for the shock to subside and for everything Aunt Ruth had told me to sink in, and I did not resolve at that point to commence any quest for justice: that came later, after I had heard more from my aunt. But back then, in early 1975, events were occurring in Europe which would later affect me. Although I would only uncover details of those events many years later in 1993, I will describe them now.

The Prak family file was closed by the Stasi in 1975, the year these five Vietnamese workers were murdered in their host town of Howerswerda in Saxony. The file was held by the Lower Saxony office of the *Verfassungsschutz*, the government department whose job it was to control all German far-right groups. In

1990, still hunting for the name Bendl – the only clue I possessed as to the identity of the Resolute Airport man, which I had obtained from the RCMP archives – I approached a friend who worked in the *Verfassungschutz*. He showed me the Prak file together with another ex-Stasi report of the same date regarding an underground anti-Semitic meeting also in Howerswerda. Later, I will explain how I came to gain access to all these files.

In 1975 Howerswerda was part of East Germany, where all political meetings were banned by the Marxist government and, if they went underground, spied upon by Stasi informers. Since a good many Nazi war criminals had been recruited into the Stasi in 1945, a blind eye was often turned on anti-Semitic acts. They were reported but not prevented. This was in direct contradiction to the stringently anti-Nazi policies of the East German government.

The Praks were a family of five from Vietnam; Mr and Mrs Prak, their two young daughters and Mr Prak's mother. Like a good many Vietnamese and Cuban visitor-workers, they had come to East Germany to take advantage of the relatively high pay-packets. At Howerswerda, they worked mostly in chemical plants and open-cast lignite mines.

The town, once a Communist showpiece, was by 1975 a bleak and grimy vista of ten-storey apartment blocks. The Prak family lived in one of these apartments, and dreamed of returning to their homeland one day, once they had saved enough money.

At 11.30pm on 20 April 1975, a group of thickset men, five in number according to neighbours, entered the Praks' flat. The report said the door lock was undamaged, so the Praks had no doubt opened the door without suspecting danger. Their bodies were found five days later, thanks to the curiosity of an immediate neighbour.

The word *Raus* was daubed on the apartment walls in the Praks' blood. Dribbles of it streamed from each letter. The two daughters had been strangled after being sexually assaulted and then their throats had been slit. Their school superior said they were eleven and nine years old. The grandmother had no injuries but for a bruise on one cheek: the police report assumed her heart had given out. What I found especially terrible was the imaginative sadism of the torturers. They had stripped Mr and Mrs Prak naked, lashed them back-to-back in the bath, defecated over them, turned the taps on low, then lit up cigarettes and settled back to watch their slow drowning. The cigarette stubs were found in the bath.

In his routine daily report, a Stasi informer from the Prak apartment block had noted the registration number of the Trabant car in which the assumed assailants had departed after their midnight mission was done. It struck me how careless any murderer must be to park his car close to the killing site. Perhaps the Prak killers had not feared any official follow up.

The second part of this file was also of great interest to me. It concerned a meeting of veteran Nazis and neo-nazi disciples at an office block in central Howerswerda's Albert Schweitzer Street, and the notes included the car numbers of all vehicles parked close to the building. Cars would not normally be parked in that non-residential zone after midnight and in winter. The Prak assailants' Trabant was among the two dozen vehicles listed. A third report was appended, which described the 'unsuccessful follow up' of the Prak murder investigation. I ignored this and concentrated on the Schweitzer Street meeting.

The report of the meeting was highly suspect since the author or authors were Stasi employees, and they were writing about a meeting of anti-Semites and nazis, some of whom were Stasi officers of possibly senior rank to themselves. Since I had no way of knowing the viewpoint of the authors, anti-Semitic or otherwise, I could not gauge the authenticity of what I was reading. However, since my sole aim was to trace one man, the overall honesty of the report would, I hoped, not matter too much, if at all.

The Stasi's history is pretty simple, and I should outline its origins if I am to explain my research difficulties when I read the Prak files.

The *Verfassungschutz* slowly gained access to old Stasi files when West Germany annexed the ex-Communist East in 1990, but many of the files were held regionally and my access was at that point limited to files from the main East Berlin Headquarters on Normannen Street.

The Stasi had been formed in the 1940s by the Soviet bosses of East Germany (GDR). They realised that a great many East Germans hated living under their repressive Marxist regime, and so they would need a vast security service to instil fear and subservience into the populace. The KGB and its predecessors in the Soviet Union had trained certain exiled Germans *before* World War II, and these men were appointed to create the Stasi. They included all three subsequent Stasi bosses Zaisser, Wollweber and Mielke.

Ostensibly the main enemies of the Communist GDR were ex-Nazis but, in reality, and as elsewhere in the West, many of Hitler's worst war criminals found their talents being utilised by their new masters.

My RCMP files research in the 1990s had furnished me with a name, real or alias I did not know, of the man I had met in 1975 at Resolute Airport. I had no way of knowing whether this Bendl was still alive and, if he was, what had happened to him. But, since learning his name, I had doggedly tried to pick up his trail on the assumption that, like most individuals who start life with chips on their shoulders and then achieve power, he would have preferred to keep his family name rather than exchange it for a false one. On the other hand, if after the war he had feared trial by the Allies, he might well have taken on a new name. Having no other information, I had to hope that Bendl was still Bendl.

Over the 15 years of my intermittent search I had followed a number of other Bendl trails, all leading nowhere. None had furnished me with photographs of my quarry, so I had no way of knowing if the face imprinted on my memory from my 1975 chance meeting at Resolute Bay belonged to any of my various leads.

My *Verfassungschutz* friend had called me in the summer of 1990 with news of a likely Bendl tracing, so I had flown to his Cologne office to search the relevant files he had borrowed from the old Berlin Stasi HQ. This was not strictly legal but nobody knew, so nobody minded.

I became very excited as I devoured the file, for *this* Bendl fitted exactly the little I knew of my quarry. Certainly his age and his origins tallied and, best of all, his Stasi missions in 1975 had all been in North America.

In the mid-1970s, after a quarter of a century of using crude torture and executions to subdue opposition to the regime, the Stasi gradually adopted high-tech surveillance, a huge mail-and-telephone snooping service, and either confined dissidents in special mental institutions or expelled them to the West in exchange for hard currency. At the same time, the HVA, the external wing of the Stasi, was enlarged to spy more effectively on the West.

Back in 1956, Bendl had been promoted to Senior Field Agent with the backing of Erich Mielke who soon afterwards became overall Stasi boss. Bendl had never looked back, and by 1986 was in a senior position in the Stasi's Department VIII which liaised with Stasi-paid spies in West Germany.

Bendl's file referred several times to his nazi views and high-level West German neo-nazi contacts. These were obviously encouraged by his Communist superiors as they helped his Stasi work in the West.

The last Bendl file entry, in August 1987, simply stated: *Geh I.M.* This, my *Verfassungschutz* colleague informed me, meant that any subsequent file on Bendl would have been held not by the main Berlin Stasi office but by Bendl's regional Stasi HQ and under an I.M. codename. I.M. meant an unofficial co-worker or civilian spy. By 1989, there were over 100,000 of them paid by, and working for, the Stasi inside East Germany. These unofficial collaborators formed a vast chain of neighbourhood spies across the whole country and even included people spying on Stasi members themselves. Longstanding Stasi officers, on reaching official retirement, were often made into 'officers with special missions'. They received excellent wages and perks, such as a car, phone and VIP apartment instead of a mere state pension. Bendl had been lucky enough to become one.

'And so where is he now?' I had asked my colleague.

'Ah! For that you will need his post-1986 file. It will not be listed under Bendl but under his new I.M. codename. All I.M.s have a codename.'

'Can the *Verfassungschutz* help locate it?'

He shrugged. 'If anybody could, we could, but it is a needle-and-haystack situation. We would need a lot of luck.'

'Could you try?'

'I will do my best, my friend. More than that I cannot promise.'

The file on the 20 April 1975 nazi meeting that followed the Prak killings mentioned Bendl, noting that he was on leave from missions abroad, and had arrived smelling of alcohol as had his four colleagues.

The meeting, according to the informer, had included a number of local Stasi officers and the sole purpose of it appeared to have been to toast Adolf Hitler well into the early hours.

I left the *Verfassungschutz* considerably encouraged that I was at last homing in on Bendl. I could, even then, hardly hear the name without experiencing the familiar churning in the pit of my stomach. How, you might wonder, could I nurture hatred and a desire for revenge for 15 long years for a wrong committed some 50 years before? Let me tell you what Aunt Ruth related to me back in 1975 – then you may begin to understand the depth of my hatred towards all those responsible.

In the early summer of 1975, Aunt Ruth came home from a spell in hospital. Based in our Nepean flat, I was working part-time for a children's centre in Ottawa and had visited my aunt on a regular basis. Her treatment was not straightforward but that June she seemed much better, and the doctors tentatively agreed that there were currently no cancers in evidence. For how long this second remission might last they could not say, but she, and they, felt she could again cope with living alone at home. That was important as in July I was due to leave for a job in West Africa. I had offered not to go but Aunt Ruth had insisted that she would feel guilty if I remained, and was adamant that she would cope as well as she had in the past.

We had been unable to talk in private in the hospital wards, but Aunt Ruth had made it clear that as soon as we were home together again she *must* continue to tell me her story. After all the years of bottling it all up, she now felt only relief to be passing the burden on to me, and during the long weeks lying in bed in the wards, she had slowly taken to the idea that her duty to the world was to make her appalling story known, both as a warning for the future and as a way of hitting back at those responsible.

I settled Aunt Ruth into her armchair and made sure the windows of the sitting room were wide open to catch the breeze. She carried on from where she had left off.

So, Doctor Meyburg took the twins away to a clinic for safety after Father was murdered. It was towards the end of October 1938 that your mother and I last saw dear Tomi and Toni. Kurt was unable to get back from his naval service for Father's funeral. Without money, for the Gestapo had closed our bank account, Mother was at her wits' end. I remember her on the kitchen bench knitting a jumper for my Uschi. She seldom spoke, and would have eaten nothing had Anna and I not cajoled her into sharing the tinned food we opened to avoid going shopping and facing local hostility.

'This is unbelievable,' Erich laughed bitterly. 'Here we are, you two sisters, your mother and me. All of us Christians and the whole world is treating us as Jews.'

'They also classify my Uschi as Jewish because of poor Father,' I reminded him.

'But your father is . . .'

'Yes, of course. He is dead. But his blood flows

through Uschi. And they know Grandpa and
Grandma are here. Last week, in the street, Mother
heard two of the parishioners call us a nest of Jewish
vipers.'

Erich and Anna were planning to move to Munich
where nobody would associate them with any
Mischling status, but their lodgings were not yet
ready. I have to admit that I was the happier for
Erich's presence in our house.

That week a sleek black car arrived unannounced
at 5am. Günther, our old dog, had died by then, so
our first warning was a shout from Erich who heard
the crunch of gravel under wheels. I told Mother and
my grandparents to stay in their rooms. The rest of
us met in the hall in our nightgowns, our hearts thudding with fear.

We heard the approach of jackboots, an unmistakable sound, and the heavy thud of truncheons on our
front door. They were SA stormtroopers, men of the
local Nazi paramilitary wing, sharp-faced and
humourless. One handed Erich a sheet of paper.
'Hurry,' he said, 'and don't try to be clever. Bring
everything listed. Any oversight will see everybody
here arrested.'

The list was mainly of utensils – telephone, elec-
trical side-lamps, typewriters, sewing machine,
wirelesses, trouser presses, even knife-grinders. We
rushed off in every direction, for Nazi officials in any
guise had an uncanny ability to create unease. There
was no question of asking what the hell they were
doing in our house at such an hour ordering us about
and stealing our property. Of course I was angry, and

the thought crossed my mind to remonstrate, but no words reached my tongue which was dry with apprehension.

When all the listed goods were piled on the floor in the hall, one of the officers nudged the booty with his foot. 'That's all?' he asked without looking up.

'Yes, sir,' Erich said, 'everything we can find.'

'Well, you'll suffer if there is more.' He flicked his fingers and two of his men dispersed to search the house. One found a toast machine. He brought it to his boss as though it were a cask of gold hidden by smugglers.

'What's this, then?' the officer turned to me.

'A toaster,' I said.

'Don't be clever, *Jud*. Why was this not brought out?'

I swallowed hard. No ideas came to my rescue and I found myself mouthing the truth. 'We must have overlooked it, *Herr Offizier*.'

'Soon you Jews will "overlook" things no more.' The officer appeared to be bored. 'Take these things to the car, *schnell*,' he said. We did so, and without a further word they drove off.

Two days later they came back for our car, once Father's proudest possession. Again without a murmur we handed over the keys.

'When they ask for our *lives*, will we go like sheep?' Erich joked.

Nobody laughed. We had all heard too many rumours, listened to the deadly lyrics of the Hitler Youth songs, and felt the murderous hatred of the anti-Semites who seemed to make up the majority of the German population, at least in our part of Saxony.

My Christian cousin Alma came to see me in her shiny Mercedes after a fortnight away on holiday with her husband. She arrived after dark for we had agreed many months back that there was no point in her taking unnecessary risks. Aryan Germans who were still friendly with Jews were themselves asking for big trouble. I had begged Alma not to keep coming and assured her that I would understand – that she would not be deserting us. But there was no stopping her. She hated the Nazis and those of her friends and family who favoured them. She was shocked when she heard what had happened to us and saw the state we were in, especially my mother, whose normally warm greeting of Alma had been replaced by a mere listless nod.

'You look half-starved.'

I explained we were blacklisted in the village shops and had no transport to go further afield.

Accepting no protest, Alma drove off and returned within the hour, her car laden with food, mostly fresh produce. By the time she left to go home, promising to return in a week, we all felt better. At least we had one solid friend, one contact with the outside world, somebody who did not hate us.

The following evening, November 9th, Alfred tapped gently on the kitchen window. He knew how easily startled we could be. We let him in at once and Anna gave him some of Alma's precious coffee. He was in a nervous state, and kept turning his felt hat round and round in his gnarled old fingers.

'What is it, Alfred?' I asked. 'Something is wrong with your family?'

'No, Frau Ruth. I am sorry, so sorry. It is the village. They have gone mad, *ganz verrückt*. You know the old Kassel brothers who live up past my barn on the lane to Röttis?'

I nodded. They, like us, were rated as Jews though the connection was faint.

'They smashed their windows, set their horses free, and when old Otto tried to stop them whipping his dog to death, they beat him with an iron bar. When they left I tried to help. He is in agony – I think his spine is broken.'

'Who were they?' I asked. I had understood most of Alfred's story but his patois was always thick as porridge, and thicker still when he was upset.

'Just people from the village – about thirty of them. No SA. But I heard them say it is to happen all over Germany tonight. Orders from Goebbels. All Jews are to be beaten, their shops and synagogues destroyed. They said there have been killings too. So I came to warn you because you are next on their list after they've done drinking at the Strauss place.'

'Thank you, thank you, Alfred. We cannot thank you enough.' Anna kissed our old gardener's wrinkled forehead, and despite the circumstances he smiled with embarrassed pleasure.

'No more than any Christian should do for his fellow man,' he murmured, 'and your family has stood by me since I was this high.' Alfred had never before been so eloquent. 'When they come, Frau Ruth, do nothing to upset them, I beg you. Let them do whatever they must, but you should hide the old folk now. Maybe your lady mother too, for she does not look herself, if I may say so. I must go now for they will turn on me and my family if they think I have been here to warn you.'

'Of course, Alfred, we understand.'

He helped Erich move my grandparents into the only place we all agreed should be safe from any search, the shelves at the rear of the henhouse. We put down new straw and covered Eli and Tilla with it so they were warm and could not be seen even were someone to peer through the hatches. Then we bolted the door and Alfred left.

Back in the house, we turned off the lights, hoping the villagers would think we were all away. Anna and Erich kept my Uschi quiet with a candlelit card game in the upper bedroom. I fussed over Mother and tried to explain why we must keep quiet. She wanted to see that Grandpa and Grandma were comfortable, for she had looked after them for many years. Beyond that she just rocked back and forth.

'Where is Kurt?' she asked of a sudden.

'With the U-boats, the submarines,' I said, surprised at the question, for nobody was more proud of her son than she was, or less likely to forget his whereabouts.

'Yes,' she murmured, 'the U-boats.'

How long we waited like that I cannot say. Once or twice I crept out to the henhouse to stop Grandpa from snoring. I had to warn him and Grandma of the danger without scaring them too much.

At an hour or so past midnight I heard the first

noise, a distant murmur as of a far away fairground. I
peeked through the curtains in the upper bedroom
and my heart jumped for they were already at the
entrance to our lane. Someone was leading with a
bicycle, but mostly they were walking, for I could see
a line of bobbing lights extending back down the lane
for several hundred yards. Alfred had said a group of
about 30 but it looked like 50, 60, or more. With
Mother in her helpless condition and Erich much
younger than me, I knew I must take charge of the
situation.

'Will you let them in?' Anna whispered to me.

'Shall I get your father's shotgun?' Erich offered.

'I will have to do whatever they say, Anna, or it will
be the worse for us. And, Erich, the Nazis took away
Father's gun many months ago. We have nothing
with which to defend ourselves, and even if we did,
there are too many of them.'

As I spoke, the noise of smashing glass announced
their arrival. Stones and kindling from our woodpile
crashed through every window in the house and we
could clearly hear the intense excitement of their
voices; a baying of hounds. Anna wept soundlessly on
Erich's shoulder.

I looked about the room. My Uschi was as safe as
she could be up here with Erich. There was nothing I
could do. I felt utterly powerless and at the mercy of
the mob below. With an effort, I forced myself down
the stairs and back to the kitchen to comfort Mother
who, as always, felt safest in the rocking chair by the
stove. Screams of hate mingled with coarse laughter.
'Cursed Jews! Jew mongrels! Christ-killers!'

There was no wind and the night was frosty so all sounds were sharp. I heard the noise of tin on tin and smelled gasoline. A sudden shudder of the curtains accompanied a flare of light outside the darkness of the kitchen and a cheer went up as our garage caught fire. Alfred stored some garden equipment in there alongside our pony trap and sleigh.

'Come out, Jews,' somebody shouted in a high shrewish voice, 'or we will burn you out.'

I told Mother not to worry, to stay quiet by the stove. She smiled faintly and nodded. I smoothed my apron down, patted my hair and opened the front door. It took a few moments to get used to the light from the flames. Torches were shone at my face.

I said, 'Good evening.' What else could I say? Catcalls came in response, and laughter.

'We'll give you good evening. Where are the other filthy Jews?'

'I'm alone.'

'Come off it.' A gruff, male, peasant voice. 'Your grandparents, the misers, they're too old to have gone anywhere.'

I began to see outlines, then faces, then individuals, most of whom I recognised: Hitler Youth, BDM and other non-Party folk, many of whom I had known since a child, or at least well enough to exchange greetings or glances in church. As I looked at a local craftsman with whom Father had done business for years, he averted his eyes, shamefaced. Others screamed mindless abuse, shook their fists and spat towards me. They did not close in on me though, and as I stood there staring back at them, I sensed the

frenzy of the first few moments begin to abate.
Perhaps they had expected some form of fight from
us or at the least, arrogance.

They appeared to have no leader, so the insults
died down and the torches moved away as their
owners, joking with one another, turned back towards
the village. They had had their fun. Whoever had
sent them out had been obeyed and, perhaps more
importantly, they had been seen by their neighbours
to be doing their anti-Semitic bit; their duty to the
Nazi Party. After all, the Gestapo frightened everyone, not just the Jews. These villagers, like all average
Germans, lived in the shadow of an increasingly terrorist regime, and they knew their neighbours could
denounce them, with or without good reason, so they
must make a show of being good Jew-haters. As the
last shouts and jeers faded away, I drew a great sigh of
relief and feeling faint leaned against the inside of
the door.

Erich appeared with my little Uschi in his arms.
'Ruth, we heard it all. You were so brave.'

'They have gone.' I hugged Uschi, Anna and
Erich, and then we all rushed to Mother. We need not
have worried; she was knitting away as though she
had seen and heard nothing untoward.

Uschi merely said, 'I won, Mummy. I beat them
twice at cards.'

Cautiously, we all went outside. The garage fire
had died down and I soon saw that little damage was
done.

'Grandpa and Grandma!' Anna said. 'We must get
them in by the stove.' We followed the path around to

the dark side of the house, and that was when it really began . . .

It was like a replay of when I was 16, walking back from our picnic in Alfred's secret glade. The house was behind us and the chicken run with its henhouses just ahead at the end of our lawn. They were waiting in the darkness behind the shrubs, and their sudden appearance was, I remember, like an electric shock, *terrifying*. Uschi screamed, so did Anna. I was stunned.

'Where are you going?' I recognised that voice well from across the years. Ernst Seidler, one-time member of the Hitler Youth, and now, as rumour had it, a special policeman for Hitler in Leipzig. He must have been on leave. I counted three other shadowy outlines behind him, all big men.

'Look in the sheds, Karl,' Seidler ordered. 'That's where they were heading, the Jewish slime.'

We stood in silence, paralysed with fear. I do not even remember feeling cold despite the frost.

'*Komm* Ernst, *noch mehr Juden.*' More Jews. The searcher had found Grandpa Eli and Grandma Tilla's hiding place.

'Watch them,' Ernst Seidler said to his friends. Then he strode to the chicken run.

'Karl, you have the can. Use it. You know how to smoke out wasp nests.'

Before anyone of us knew what they were about, there was a sudden thud of ignition and a burst of flames. I shot forward and, dodging Seidler, rushed to the rear door of the henhouse to undo the bolt. As I tried to slide it open, I was grabbed round the neck.

The flames roared up, helped no doubt by the dry straw in the roosts. The chickens screeched and fluttered violently against their prison walls.

'*Hühnerbraten*,' one of the men laughed. Roast chicken.

'You murderers!' I yelled, and beat my arms against my captor. 'Let them out. They are harmless old folk.' Then I saw Erich appear. He had found a piece of wood which he brought down on the head of my assailant. The wood, rotten, smashed into pieces and Erich's spectacles flew to the ground. Without them he was as blind as a mole. Two of the other men closed in on him. One had a bayonet and he plunged it deep into Erich's stomach.

From inside the sheds I heard a thin scream from Grandma Tilla, then a feeble battering from within against the burning wood. One of the chicken hatches flew open and, briefly, I saw Grandpa's face, his eyes tight closed against the searing heat and his beard on fire. I clearly caught his words. '*Den zweiten Fensterladen auch. Mehr Licht. Mehr Licht.*' He was quoting Goethe as he died. Grandma made no further sound and must already have passed away.

The men dragged me back to the lawn by my hair. I could see it all clearly by the light of the leaping flames. Anna, curled up on the grass, her arms around Uschi, who was screaming her heart out. I did not recognise the two men, uniformed like Seidler, who stood over Anna, with their heavy truncheons to hand. But the fourth man called Karl was a younger brother of Seidler, and though big for his age, was probably no more than 14 years old. He was clearly determined to win his spurs in the presence of his peers for he kicked hard at Anna's buttocks, and as she cried out, he seized my little Uschi by one leg . . . held her high over his head and flung her into the inferno.

I must have lost consciousness at the sheer horror of it all, as when I came to my senses, they had lashed my hands together and torn off most of my clothes. One man held me around the neck as Ernst Seidler raped me. The other two Nazis attacked your mother, Seidler's younger brother raping her. When he was done, he spat on her and called her a Jewish whore.

What petrol was left, they splashed around our sitting room and soon the house too was on fire. I heard our old clock strike the hour. It was two in the morning and our whole world had changed forever.

Alfred came back just before dawn. The time when the cocks would have crowed, but they, like Uschi and my grandparents, were charred remains in the skeletal black wreck of the henhouse. He found us on the lawn where we lay clasped together, your mother and me, cold as the grave but not caring, and led us gently to his potting shed where a kerosene burner glowed blue to keep the frost from the seedlings. 'Here, Frau Ruth and Frau Anna, you stay here while I make you some coffee. Where are the others?' We told him and he shook his head in disbelief. 'And your mother?'

Anna and I looked at each other. In our state of shock and grief, we had not thought of her at all.

'She was in the kitchen when they came.'

'But the fire?' Alfred asked. 'The house is burnt out.'

'She might have left by the front door. They were all here at the back.'

Alfred was gone for some minutes and we could hear him calling for our mother. He came back with her, his arms around her shoulders.

'I think her mind has gone,' he said. 'She was in the shrubs singing nursery rhymes.'

Months later, from Mother's ramblings, I worked out that she had seen everything that had happened on the fire-illuminated lawn from inside the house. She had already been under great mental stress and that night surely tipped her over the edge. We gave Alfred Alma's phone number and he called her from the village. Between the two of them, they kept us alive in that little shed. Even today the smell of kerosene reminds me of it. It took Alma two weeks to trace Uncle Ludwig by leaving a message at his old address which was up for sale. Just as he had said, he was taking the secrecy of his new job very seriously and had left no forwarding address with his estate agent nor with anybody else. But he came as soon as he found Alma's message.

'You must leave here at once. Rais has plenty of spare bedrooms and we have enough stores to feed a regiment. You poor, poor dears.'

Before we left our home, our only home, Uncle Ludwig said prayers with us over the simple graves that Alfred had dug in the lawn for the remains of Uschi and my grandparents, and the body of Erich. At the end of the war, your Uncle Pete and I had them re-buried before we came out here.

Uncle Ludwig's car was large and grey. 'I'm

allowed in and out of the Clinic, as we call our new home,' he told us, 'but nobody else is. There is a guard on the inner gate, and although neither Rais nor I have yet been submitted to a thorough search of the car, there is always a first time. You cannot be too careful.'

He laid us down on rugs in the spacious rear compartment of his car and covered us with a tailor-made, plywood and carpeted 'floor' on which, he said, he would place his briefcase and various files. He assured us that this had worked well with previous 'refugees' he had smuggled into the Clinic. It was cramped, but the journey was smooth and fairly brief, certainly less than an hour.

We were to live in the Clinic and its walled grounds through much of the war. You, Derek, were born there and gave your mother and I great pleasure. We suffered times of terror there too, but for us and those other lucky few saved by the bravery of Ludwig and Rais, the place was a haven of safety in an otherwise utterly hostile world. Mother's physical health remained good but her mind never healed. I think she was happy enough in whatever dream world she spent her days. Uncle Ludwig, one of Germany's top child psychoanalysts, assured us there was nothing anybody could do for her but keep her in a quiet environment.

Rais told us that Jews throughout the Reich had been assaulted over a three-day period that November. A German diplomat in Paris had been shot by a Jew, and Goebbels had orchestrated the violence everywhere to crank up the speed of the

Judenfrei process: the ethnic cleansing of Germany. Although our family had been unable to obtain emigration papers, at least 300,000 of Germany's half a million Jews *had* already fled the country, and this latest provocation was intended to get rid of many more.

Hitler's specific rationale for encouraging rich Jews to emigrate was to gain their vast wealth for his war machine. No Jews could leave without paying huge 'taxes' and leaving most of their belongings behind. So, to emigrate successfully, you needed foreign friends or relatives to sponsor your visa and the money to afford the bureaucratic robbery en route. We had originally had the funds but not the foreign contacts. Now we had neither.

Rais had driven through Plauen and she described what she had seen; fires and broken glass everywhere from the shattered windows of Jewish homes and businesses. The new synagogue on Senefelder Street, the pride and joy of the community, had been burned to the ground.

Any non-Jew who tried to save things from the flames was threatened with violence. There were bloody-faced, beaten Jews everywhere and they were terrified. The next day they were ordered, on pain of deportation to the camps, to clean up all the rubble and the smashed glass. Furthermore, all over Germany, they were fined millions of Reichmarks to atone for all the damage, as if it were they who were to blame.

Nobody helped the Jews. The police, the fire service and the hospitals stood by silently, as did the populace, some through hatred and others through fear. Even some eminent citizens, whom Ludwig and Rais used to call friends, had been personally involved with the pogrom, gleefully beating up Jews and looting their possessions, especially oil paintings and antique furniture. Bedding and cheap items had been thrown out of windows. Rais had seen blankets and pillows in the trees of Plauen as she drove by. She told us, 'Ludwig says thousands of Jewish old folk, sick patients and orphans were chased out of homes for the elderly, hospitals and orphanages into the freezing night. Some thirty thousand male Jews have been sent to concentration camps like those at Dachau and Buchenwald. If their families are rich they can be "bought out" of these prisons at a hefty price.

'Last week we lent money to my old tailor's wife to buy back her husband from Dachau. He had only been there for three or four weeks but he came back a physical and mental wreck. His famous sense of humour has quite gone, his spirit has been crushed and he looks as shrunken as an old ape. God knows what they did to him and the others for he is too frightened to tell even his wife. All those who were in the camps were threatened to keep quiet, and some have since committed suicide. Others, whose families were too poor to buy them back, have died, and their widows have received invoices for four Reichmarks, the cost of having their husband's ashes posted home.' She and Ludwig were visibly shocked by what they had seen and heard.

The three of us, Anna, Mother and I, each had

our own little bedroom in the Clinic, but we shared a large kitchen and lounge with whoever else was around at the time. The cook, Maria, was an ardent *Sozi*, or Social Democrat, who had studied domestic science with Rais four decades earlier, stayed friends with her, and joined her household five years earlier when *Sozi*s were being hunted by the Nazis even more zealously than the Jews. Maria was originally Italian and her German husband had left her some years ago.

About a month after our arrival, Ludwig sat us down together in the kitchen. 'Rais and I have tried to decide how much we should tell you about the background to this place for your own good. Should you, or Maria, or indeed anybody else we give sanctuary to, be discovered here by the authorities, we think you will be killed, as we will, whether you know everything or not. We can see no reason therefore why we should not put you fully in the picture.

'So long as the Nazis are in power, you as Jews, and Maria as a *Sozi*, will be at risk. We will look after you for as many months or years as it takes, but we must all be very careful at all times. Never relax your guard. Never go outside the inner walls or near enough to the guard hut just outside the walls for a guard to see you.

'My work here is not, as I originally thought, for the government nor even for the Gestapo. It is entirely for the personal service of three very senior Gestapo officers. I am not talking of Himmler or Heydrich, but these men are of a similar status and extremely powerful, especially in Saxony. They met at a clinic for child schizophrenia where each was taking his son for treatment. I worked at that clinic and was one of those responsible for treatment of the three young boys. All were badly afflicted, with little hope of any cure. The parents' problems grew more and more acute as it became obvious that Nazi policy was heading towards sterilisation, to be followed in all likelihood by euthanasia, for a vast range of disabled people, including anybody suffering from schizophrenia. The three officers agreed to pool their resources and secrete their children without their mothers, in a place so secure that even the Gestapo would never learn of its existence. They would also hire the very best medical help on a full-time basis to cure the children as soon as was humanly possible.

'They chose an area in the heart of their own jurisdiction in the most pro-Hitler part of Germany, here in Plauen, and classified this place as an untouchable safe house for debriefing Gestapo informers. That is why, unless any of us makes a stupid mistake, this house will be just about the only place in Saxony immune to Nazi searches and harassment. And, so long as I can carry on convincing the officers that I have a long-term chance of curing their children, they will retain my services. They know my wife and I will keep our mouths shut. Why should we not? We have Gestapo protection, a good food allowance, a lovely location, and I have a chance to carry out my life's work, hopefully for the good of schizophrenics everywhere.

'So long as you stay in the house or the back garden, nobody will ever know you are here. I hold the key to the green door giving access to the front of the house where the children, their nurses and maid are quartered.'

Aunt Ruth smiled for the first time in a while. 'So, you see, Derek, we were in clover thanks to Ludwig. Hell on earth continued for the other poor Jews and *Mischlinge* in Plauen, as indeed it would for Jews all over the Third Reich. You were born on Monday 14 August 1939, and Rais brought us a bottle of champagne to celebrate. You had your mother's blue eyes and good looks as well as two doting ladies to spoil you rotten.' She stopped there, for it was time for her pills and a nap. I switched off the recorder and sat by myself for a long while. I had a lot to digest.

I will not attempt to philosophise nor to meticulously record my thought processes, for I am not by nature introspective. I know that I began to change at that time and became obsessed with a need to know everything about my past. In particular, who was responsible for the horror and what justice had been meted out to them, if any.

From that week on, I never travelled anywhere without Holocaust literature in my bag. I watched old movies of the Nazis and the Jews, and my social and sporting life ground to an unhealthy halt for I had stopped answering phone calls from friends. Above all, I began to nurture a hatred for the Seidler family and for all those faceless, nameless Nazis who had destroyed my family. A vast injustice had been done and, as far as I could learn, the perpetrators were in most cases unpunished and living prosperously. I craved the ability to do something about it, and until I could think of a positive course to take, I resolved to learn all that I could about the Nazis. Who were they? Why did they do it? Did they still exist? Was it just the Nazis who were responsible or the majority of the German people? In the course of my increasingly avid reading activities, I came across many books by self-styled historians 'proving' that there never was a Holocaust. I burned with fury to read such rubbish.

My time in Ottawa was divided between my work for the children's home, the city library and looking after Aunt Ruth. Every time she spoke faintly or seemed more tired than usual, I feared that her period of remission was ending.

The date for my West African contract approached very quickly, and I promised my aunt I would write frequently and phone when I could. I knew both her welfare visitors well and trusted them; they had my Poste Restante address in Luanda, the capital of war-torn Angola, where I was to work with refugees.

On my journey to West Africa, I made a detour to Europe and, having rented a car from Hamburg Airport, I drove south to Belsen, the nearest Nazi death camp. Given the time and funds at my disposal, I had decided to concentrate first on the camps in West Germany, rather than risk delays due to Communist bureaucracy trying to visit the Polish master-camps like Auschwitz.

The books I had read had made it clear that the worst extremes of Nazi brutality had occurred in these camps. Compared with the elaborate set-up of huge killing camps such as Auschwitz, Belsen had been merely a makeshift holding camp. Nevertheless, prisoners there were tortured, starved, worked to death or shot, as they were at all the German death camps and in the ghettos that served as purgatories to the hell that followed.

I did as much research as I could about Belsen and about the whole camp system, and learned that after the war, German citizens mostly denied knowing about the camps or the atrocities. It was the fault of 'them', the Nazis. So, who were these Nazis? Surely they were German citizens or ethnic Germans from subject countries. How many of them, I wondered, had actually worked in the camps and could not therefore plead ignorance?

The Belsen fact-sheets made available to visitors provided a grim picture of the Nazi prison system. There were 10,002 positively identified and named camps and ghettos, with a further 900 destroyed to the point of obliteration by the Nazis just before the war's end and thus unidentifiable. Of the 10,002 that had been identified, 1,600 were labour camps reserved for the killing of Jews through overwork. There had been 51 main concentration camps with 1,200 satellite camps. Auschwitz had 7,000 guards, Dachau had 4,000 and Mauthausen over 5,000. An average of one guard to 100 prisoners was standard SS practice, so at least half a million German or ethnic German citizens, in addition to a number of anti-Communists from countries like Latvia, were involved in the vast killing machine. Of these guards, some 4,000 were executed or imprisoned after the war, so a huge number of sadistic murderers had been allowed to live out their lives entirely unpunished.

I looked about me. Summertime at Belsen death camp. Of the touring coaches in the nearby car park, most I noticed came from Germany. So it was safe to assume that a number of the summer-clad tourists strolling about this place of remembrance and taking photos of each other in front of blown-up black-and-white photographs of pile upon ghastly pile of emaciated bodies, were Germans. Many laid out picnics of schnitzels and beer. I wondered if any of them felt any shame at all. But then of course why should they if it was all the Nazis' doing?

Did we Canadian whites feel shame when we visited the graves of the half-breeds of the Louis Real rebellion in the days of our grandfathers? Did the British feel guilty when they toured the memorials of the South African Boers? The more I studied the enormity of the Nazi Holocaust, the less such comparisons were meaningful.

I overheard a group of students, from different countries but from a single coach, discussing the Belsen photographs and captions as they sat on the grass. It is said that no flowers grow nor birds sing at the camps, even now. I could not say whether this was true for my ears were full of the comments of my fellow visitors to this tragic site. It is also said that certain grasses grow only at the camps due to the richness of the soil fed by the burial of so many human remains. I did not notice this either, but I did try to learn what these students thought of it all, 30 years after the events.

My German was pretty fluent from my early teenage years when Aunt Ruth and I still spoke it daily. As I had learned English in school and Aunt Ruth had studied it diligently in night classes, we had gradually spoken our native tongue less and less, but back in the land of my birth for the first time in three decades, I had no problem in understanding most of what I heard. The students all spoke in English or German, and I eavesdropped at the fringe of the group as did one or two other lone visitors.

A middle-aged man in slacks and sweater with a Nikon camera slung around his neck was close by.

'You American?' he asked.

'Canadian,' I replied.

'Hi. I'm Greg Wilson. Good to meet you. Your first time here?'

I nodded. I wanted to listen to the students.

'First thing you'll learn about the Germans is that they remember nothing. The war never happened when it comes to the camps. They're a nation of amnesiacs.' He took off his spectacles to polish them and I saw his eyes were brown and green together. His smile was easy and natural.

'Funny thing is, we fought a war against the Nazis to put a stop to all this.' He waved at the camp buildings. 'Yet now, in Germany, there are no Nazis. They've disappeared entirely, to the last man and woman! You certainly can't meet *anybody* who voluntarily joined the Party or actually voted for Hitler. I know because I've tried.'

He looked behind him briefly then he touched my

elbow. 'Call me Greg,' he said. 'What did you say your . . . ?'

'Oh, sorry. I'm Derek. Derek Jacobs.'

'Jacobs.' He thought for a second. 'Excuse me for asking, but are you also a Jew?'

I shook my head. 'Not exactly, but my family suffered as part-Jews here. We emigrated in 1946.'

'So you were one of the lucky few. You and me both.' He glanced about the student groups with what seemed a practised eye. 'Not many of these are Jews but quite a few are Germans. Their parents would probably be embarrassed to be here with them. War-generation Germans often make a rule never to talk about their war memories to today's teens because they end up shouting at each other. Before the parents even open their mouths they *expect* to be condemned as guilty by their children. The kids have formed a moral verdict already so the parents just keep their thoughts to themselves. Anything they try to say in their own defence or Germany's sounds grotesque to a student of today. The safe line to take is to forget and to profess their love for all Jews now living in Germany.'

He lapsed into silence. I was listening to an Australian who was conversing in English with a spotty German teenager.

I felt that Greg was watching me watching the students, but I was soon wrapped up in the student discussion. They were talking about the Passion play at Oberammergau. Either they'd all been there or they'd watched a video of it.

'I've been into Oberammergau village,' the

German student said. 'I've spoken to the players and
the villagers, and not one of them admitted having
heard of any death camp. Not even Dachau, which is
less than one hundred and forty-five kilometres from
their valley. Just like my parents they said they knew
nothing and got annoyed when they took my questions to infer their guilt.'

'But their Passion play is all about guilt,' the
Australian said. 'The collective guilt of all Jews forever for killing Jesus.'

'That's right, but they don't like it when someone
implies *they* should feel collective guilt for the murder
of six million Jews.'

'It's not just in Oberammergau.' Another German
youth sat up, Coke bottle in hand. 'All that generation
see only what they want to see. As Helmut says, all
our parents do it. My mother tried to tell me that
only bad Nazis killed the Jews, and that all the good
Germans were at the front. If they had only been
here, she implied, they would never have allowed the
Holocaust to take place.'

'Our parents knew they were *Übermenschen*, superior to all other races, and they were happy in
Hitler's disciplined pre-war world,' the spotty
teenager added. 'They liked straight white lines on
pavements and litter bins in lines, but such neat and
orderly values made them clay in the hands of the
Führer.'

'Even to the extent of this sort of cruelty?' The
Australian waved a hand at the photographs.

'Oh, of course,' the teenager answered, warming to
his subject. 'For a guard to perform well in a camp

like Belsen, he or she, to use Himmler's words, "must be ruthless, obedient, loyal and without moral scruples towards sub-humans."'

'We weren't angels either,' an American youth piped up. 'We burned one hundred and thirty-five thousand civilians alive in Dresden. And don't forget our firebomb raid on Tokyo – another eighty-five thousand dead – or Hiroshima, where there were seventy-one thousand victims.'

'Ah,' said the spotty teenager, 'now you're talking atom bombs. Just think what Hitler could have done with some of them.'

A plain German girl wearing heavy make-up and a skin-tight tank top tried to put things in perspective. Self-denigration was going over the top, she probably felt, especially with so many foreigners present. It was becoming embarrassing. The German economic miracle, not to mention the Bundesrepublik's sporting brilliance, did after all prove who was still the *Übermensch* in the mid-1970s. Why spoil it all with a one-sided debate on the folly of the previous misguided generation? 'My cousin,' she proclaimed, 'was executed by the Nazis for conspiring to kill Hitler. There were plenty of brave Germans who, like him, risked their lives to stop Hitler.'

Her comment cut no ice with the Australian, who must have done his homework on von Stauffenberg and the other anti-Hitler officers. 'All due respect to your cousin, Ursula, but if you read the Dipper Report based on the statements under interrogation of von Stauffenberg and his co-conspirators, you will find that, however much they may have disliked

Hitler, they were nonetheless in full agreement with the Nazis' policy of ridding Germany of Jews.'

'Right, Mick. That's right,' the spotty teenager joined in. 'For millions of Germans, killing Jews was necessary for the good of the German race. Many anti-Nazis approved of the Jewish extermination even if they disagreed with all other Nazi policies. Keeping the *Volk* pure by ridding the Reich of Jews, gypsies and other "impurities" was a national project. Annihilation of Semitic bloodstock made good sense to our ordinary citizens. Probably even to Ursula's cousin.'

This raised a ripple of nervous laughter and the debate split into separate discussions. In the background the giant photographs of the corpses continued to accuse whoever looked upon them.

Back then, I believed that if I read and searched enough I would find the answers to all the questions that plagued my waking hours. And if I could not avenge all these dead Jews for the horror they had suffered, then at least I could find and bring to justice my own family's killers.

I left the student group and wandered to the very edge of the camp, where the wire fence had delineated the perimeter of suffering; of misery and death. I sat down on a stone there to reflect.

Curiously, Greg the American, with so much else to photograph, was taking a photograph of me.

CHAPTER FIVE

I was born on a sultry day split by thunder echoing above the forested hills around Plauen. My birth was normal and the subject of great joy for my young mother and Aunt Ruth. My grandmother, in her detached and wandering state, showed no interest in my arrival other than a childlike fascination with the large violet birthmark on one of my legs, which Uncle Ludwig diagnosed as congenital and likely to be with me for life. He asked my mother if he could study my development and play, and she agreed. It would, I suppose, have been difficult to refuse, since our safety was entirely in my great-uncle's hands.

When Aunt Ruth told me about my infancy and childhood back in 1975, she probably hoped that she would rekindle some memory of my own. Perhaps she did, but I think it more likely that in the 18 years which have elapsed since then my mind has assimilated her stories of the Clinic, and I may now be regurgitating them as though they were actual memories. Either way, I retain no clear picture of Uncle

Ludwig. As an eminent child psychoanalyst, his six years at the Clinic with three captive schizophrenic patients, at the outset aged between four and seven years, must have been very helpful to him. His analytical methods, Aunt Ruth explained, had been a mixture of Freudian and Kleinian techniques.

In the 1930s the psychoanalytical capitals of the world were the Freud school in Vienna, and London, where Klein had settled. In the latter part of the previous century, Freud had developed psychoanalysis to study hysterical illnesses and did so using two basic theories: infantile sexuality, and the existence in every human being of an unconscious mind which reveals itself in dreams, language and behaviour, and allows insights into the workings of the conscious mind.

In 1918, Melanie Klein, inspired by Freud, started to analyse her own daughter and then other children, using his theories. By the late 1930s, she, my great uncle Ludwig and others were experimenting with their own independent ideas, and their research was new and exciting. In Germany and Austria, Klein's innovative methods had been viewed as controversial, so she had moved to London where her colleagues were more open-minded and more convinced of the importance of child study. It was Wordsworth, not Freud, they reminded Vienna, who had written, 'The Child is father of the Man.'

Klein's longest analysis of a single, neurotic child lasted two years and the girl was six when the treatment started. Ludwig's charges at the clinic were of varying ages and, due to the peculiar nature of their situation, he was never interrupted or pestered by their parents. Like Klein, he believed that his work with these child patients would only succeed if he became their parent figure. Also like Klein, his aim was to tap into the primal elements of the mind through meticulous observation of their psychotic outbursts and the patterns of their play. Ludwig would record whatever the children said, however trivial or unpleasant, for he believed that every utterance could give him further access to their unconscious thought processes.

He used a numbered set of objects or toys in all the play sessions, focusing on one child at a time. These items included pencils with paper, jugs with water, and scissors. For hour after hour, he would note every move the children made and their facial expressions. His expertise lay in interpreting the interplay between reality and fantasy in each child's complex internal world.

When the Gestapo children had all passed early childhood, Ludwig still needed to observe infantile behaviour, for he believed that the key fixation points of most psychoses stemmed from the months of infancy. So, for a while, I also served as a 'Ludwig child'. He searched for comparisons between my toy-play reactions as a normal infant and those of the schizophrenic children.

His wall graphs displayed a fantastic spider's web of different coloured lines delineating normal and psychotic behaviour patterns. Rais and Aunt Ruth had great fun in the evenings making him summarise his day's work so that they could understand what on earth he was doing. As a result he must have become the most intelligible analyst anywhere.

Aunt Ruth had told me that she used to listen to the BBC on Ludwig's wireless throughout our years in the Clinic. In 1940 and 1941 the news was usually good for the Nazis, which meant it was bad for us. Since we could not tell truth from fiction on the state-controlled German channels, we knew more about the war situation in far-flung places, like Crete, than we did about Plauen. And then, in the winter of 1941, Doctor Heinrich Meyburg met up with Uncle Ludwig, when the latter was out shopping with Rais.

Ludwig had a great deal to tell us when they returned. Two months earlier all Jews had been ordered to wear yellow stars on their clothes, but on the streets of Plauen, Ludwig had not seen a single Jew.

He said that all Jews had been evicted from their homes to four ghetto houses inside the city. They were allowed to take only bedding, some pots and dishes, and a few clothes. All their other possessions were confiscated by the Gestapo. Haphazardly, the Jews were gradually being sent from these ghettos to the death camps. Not for a moment were they free from fear. The ghetto houses included abandoned factory blocks. Concrete floors, dripping green walls and broken windows. All Jews, from babies to 90-year-old cripples had to live there. A Nazi official guarded the entrance and allowed the Jews in and out only briefly each day. There was also a strict curfew in Plauen and very little time to get food. With a

Jewish ration card your only allotment was cabbage, potato, and dark bread.

Ludwig recited what Heinrich had told him, ticking off each point on his fingers, one by one. 'Jews in Plauen are forbidden to drive, use any telephone, read newspapers, receive letters, or meet together in public places apart from the Jewish cemetery. *Mischlinge* are especially hated by our good mayor, who has forbidden their burial in any Christian graveyard in Plauen. If the Jews leave the ghetto to visit a friend or collect their rations, they are, in all places, *Vogelfrei* or fair game to the bullies. Many are beaten up in broad daylight. Nobody helps them. SA stormtroopers are less in evidence due to the war situation, but Hitler Youth roam the streets yelling for Jewish blood.'

My aunt asked if anybody in Plauen was speaking out against such inhumanity, but he told her the simple answer was no. Nobody at all. Individuals like Heinrich were rare and he was only able to covertly use his medical skills on desperately ill Jews by keeping quiet, or he too would have been sent to a camp. Lots of previously sympathetic Germans had succumbed to Nazi pressure through fear, others through greed, taking advantage of cheap or confiscated Jewish property. The majority could see what was happening, but just shrugged and looked the other way. That was true of 99.9 per cent of all 79 million Germans, not just our Plauen citizens.

The other 0.1 per cent of the German population were the several thousand, truly brave and wonderful human beings who were prepared in the midst of so much fear, danger and suspicion, to help the persecuted, whether they were Jewish, opposition politician, gypsy or whatever. Heinrich was one of them and he had a friend who was part of a tiny group called the Bund. The doctor asked Ludwig if he was prepared to help out at the clinic by occasionally giving sanctuary to refugees in the Bund's rescue pipeline.

When Ludwig told us of this, he said he would only agree when he'd spoken to the rest of us. Aunt Ruth could still remember his words: 'There are German *Spitzel*, informers, everywhere. All over Nazi Germany, there are now Gestapo cellars to loosen tongues and Gestapo stool pigeons, traps, decoys and anonymous agents. At present we know we are safe in this tiny sealed community, because none of us will betray one another. However, once we accept outsiders from Heinrich's Bund, there will always be a risk of betrayal.'

My aunt went on, 'I was horrified, as you may imagine, that Ludwig should even contemplate risking the lives of us all, his own family, to do the doctor a favour and take in outsiders. How could he check up on these people's backgrounds? Any one of them might betray us to the enemy.

'On the other hand, denying to other persecuted souls the safe haven for which we were so grateful would be condemning them to the very fate we were avoiding. That would make me as culpable as all the other millions of Germans who were refusing to confront the horrors being done in the name of their nation.

'After a brief discussion it was agreed unanimously

that we would go along with whatever Ludwig decided. When Maria left the room to prepare the evening meal, Ludwig sat beside your grandmother and, holding her around the shoulders, told us some bad news.

'Heinrich had for some time been keeping him informed of the welfare and progress of Tomi and Toni at the Bayerische Clinic. Two years before Hitler had begun to carry out his "T4" euthanasia programme, which took its code-name from the Tiergarten 4 address of its parent organisation in the Berlin Chancery, and which ordered the murder of a million German invalids including *all* children born with any defect. Over 200,000 T4 victims had been killed, mostly by lethal injections, by the time that growing public pressure forced the Nazis to abandon the programme.

'Tomi and Toni had been registered in their clinic as Christians and their care had already been paid for by Father before his death. Heinrich told Ludwig that some months earlier, the twins had been taken away from the clinic by T4 staff, who raided the files of all such establishments across the Reich and murdered thousands of the hitherto 'safe' inmates. Heinrich had heard that Tomi and Toni might have a chance of survival for they had been sent to a special research clinic in Poland where medical studies of twins were being undertaken.'

Aunt Ruth halted her story and asked me, 'Have you ever had that trapped feeling, Derek? As though the walls of your room are closing in, and the ceiling . . . but you cannot move? Well, Anna and I both felt that way that day. Our family was falling victim to the Nazis, one by one. Mother was lapsing ever deeper into her own mad world, people like us were being murdered as though we were vermin and now the one thing we depended upon, our security from betrayal at the Clinic, was being put at risk by taking in refugees who might be Nazi spies.'

'What about your emigration efforts?' I asked her.

'Oh, no!' My aunt gave a wry laugh. 'We'd been trying to escape that way for over ten years. Hänschen had used all his contacts, as had my father and latterly Uncle Ludwig. Our main problem at first was our lack of relatives abroad, not a lack of money. For years our main hope was the United States, but you needed to make their annual quota, which was difficult, because the Americans allowed only a minimal number of German Jews to emigrate there each year. Then you had to have a stamped visa and, finally, an affidavit from a relative in America guaranteeing financial support. This last proved to be our stumbling block.'

'Did *any* Jews get out?' I asked.

'Oh, yes!' Aunt Ruth answered. 'By 1938, over a third of all Jews had left Germany. They held auctions and sold priceless possessions at rock-bottom prices, often to senior Nazis. With the scant proceeds, they paid the exit tax and bought foreign currency for less than five per cent of the value of their blocked German money. Most rich German Jews spent their entire savings getting out. By 1942, only the super-rich, who had contact with corrupt top officials, stood a chance of emigrating.

'We were trapped in Germany. Our whole world consisted of just ourselves, a few rooms and a little walled garden. The Reich looked like it would last forever. The British and their Commonwealth were weak compared to the all-powerful Nazis.'

'Sometimes,' I told my aunt, 'I think I can remember being in a little garden. A place with many pink and yellow flowers. But it may just be the fragment of a dream.'

'Do you remember Reinhardt from Leipzig, Derek?' she asked.

'What did he look like?'

'Short, stubby, bald and endearingly simple. He used to wheel you round and round the little lawn in a barrow, and when you laughed too loud, he'd stop in mock horror, clap his hands over his ears and purse his fat lips together to *Sssh* at you. He feared that the guard or the other children, the "schizo-kids" we all used to call them, might hear.'

I shook my head and Aunt Ruth then told me Reinhardt's story.

'Four outsiders in addition to Reinhardt shared our Clinic refuge with us during the last half of the war, each having suffered persecution and lost members of their families to the Nazis. Two were sad, stunned individuals, who would gaze at the bedroom wall for hours on end. Where they went when they left the Clinic, I don't remember or perhaps I never knew. The third was a farmworker's girl in her mid-teens, who had lost her entire family during an SS Jew clearance. Her father had hidden all the family in a haystack, but an Aryan neighbour had seen this and

told the searchers. Somehow, when the others were
dragged out screaming, as one by one the probing
bayonets detected their presence, the girl had
escaped.

'The neighbour had returned once the hunters
were gone and offered the girl refuge in his own barn.
He brought her bread that same night then, when her
gratitude did not extend to sex, tied her up and raped
her savagely. She'd crawled away and a lucky chain of
circumstances led her to the Bund and finally to the
Clinic. We all called her Liebchen and spoiled her.
She grew to love Mother who taught her to knit. I
never heard them actually converse, for by then
Mother was hardly coherent, but their wounded souls
grew gently together.

'Reinhardt came to us in May 1942. He was different from the others. He seemed shy to begin with, but
we treated him well and the protective, glowering
frown that he wore for the first few months lapsed
into a look of eager expectation as he waited for one
of us, especially you, Derek, to say something to him.
You were three then, and talkative, to put it mildly.
We learned that Reinhardt was the only son of a
Leipzig policeman who was bitterly disappointed
when Reinhardt proved to be a poor scholar and had
cruelly ignored him thereafter. When he was twelve,
his school had thrown him out as an "unteachable
idiot", and his mother had treated him like an unpaid
skivvy.

'In the late 1930s, one of his father's police colleagues had jokingly put "the idiot" forward as a
recruit for the rapidly expanding German Order

Police, one of Himmler's mobile police formations that included a great number of unqualified country folk, many of whom were middle-aged and completely un-Nazified.

'So Reinhardt found himself in an utterly bewildering world of authority and discipline, and wearing, to his enormous pride, a smart new uniform with shiny buttons. He listened to his new colleagues with awe as they told tall stories of past heroics. Some had been town or country policemen, others firemen or mere auxiliaries. Their job in the new Order Police was initially to "enforce the law and protect loyal Reich citizens". Reinhardt began to notice, for the first time in his life after being the butt of everyone's jokes, that people now respected him. Of course, it was his uniform and his gun that did it, but he revelled in his new-found power. Now he could get his own back on the human race, and the nastier he was, the less his police mates joshed him.

'In September 1939, Himmler ordered Kurt Daluege, the Order Police chief, to take six thousand of his men into Poland, right behind the army troops. Two months later, Poland was crushed and its Jews became sitting ducks. Daluege increased his police force to twenty-five thousand, the better to carry out the pending duck shoot.

'Burning synagogues occupied much of Reinhardt's unit's time. At first they only shot Poles who posed some sort of problem. Reinhardt found these occasional killings even more exciting than beating people up, although the feel of his truncheon cutting into flesh and the sound of his victims' cries were undeniably satisfying. He had suffered the cuffs and ear-twistings of his parents since childhood, but now the boot was on the other foot.

'In late 1941, Reinhardt's unit was moved into the Soviet Union along with eighty thousand other special killer groups, or *Einsatzgruppen*. Himmler had had a huge task put on his plate by Hitler: to *exterminate* Soviet Jewry. He needed policemen good at killing men, women and children, at close range, day after day. Reinhardt and thousands of other non-Nazi, non-SS, simple policemen happily complied by means of brutal ghetto clearances, mass executions, and countryside hunts in the manner of pheasant shoots.

'Hitler's army first swept all before its Blitzkrieg force of three million soldiers, and Himmler's *Einsatzgruppen*, SS, Order Police and certain units of the *Wehrmacht* then murdered the Jewish population behind the new German lines. They would kill individuals, families, whole village populations and prisoner groups; sometimes a hundred, sometimes twelve hundred, even thirty thousand in a single purge.

'The suffering is impossible to imagine. Many of these brutal events are now long forgotten, even huge and messy massacres. But Derek, don't think of Reinhardt and his fellow, middle-aged policemen as stereotypical Nazis or SS, because most were not. They were merely simple folk helping to keep Germany and its newly acquired lands racially pure, and avoiding the perils of the real war. Week after week, month after month, through three deadly

years, they continued their human cull. Many Order
Police were awarded the Iron Cross, but few of them
were ever shot at. Their finest hour was probably in
1941 at Babi Yar, where Reinhardt's unit killed one
group of thirty-three thousand eight hundred and
sixty prisoners.'

Aunt Ruth did not tell me Reinhardt's story in one
sitting; I let her set her own pace, for I was ever conscious of the toll on her health that reviving these
memories might cause. Not that there was any stopping her, now that her goal was for me to know her
story in all its fine detail. As each recording tape was
finished, I catalogued and dated it.

There was so little to do in the sitting room of the
Clinic during those empty years, that Reinhardt's
story would have hung in the air, both fascinating and
appalling his spellbound audience. At the time, I
would doubtless have been excluded as too young.
When Aunt Ruth finally related Reinhardt's experiences to me in our Ottawa flat, I was filled with
repugnance for the man, misguided simpleton or not.
And as she continued to tell me about his life, I found
myself more and more confused in terms of being
able to neatly blame the Nazis for the atrocities
described. Most of Reinhardt's fellow killers were
clearly no more Nazi than he, nor were they all easily
moulded youths. Although Himmler, the man in
charge of Germany's huge police terror machine, and
his second-in-command, Heydrich, were in their early
forties during the war, most of the Order Police killers
were considerably older and quite capable of making
up their own minds as to the morality of mass murder.

'If Reinhardt had told his boss to shove it and had refused to go on shooting defenceless Poles, would he have been executed by his officers?' I asked my aunt.

'Oh, no. He was very clear about that. His company major often stressed to the men that they should apply for other duties if the killing work worried them. Some of Reinhardt's friends actually did apply for other postings, and none were ever punished.'

'So why didn't Reinhardt ask for a different posting?'

'Of course I asked him that. He was always very honest, but he didn't ever seem to feel a need to explain himself. He just wanted to tell us everything. He certainly had no idea that his duties would include killing when he first joined the Order Police. And then, when his superiors ordered the first killings, it was merely to execute "partisans" who had ambushed army units. Later these "partisans" included many women, children and old cripples. He was told that killing them was necessary for "the good of Greater Germany".

'At other times, Reinhardt assured us he had never killed Jews simply because they were Jews, but because they had "helped partisans". His major often boosted anyone whose killing instincts were flagging by reminding them that back in Germany, their own families were being bombed, and their own wives and children were being murdered by the enemy. So, what was the problem exterminating Polish or Russian boys and girls? Reinhardt also admitted that his standing in the company was based on his reputation for brutality. Peer pressure was at least one key to his motivation and quite a powerful one, I imagine, since it impelled him to carry on killing children on a daily basis for over two years. He never experienced a single bullet fired back in anger or a fist raised in defiance against him. All he heard were the cries of anguish, the begging for mercy and the terrified moans of his naked victims awaiting death in long queues.

'His major was obviously good at motivating his men, for he gave Reinhardt and the others extra tots of brandy after a day of killing and held parties "after work" in their billets. They would sing German songs about home, their children and christmas trees. Sometimes, their lieutenant would stand up and quote German poems to remind them that the Reich was Europe's cultural centre. And occasionally, a medical officer would lecture them on killing correctly, using a diagram and marking the neck or temple as the best target. They were also advised to use their bayonets mounted since this kept the rifle barrel the correct eight-inch distance from the victim, which helped to avoid misfires.

'Nonetheless, Reinhardt told us, the officers preferred to use their pistols, so they would hold a baby at arm's length or an adult by the hair. Others preferred to make mothers hold their babies in between their breasts, so that one shot would pass through the baby's skull into the mother's breast thereby saving the Reich the cost of a bullet. He said that the shootings were seldom clean. Usually the skulls would shatter and Reinhardt's colleagues sometimes vomited at the spectacle of exploding heads; flying bone and brain spattering their faces and clothes, and the screams of those inexpertly shot mingling with the dreadful wails of the crowd of naked prisoners waiting to die.'

'Why on earth did he tell you in such gruesome detail?' I asked my aunt.

'I believe for the same reason as I now find myself choosing to repeat the detail to you. I think I want to be sure that you *really* understand the utter horror of what Reinhardt did. Time and time again. Voluntarily. Dear, simple Reinhardt, whose life had been spent as a bullied, harried drudge, suddenly found himself doing something he believed was meaningful. Something which he could recount to an audience, knowing that he would hold their attention and really make an impression. I am sure he did not feel guilt over what he had done, because nobody ever punished him for doing it. On the contrary, he was praised for his diligence in carrying out his orders in the uniform of which he remained so proud, even when things eventually went wrong for him.'

'Perhaps the very fact that he never shot people as individuals, but merely as part of the day's work, helped him feel no guilt?'

'But he did shoot them as individuals also. He recounted one method his company often used to dispense of large groups of victims; a method that seemed almost designed to ensure close personal contact between killer and victim before and during execution.

'Once the group of prisoners to be shot had been

marched to the selected forest killing ground, and made to strip off their clothing, they would be forced into a single file. A group of twelve policemen would then march alongside the first twelve prisoners until they reached the chosen spot, usually beside a pit or ravine, but sometimes just a clearing.

'As they walked side by side with their victim to the execution site, each policeman could hardly fail to notice the individual, naked person at his side even if they kept quiet. Since the majority of those killed were women and children, and since most of the middle-aged policemen were married with their own children, it is possible that sometimes the thought of blowing the brains out of a particular prisoner might become distasteful. But no, thousands of these policemen went on and on shooting thousands of little naked children at close range, and were repeatedly splattered with their gore in the process.

'"I used to smoke a cigarette in between killing little girls," Reinhardt told me once, "and I once let a German Jewish boy take a puff before I shot him."

'Sometimes Reinhardt's unit was shown a Soviet town or village on the map, always in an area already conquered by the army, of course, and they would arrive there by night. Local anti-Semites would then reveal where the Jews were and, often before dawn, the day's work would begin.

'Families were kicked out of their homes. Sometimes they tried to hide, and were shot or clubbed to death, as were old people who moved too slowly. Others made a dash for it outside and were killed there. But the majority were herded into the main square to be crammed into lorries. Once or twice, Reinhardt's company was short of ammunition so they decided to incinerate the gathered prisoners. This was usually done by driving them into the local synagogue and setting fire to it. In one such inferno near Minsk, his unit got rid of eight hundred and fifty people. The Germans had at that time over four hundred police units like Reinhardt's working full time to eliminate Soviet Jews.

'Reinhardt was surprised at how willing the vanquished Soviet peoples were to help his unit find and kill their local Jews, especially the Latvians, Ukrainians and Lithuanians. He told of many "big days". One I particularly remember, because Reinhardt said the flies and mosquitoes were troublesome. They had collected a total of fourteen thousand Jews in some town or other, driven them to a field a kilometre outside the suburbs and made them dig three big pits. Those without spades had to use their hands. Mothers were made to leave their babies lying in the muddy field while they worked. The screaming of the infants made the Germans angry and many babies were silenced with truncheons. When the pits were eventually ready, some sixty policemen did the shooting. This took a long time and many of the remaining Jews grew desperately thirsty.

'"Mummy, please get me water," they cried, and "Papa, what will they do to us?" How do you answer your child in such circumstances, as you await your deaths, as the gunfire and the screaming continues, hour after hellish hour?

'The work in that open field was hot and tiring for

Reinhardt. At midday, he and his friends were allowed an hour's rest and given schnapps. They sat around and smoked, in between the great horde of still living Jews and the mass graves now swarming with flies. Reinhardt had his break with his legs dangling over the side of one pit and watched Latvian auxiliaries searching bodies for loot. A surprising number of Jews, including little children, had not been finished off and still writhed about. The Latvians ignored them, but they died soon enough due to suffocation by the next layers of bodies that landed on top of them.

'The curses of the Latvians and the desperate pleas from bodies that still moved, Reinhardt said, still came to him in dreams. They only killed twelve thousand that day as the pits were overflowing. They finished off the balance the next morning.

'I remember asking Reinhardt if he was ever given leave from such awful work. His group were apparently often allowed to have Sundays off so they could relax. Can you guess, Derek, his reply, when I asked him what they did on those days off?' my aunt said.

I shrugged. 'Got drunk, I suppose.'

'Well, yes, they often did, but on Sundays they usually organised hunting parties in competing groups. They'd set off with picnic lunches in their packs and light gear, no helmets, and an agreed number of bullets per man. Then, at the end of the hunt, they would "count ears" between each group. The winners would receive the agreed alcohol or money prize at a party that evening. The ears belonged, of course, to the Jews they had "bagged" during the day's hunt and two little ears were worth a single adult ear. Some of them cheated to save bullets by using *Nussknacken* clubs, skull-crackers.

'Sometimes the hunters would comb a wooded area, because that was a favourite hiding place for Jews who had managed to escape the massacres, or else they would return to some ghetto and conduct a "game" of hide and seek for Jews who had hidden under trapdoors, in false ceilings or under woodpiles.

'"I've got one," would be the jubilant cry of a hunter. Or, "Help me pull this girl out. She's jammed in the loft and holding on like a monkey." Often there would be rape or torture before the quarry was dispatched and "eared".'

'I cannot believe it,' I told my aunt. 'It is make-believe. Nobody would behave that way. It sounds like propaganda from the Allies.'

My aunt sighed. 'You are neither the first person nor will you be the last to disbelieve what happened. And remember, you and I are Germans. I am talking about our own countrymen who did these things, not some alien scapegoat called a Nazi.'

Later on, when I read the official war-crimes tribunal records in Ludwigsburg in Germany, and at Yad Vashem in Israel, I no longer doubted Reinhardt's stories. And the brutality of the German bullies was infectious; wherever they went, they spread their reign of terror by allowing others to share in it. Thus, as Reinhardt had told my aunt, various Polish, Soviet, and even Jewish turncoats were often as inhuman to Jews as were their German overlords. Especially the

Latvians, who liked to kill with imagination. They killed for sport and for target practice; they shot women in the stomach and timed their death throes, and they killed children slowly in front of their parents or vice versa.

My own reading of the official war reports, which anybody could study nowadays, had not made as great an impression on me as had Aunt Ruth's recounting of Reinhardt's stories, but the cold historical facts had been impressive nonetheless. For instance, *a single pit* that the Germans prepared in Poland was designed to take 28,000 bodies. In November 1941, an especially hard winter helped many Jews survive longer because the pits were too difficult to dig. The official estimate for Jews who were buried *alive* was 2 per cent. Large-scale massacres in 1941 included: Kamnets-Podolski 23,000 dead; Rovno, 21,000; Minsk, 19,000; Riga, 25,000; and in early 1942, Kharkov, 14,000. There were many thousands of lesser mass shootings all over Eastern Europe and over four million prisoners died in the camps. So Reinhardt's experiences had been but a tiny part of the horrific killing machine of the glorious Reich.

By the spring of 1942, Hitler realised that his dream of total extermination of the Jews was being carried out too slowly. Shooting was not an efficient method, and Germans could not be criticised for lack of efficiency. So, the custom-built death camps began to open their gates. By the end of 1943, one camp alone could gas and burn 12,000 human beings, day in, day out, without pause.

Reinhardt's Order Police unit was withdrawn from the Soviet Union for retraining in April 1942. Back in Leipzig for a brief leave, Reinhardt met up with a Catholic girl, with whom he had enjoyed a brief fling before joining the police. When he proudly regaled her with his stories of murder and cruelty, she was utterly shocked. 'You must go to the priest,' she told him. 'You must confess your great sins, for if you die, you will go straight to Hell.' Reinhardt told her priest everything and the latter, presumably not believing him, went to the Gestapo and denounced him as liable to endanger the Reich's fine reputation.

Reinhardt was out when the Gestapo came visiting and, when he got back, his mother told him never to come home again. He was not only an idiot but a traitor to the Fatherland. Reinhardt rushed back to his girlfriend who asked for help from her doting father; an active underground Communist with contacts to the Bund. He used them, or, as Reinhardt joked, misused them, out of love for his daughter. So Reinhardt came to the Clinic.

Our own security at the Clinic depended on our isolation from the outside world, and so long as we never strayed beyond our accepted safety zone, we remained undetected by our enemies. By mid-1942 we knew without a doubt that any Jew caught in the Nazi net was liable to end up dead in a concentration camp. So we took our security seriously, and I was watched like a hawk at all times by my mother or aunt. I was never to leave the back garden nor scream loudly like normal children do.

Unfortunately, a new arrival at the clinic put us all

at risk one lovely day in early June 1943. Bippi, from Plauen, was a Jewish homosexual who was being sought by the Nazis. He had escaped from the local Flossenbürg labour complex after three years spent in other camps, mainly the notorious Auschwitz, and a fellow escapee, a Communist from Essen, had sent him to the Bund. They in turn had passed him to us at around the same time as Reinhardt.

Bippi's sexual urges were not reciprocated by anybody in our household, and a recent black eye from Reinhardt testified that Bippi was becoming desperate. Nonetheless, we were flabbergasted at his stupidity when we learned from an extremely alarmed Ludwig that Bippi had left him a note that morning saying that he would be gone for a day or two in order 'to attend to business', and that he would be sure not to alert the guard either on his departure or his return.

'If he is captured in Plauen,' Ludwig warned, 'the Gestapo will question him. We will just have to hope for the best. There is nothing we can do right now but pray.'

'Can I join you?'

Startled from my reverie, I looked around. It was the American with the Nikon camera; my fellow visitor to Belsen. I stood up slowly, cramped from sitting on an uncomfortable stone. 'I'm sorry, I was miles away. It's Greg Wilson, isn't it?'

'Yep, that's right. So what do you think of this place where so many of our brothers and sisters perished?'

I raised my hands. 'What can one say . . . or even think?'

'Listen, why don't we get a cup of coffee somewhere? The midges are coming out and this place will soon be closing for the day.'

Comparing notes in a local café, we discovered we were both heading on to Hamburg.

'It's a small world,' Greg commented. 'I'm staying at the *Vier Jahrezeiten*. Why don't you meet me there for dinner? On me, of course, since it's my hotel. If you're catching a plane to Africa tomorrow, you'll want an early night, but we'll have plenty of time for a chat. I can at least promise you the very best of meals before you begin your African privations.'

And so it was that I fell into the net of the Secret Hunters.

CHAPTER SIX

We drove separately to the *Vier Jahrezeiten* in Hamburg.

'The best in the West,' Greg assured me. 'I use it whenever I'm over here. The British Army kept the place as their headquarters for seven years after the war then handed it back to the Haerlin family, once they had been officially de-Nazified. They still own it. The founder of our group, a Russian prince, found it very useful because everyone who was anyone in Hamburg came here. They still do.'

We went up to Greg's room.

'Normally you'd need to be a millionaire to use this sort of place.' Greg had noticed my reaction to the opulence of his suite. 'This is an *Alster-raum*, one of the finest in the hotel and I get to use it at a fantastic discount because of our history with the management. Feel free to freshen up. I must make some calls.'

He made himself at home behind a huge walnut partner's desk with an antique reading lamp, while I marvelled at the voluminous bed, the Victorian shoe-stands, bathroom thermometers and opulent furnishings of a bygone era.

We dined downstairs at an open grill, seated in sturdy wooden chairs, the panelled walls around us hung with old maps, wooden buckets, great iron farm implements and outsize tin plates. The food, Greg assured me, was typically Hanseatic. It was certainly interesting, and included *Rinderroulade*, pea soup, roasted *Scholle* flat fish, green eel, *Matjes* sour herrings and *Rote Grüeze*, red custard.

Greg addressed the grill-chef as Herr Höderle, the concierge as Herr Schlage and the director, who came to greet him personally, as Herr Prantner. I was impressed, which I imagine was Greg's intention. I was being softened up.

After dinner, we moved downstairs to an elegant, panelled drawing room adjoining the hotel lobby. The headwaiter, Herr Schmeisser, served us brandy in huge glasses and Greg eased into a gently inquisitional mode. I told him my life story. I had nothing to hide, after all. He nodded politely at my personal anecdotes about Ottawa, Asia and Africa, but lost his glazed look when I moved on to my meeting at Resolute Airport and Aunt Ruth's revelations.

'Until your aunt told you all this, you had *no* interest in the Jews? Or in Germany?' Greg queried.

'None at all,' I told him. 'Why should I? I was Canadian. I am Canadian. I remembered nothing of Europe.'

Two great oil paintings were hanging either side of the fireplace next to us.

'That's Heinrich,' Greg explained, pointing to the left-hand picture, and I felt this was not the first time he had shown his guests his knowledge of European history, his appreciation of German culture, in short, the depth of his very un-American cosmopolitanism. 'He was Prince of Prussia and a frequent visitor here. And *she*,' Greg indicated the portrait to the right of the fireplace 'was his wife, Irene, the sister of the last Russian Empress. The Prussians, you know, have an awful lot to answer for. Their aggression can be said to have contributed largely to sparking off the horrors of both Marxism and Fascism.'

For a while we lapsed into silence. Africa was a thousand miles from my thoughts. Greg's next words brought me back to the present with a jolt.

'Do you feel that those who hurt your family should be punished?'

'Punished?'

'Yes. If they went free after the war, you can be sure that the Nazis who murdered your mother are now enjoying the good life in Buenos Aires, Hamburg or Vienna. Do you think they should suffer no penalty, or that like Eichmann in the 1960s, they should be hunted down and imprisoned?'

My answer was immediate and came from my heart. 'If a suitable prison, simulating Auschwitz conditions, is available, then, yes, I would hunt and jail them.' I paused, remembering Aunt Ruth's distress. 'No, not even Brezhnev's gulags, would be hellish enough, so I would *hang* my mother's killers, *slowly*.' I took a deep breath and looked Greg straight in the eyes. 'Like they hanged their victims at

Auschwitz, so that they would also take ten minutes to die.' I continued to hold his gaze, and added, 'or longer.'

Wilson nodded, appreciatively I thought.

'So you approve of Wiesenthal and other such Nazi hunters even though some thirty years have passed since your mother's death?'

'If Wiesenthal offered me a job tomorrow, I would take it. It can never be too late to deliver justice where it's due. How can a Nazi criminal become too old to be punished? No Nazi heart ever unfroze due to the *age* of a Jew.'

'Wiesenthal's line of work pays only a pittance, you know.'

'I could make do. I have no dependants other than my aunt in Canada and she now gets her senior citizen's pension.' I laughed at Greg's solemn face. 'Why all this Wiesenthal talk, Greg? Are you offering me a job?'

He grinned. 'You could say so.'

'You *are* serious? I thought you said you're a lecturer.'

'I am,' he affirmed. 'But the Holocaust, which is my subject at college, is also what you might call my hobby. I spend my holidays in places like Belsen looking out for young Jewish people. I am what we call a trawler . . .'

'So this dinner, the wine, this is all a set-up?'

Greg raised both his hands.

'Hold on, Derek. Don't be hasty. Hear me out . . . okay?'

I waited.

'What I'm proposing is, I believe, an opportunity you will jump at. And if you don't, your only inconvenience for my having cornered you at Belsen will have been a free dinner on me at one of Europe's top hotels. Is that so bad?'

I could see his point. 'How come you thought I was a Jew? I don't look like one. I'm not one, in fact. I saw a great many tourists a lot more Jewish-looking and a great deal younger than I who you could have picked on.'

'Ten years ago, perhaps I would have missed you, but I've developed a good eye. Some of my best recruits have been, like you, outwardly un-Jewish. Not many, I admit, have been Christians, but I would prefer any single, middle-aged Christian with the right attitude, to a hundred young Jews without the inner desire to hunt for justice.'

'You like that word – "hunt". Is that what your recruits do, go hunting? What do they do when they catch their quarry?'

Greg gently replaced his Dresden-china coffee cup on its saucer. 'I can answer all your questions, but first, just in principle, how do you feel about such a proposition?'

I shrugged. 'Don't take offence, Greg, but we've only just met. How can I tell if you're serious? You could be anyone. Joking apart, you could be mafia or Revenue Canada. You could even be one of those joke TV presenters. Maybe your camera crew is filming and taping our conversation right now and hoping that I'll jump hook, line and sinker for the bait, so you'll get a good laugh from your audience.'

'Of course you're right. I might not be genuine,' Greg agreed, 'but I will give you impeccable witnesses and irrefutable proof later as to who I really am and who I represent. Would you at least like to hear the background of the organisation I'm asking you to join?'

Of course I said 'yes'.

Greg took me up to his room where he carried two chairs into the bathroom and turned on the washbasin's cold tap.

'Old habits die hard,' he explained. 'I don't expect there's a single bug in *Vier Jahrezeiten*, but then you can't be too careful. Everything I will now tell you is best not repeated. If, of course, you do tell anyone, it will not harm our organisation, and until you prove your reliability to us . . .'

'Us?' I prompted. 'Do you have a collective identity?'

'Wait,' Greg smiled patiently but firmly. 'As I say, until you prove your reliability, there are many things – things that could harm us if they were to reach the media – which you will not be told.'

For half an hour I listened with fascination to Greg explaining the covert war waged in 1944 against the Nazis in occupied France by the agents of the Special Operations Executive (SOE), which had been based in London and worked with the French Resistance. These operatives had been highly trained individuals from many countries and were zealously hunted by the Gestapo.

In the period immediately after the war, a third group, comprising mostly American, British and

French operatives, had worked with SOE and the Resistance to hunt down specific Nazi war criminals who had murdered Allied soldiers, French civilians and SOE agents in the South of France.

This group came to be known as the Secret Hunters, and their main quarry was the Nazi murderers of soldiers from the British Special Air Service Regiment (SAS), who had operated behind German lines in the forests of the Vosges Mountains.

In May 1945, the SAS commanding officer, Colonel Brian Franks, sent a small team of SAS men in a jeep and a truck back to continental Europe from England.

Colonel Franks appointed as boss of the group an SAS intelligence officer, Major Bill Barkworth. The Barkworth group was given the grand title of the SAS War Crimes Investigation Team and they immediately began their search for the men who had murdered their comrades over the previous 12 months. They started the hunt in the French-occupied zone of the defeated Reich, and worked tirelessly for two years, befriending in the process a number of individual French Nazi hunters, and members of the US War Crimes Investigation Team.

Although Greg was selective in what he told me at the *Vier Jahreszeiten* back in 1975, I will also record at this point what I later learned about the Secret Hunters. Until 1947, their leading light was still Major Bill Barkworth, but that year the British disbanded them and, like the SAS themselves two years earlier, the Secret Hunters ceased to exist. The fact that they re-emerged in 1948 was due to a

Russian prince, Yurka Galitzine, whose mother was English.

In August 1944, Galitzine was a 21-year-old captain working for the Political Warfare Department of Supreme Headquarters Allied Expeditionary Force (SHAEF). He landed as part of the Allies' Operation Dragoon at the coastal village of St Tropez, and became a member of a three-man task force together with an American and a Frenchman. Their job was to report, for Allied propaganda purposes, exactly what crimes the Nazis had committed in the area.

From Nice, where Galitzine had visited the recently evacuated Gestapo Headquarters, he reported that, 'There were eleven bodies in the Gestapo cellar. One was the daughter of Mayor Valiano. She was six months pregnant and had been raped after death.' Shortly afterwards, Galitzine's T-Force located the entire Gestapo records for south-eastern France in Strasbourg. Since that was where the Nazis had murdered the SAS men, these records were later to prove vital to Barkworth's Secret Hunters.

In December 1944, Galitzine, travelling with the US Seventh Army, came to a Nazi concentration camp in the Vosges Mountains where 24,000 prisoners had suffered and died. He developed a deep personal hatred for Germans during the weeks he investigated the atrocities at this camp. His reports, which I read in the 1970s, were not openly published in Britain until 1986. They included references which explain Galitzine's frame of mind:

The SS officers beat, tortured and killed the prison-
ers at will. The Russian inmates were treated worst:
their food included grass and dung. Hangings were
carried out daily. On 1 September 1944, the Nazis
killed 92 women and 300 men in one night and
stacked the corpses in a cellar. The blood level was 20
cm up the walls . . . They built an experimental gas
chamber in the nearby Struthof hotel. Most victims
there were women. First they stripped and raped
them. Then they were crammed into the gas chamber
and watched through a peephole . . . We found 120
bodies at the Anatomical Institute of the Strasbourg
Hospital. The Head of the Institute, one Professor
Jung, had been sent the bodies from the camp, killed
to order and injected with a preservative serum.

Galitzine had also found a number of body parts
preserved in jars. His report on the concentration
camp, compiled long before the public knew of the
existence of such places, was received by his bosses at
SHAEF HQ in Paris with apparent indifference. He
was ordered to tell nobody. Even when I met him in
London last year, 1993, he still had no explanation as
to why his Allied bosses, who had after all tasked him
to find evidence of Nazi crimes, did not use this
damning material back in 1944. His guess was that
such propaganda, if released by SHAEF, would have
caused the Germans to resist defeat even more
doggedly in Europe through fear of Allied reaction to
what they had done.

So Galitzine was told to keep quiet. He was
deeply frustrated, but after the war's end, he jumped

at the chance to join the War Crimes Investigation Branch at their offices in 20 Eaton Square in London. By the end of the summer of 1945, he had become closely involved with Barkworth's Nazi-hunting team and, when the SAS were disbanded that October, their colonel and Galitzine defied the War Office by unofficially keeping Barkworth's team going with pay and equipment. They managed this by taking advantage of post-war administrative confusion.

The Foreign Office, to Galitzine's disgust, was against any retribution. Whatever crimes the Nazis had committed during the last war must be forgotten, if not forgiven, because Germany was now the vital bulwark against the new enemy: Soviet Communism. Galitzine realised that, if justice was ever to be done, it must be through private initiative. He and Colonel Franks installed a radio and signaller in the attic of 20 Eaton Square, and called Barkworth's unofficial group the SAS Secret Hunters.

Over the next two years, Barkworth's disdain for 'official channels' earned him such hostility that his men were forbidden to operate at all in the British zone of occupied Germany. He and his deputy Dusty Rhodes, once went to witness the execution of a Nazi they had caught by the famous hangman Pierrepoint in Hamlin Prison. Rhodes was asked if he was there out of revenge. 'No,' he said, 'revenge is not involved. We have a job to do, to bring these people to justice. We don't seek revenge.' The two Secret Hunters never watched another of their quarry being dispatched. The evidence they collected was always passed to legal people at British Army of the Rhine under Major Alistair Hunt.

By the summer of 1947, when the Secret Hunters were disbanded, they had accounted for all the murderers of the SAS men, and of a number of SOE operators as well. In all, the British courts tried 1,085 war criminals and hanged 240 of them, a pitiful fraction of those guilty and still at large.

When the British government finally packed up their War Crimes Group in Germany in 1948, they still knew of 10,000 known torturers and murderers whom they had failed to apprehend. Many of these had been concentration camp staff, or specific killers of British soldiers in Stalagluft III. Of course, the Germans usually murdered the non-Jewish British in a far less brutal manner than they did the Jews but, nonetheless, one can understand Galitzine's frustrations at the time.

He left the army deeply altered by his experiences. All his attempts to goad officialdom into continuing the hunt for the many thousands of Nazi criminals starting new careers in Europe and elsewhere came to nothing. He set up a public relations agency in London's Mayfair and Bill Barkworth emigrated to Australia. Galitzine did not, however, call it a day. In his own words, he had experienced a lot of very scarring experiences. 'I didn't recognise the difference between Germans. To me all Germans were cruel, and as a result I was very vengeful.'

Using his many wartime connections in France, Galitzine quietly set up a new version of the Secret Hunters. His specific aim was to locate and bring to justice as many escaped Nazi war criminals as possible, no matter how long it might take to do so. By the early 1950s, the group was firmly established and bringing in results, slowly but surely. Galitzine, well satisfied, retired from the active scene. His successors were mostly French and American at the top, but international at field level.

I had interrupted Greg to ask the age of his field workers. 'I assume that's what you have in mind for me?'

He smiled. 'There is no age limit for someone still capable of getting the work done. Once you are with us you can stay until you die or you can leave when you wish. Likewise, you can take on some of the jobs we offer you, but not others. None of us is paid, but all our expenses are covered. Few of us are full-time Hunters. Sometimes you may not hear from Lyons, our base, for several years and then, out of the blue, your talents will again be called upon.'

'What does the work entail? Is it within the law?'

'Whose law?'

'Well, whichever country is involved at the time.'

Greg's reply was ambiguous. 'Our law is God's law. We obey the Ten Commandments . . . when feasible. Our rule is "an eye for an eye", not "turn the other cheek".'

'That's the Jewish way. I'm a Christian.'

'Purely incidental, I assure you.'

'And the actual work?'

'The tracing of Nazi war criminals; often observing them, and then compiling reports against them. Locating witnesses and amassing dossiers. At that point we hand over the information to the relevant authorities, or do so through the Wiesenthal organisation and another all-Jewish group about whom I can give no details. In the 1960s, one of our teams was involved with the groundbreaking Eichmann case, and in the early 1970s we began work on Klaus Barbie, whose crimes included atrocities in Lyon, our base. We will nail him sooner or later. Every year our Nazi work gets harder as the old killers, none of whom show genuine remorse, fade further into obscurity.'

'So you will soon be redundant, unless you intend to follow up Cambodian killers?'

'If Nazis were our only concern, I would agree: God would net them all before we could. But last year our Nazi watchers in Germany and elsewhere, especially in Canada I should mention, became worried at the renewed effort some of our remaining targets are making to kindle new fascism in West Germany. They see an opportunity to reinvigorate nazism once Communist East Germany democratises, as they believe it eventually will.'

'I have no skills you could use. I'm not secret agent material. Even a geriatric Nazi would run rings around me.'

'You don't like the idea?'

'I didn't say that. Can I think about it?'

'Sure.' Greg got up and turned off the tap. 'Make yourself at home and I'll make some more calls.' He looked at his watch. 'You have a couple of hours before you need to be at the airport. Can you make up your mind by then?'

I went back down to the lobby and out into the streets. I think better when I'm jogging or even strolling. What decided me was the knowledge that my aunt, the only person who mattered to me at the time, would soon be dead. Secondly, I had promised myself and Aunt Ruth that somehow I would catch the people who had destroyed my family. If they were still alive, anywhere, I would locate them. These were strong words, but in the weeks and months since I had uttered them, what had I achieved with all my reading and the visit to Belsen? Zero. Seidler was just a name gleaned from Aunt Ruth with no clue as to his history or current whereabouts and, at that time, I still had no name at all to attach to the man at Resolute Airport.

As a member of a group which had been involved with the successful tracing of Eichmann, surely I would be on a far better footing to follow up my personal vendetta, in addition to the general satisfaction of helping to catch other Nazi criminals.

Back in Greg's room, I put it to him that I would be keen to join up if the group would help out with my search for my own family's murderers. Greg said that others would decide on that, but he did not see it as an obstacle. On the contrary, it was powerful proof of my commitment.

Four months later, on a bleak afternoon in January, I arrived back in Ottawa from Angola on compassionate leave. I was too late, however, for Aunt Ruth had died early the same morning.

Grief-stricken, I met with her welfare sister and

arranged the funeral through an agent I found in the phone directory. Only the best for Aunt Ruth: she may have lived simply enough, but by making a big dent in my savings, I made sure that she passed on to the next world with due pomp, in a teak coffin with silver handles. Three of her knitting circle saved me from being the only attendant at her funeral.

I made two promises over my beloved aunt's grave and I have returned every year since to renew them. I would avenge all her suffering and I would make her story known to as wide an audience as possible.

For the next 17 years, I continued my work for refugees and children world-wide, being contracted to several agencies and charities. Sometimes I would perform only basic menial work, even cooking, in overcrowded tents, and often had to wade from family to family through stinking mire. The work that made me happiest was caring for children, ensuring food deliveries, locating doctors and equipment, saving lives and keeping families together. I seemed to have a way with kids in the great, sad, disease-ridden camps of the world.

In between my refugee jobs, I worked, mainly in Europe, for the Secret Hunters. I knew my appointed controller by the name of Laro. I'm not a great supporter of Quebec – the inhabitants complain too much, and since de Gaulle's famous visit, I've never been a Francophile – but Laro, who is very French, is a wonderful character and we have become good friends.

I regret nothing I have done in the name of the Hunters. I have killed only in self-defence and have deceived only the deceitful, but even now there are things I cannot put into writing for they might be misunderstood, or they might cause harm to my colleagues. So, I will stick to describing the Hunter work that affected me personally.

In late March 1993, I was sent to Rwanda on a job for the Canadian government, who had previously sponsored the Rwandan College in Kigali. I was later to learn that the same week that I left for Rwanda, two events took place, in Marseille and New York, which would directly affect my own future. I will describe them separately even though, as is so often the case in life, the events were interlinked.

Jan Meier was a *blokkar*, a Vlaams militant from Antwerp, who killed to make money, but specialised in 'foreigners'. In the 1980s the Vlaams Blok, Belgium's ultra right-wing party, polled 25 per cent of the vote in the key city of Antwerp.

The Blok also appealed to those inhabitants of Brussels and French Belgium who hated the presence of the 'foreigners', mostly Arabs. In the 1990s however, Meier, once a mercenary in the Congo, tired of his Blok colleagues, whose stolid Belgian mentality prevented them from supporting the aggressive methods of political advancement that he favoured. So he abandoned his last lingering hopes of power through politics, and focused on what he was best at: organising men and equipment for illegal activities and, of course, removing foreigners.

Meier worked, as most top-notch contract killers do, through a trusted and carefully controlled grapevine, with a cut-out system designed like a one-way butterfly valve: genuine clients could reach him but the law could not.

He had recently returned from Milan where a super-rich renegade of the Lega Nord, a party dedicated to the overthrow of the Italian state, had invited him to put away a Sicilian troublemaker. When Meier had announced his price, the client had turned ashen and no deal had been reached. Very rich people, Meier reflected, can waste an awful lot of time through their meanness. Anyway, he looked forward to this Marseille job. He always liked working for the big boys of the Far Right.

On 26 March 1993, he reached the northern outskirts of Marseille at dusk and drove through heavy local traffic. For 20 minutes he focused on his tail, as was his habit on reaching any given target town or city. He would arrive at a busy time in a vehicle he'd rented using one of his false identities. He then checked that he was 100 per cent clean; that not even the best agent in the game was on his heels. That way he entered each new mission pristine and uncompromised.

At 9pm he dined alone at a seafood restaurant in the narrow pedestrian streets close by the Quai de Rive Neuve. He knew Marseille well but, just as any cautious man never uses the same prostitute more than once, so Meier never ate twice at the same restaurant.

He ordered moules with garlic and herbes de Provence, followed by bouillabaisse du Ravi, relishing the distinctive flavour of each of the six different fish, and then enjoyed a fine cassis blanc-de-blanc, before finishing with Turkish coffee. Deep in thought, he studied a map of the local coastline.

When he was ready, he paid in cash and drove east along route 559 to Cassis where he parked close to the beach. Then, savouring the night air and the sounds of the sea, he walked with a backpack west towards La Madrague. Three hours later, he followed the course of a creek until it dropped into a steep gully and plunged down to the sea.

He unravelled a thin nylon line, anchored it to a rock and using a simple *descendeur* climbing device, abseiled down the cliff to a wide ledge where he took out the contents of his pack. His Magellan GPS Pioneer satellite navigator told him that his position was accurate to within 160 feet. Not that he doubted his own navigational abilities, but double-checking was an ingrained habit and along these cliffs there were a number of similar *calanques*, or creeks, each with its own little beach outlet. Scanning the opposite side of the ravine, he picked out two stepladders descending to sea level.

Towards 3am, at low tide, and without needing the aid of his monocular night-sight thanks to the full moon, Meier spotted the approach of a sturdy fishing boat even before he heard the low chug of its inboard motor. In addition to the helmsman, he counted 14 people on board, including women and children, all illegal Arab immigrants. Then, a couple of hundred yards behind them, the sleek outline of a smaller, high-speed minder-craft. He would ignore the crew of this second boat unless they became a nuisance, for this time his instructions were not to harm the management, merely their human traffic.

Waiting until the bigger boat nosed towards the beach below him, Meier pulled the pin from a fragmentation grenade, and then lobbed it towards the middle of his target. For good measure he threw another two grenades, ducking on his ledge as the first explosion split the air.

A brief glance below indicated a successful mission. Half-expecting a searchlight from the minder-craft, Meier checked the readiness of his three-piece sniper-scope rifle. But no reaction came from below, so he repacked his gear and, with his *ascendeur* device, silently climbed back up his rope using the shadow of the cliffs for concealment.

When he returned to his car, Meier made a call to his agent. The job was done, so the second and final tranche of his fee must be transferred to his bank account within 12 hours. Meier suspected that his client would now apply heavy blackmail and protection demands to the immigrant racketeers. A lot of money was to be had from the lucrative trade in *sans-papiers*, the smuggling of hundreds of thousands of illegal refugees into France from North Africa.

He drove east towards Toulon and later made another call, to Helmut Bayer in New York. The two had liaised together over the years. Both were in their mid-fifties and shared the view that a Fourth Reich was the answer to the world's problems. Bayer's people also paid well for Meier's administration services and trusted him implicitly.

When Meier finally pocketed his phone he

whistled to himself. This was something altogether new. Bermuda! Bayer never ceased to amaze him.

Dean Witter was intelligent and charming. Heavy lensed spectacles and a receding hairline made him look a good deal older than his 36 years. He adored his wife Jane more than was good for him, for she was seven years his junior and a fine looker with a voluptuous figure men yearned to get their arms around. He constantly found himself unable to believe the good fortune that she loved him back.

They had been married more than 10 years and Dean's aim in life, his obsession, was to keep her in love with him. Since *her* dream was to own a real estate agency in Greenwich Village, and as she did score as many financial disasters as notable successes in that profession, Dean soon found the best way of binding her to him was to regularly fulfil her oft-recurring requirement for cash injections. He managed this through what he called his 'investment schemes'. He was a con man of the nicest type.

Born in Augusta, Georgia, of humble schoolteachers, Dean had become a salesman in Saint Paul, then Chicago, and finally Manhattan, which was his personal Mecca. He had met the 19-year-old Jane while trying to sell an industrial vacuum cleaner to the estate agency for which she then worked. The sale went nowhere but they had made love the following weekend and married a month later.

They had been eager to start a family but had been unable to conceive a child. After eight years of *in vitro* fertilization treatment, Jane finally became pregnant, but their joy died when their daughter was stillborn, and Jane's focus on running her agency, her own 'baby', became intense, devouring her every waking hour. She needed capital and, so long as Dean provided it on tap, she would snap up the best bargains on those rare occasions that they surfaced, in the East Village, Alphabet City or indeed anywhere near fashionable Greenwich Village.

Dean's scams were many and various to satisfy Jane's cash-flow needs. The fact that he had never yet had a brush with the law testified to his success. And he never overdid things. Moderation was his watchword, and his constant ability to switch what he called his 'scam-fields' from one profession to another, and never to repeat a fraud, however successful, had helped him to go undetected.

He also believed in good luck. Golden opportunities were both rare and fleeting, and must be grabbed with both hands if full advantage was to be had from them. In November 1992, at a Boehm porcelain exhibition, in their gallery on level 2 of the Trump Atrium on 5th and 56th, he spotted the twinkle of stardust.

Helen Boehm porcelain attracted collectors from all over the world, but especially North American aficionados with a great deal of loose wealth: those very individuals upon whom Dean Witter depended. So he had turned up at the Big Apple Boehm Bash in his Dallas rig, complete with lazy drawl, bootlace tie and cowboy boots. Jane needed half a million dollars by the New Year to put towards some dilapidated but, she believed, promising basement rooms on 10th

Street. The thought that she might miss out on this potential trove had made her very jumpy, so Dean rejoiced that he'd had the good fortune to meet his new Boehm acquaintance, Brian Simpson from Pennsylvania.

After pretending, catalogue in hand, to admire the Boehm collection, but actually with eyes only for his fellow visitors, Dean was about to target a rotund Miami collector sporting a 12,000-dollar Piaget time-piece, when he inadvertently collided with a neighbour and spilled his champagne. His apologies were accepted with an unruffled grin, which in itself was quite surprising in this room full of egotistical fat cats.

Dean smiled back and introduced himself. The two men clicked and, after a chat about various Boehm pieces, they ambled out of the exhibition in Patchin Place and went to Balducci's, a nearby deli. 'Pricey but spicey,' laughed Dean's new acquaintance. 'I recommend it.'

Brian Simpson, a craggy individual in his late for-ties, explained that he was only recently rich. 'I got a State Senatorial scholarship to my area land-grant college, Penn State, and became a geologist.'

Simpson was proud of his making good so Dean did not have to work hard, he did what he was best at, listening and prompting as imperceptibly as steering a glider. For 20 years Simpson had lived an interest-ing enough existence in many parts of the world, often in colourful or remote spots, plying his profes-sion for various mineral and oil corporations. Then, that January, an Angolan oil concern had hired him for exploration work in Cabinda. He refused to go into the exact nature of his discovery, but it had to do with oil and it coincided with a sudden retreat by Angolan government forces under pressure from UNITA rebel units. Simpson was paid a great deal by a European oil company for his information and his agreement to keep it confidential. Since then life had been fun. Krug champagne and Boehm porcelain were Simpson's current hobbies.

They both shared a liking for Carlsberg lager, not on Balducci's repertoire, so they wandered down Christopher Street until they found a Carlsberg haunt. Dean's excitement had been sparked not by Simpson's Cabinda story, but by a much earlier tale from the 1960s.

'I was posted to the National Science Foundation,' Simpson had reminisced, 'on a two-year job in the Antarctic Peninsula. The NSF has a remote base camp down there on Anvers Island and I can tell you, you'll not find a more wildly beautiful place in the world, but it's dangerous too. Our hut was down by the beach, Bonaparte Point we called it, officially known as Palmer Station. Anyway, back then, we were visited by two Brits in a boat from another island base. One was a geologist and I joined them for a week's field trip on the islands. The weather that January was as good as you could hope to find in those parts and we were able to land at a useful-looking island, where we all did a spot of individual rock-chopping. On the last day before we turned back for Palmer, some eighty miles north, I found a freak ore site which, some day, would have made me rich!' He paused and pursed his lips, looking almost rueful.

'What went wrong?' Dean had asked.

'Oh, nothing went wrong! I knew I had struck gold, literally, but I was also aware of the mining regulations for Antarctica. Removal of minerals is banned. I kept quiet about my find, but I never forgot the location, a low humpy isle not far from an old British hut occupied in the late 1950s. Of course, I never went back, but I never stopped dreaming about it. It was my secret. Now with my Cabinda deal, I'll never want for money. And I've grown to like my comforts. Antarctica's short on five-star hotels.'

'So if you found a gold mine up for grabs, surely anybody with a bit of knowledge could do likewise? Alaska all over again!'

'No way! Alaska is easy to reach. For this you'd need to have a boat capable of coping with the South Atlantic rollers, the biggest seas in the world, and your skipper would need polar seas experience. Then you'd need me to find the seam.'

'Would you come if I prepared everything?' Dean laughed to show he was not serious.

'I don't think so,' Simpson mused. 'If you were caught, you could be in big trouble. Me, I'm a law-abiding citizen. No, my seam will just have to stay right as it is. *The fish next to 140* . . . That's how I remember the location.'

'Why do you say it was a freak find? Is there no other gold down there?'

'D'you want a geology lecture?'

Dean nodded. His brain was already racing. His neck felt warm as it always did when a new scam began to simmer.

'Well, another Carlsberg and pretzels will oil my throat. Prepare to be sent to sleep!'

Dean ordered the beers and listened intently. A photographic memory would be overdoing a description of his retentive powers, but he did pride himself on near total recall once his focus was beamed in on good scam material; information he might later need to regurgitate more or less verbatim.

Simpson drew a rough map on a page of his diary. 'This here is Antarctica,' he explained, 'a continent bigger than all India *and* China and mega-rich in minerals. This bit that sticks out like a scorpion's tale is the Peninsula. Being further north than the main body of Antarctica it has a less ferocious climate so, over the past eighty years, a number of field geologists have been able to study a tiny percentage of the exposed rock areas, mostly along the coastline, where giant snowfields haven't buried them.'

Simpson rambled on . . . metals are to be found in almost every part of the world, especially in places where volcanoes have allowed hot matter from the Earth's bowels to penetrate the crust and reach the upper surface . . . Gold is one of the metals spewed up in this manner, and two of the world's gold-rich zones are southern Chile and New Zealand . . . Since both regions and their respective tectonic plates sandwich the Antarctic Plate, the presence of gold in Antarctica would not surprise a geologist.

Gold is very often found washed up many miles

from its mother lodes by glacial meltwater, but secondary sites of this nature, known as 'placers', will usually prove slow to garner . . . Simpson's seam was a rare mother lode. He called it rare, because he had never heard of any other discovered in Antarctica.

When the southern continents split up many millions of years ago and eventually drifted to their current locations, the Antarctic Peninsula was part of the Chilean Andes. The rocks of both zones, though now so widely separated, should be as similar as surgically split twins. Considering Chile's position as one of the top fifteen global gold producers and Argentina's long history of silver and gold mining, gold should also be present in the Antarctic Peninsula. Both regions exhibit igneous intrusive rocks of varied and uncertain ages and both are mineral rich. For instance, Chile was the largest copper producer in the world and, although no mining company had ever prospected professionally in the Antarctic Peninsula, chance specimens of rock had been found containing exceedingly rich copper ore on the islands close to Brian's own find. Much of the area exhibits rock of the Jurassic age and because a good deal of the gold discovered in New Zealand was Jurassic in origin, Brian saw a strong likelihood for deposits of Jurassic gold from volcanic origins in the Peninsula.

'Geographically speaking,' Brian continued, 'you get gold both above and below the Peninsula, so why the hell not expect it in between?'

'So why isn't it being heavily mined already?' Dean asked.

'Like I told you. There's an old saying: Antarctica is a continent with no laws but thousands of rules, and mining is forbidden. All the Antarctic Treaty Nations would be up in arms if they discovered that some commercial firm was moving in with heavy mining gear. As a result, huge ore deposits may continue to lie there undisturbed for decades. Also, those few geologists who, like me, have spent a few days or weeks in the short Antarctic summer hammering away and writing reports, have to date summarised the general features and rock typing as unlikely to host high-value ore.'

'So no official gold sighting has been recorded?'

'Nope. Not commercially viable stuff. A few low-grade occurrences . . . yes. And a massive pyrites site on the coast.'

'Pyrites?'

'Sure. Better known as "fool's gold" because it looks similar, but is worthless. However, where you find pyrites you can often find gold. They go hand in hand, because the heat and pressure processes that give rise to pyrites are associated with those which yield gold.'

Brian wagged a finger at Dean. 'It's also pretty much common knowledge that some NSF geologists were told to keep any discoveries they made of commercial value confidential to all but their departmental boss. As a result, they will tell you flat that there is no worthwhile ore deposit in all Antarctica. That's garbage, my friend. The simple truth is that they know very little about the geology of the area, and existing fieldwork reports are based largely on maps made back in the 1950s and 1960s. Due to the obvious difficulties caused by polar conditions and remoteness, only favoured locations were visited, so an awful lot has been left to mere deduction from generalised observations.'

'Could you get at your gold without a shipload of heavy mining gear?' Dean purred his key question.

'Certainly. That's the joy of it. I'm talking a *primary* site close to sea access. A rich vein with surface exposure as yet uneroded. A dream site, Deano, maybe not exactly a pick-and-shovel job but, certainly, no more equipment than could be taken in from a small ship anchored off the island when the pack-ice is loose.

'The ship could be made to look like a tourist vessel without too much trouble. You won't find Revenue officers down there! And there's not one police officer on the entire continent.'

Dean took Brian's address, swapped a few porcelain acquisition stories with him and parted before the downtown rush hour began. The next day he immersed himself at the library and ordered maps. The scam was under way. He signed on with Abercrombie and Kent – the luxury cruise and exotic holiday agents – for a Christmas cruise from Barbados. Jane, acknowledging that Christmas was a useless time for selling property, accompanied Dean, and as usual, involved herself fully with the planning of his next 'fleecing' operation. After all, the proceeds were for 'the agency', and she often spotted flaws that Dean had overlooked. They both agreed that they worked very well together and, by the luxury swimming pool on board the cruise liner, the eyes of their potential male targets could not fail to be impressed by, and hunger for, Jane's superb body.

The Witters were after the same niche market that Geoffrey Kent, boss of Abercrombie and Kent, so assiduously sought: those multi-millionaires who are *not* attracted to the world's most collectable works of art. The ones who instead lust after the excitement of being explorers and/or treasure hunters. They pay for super-guides to lead them on searches for Inca gold, arrive in the remote search zone by helicopter, take on files of jungle coolies and mules, dress in heroic clothes and wield fearsome-looking rifles. Of course, they never find the treasure, but they have 'been there and done that', and have the photos and videos to prove it. Some favour deep underwater adventures or big game safaris, others cross high mountain ranges in balloons, yet others descend roiling Tibetan rivers in jetboats.

By the end of their week's Caribbean cruise from Barbados (which included a charter flight over the Angel Falls and a nifty longboat journey up a tributary of the Orinoco, all within a 12-hour side trip from the ship), the Witters had made firm friends with a dozen very rich adventure-seekers, all of whom had separately agreed to meet Dean back home in the US to listen to an amazing project he had in mind.

On his return to New York, Dean lost no time in preparing his folders and doing his homework with meticulous care. He forged certificates to show he had a doctorate in geology and various other qualifications in that field. By mid-January, he had visited four of his potential 'suckers' and he was pretty certain that each would pass on the outline of his scheme to their similarly disposed pals.

He reckoned on planning his voyage for the following September, so he would need most of the necessary funds up front within the next two or three months. He had never had a better scam nor one as foolproof. He borrowed money to keep Jane happy until the sucker funds arrived and waited to see who would fall into his net. In February there were three near takers, but early in March, he felt the first *real* tug at his finely baited lure. He recognised genuine signs of interest from his very first meeting with Helmut Bayer, and had him vetted by a private eye in the usual way. Bayer checked out as a retired businessman, an ocean-faring yacht fanatic and a long-time adventure-seeker with a preference for Brazil- and Ecuador-based treasure hunts.

What Dean did not discover until a good deal later was Bayer's full background. In 1947, aged 24, he had been recruited by the US government along with 3,000 other ex-Nazis, as part of their Operation Paperclip, to lead research into a number of anti-Soviet projects, from mind control to rocketry. Early in the 1970s, he was approached by the Stasi who asked him to become one of their spies. Under a *nom de plume* he gained covert access to IBM. He and his Stasi controller, Karl Bendl, became friends and the commercial secrets which they passed to East Berlin did neither of them any harm.

In the mid-1980s, Bayer unearthed for his Stasi paymasters various coded accounts and correspondence files, mostly from the 1930s and early 1940s, revealing direct collaboration between Hitler and the then IBM chairman, Thomas J. Watson, who had taken control of the company from its creator, a German-American technology genius named Hollerith.

Largely through Dehomag (the then German branch of IBM), Watson and Hitler, who met and corresponded frequently between 1933 and 1940, masterminded the design, distribution and use throughout the Third Reich of IBM Hollerith 'death machines'. Using a punch card for every Jew and any other enemy of the Fatherland, Nazi machine operators, tutored by Dehomag, were able to administrate the complex process of genocide.

Without IBM, Hitler would still have murdered his enemies wholesale, but not with the devastating efficiency and speed that he managed thanks to Watson's complicity.

How the Stasi and their Soviet masters benefited in the early 1980s from Bayer's revelations has never been established. Perhaps Brezhnev used the threat of tipping off the Western media as a lever in his dealings with Reagan. Whatever the outcome of his espionage, Bayer retired in the mid-1980s with a large portfolio of shares, which he sold not long before the world stock markets nose-dived.

In retirement, the wealthy Bayer enjoyed two hobbies, ocean yachting and avidly supporting neo-nazi groups in Europe. He particularly enjoyed the warm comradeship and respect he frequently garnered as an honoured fund-raiser at their annual get-togethers. At one of these events in Cologne in mid-March

1993, Bayer met his old ex-Stasi colleague Karl Bendl. The latter was in the process of fund-raising to maximise the massive, early 1990s resurgence of nazism in eastern Germany. Bayer, who was due to meet Dean Witter to discuss the yacht trip to a polar gold mine, suggested Bendl might be interested.

'Who is this Witter?' Bendl asked.

'I met him on a cruise recently. He's a Texan geologist, with a beautiful wife, and he's on the lookout for a partner to exploit a gold seam he recently discovered on the Antarctic coast. Not strictly legal, but if it works, there could be huge profits.'

'Have you checked him out?'

'Sure.' Bayer did not wish to seem stupid. 'He's quite rich, but really just a geologist made good. He's literally sitting on a potential gold mine, but he doesn't have enough cash to get an expedition together. His credentials all check out and, remember, he didn't approach me. I just ran into him by sheer coincidence. This is not some carefully engineered anti-nazi plot.

'You're saying you would pass this Witter on to me?'

'It's for the cause. And my interest in his scheme would be more for the experience of the voyage than any potential profits.'

'That is very generous of you, Helmut. It certainly seems interesting. Could I meet the man? I'll be in the States the last week of this month.'

'Very well. I'll fix up a meeting.'

Juneth Glasgow, manager of the Explorers Club, had worked hard for months on the complex organisation of The 89th Explorers Club Annual Dinner. As usual, the venue was the Grand Ballroom of New York's fabulous Waldorf-Astoria Hotel.

Guests from all over the world would be in black tie or native dress and the event theme was to be 'The Great Apes'. Famous attendees would include anthropologist Jane Goodall, Sigourney Weaver, star of the film *Gorillas in the Mist*, and Professor Donald Johanson, America's leading paleoanthropologist.

Juneth was not happy with table hosts who made last-minute changes to their guest lists, but since many of them were incredibly rich, 'would-be explorers' who sometimes made healthy donations to the club, she had to accept their casual behaviour. This did not stop her worrying however, as over 900 guests were expected and people had paid a minimum of $2,500 for a 10-person table at this prestigious event in the New York social calendar.

She checked the exotic menu in its final format. A great deal of work had gone into its preparation. The 11 courses included such rare delicacies as Olduvai bone marrow, Nouabale bush pig, Indonesian Fiddle or Hornbill bird's eggs, Congolese perch, Sumatran bamboo shoots and Dokie Swamp snails.

On the afternoon before the dinner, one table's host announced four new guests, Bayer, Bendl and the Witters, so Juneth was forced to break her 'firm' limit of ten per table.

At 6pm the limos began to disgorge their rich and often famous occupants at the Waldorf. Suppressing their slight nervousness, the Witters waited at the Earthwatch stand in the hotel's east foyer, as they had been bidden that morning by their host (and prospective target), the wealthy yachtsman Helmut Bayer.

Not long before 7pm, Bayer turned up with another man at his side. As they approached, Jane squeezed Dean's hand. 'I don't like the look of Bayer's companion,' she whispered.

The man in question was well-built and silver-haired, with hard grey eyes that Jane later described as 'about as warm as a block of ice'.

'Please meet my good friend, Karl Bendl.' Bayer made the introductions. 'Karl comes from Berlin, is far wealthier than me and is greatly intrigued by the idea you put to me during our recent and delightful visit to the Orinoco. I hope you do not mind my bringing him here to meet you.'

Conversation during the ensuing dinner was kept away from the topic of Antarctica. The Witters felt themselves to be very much under observation, and not just because of Jane's purposefully plunging neckline. But they were used to being scrutinised during the key phase of a scam, and they both flourished under the pressure, exuding an easy charm. Anyone could see that their honesty was genuine, and their self-confidence rock solid.

After the dinner was over, the four of them took their leave from the host of their table and adjourned for coffee in a private room as pre-arranged by Bayer. A good sign, the Witters later agreed, of Bayer's commitment.

For two hours the Berlin tycoon and the yachtsman meticulously questioned Dean. The latter's wife was studiously ignored by both interrogators but, nonetheless, offered a good deal of pertinent information to back up her husband's responses.

'What is the location of the seam?' Bayer asked.

'Along the coastline of the Antarctic Peninsula known as the Graham Coast. No offence intended, but I don't tell anyone the precise location. I will guide you to it though. I need half the funds paid into my bank account over the next month, and the balance on the day I reveal the gold seam's location.'

'Which bank account?'

'Here in New York. I, we, don't bank anywhere else.' This, the Witters knew, would act as convincing testimony to their honesty, since they could easily have suggested an overseas account to avoid the taxman.

'What funds are you looking for from your partner in this venture?'

'Two million US dollars in total and the costs of mounting the expedition.'

'And what does your partner, whether it is me or some other party, get out of this deal?'

'All the proceeds of the mine and all legal responsibility in the event that your illegal mining activities are discovered by officials. We, Jane and I, cannot afford to be involved in the mining, so we don't expect a percentage of the takings.'

'Fair enough,' Bendl commented. 'Are you *both* intending to make the voyage?'

Jane replied without hesitation, 'Of course. We do everything together.' It was clear that she would brook no argument.

Bendl exchanged glances with Bayer. Neither man had expected this.

Bayer changed tack. 'Do you have an idea of the potential output of the vein?'

Dean passed him a carefully prepared file full of facts and figures and the forged certificates showing his geology qualifications. Both men scanned the summary page, but if they were impressed, they managed to maintain poker faces.

'When would the voyage need to start?'

'Depending on where the vessel leaves from and its projected speed, we work backwards from the sea-ice factor. The seam can normally only be reached by sea in December, at the earliest, but, in an average year, only in January or February. We cannot count on reaching the location by boat alone on the initial reconnaissance trip, so we will need manpower and equipment sufficient to haul light outboard-powered vessels over ice-floes between stretches of open water. The mother ship might have to be anchored a hundred miles or so from our goal.

'Some years, however, the conditions are more favourable and so we should plan to be in position to take advantage of unseasonably loose ice as early as late November.'

'What sort of boat do you have in mind?' Bayer asked. 'I know of a sixty-foot, ice-strengthened yacht that took friends of mine to Antarctica a few years back and has sat unused in a Bermudian boatyard ever since. Would that do?'

'How many crew does this boat hold? We'll need

space for a dozen people and at least two twenty-foot inflatables.'

Bayer nodded. 'I'll check that out, and the availability of the vessel. How do you see preparations being handled?'

'I would leave all that to you. You have our contact data. I'll give you all the key information, apart from the exact location of the seam, as soon as the first instalment of the funds reaches my bank.'

There were many other questions and it was 3am before the Witters left the two men at the Waldorf. It was agreed that barring 'unforeseen elements', as Bayer put it, the project should go ahead without delay and the first payment would be made within the next few weeks.

Later that morning, Bayer took a call from Meier in France and then telephoned two wealthy ex-Nazi businessmen in Argentina.

On their way back home in a yellow cab, Jane and Dean hugged each other with joy and relief. It had worked. One million dollars in the bank. Other scammers would have demanded at least five million, but their motto was moderation in all things. That way nobody got too serious or too nasty.

'So what do we do, angel face, when the day comes and we actually reach the seam?' Dean asked suddenly. 'We might be handing the Germans a fortune if it turns out to be a real big lode. Then the joke would be on us.'

'Let's cross that bridge when we come to it,' Jane replied. 'But I have to admit, I don't like the Berliner at all and I couldn't work out quite how he fits into the picture. Who's the boss, Bayer or him? Do they both intend to go south? There's a lot of questions I'd like to have answers to.'

'I'll pop him overboard if you don't get on with him,' Dean joked. Nothing was going to dampen his savouring of the moment. His darling Jane was full of admiration for his successful handling of this one. What more could he want?

CHAPTER SEVEN

I arrived at Kigali Airport towards the end of March 1993, and was met by an Oxfam worker who drove me into town for the night. The next day I was joined by a lady from the charity CARE, and together we reported to the group travelling in a convoy of three jeeps organised by *Médecins Sans Frontières*.

I first noticed Veronique Mahos on that drive north-west to the province of Ruhengiri, our designated work zone. I think I saw her glance my way at one point, but that may have been mere wishful thinking. I learned from one of the drivers that she worked with *Action International Contre la Faim*.

Before I had left Kigali, the man from Oxfam had delivered a warning: 'Don't think it will be like the 1980s when you were last here, Derek. Things have changed for the worse.' That, I was soon to discover, was the understatement of the year. What I saw and heard over the next four months in Rwanda shaped my reactions to later events. Even though I had listened to Aunt Ruth and knew the grisly depths of man's inhumanity to man, Ruhengiri was to make a profound impact on me; the sounds, sights and smells of that horror remain with me to this day.

Rwanda is a small country the same size as Belgium, densely populated and aggressively farmed. They call it 'the land of a thousand green hills', and I breathed in the beauty of the place as we sped on excellent roads through a veil of morning mist.

Ethnic conflict in Africa usually occurs between two clearly defined tribes, but in Rwanda the two main tribes are well mixed. They have intermarried for centuries so the differences between Tutsi and Hutu are often indistinguishable to the eye. There was no trace in Rwanda's pre-colonial history of systematic violence between the two tribes.

In the 1890s, Rwanda was a colony of Germany, who favoured the more sophisticated, cattle-owning Tutsis over the land-tilling Hutu majority. After World War I, the UN handed Rwanda to Belgium, which already ruled the neighbouring Congo, but the Belgians interfered with the Hutu–Tutsi status quo, favouring the Hutu.

By the time the Belgians gave Rwanda its independence in 1962, thousands of persecuted Tutsis began fleeing the country, and the vacuum they left in the political arena was filled by the regional tensions between the northern and southern Hutu tribes. After 10 years of increasingly violent rivalry, an army coup thrust Major-General Habyarimana into power and he ruled as a virtual dictator.

This had been the situation when I worked there in the 1980s, helping at an orphanage in Gisenye province, where everybody intermingled peaceably enough. In 1990 however, Tutsi refugees from the 1960s' troubles formed the Rwandan Patriotic Front, or *Front Patriotique Rwandais* (FPR) in Uganda, and attacked Rwanda with limited success. This initial invasion attempt was followed by a series of armed incursions which unnerved the Hutu dictator's ruling clique.

In the early 1990s, this clique, a small grouping of Hutu in influential positions, deliberately set out to exterminate the Tutsi race by mass murder. Since a great many moderate Hutu across Rwanda were also openly hostile to the government, they too were marked for assassination.

The clique evolved a mass killing system shaped to create maximum psychological terror and planned to the finest detail. The entire Hutu population was to be mobilised to kill their Tutsi friends and neighbours as a civic duty. Anybody who refused to become an executioner would themselves be murdered.

All moderate Hutu leaders or people attempting to shield Tutsis were to be killed. The resulting cleansed Rwanda would be pure Hutu, and all citizens would be bound together through their communal involvement in genocide. The extremist clique which planned all this was lucky in that the Belgians had already created a country where citizens could be easily disciplined through the introduction of ID cards, and had established a simple chain of government, where regional parish bosses reported to provincial ones, who in turn reported to Kigali.

The slaughter was meticulously organised from the top, using the army, the police, the local mayors and, above all, regional groups of thugs called the Interahamwe who were recruited from every village in the land.

Each new border incursion by the FPR gave the clique a new excuse for a dress rehearsal of their killing system. Between 1990 and my visit in 1993, they had assassinated several hundred Hutu moderates and thousands of Tutsis in small regional massacres.

A few weeks before I came to Ruhengiri, an International Commission of Enquiry on Human Rights Violations toured Rwanda. As soon as this fruitless and futile quest was over and the Commissioners had departed, the clique began a new round of massacres. Unaware that I was headed straight for danger, I settled into a rewarding job with four other aid workers, assisting in different hospitals and orphanages in Ruhengiri and its neighbouring province of Gisenye.

Veronique was one of my co-workers and came from Provence. Despite my reticence about all things French, I found everything about her attractive. Luckily, she seemed to reciprocate my feelings and we worked well together.

At 54, I was 10 years older than 'Nique', as she liked to be called, but we had both reached middle age without being snared by the many brief or not-so-brief flings that we had enjoyed. We had both weathered the years well, possibly through avoiding marriage and its related stresses. I was fit, sparky and lean, with at least half a head of hair to cover my skull. Nique was still sexy, curvaceous and playfully responsive to my slow but sure advances. This slowness was partially due to the nature of our group's work schedule: a great deal to do, inadequate equipment, too few vehicles and too much local inefficiency.

Nonetheless, by the end of the first month Nique and I were sleeping together and behaving like young lovers. We didn't need to talk much, and we touched a lot. Even a glance from her long-lashed, hazel eyes, as we assisted with appendix operations, shifted endless bags of milk powder from trucks to stores or sat talking to starry-eyed, thumb-sucking orphans, made my heart beat faster.

But we were working inside a ticking time bomb. The ruling clique was almost ready to give a nationwide signal for genocide.

The conditions necessary to create a genocidal mind-set within any given population are a depressed economy, uneven distribution of wealth, the existence of an identifiable minority, the strong political ambition of an oppressor group, and impunity. On top of all that, the genocidal leadership needs a base of social deprivation and tension which it can exploit to its own evil ends. It must excite a sense of unjust suffering among the masses, and focus the resultant anger against a specific group. Preparing a population to commit genocide against lifelong neighbours is a complex job that takes time. Natural feelings of revulsion and guilt must be overcome. Hitler took at least six years to achieve this; the Rwandan clique had so far taken three.

The level of education of the relevant population probably defines the level of sophistication required to mobilise them as killers. Remember that most such killers are average, gentle, decent people like you or me, not brutal psychotics. It is no more natural to murder a neighbour than it is to bungee jump. We have to be mentally trained to kill, to be taught why it is right and then be motivated to act at a certain time. Normally it needs the justification of a 'war' to convince us to join bands of killers (called armies) and accept training in how best to shoot, bomb, bayonet and effectively kill or maim the citizens of those very countries in which we may have been taking annual holidays for years.

In Rwanda, the government was indoctrinating the masses at national and local levels into believing that they were indeed at war. The government-controlled radio stations, newspapers and TV were ceaselessly preparing their audiences for action. Militias were being trained to kill in every district. The Tutsis, the designated enemy, were painfully, fearfully aware of the impending Armageddon, yet they could do nothing but wait and hope. The army and the police, indeed every armed authority in Rwanda, were Hutu controlled. There was no escape for a Tutsi.

Of course, the ruling Hutu needed its killers to be well trained and armed for the massive task ahead since the Tutsis could not be expected to lie down meekly and be slaughtered. As with the Nazi policy of *Nacht und Nebel*, or darkness and fog, a policy of deception should hopefully confuse the victims, and a rash of intermittent mini-massacres before the big one might terrorise them into submission. This could fail however, so total superiority in weaponry must be assured before the starting gun could be fired.

There were three main arms suppliers, Nique told me. South Africa was supplying Rwanda's main killing force, the Hutu army, with grenades, machine guns and mortars; not through any political affinity with Rwanda but purely for commercial gain. The very week Mandela came to power, convoys of arms headed north on their way to Rwanda.

Egypt was another eager arms supplier but, Nique sadly confirmed, her own country, France, was the mainstay of the Rwandan government's genocidal plans. 'Our role and responsibility for what is happening is tragic and overwhelming. We are feeding the Devil. These evil people are being financed, trained and armed by us, even though everyone in Paris knows what will happen sooner or later. We *welcome* the extermination of the Tutsis because they threaten our influence here.'

She explained France's motives. 'Unlike the British and Portuguese, we have maintained close relationships with nearly all our former colonies in Africa, and we treat Belgian colonies as our own; a part of francophone Africa. Our intelligence services run this place for the ruling clique. Our government used the nationalised Credit Lyonnais to channel funds to the killers for their arms' purchases. The reason is simple. We value our influence, our trade benefits, the use of our culture and language, our position of privilege and of course, above all, we fear and hate Anglo-Saxon encroachment. *Les Angliches* and *Les Ricains* are the enemy at the door.'

'But the Tutsis are not Anglo-Saxon, surely?'

'Derek, you are so innocent. Of course they are. The FPR Tutsi refugee army comes from Uganda, and what is Uganda? It is anglophone. The Tutsi refugee leaders speak English. If they were to take over Rwanda from the current Hutu dictators, then, *voilà*, Rwanda would soon become a part of English-speaking East Africa. France must do and does do all she can to prevent such an appalling scenario! Do you not remember the party in Kigali last week? Could you not feel how uncomfortable the French diplomats were when English was spoken around them? You can go to Djibouti or the Ivory Coast or anywhere under French influence and you will find the same thing.'

'It is the United Nations,' I pointed out, 'not France, who will decide things here. Their talks are going on right now. The UN will not allow large-scale killings.'

'*Alors!* Who have you been listening to, my poor darling? Where have you been?'

'Working very hard like you. Or else, in bed . . . with you!'

'Thank God for that. It is the only sane thing in this mad place. But don't change the subject. You are very deceived if you think the UN are the big wheelers and dealers out here. Maybe in name, yes, but the truth is that we, the French, control UN policy here! We are a permanent member of the Security Council and can thus define the agenda in the same way the US does on the Israeli question.

'In the past, we have always turned a blind eye when our Hutu friends have massacred Tutsis. We, and therefore the UN, will continue to do this. The other members of the Security Council will not stop us. The UK never interferes in francophone countries, Bill Clinton's hands are full elsewhere, and anyway, the US is against military intervention in Africa after its recent troubles in Somalia. Russia and China never make a fuss about human rights because of their own ongoing abuses of them.'

As the weeks went by our patients whispered of intimidation and murders in nearby hilltop communities, or *cellules* as they called their villages. They talked of recently assassinated Tutsi and moderate Hutu leaders. In April a minister was reported as saying, 'I am planning now for the apocalypse. The *Akazu* is almost ready.' *Akazu* was a local name for the ruling clique whose goal was absolute power through absolute terror.

The RTLM radio channel we listened to each evening included a report in which a local burgermeister, one of the all-powerful regional mayors, said, 'The only remedy now is total extermination of the enemy and their Hutu supporters. We will kill them all. Wipe them out. Our knives are ready.'

In the local markets, Hutu customers could buy a grenade for the same price as two beers. Weapons were on sale everywhere, as available as avocados and mangoes, but only to Hutu. The Rwandan journal *Le Flambeau* announced that government extremists, 'are plotting to exterminate all political adversaries and the defenceless population of the enemy. This will be the final solution.'

'How can a Hutu tell who they should kill?' I asked Nique. 'To me, the majority of Rwandans look alike.'

'Well, how does an IRA killer in Ireland know who is Protestant? They do their homework first, ask neighbours, prepare lists. Here it is easier, for you can look at a person's ID card, and in some cases Tutsis definitely are taller with straighter noses and longer fingers.'

The trouble began in late April with a visit to our region by a Rwandan governmental party leader named Leon Mugesara, who had studied for a time in Canada. He had seemed a nice enough fellow, intelligent and friendly, but then I heard him on the local radio the day he arrived in Ruhengiri and changed my opinion. In Hitlerian tones, he urged his listeners to rise up against their Tutsi neighbours and dump their bodies in rivers.

That night, out shopping in the local market, I tripped over what I assumed was a drunkard lying in the street. When I arrived back at the orphanage, I found bloodstains on my trouser legs. My drunkard had been a corpse.

Nique returned with two others from our group after visiting Nyando in the Gisenyi district. They were unusually subdued. She told me they had been stopped by six villagers armed with machetes. 'They made us get out of the jeep, and searched it. One of the machete men said, "Maybe you are hiding a Tutsi?" Then he smiled menacingly and ran his fingers across his throat. We kept quiet and they let us go. It was very unsettling.' She shivered.

The next day we drove to a clinic for refugees

where Nique had earlier worked as a nurse. The building was spotless, and since the cook was away sick, some of us who loved cooking, like me, took turns to help out as chief chef. After supper, we joined the 150 or so refugees in the dirt clearing beside the clinic for a few simple prayers and a singsong.

The next hours and days were a nightmare that my mind still replays in my sleep occasionally, so that I awake in a sweat. My trauma only lasted a few *days*, however. For many Jews, the horror had continued over *years*.

One moment we were singing and laughing, the next, there was silence and fear on the faces of our hosts, who were mostly, but by no means all, Catholic Tutsis.

We became aware of voices approaching from another part of the village. Nique's hand closed over mine. Our thighs pressed together. Although the day had been warm, we were wearing slacks against the insects.

The darkness all about our lamp-lit circle became animated as a number of shadowy figures materialised on the three open sides of the yard. Behind us, the front wall of the clinic reflected our silhouettes.

A young male voice shattered our apprehensive silence and realised our worst fears.

'Look! They are Tutsi. See their white Belgian friends. We have a nest of *Inyenzi* ready to be cut.'

'No,' said another. 'I see Tutsi children of Hutu mothers, and there is Jean from the post office. He is Hutu. We must check them all.'

'Kill the Belgians, the Tutsi-lovers.'

'No, be careful, maybe they are French.'

The arguments went on. I thought about escape, but we were surrounded. Maybe two or three hundred men and women jostled ever closer in the yard. Our people cowered together against the clinic wall.

'Who are they?' I asked Nique.

'Some are from the *Interahamwe* militia,' whispered Jerome, a Hutu helper at the clinic. 'Some are local people from the Parmahutu party, all bastards, but most are just local Hutu. They have been stirred up. Mugesara is to blame.'

Suddenly, a young girl ran screaming into the clinic. Her child was in bed there with a fever. A group of Hutu from the crowd quickly pushed past us to follow her. They soon came back out and, in front of us all, they held her down while one of them tore off her dress and pushed a kitchen knife slowly into her stomach. I can hear her terrible cries even now. Another man held her little daughter by the hair and swung her in the air, while a colleague swatted her again and again with a *masu*, a wooden club with long nails protruding from its end. The child made no sound, but blood spurted from her many puncture wounds.

'The cockroaches will try to escape us,' an old woman shouted. 'Let none escape. Kill them all. Cut them up.'

Jerome whispered, 'That is a member of the Zigiranyirazo family, a cousin of the man whose gang is accused of killing Diane Fossey, the white lady doing monkey research here. She has many Tutsi friends among those here, but now she will have them all killed.'

'Come out if you are Hutu,' the cries went up. 'Show us your proof.' 'ID cards!' 'Prove you are not *Inyenzi*.' A dozen or more of our group produced their Hutu cards. They were spat at and warned to keep away. 'Tutsi-lovers will be killed in future.'

One man with a Hutu card was hit on the side of his head with a *masu* and died at once. His killer said, 'His card must be false, for he is too tall to be Hutu.' Nobody objected.

Jerome said, 'That man, Joseph, who killed the tall Hutu, he was my friend. We were at school together. He must be drunk.'

There was a lull in the violence. I was numb with fear, a feeling like none I had ever experienced. The crowd murmured. A low evil sound of anticipation. Then, two of their number seized a pregnant woman from the midst of our group, stripped off her dress and slashed again and again at her stomach with their machetes. Nique vomited.

Two more Tutsi women were selected and cut open in front of us. Their hands and feet were hacked off. Neither died immediately. They lay bleeding and begging for help. The psychological terror of all of us who witnessed this was immense.

'We will take ten of you now to work on,' a short squat Hutu declared. Perhaps he was the leader. 'Tomorrow we will return for more.' We were rounded up and locked in the clinic.

That night was perhaps the worst of my life. I tried to think. There *must* be some way out, but the building was surrounded by Hutu militia with machetes and knives, and we were all weaponless apart from some kitchenware. And any display of defiance would, I feared, only spark a massacre. I tried the telephone but the line had been cut.

'Surely,' I asked Nique, 'they will not return. They're just drunk. Tomorrow they'll regret it. They've murdered five of their own fellow villagers, and they'll definitely be arrested tomorrow.'

Nique shook her head. 'Five killings is nothing. Eight weeks ago in Gisenye they killed two hundred and eighty people in only one village. And don't count on the police. They are Hutu-controlled and won't interfere. Here in Ruhengiri, there are very few Tutsi. We are isolated. Our only hope is to make them believe we are both French. Of course, I have no passport with me, just when I have most need of it.'

None of us slept that night. In the morning they cut off the water. Soon the four lavatories began to stink. At nine o'clock the crowd returned, eager for blood. This time they took four Tutsi businessmen, all well educated. I had noticed on the previous day that the three women who had been assaulted had all been smartly dressed. We closed our eyes, but heard their cries and the dull thuds of machetes. The bodies were left for the flies outside the clinic.

Our captors had forgotten to switch off our electricity so we all moved into two rooms with fans. A tall Tutsi doctor visiting from another province told us of past Hutu depravities elsewhere in Rwanda. Others joined in with their own tales of horror. Nique and I did not interrupt, but I could think of no less suitable topic of conversation given our circumstances. The doctor was called Emmanuel. He said that the Hutu killed with as much cruelty as possible. He listed their barbaric methods: 'They love to hunt us down. There can be no hiding place for us. They burn alive children hiding in ceilings or haystacks, and they cut off feet, hands, breasts and testicles. They throw people into latrine holes to drown, or they slash with machetes so that death is slow and agonising. They set fire to the bush if people try to hide in the country, and they leave young boys out of reach of water with both hamstrings and Achilles tendons slashed.'

We all listened, queasy with fear, as Emmanuel continued. 'They rape girls of five. They torture women before rape and they rape badly wounded women. They even rape women who have been killed. Afterwards, they fling their living victims into death pits full of corpses, where crows and dogs feed on them. My daughter was gang-raped in Bugesara last year. They ruptured her uterus. Many of the rapists are HIV-positive.'

'There must be some way for us to escape before they return. Somebody must help us.' This was the voice of another well-educated man, who was exhausted by fear and hoarse with thirst. Outside the air thrummed with flies feasting on the bloody corpses swelling in the afternoon heat.

'There are many good Hutu,' Emmanuel said. 'We all know that. But what can they do? Every month the *Akazu* murders any Hutu who criticises the government. A Hutu who sides with us is signing his own death warrant. If he refuses to kill, he will be killed. The *Akazu* are training their people to murder as their civic duty. It will become the correct thing to do, "Kill a Tutsi every day".'

'He is right,' a high, nervous voice came from a corner of the crowded room. 'I saw villagers this morning watching the slashing of men they have been at church with every Sunday – faithful Christians, good Christians. How can they do this? Emmanuel is right. May God save us.'

'I fear,' said Emmanuel, 'that God is occupied elsewhere.'

'In Bugesara,' a young man said, 'I was walking back home from the shops on the usual path, when some neighbours stopped me and my cousin by marriage. She was Tutsi. They told me to kill her or they would kill me. I refused so they hit my legs with a *masu*. Then they switched to my back so I took their knife and started to stab my poor cousin. They all joined in with their machetes but she took a long time to die. They left me alone eventually. What else could I have done?'

'Did the *masu* hurt?' somebody asked.

'Of course. The nails are long and the ends go through your skin into your bones. But unless they hit your head, they won't kill you at once and you don't lose too much blood. No, the machete is the worst, the most painful.'

I had often heard Tutsis talk about the machete in fearful tones, and a nurse friend who had attended victims of such attacks had told me that many survivors were now HIV-positive. This was due to the killers using their blades to chop madly at victim after victim, their machetes dripping with infected blood. Many Hutu militia considered it a failure to leave their victims dead, preferring to cause maximum suffering rather than immediate death, so they severed limbs, slit tendons and stomachs, and denied the final mercy blow. Many Tutsis begged for a bullet to end their agony. Others, when cornered by *Interahamwe* killers, offered all their money to be shot rather than die by a machete blade.

A good joke for the Hutu was to cut the feet off a Tutsi and say, 'You're not so tall now, cockroach.' Or to slit off their nose or fingers, and likewise to remark that their prominent Tutsi features were no more.

Degradation of Tutsis was important to many of the killers, and a favourite method of dispatching Hutu prisoners was the pit latrine. Every Rwandan country *cellule* had pit latrines, sometimes 20 feet deep or more and impossible to escape from. The wounded, the pregnant and children were frequently thrown into these foul black trenches and drowned when they could no longer keep afloat.

'I was caught in an attack in our own village last year.' A tall man started to tell his story. 'There were eight of us, all related. Five of us fled to a nearby swamp but my sister and her child were cut up as they ran. We found her body later with the child's head placed between her legs. At night we crept out of the swamps to find sorghum stalks to eat. My uncle was caught nearby and we hid as they carved him up. Then they found us too.

'They cut my neck and chopped off my fingers. They thought I was dead. For an hour they ran around in the bushes screaming, "I've found one. Kill him. Kill him." Just like a rat hunt when we were little. I was lucky to survive – all the others died. Those who attacked us had been our friends and neighbours since we were children. Now they own all our cattle.'

At dawn on the third day, those of us who were left, exhausted and thirsty as we were, tried to barricade the entrance to the clinic. We made quite a good job of it with some furniture. Later, we heard a crowd of Hutu wandering around outside and laughing. They tried to remove a heavy dresser, but we had sticks and put out the eye of one of them who reached in to try to remove it. They went away and came back with some soldiers who machine-gunned the pile of furniture. Some people behind the barricade were struck by the bullets. Then, the soldiers lobbed grenades in and soon there were bleeding corpses everywhere.

A few of us crawled into a tiny storeroom. Nique and I kept close together. Emmanuel was with us, but he was bleeding from a shrapnel wound. More and more injured people crawled into the storeroom, and some lay on top of us.

Our attackers gained access to the clinic and started to butcher everyone. I listened to the screams of two sisters clinging to each other as they were struck repeatedly by machetes. Many of the victims begged for mercy or to be shot. Every so often we heard the rasp of metal on whetstone as the killers re-honed their blades, but they failed to find us.

To my enormous relief, they at last tired of their work – which was no doubt as strenuous as chopping firewood – and went away, even though there was still movement and noise in the room. We waited for a while, and then breathing heavily in the fetid air, Nique and I forced our way out from under the dead and the dying in the storeroom. But then we found that bodies on the other side of the door prevented us from opening it. In desperation, I battered the perforated zinc panel halfway up the storeroom's door until it tore off and we were able to squeeze out and into the concrete passageway.

The heaps of mangled bodies around us were slippery with blood and excreta, and exuded a loathsome stench. A woman in one corner motioned at me feebly. The right side of her face had been cut open. A girl of about seven years stood up and I saw that she had only half an arm; the other had been hacked off at the shoulder. She kept calling '*Baati. Baati,*' but nobody responded. I saw that four other people were breathing, but all had missing limbs or gaping wounds.

In another room, a teenage girl cried, 'They shamed me first. They said they will come back tomorrow and, if I am alive, they will do it again.' Her Achilles tendons had both been slashed. A little baby cried fitfully on the floor, its tiny fingers clasping the foot of a dead man.

Nique gripped my wrist as we crawled over bodies towards the end of the passageway. She held a finger to her lips.

'*Pas un bruit,*' she whispered. 'Be quiet.'

Moving over to her vantage point, I saw why she had silenced me. We froze, and for the next few minutes, which seemed like an age, we watched a ghastly scene in the clinic's lounge. The fan was still revolving with a steady whine and two *Interahamwe* civilians were silently and methodically looting the bodies. One of the looters carried a machete and, each time either man found someone alive, he held the survivor's head up by the hair and drew the machete across his or her throat.

'I saw that killer on the first night,' Nique whispered. 'He is no more than eleven years old.'

After the two looters had left, there was silence, but no assurance that the killers had gone. We returned to our storeroom through the hole and replaced the panel. The smell inside was suffocating. Every breath I took reeked of blood and death. The raped girl had said the attackers would come back, so we slithered beneath two corpses and tried to ignore the foul matter that soiled us, mingled with our sweat and entered our eyes and mouths.

A raging thirst gripped us both and eclipsed all our other worries, but we stuck it out until morning and when at noon nobody had returned, we again crawled out of the room and into the passage. The girl and the others were dead now. In the lounge area the only corpse-free spot was where we stood. A spear remained in the stomach of a pregnant woman. Her fists were clenched around its haft but she was clearly dead. Strewn around the room in pieces were babies and little children.

I noticed a movement near the window, and a

sudden snarl revealed a ravenous dog tearing at the flesh of a torso.

We emerged with caution from the lounge, both of us armed with discarded weapons we had found among the bodies. At the outer doorway I was blinded by sunlight, and when my focus cleared, I could see nothing but dead people in the clearing where only a few nights before we had joked and sung.

'*Pas Tuez*,' a little voice whimpered nearby. A boy cowered at my feet staring in terror at my machete. One of his hands was attached to his wrist only by a thin lace of sinew and tendon. His shoulders were also gashed, and I noticed that the arms and hands of other victims had been slashed, presumably as they had tried to protect their necks and faces. Thinking we meant to harm him, the child ran limping into the bush. The smell of rotting bodies filled the air.

In the village, we found an old Hutu lady in bed, just as she had been when we had visited her with medicine on the morning of the attack. She told us that all the villagers except the sick had gone to another *cellule* because of a rumour that they might be punished for the killings.

'They know you are alive,' she said, 'but the leaders now know you are French not Belgian. They want you to tell the papers and the TV about what has happened because they think it will spark big fear among the "cockroaches" all over Rwanda. That is what they want.'

'What shall we do?' It seemed odd to ask such a question of this sick old woman, but she appeared to be fully informed about the situation, which was more than we were.

'They took your car, but put it back where it was when they learned you were French. Maybe you should go before they change their minds about what is best for you.'

We found the car and drove out of the village. There was no roadblock and, elsewhere, all was as 'normal' as ever. I felt like I had emerged from hell. We stopped at a stream, and drank and drank until our immediate thirst was slaked. Then we stripped off and lay in it, letting the cool water wash away some of the dirt and the smell.

Once back on the main road, we pulled up and talked about what to do.

'We must tell Martin at MSF at once,' said Nique between convulsive sobs.

'What can he do?' I asked. 'What can anyone do?'

'Derek, *tu es bête*, of course they can stop this happening again.'

'But, my love, they can't. Think about it. Every month there are killings of individuals, of families, of tribal groupings. You know this as well as I do. Sometimes a massacre of two or three hundred Tutsis hits the headlines and is recorded, but nothing is done. This will be no different and the old Hutu woman seemed honest. She was grateful to us and would have no reason to lie. They *want* the word spread. It will serve to increase the terror of all Tutsis throughout Rwanda. That's exactly what the clique wants. And of course, the President will deny any involvement as always, and the UN will blame nobody as always.'

'But we *can't* just say nothing,' Nique cried. 'It is a nightmare. Worse than anything I could ever have imagined. I will never be able to sleep again.'

I said nothing, but I felt like so many people must have felt each time they saw maltreatment of the Jews, and knew that nothing they could do or say would change things.

Surrounding our jeep were lush and verdant fields, rivers and streams, cassava and banana plantations, coffee and sorghum fields, and little peaceful villages bathed in the magical Rwandan sunlight. Yet death was all around us too. I reeked of it. In fact, for months after I left Africa, I would break out in a fearful sweat and the stink of death would fill my nostrils. I could be eating and suddenly smell its loathsome odour on my fork; then I could not finish what was on my plate.

When we returned to our base, I promised Nique I would at least try to alert the authorities about the tragedy we had witnessed.

That week, I drove to Kigali via Gitarama and gained an audience with the Hutu Archbishop Nsengiyumva, who was known to have influence with the government and wide international contacts. He was polite, hospitable and upset that someone who had come to help his country was in such a disturbed state. However, he appeared to be wearing blinkers.

'I have already heard about the incident,' he assured me, 'but you are quite wrong in blaming Hutu troublemakers. The attack was in fact a raid by an FPR unit who had learned of your presence there and wanted to use you to turn the international community against our government.'

'But with due respect, Monseigneur,' I interrupted, 'I *know* that the attackers were Hutu.'

'Nonsense.' He brushed my words aside. 'It is easy to make mistakes. Why do you think you and your friend were spared, and everyone else was killed? Of course it was so that you would report the incident. This attack against the reputation of our government is preposterous! It is nothing but another Tutsi plot to gain international sympathy.'

'But—'

'No, no.' The archbishop was not going to listen. 'These Tutsis have no place in Rwanda. They are a troublesome minority from Ethiopia. In a democracy, the majority will is the legal way and minorities who do not go along with it must leave, or face the consequences.'

My further remonstrations were stonewalled. I was wasting my time with the Church in ultra-Christian Rwanda and drove on to Kigali to my Oxfam contact, who suggested I should attend a diplomatic cocktail party that very night. After he'd made two phone calls I was able to present myself as an accredited guest.

The room was thick with tobacco smoke and uniformed waiters circled continuously with an array of beverages. Diplomatic staff representing many nations were there, and a sprinkling of western businessmen. After twenty minutes or so, I was able to identify people from the UN and from the French Embassy. One UN staffer, who claimed a close association with the Special Representative, Jacques-Roger Booh Booh, insisted that 'knowledgeable sources' indicated that the event I had witnessed was an FPR attack.

'No!' I was adamant in my response. 'The killers were Hutu. The FPR was in no way involved.'

He snapped back at me in disbelief. 'How do you expect me or anyone else here to believe you? How could the Hutu government, who give the donors of foreign investment the greatest return of any country in Africa, be preparing genocide under our noses? Do you think we are stupid? Where would they find the time to organize such nationwide genocide, when they are fully occupied implementing our aid projects? No. Be serious. I can see you are upset, but you've got this wrong, believe me.'

I turned away from him in disgust, and cornered an official from the French Embassy. I listened aghast as he gave me the same response, though this time it was punctuated with many a Gallic gesture.

I left Kigali that night in frustration. All around me, mass murder was being clinically planned and rehearsed, but those authorities that had the power to prevent it were unwilling to do so.

They say that shared suffering makes the bond between two people tighter, but with Veronique and me this was not so. We found it difficult to talk whereas previously we had loved to converse together about almost anything, or merely to sit together. But not after the killings. Nor could we make love. Even the silences weighed heavily, as each knew what the other was thinking about. We could not talk about the killings yet, and to talk of anything else seemed superficial.

We began to keep away from each other, so when the call came from Laro I did not, as otherwise would have been the case, turn down his offer of a 'job'.

Veronique smiled sadly when I told her I would be leaving, but she nodded and agreed it would be best for both of us to be apart, at least for a while, until the memories grew less painful. I think she still believed I should have pressed the authorities harder about the killings, but she had no answer when I asked her *which* authority would do anything to help a single Rwandan Tutsi? The fact that she knew her own country was so clearly to blame for its blind support of the evil governing clique made her all the more determined to stay in Rwanda, come what may, and to give assistance to persecuted people wherever possible. That way, she could atone for being French.

For my part, the dreadful proof in Rwanda of the human capacity for great evil, and my frustration at being unable to even seek justice for the poor helpless Tutsis, served only to increase my desire to avenge my own family for *their* suffering.

Laro had instructed me to fly to Paris. I would call at my safety deposit box there and then head for Lyon. After I had done whatever needed to be done, I knew I would go back to Veronique for my heart already ached for her.

CHAPTER EIGHT

Sleep was elusive on that flight from Africa to France. I tried to force my mind from dwelling on the horrors of Rwanda, but images of other horrors besieged me instead.

I thought of what Aunt Ruth had told me about Bippi before she died. His story is now a mixture in my mind of what my aunt told me and what I have learned from the tales of other survivors.

The month of August of 1943, when I was four, was hot and humid in *Vogtland*, and on a normal day Aunt Ruth would have given me my lessons in the shade of the garden hedge. But we were expecting the worst. The stupid Bippi, our fellow refugee, had gone on 'an outing' into the city against the specific instructions of the Clinic's director, my great-uncle Ludwig. If the Gestapo caught him, he would be tortured and no doubt tell them where he'.d been hiding. His Auschwitz Jew tattoo meant he would never be able to bluff his way out of trouble.

If we were raided as a result of Bippi's excursion, the three senior Gestapo officers unofficially running the Clinic for the benefit of their schizophrenic children would be in major trouble too, but that was no consolation to us.

Only my grandmother showed no signs of concern due to her wandering mental state. Liebchen, the teenage Jewish girl, sat beside her and their knitting needles clicked in unison; the only sound in the room for much of the time.

'That stupid ass of a Bippi,' Reinhardt growled. 'He knows the danger he's putting us all in, but he still can't control his urges. He's probably gone to find a pretty Plauen boy. I'll *kill* him when he gets back.'

'Please guard your tongue, Reinhardt,' my mother murmured, nodding in my direction.

'*Verzeihung*, Frau Anna, excuse me. But Bippi has done us wrong.'

Neither Bippi himself nor the Gestapo had appeared at the Clinic by midday, so Ludwig suggested we all try to rest, and returned to his work with the children in the other part of the house. The Plauen curfew would begin at 8pm by which time, we desperately hoped, Bippi would be back.

Three hours after dark, a gentle knocking sounded at the kitchen window and Maria, our cook and fellow refugee, screamed in terror. Then, recognising the grinning face of Bippi, she clasped her hands to her ample Italian chest, forgetting that she was holding a wet dishcloth.

Soon we were all laughing at and with Maria,

releasing the pent-up tensions of the past few hours. All of us, that is, except for Ludwig, who was furious and confronted the shame-faced Bippi without delay.

'What in God's name do you think you are doing? Where have you been and why? Do you not realise you could easily have had every one of us killed? In fact, we still could be, as the Gestapo may have had you followed. Tell me *exactly* where you have been and who you have seen. Afterwards I will decide what to do with you.'

Bippi's habitual affable grin was for once absent. He sat at the kitchen table looking almost contrite, as Ludwig towered over him like an Inquisitor aching to apply hot irons.

'I went to visit my old *Mischling* friend Richard in Wettinstrasse near the school.'

'Which school?'

'The Lessing and Schiller. He teaches there. They never discovered his *Mischling* status nor his sexual preferences or he would have been sent to the camps like me.'

'Why did you need to see him so badly?'

Bippi looked down at his hands. We were all aware of his homosexuality, although at four years of age I did not of course know what was involved. Ludwig did not press the point.

'So, you are happy to hand us all to the Gestapo just to satisfy your basic urges?'

Bippi shook his head. 'No. No, Herr Ludwig. I just did not think. I love you all and want no hurt to come to you. I thought only I would be in danger, and I was happy to take that risk to see Richard again. But now, I do realise the consequences for you, and I am very, very sorry. It will never happen again, I promise you. However long the war lasts, I will never break your rules again. I will never leave these walls.'

'So, how *did* you get to Wettinstrasse? That's the other end of town. You *must* have been seen.'

'No, Herr Ludwig. Naturally, I did not wear my *Davidstern* for there are now no Jews walking about openly in Plauen. To wear the star would invite immediate arrest. Before dawn, I sneaked across country and through back gardens to the Leuchtsmühlen bridge. Then up the Leuchtsmühlen way beside the river until I reached the Johannes *Kirche*. I know every corner and back route from my childhood. Once the curfew hour was up, I walked boldly and used these,' Bippi held up a *Vogtländer* postal cap, coat and satchel, 'which Maria found in the attic when she first came here.'

Maria nodded. 'That is true, Herr Ludwig, but never for a moment did I think this rascal would use them for such a purpose.'

'So, you reached your friend with no trouble?'

Bippi agreed. 'No trouble at all, sir, in fact nobody even looked my way. People avoid eye contact with each other now, you know. I noticed that. I went to an old Tante Emma Lade confectionery shop I used to frequent, to buy Liebchen a gift, and I saw how the customers came in, collected their orders and left. Nobody talked to or looked at each other, nor did they even chat to the vendor – a new man and an Aryan so I left without buying anything.'

'And then?' Ludwig was remorseless.

'I cut across Goethe Platz to Albertstrasse and found my friend Richard. I hope you will not mind if I do not use his full name. He was not at all happy when he recognised me, but he bustled me into his apartment. He said I must go at once and that he was being watched. He is, he thinks, one of the very last surviving Jews at large in Plauen. He could not be certain that the Gestapo were on to him since he has good forged Aryan papers and his last Jewish relative died over twenty years ago. But he is paranoid, suspicious of everyone and everything.'

'Maybe he is now a paid informer?'

'Oh, no, not him. He was a friend of Herr Max Perl, one of Plauen's Jewish community leaders and, anyway, he'd be useless to the Gestapo. He said that by 1939 all the city's Jews had been confined in the four ghetto houses and then the Gestapo had sent them off to labour camps in batches. By early this year, the majority had gone. Only a few individuals, mostly *Mischlinge*, survive outside the ghettos. Two such people, both friends of Richard, were picked up recently by catchers.'

'Catchers?'

'Yes. The Gestapo employ Jews to pose as underground Jews. They are trained to hunt us out from our hiding places by the notorious Gestapo boss from Zwickau, *Oberleutnant* Agsten.'

'You've done a pretty good catching job on *us*.' Reinhardt glowered at the recalcitrant Bippi.

'I am sorry. Very sorry. I regret it, please believe me. I will never, never go away again.'

'You should indeed be sorry, Bippi.' Uncle Ludwig

stared at him gravely. 'The Bund sent you here and I do not know when they will next make contact. I have no way of communicating with them, so you can stay here under sufferance until I do hear from them. But I cannot risk having you here a moment longer after that. The Bund must find another refuge for you. The safety of the rest of us cannot be left at the whim of your uncontrollable urges.'

Bippi looked utterly crestfallen, but he nodded. 'Of course, Herr Ludwig, thank you. I understand. I am sorry.' He carried his postman's gear away to the camp-bed in the tiny boxroom he shared with Reinhardt.

Ludwig clasped Rais to him. He was a kind man who had been forced to be ruthless. At the time, we all fully agreed with his decision, fresh as we were from the fear and apprehension Bippi's excursion had caused us.

Aunt Ruth had found Bippi's effeminate ways endearing. At first my mother had kept me away from him, but it was soon clear that there was not the least likelihood of his molesting me for he was no paedophile. Bippi soon became my guardian in the garden whenever my mother and aunt had wanted time to rest or to help Maria. I found him hilarious, and listened to his funny stories for hours on end.

'*Why* did he do it?' Aunt Ruth sighed. 'We all love him. He is part of the family. We will be so sad when he has to leave.'

Reinhardt cleared his throat.

'*Sei Ruhig!*' Aunt Ruth glared at him. 'Shut up,

Reinhardt. You go and tell Bippi to come down here again.'

When Bippi returned, no doubt expecting to be told to pack his bag at once, my aunt spoke to him kindly.

'Come, Bippi. Let's go outside where it's cool. I want to learn more about you, and I know you won't talk in front of this barbarian.'

Bippi had never told us how he had survived Auschwitz nor indeed anything about his early history. He was wonderfully talkative on just about every topic under the sun except for his own experiences, but now he knew that he was soon to be expelled from the only safe and friendly refuge he had experienced in years, he revealed what he had suffered.

Mixed in with these revelations from Bippi, are historical details of the events concerned and some of the memories of Auschwitz survivors that I myself have researched over the past few years.

After school, Bippi had been apprenticed by his widowed mother to a small lace factory in Plauen, where he thrived in a largely female workforce who loved his bubbly, happy nature. None of them knew of his homosexuality, which was considered a hideous crime in Germany even before Hitler's arrival on the scene.

Like other Plauen Jews, he and his ageing mother suffered increasing hostility from non-Jews throughout the late 1930s. In 1939, they were forced into a ghetto, and then sent to Auschwitz in 1942.

On arrival at the camp, Bippi tried hard to hide his homosexuality, for he knew that only one type of human being rated lower than a Jew with the SS guards and that was a 'queer' Jew.

Although as far back as 1930, Hitler's half-dozen top Nazi leaders had included homosexuals, the fact was always covered up. All 'queers' were sent to the camps where, over the course of the war, some 50,000 of them perished in misery. In the armed forces and the SS, homosexuality incurred the death penalty.

'Frau Jacobs.' Bippi's hands were clasped together as though in prayer. 'You know nothing of Auschwitz. May I tell you about the camp and what happened to me there?'

Aunt Ruth nodded. Bippi's memories of the death camps then poured out in a torrent of clearly etched vignettes. For him to share such unspeakable horrors with a sympathetic person was probably therapeutic.

'Auschwitz is one of six large killing camps inside Poland. The Nazis created it over a period of two years starting in 1940 and using many thousands of Polish and Soviet prisoners for the work. *All* of them died of brutality, starvation and disease. I was selected to join a group who had to exhume and burn their corpses, which lay just beneath the earth all around the camp huts. We dragged their decomposing bodies to pits we had dug and set fire to them. We had neither gloves nor masks, and often had to kneel in rotting flesh. The SS beat us as we worked.

'The camp covers sixty-four square kilometres and must be one of the largest graveyards anywhere. It is situated on a damp and swampy plain. By the time I left, there were Jews from most of the occupied countries in the Reich. Lots of minor camps inside the main Auschwitz boundaries are separated by barbed electric fences. The Nazis are extending the camp right now to become the biggest death factory in the world, the central killing site for Jews transported from all the German-occupied territories.

'The secret of Nazi success at Auschwitz has been keeping the world from discovering that the camp's specific purpose is to *kill*. Jews have been persuaded to think it is merely a *work* camp with food and accommodation for families. That way, since anything seems preferable to starving in a ghetto, they flock there willingly and unwittingly lead their children to their deaths.

'My own deportation order arrived at the same time as my mother's and we carried our chattels to the railway station in Plauen. My mother needed two walking sticks and often stopped to rest. Like the other Jews from Plauen's ghetto houses, we were looking forward to an improvement on our cramped, cold partition-wall room in the Albertstrasse cellar. Anywhere else must surely be an improvement, we thought.

'I learned later at Auschwitz that we were very lucky at the Plauen *Umschlagplatz*; the place where all Jews to be deported met and awaited trains. In some cities, people waited at such deportation points for days and nights in great heat or cold, with no water or lavatories. When they complained they were beaten up. We only waited one day. Then we heard a train whistle, and an engine pulling eight boxcars appeared. As they shunted into the station we smelled a suffocating wave of chlorine. Immediately, SS guards began to push us all into the heavy boxcars. Some children screamed in fear, and we were jammed in so tight there was only standing room.

'I managed to get Mother quite close to a ventilator slit in the wagon's side-wall. More and more people were crammed in and it became difficult to breathe. I felt the onset of claustrophobia. Why, I wondered, did the wagon smell so much of chlorine? Shots were fired to encourage the last few passengers into the carriages. Then the heavy steel door was slammed shut. That was truly a terrifying moment. People cried, groaned and called out the names of their loved ones in the dark, and some even vomited.

'I felt parched, dirty, exhausted and bewildered. Panic enveloped me. Where were we going? Plauen was all I knew. My mother and the other frail folk on board . . . how were *they* feeling? And the little children, some of whom were clearly alone and weeping bitterly?

'I knew our situation was bad. No window, just a single, barred ventilator slit. One bucket. No doctor, although many people were already sick. The woman beside me had wet herself in fear. She was frozen with embarrassment, but there was no privacy to attend to herself. We were all degraded, stripped of all dignity, all self-confidence. Crushed against the woman was a little girl, her large, wounded eyes staring upwards. She had a doll on a string about her neck. Her mouth was wide open, struggling for breath.

'There was no straw on the wooden floor. No way of lying down . . . you would be trampled on. I tried to support Mother. She sagged against the wall. A faint shaft of light fell on her face from the ventilator.

'In the morning, after that first ghastly night, the death-count was eighteen. Mother somehow survived. There was no water and the only toilet bucket was soon full. The ventilator slit was too small to allow us to empty the bucket through it, so its contents were poured into one corner. It ran all over the floor. People had to soil themselves after that. We all did. I cannot describe the stench by the second day.

'We stopped in sidings and without the slight draught caused by the train's motion, the air became almost impossible to breathe. More people died or fainted, so I was able to lie Mother across two corpses. There were constant cries for water, especially from the children. Somebody relieved themselves onto Mother and me. I swore at them and lashed out in the dark.

'We were very fortunate that we reached Auschwitz in only three days. I heard of other trains that took eight days to make the journey and less than a dozen out of a hundred passengers survived.

'Our train halted. The great door opened, blinding us with light and we were assaulted by the sudden sound of barking dogs and screaming guards.

'"*Los!*" "*Raus!*" "*Judenscheisse!*" "*Schnell!*"

'I tried to find our belongings but the violent rush to get out caught me by surprise. It was all I could do to protect Mother from being trampled. I lost her sticks. People behaved like animals. "Water!" they screamed, pulling each other by the hair, treading on corpses and tripping over bags.

'Prisoners in striped clothes pulled us down from the wagon, showing us no sympathy, only fear for the SS guards behind them. Large dogs snarled and jumped against their handlers' chains.

'"*Raus! Raus, alles liegenlassen!*" the guards kept shouting. "Out! Leave everything!"

'I saw two machine-guns trained on us. As if, in our stunned, drained state we could cause trouble!

'Although I felt a huge relief at leaving behind the close stench and the foul dead air of the boxcar, I found myself wondering at a new all-pervasive, cloying odour of decomposing meat, as though we had arrived in the neighbourhood of some great abattoir. I was allowed no time to think about this smell for a guard ordered my mother and all the other females from the train to form a separate unit. There was no point in protesting. I blew a kiss at her and shouted, "I love you." I saw her smile back weakly as she hobbled away in pain without her sticks.

'We were formed into lines and whipped at any sign of delay in following the constantly shouted orders.

'A smart SS man wearing spectacles flipped his cane to the left or right and divided us without a word into two groups. Another officer across the yard was doing likewise with the women. Some people panicked as they clung to a child or sister, but they were beaten apart and forced into separate lines. Lorries arrived and truncheons forced the line on the left to board them.

'The men and women remaining behind when the lorries roared off were, I noted, all over the age of about eighteen, generally strong-looking and none wore glasses. I was one of this group.

'A day later we all learned from other prisoners that our loved ones had been taken away to be murdered and incinerated in ovens, as the Germans burned all those who could not work. The smoke we could smell and see belching from the chimneys was all that remained of our parents, wives, husbands and children. They died stinking from the train and they died thirsty. My mother was already ashes, but had at least, as I now know, escaped the slow terrible death that awaited those still alive.

'We never saw our luggage again. Trucks took it to a sorting centre where any valuables were extracted to help the Reich's economy. A group of prisoners, working at the run, removed the soiled bodies from the boxcars along with those left dying. All were taken on trailers to the furnaces for burning.

'We were marched away from the arrival ramp. All around us was a forest of barbed wire and giant searchlights. The land was flat and at all hours the chimneys did their work. You could never forget them. The smell was always present. New freight trains kept coming, bringing more human fuel for the incinerators.

'Later, on a work detail to the nearby Birkenau camp, I was to see nine thousand women, all naked and skeletal, seated in silent rows. It was winter then and the ground was frozen. There was a typhus inspection, I learned. They gassed over five thousand of those women that night.

'Never a day passed after the autumn when I didn't

see long columns of prisoners heading for the smoking chimneys of Auschwitz. Sometimes they
hummed or chanted but more often they wailed with
fear and, seeing us behind the wire, screamed for us
to save them. Our souls shrivelled up as they passed.
They would enter a hall, strip off, undergo crude
body searches, have their heads shaved and, finally, be
forced to rush naked in their hundreds to the gas
chamber, under the lashes of SS whips.

'Those of us who had been selected for labour
rather than immediate execution, began the Auschwitz
welcoming ceremony without food or water, and
already traumatized by our nightmare train ride. What
happened to me then was the fate of a hundred thousand others. It was worse for the females, as I later
heard from an eighteen-year-old girl in the camp.

'The girls were lashed into a hall swarming with
SS men. "*Ausziehen! Alles!*" "Get undressed! All
your clothes!" Most girls had never seen their own
mothers naked. Certainly, no man had ever watched
them undress. Some refused or left their bras on.
Shots rang out and a fat woman with her pants on lay
dead on the concrete. Blood ran away to form a pool.
Everybody took their remaining underclothes off at
once, embarrassment forgotten. It was so cold in the
halls. A thousand naked, fearful women rushed from
horror to horror. Next, the yelling guards whipped
them into another hall lined with benches, where
prisoners, some with crude shaving-machines, others
with razors, attacked the body hair of each newcomer.
Their scalps, armpits and pubic mounds were all brutally shaved leaving deep cuts.

'"*Los! Blöde Lumpen!*" "Move on, you rabble!" The whips lash out and they are rushed on to a shower hall. More prisoners arrive to pour Lysol disinfectant over the newly shaven bodies to kill any lice. Many scream as the liquid runs into shaving cuts and into their eyes. Then ceiling faucets send streams of freezing water onto the already shivering women. Now that they no longer stink from the train journey, some of them are searched gynaecologically for hidden valuables in front of the sneering SS guards.

'Now mothers cannot recognise their own daughters for everyone has a white, cabbage-like skull. Although there are some distinctive pendulous breasts and large stomachs, and nose shapes are unchanged, most of the bald, naked women are similar in their unattractiveness. Friends pass each other by. A babble of name-calling is necessary, like sheep calling for lost lambs.

'Another move is achieved by the whips. This time, in yet another dank hall, the women find a heap of long grey shirts to pull over their shivering wet bodies. These garments make a mockery of the shower and disinfectant, since they are soiled with the blood and excrement of their previous, now dead, owners. And they crawl with lice.

'A second pile, this time of wooden clogs, confronts the women. No time to pick up a matching pair, or a suitable size. The cut of SS whips sees to that.

'Then, photographs. One facing the camera and two profile shots holding up a card with a registration number which thereafter replaces the woman's name, for she has at this point become an Auschwitz prisoner. Soon afterwards, the number is deeply tattooed in blue ink onto their left forearms. When there were too many Jews arriving daily, they stopped taking photographs but still tattooed them.'

Bippi pulled up the sleeve of his cotton shirt and showed Aunt Ruth his own number.

'This will be with me till the day I die,' he said, 'and if I am to be thrown out of the Clinic that day will not be long now.'

Aunt Ruth said nothing. She was thinking that, but for the grace of God, we might all have ended up in Auschwitz too.

Bippi continued, 'Each of us had to sew a piece of cloth to our prison garb denoting our category. At Auschwitz, I was lucky, for they treated me merely as a Jew, not a homosexual. So, my symbol was a Jew's yellow triangle. With the other new arrivals designated for labour, I underwent an initial quarantine, kept away from other prisoners. This was an introduction to a new kind of hell. At night we were jammed onto plank platforms; packed in like sardines, we were too scared to relieve ourselves since even after a brief absence, we could never squeeze back on. The barracks were unheated even in winter, but the overcrowded platforms at least gave the comfort of some body heat from the other bony-ribbed occupants.

'At four-thirty every morning, we were beaten out of the barracks, and had to make a mad dash to a nearby open area where we lined up in ranks of five. For four or five hours we would then wait for the SS to count us, and everybody else in the main camp too.

In winter, it was cold, *very* cold. Bald heads, no underclothes, no socks in our crude clogs and no body fat for insulation. Freezing winds, drenching rain, even snow. In summer, great heat, thirst and sunstroke. Nothing allowed you the right to stand at ease, much less to move or to faint. If you had diarrhoea, too bad. *Any* movement led to your death or a severe beating.

'Today, Frau Jacobs,' Bippi's smile returned briefly, 'and *every* day, I *luxuriate* in the feel of warm clothes, the joy of drinking enough not to be thirsty and to have sufficient food. To be warm in winter and cool in summer. Life is *so* wonderful here.

'The roll-calls sometimes took nine hours. Many people collapsed, some died. There were twenty-nine thousand prisoners to be counted and recounted, always including the daily toll of corpses. On a hot day in the middle of summer, the police chief Himmler inspected us. He witnessed the flogging to death of a woman, six hangings and a batch of gassings, then he left. That month, four thousand inmates died, many from typhus.

'The SS guards were inhuman, trained to a level of brutality where mercy was unknown and sadism the norm. Beneath them were *Kapos* and barrack or block seniors, like school prefects. These were prisoners with perks; a minor ruling class who aped the SS ways and killed or maimed with equal zeal. We never looked into the eyes of these people, even those who were Jews. Not all *Kapos* were beasts but most were certainly opportunistic traitors.'

Aunt Ruth interrupted, 'I have a question, Bippi.

In the midst of such awful fear and hatred, were personal friendships possible?'

Bippi gave a bitter laugh. 'Can the occasional flower keep growing in a field of rampant weeds? Perhaps, in exceptional cases, but for the most part, no. To survive in such a diabolical place, an individual must obey the law of the jungle. If you were lucky enough to have a relative or friend still with you, or even someone with whom you had some common bond, like religion, a home town, or a profession, then you could confront the terrors of Auschwitz together and draw strength from one another, but such a relationship was best kept devoid of any emotional attachment. Too often the other party would die leaving you bereft of all support, and grieving their loss.

'The best way was to cultivate an alliance of convenience with somebody in a position of advantage. Perhaps a clerk or a kitchen worker who could steal an extra crust for you. When they died, as the vast majority of inmates did, all was not lost, so long as you had not allowed yourself to become too dependent.

'People I had known from before, nice people, became savage. Breakfast was a bowl of bitter green liquid shared between six prisoners. Two gulps instead of one could easily keep you alive longer, so it was advisable to be selfish. Indeed, it was *wise* to be selfish.

'There were many prisoners without shoes, and once frostbite set in they would be dead from gangrene within a week or two, or shot by the guards for not keeping up. So there was a constant stealing of shoes. I slept with mine between my thighs. Weaker prisoners were killed at night for their shoes.

'In Auschwitz, you cannot expect help from anyone. You, yourself, are your only real friend. Your brain and your willpower are your only hope. Plus lady luck! You must be hard if you want to survive. We lived day and night like animals. We slept six to a blanket, so if one man turned over, the other five must too. We were *truly* miserable! A human who has not lived in a camp like that does not even begin to understand the meaning of the word "misery". I used to be a happy, strong person by nature. My family told me so. But in that place, I was always *frightened*. If a day went by without deep physical pain, suffering and mental anguish, then that was a minor miracle.

'Have you ever visited a ward in a mental hospital and listened to the *noise*? An Auschwitz block was much, much worse. Tempers were always short and on edge. Grief would explode or rage be sparked off by the most trivial events. Frustration, sickness, lice, thirst, and constant hunger and fear brought out the worst in us.

'And moreover, each of our sleeping blocks held a huge number of people from a dozen countries, all speaking different languages. Many did not speak Yiddish or Hebrew, so communication was impossible and there was never a moment of privacy. You could not defecate or even commit suicide unobserved.

'And suicide seemed a sensible option. Why die slowly and in pain if you could avoid it? We were never far away from a high-voltage electric fence. I watched many men hobble (few could *run*) towards the fence, and those that made it unobserved were rewarded by an instant crackle as they roasted in its current. The Nazis hated these "moth" deaths as they had to pull the corpses off the wires with long wooden poles. They discouraged prisoners from trying it by shooting in the legs those whose attempts failed, and then hanging them in public.

'You might think it was easy to reach the wire unseen, but the camp was a quagmire of mud. For much of the year everyone was caked in it as well as the oily soot perpetually pumped from the chimneys; the grease of human fat. The streets between the blocks were covered with deep mud whenever it was wet for Auschwitz was built on marshland.

'The mud would claim over a hundred prisoners each week in the rainy season. When you were weak and sick and fell over in that gluey morass, there was no getting up without help. And who would risk weakening their own frail state to tug you from the sludge?

'I did once try to pull a friend out of the mire, but I had too little strength and quickly gave up. Later in the day, I saw him on a pile of dead bodies stacked beside the latrines. He was still alive, and his mouth moved as I passed by. I think he was begging for water. That was a joke. If there had been water, I would have drunk it myself, but there was usually no drinkable water available anywhere in the camp. In winter, our thirst was kept just bearable by the evening soup and paltry coffee rations, but in the heat of summer the salty soup merely aggravated our raging and incessant craving for water.

'As for washing, that was a luxury I never experienced, not even when I was assigned to litter duty. The "litter" consisted of corpses which, like cigarette ends in a city, were constantly replaced by new arrivals. We dragged the bodies to collection points and stacked them neatly in rows of six and layers of five. Many were not yet dead but they soon would be. Rats and crows and cockroaches attended to our stacks, and in summer, the stench of rotting flesh competed even with the smell of the chimneys.

'Since we could not wash, our bodies became havens for fungal infections and lice. We itched day and night. The lice loved armpits, crotch hair and scalps. Even eyebrows! They infested our beds and clothes, especially at the seams. A single bite from a typhus-carrying louse could kill, but I remember mostly the terrible itching that they caused; impossible not to scratch, even though to do so caused pus-filled sores that festered and seldom healed.

'Most of all, I loathed the latrines. Ours was thirty-six metres long and used by seven thousand of us. There was a similar arrangement for the women. Every morning, we were allowed twelve minutes to defecate. In the freezing cold, we stood in line, edging towards this noisome hut which housed a deep trench, along the length of which ran a single squatting pole. If you could find an unoccupied place you lifted your clothes and perched upon the pole. Nearly all of us had diarrhoea most of the time, so we soiled each other. The pole was itself slippery with muck, as were our hands, for there was no paper. The weak fell into the trench. Later in the day the latrine patrol, knee-deep in excreta, removed the bodies. Of course, we all stank of faeces and our clothes, which we never removed, were ingrained with it.

'I saw people meet in the latrines to exchange scraps of bread for sex. Ask any Auschwitz survivor. Women with cross-camp duties met up with *Kapos* in our camp and were given useful items, a cup or a spoon, in exchange for some sexual act. They lay down in that foul place in full view of the constant stream of visitors. I know you will not believe me, but I swear all that I tell you, Frau Jacobs, is true.'

Bippi no longer checked with Aunt Ruth as to whether she wished him to carry on. His memories were now flooding out as from a breached dam. It was as though he believed nobody at the Clinic would be cruel enough to banish him if only they knew the full horror of Auschwitz.

'Because we were overworked, underfed, dehydrated and vulnerable to disease, we of course lost weight, strength and hope. Inevitably prisoners would reach a certain point from which, without intervention, they could only fade away and die. At this stage they earned the nickname *Muselmänner*, Muslims, for men, and *Schmuckstücke*, jewels, for women. They had become the living dead and were ripe to be culled.

'Every so often, the Germans would thin from our ranks anybody deemed incapable of hard work. Whistles would sound around the camp, we would rush out of our blocks to line up on parade, and guards with killer dogs would drag away weak and sick-looking prisoners to be murdered by phenol injection or gassing. The phenol victims were stacked in piles all over the camp for eventual disposal in the ovens.

'I could always tell when a man had become a *Muselmann* and would fail the next selection. I stole bread and soup at every opportunity so as not to reach that stage. Such men looked like skeletons clad in sagging grey skin, covered in stinking, lice-infested rags, suffering from diarrhoea, open sores, and running discharges from nose to chin. Bulging, lifeless eyes stared from sad, empty faces entirely devoid of hope. The last glimmer of survival had been extinguished and they would die within days.

'It was possible, if you were still strong but had caught some sickness, to go to the hospital and avoid heavy labour for a short period. But this was a dangerous option, as SS guards often slaughtered the hospital inmates en masse. I was lucky, for I survived a severe bout of gastro-enteritis away from labour through a brief spell in the infirmary. Nonetheless, I would not recommend the place except as a last resort. Its patients suffered from pleurisy, pneumonia, frostbite gangrene, urinary blockages, ulcerations and abscesses from vitamin deficiencies, tuberculosis, and a variety of horrific skin disorders.

'I was lucky to have claimed a top bunk, since the often moaning or screaming patients were crammed together and their weeping wounds, dysentery and various infected discharges seeped through the planks beneath them and onto the beds below. The stench of rotting flesh and excreta, and the general overcrowding, attracted hordes of rats which gnawed noisily at the recently dead whose bodies had been immediately heaved out of bunks by those still living.

'Shortage of water made for a lack of sanitation and the poor prisoner orderlies stood little chance of saving lives. They offered us comfort but little else. Typhus lice crawled all over us. Itch, itch, all day. Thinking of it makes me feel itchy right now. Of course, the typhoid epidemics worried the SS so they gassed anyone who showed any symptoms.

'I had a friend, a Polish, Jewish lady, who had access to our camp due to her clerical work. Listening to her, I gained the impression that Auschwitz was even worse for women than for us men. In addition to all the standard torments, they had to put up with pregnancy, abortion, invasive gynaecological examinations and, at least for their first month in the camp, the problem of menstruation; a source of amusement to the SS guards. There were no sanitary supplies, of course, nothing but odd scraps of dirty paper, wood shavings, a leaf maybe, and certainly no tissues or scraps of material. The dirty cotton smock issued on arrival was a woman's only clothing. No knickers were permitted, nothing to prevent the blood from dripping down their legs. Luckily, they rarely menstruated more than once because that bodily function ceased abruptly due to shock, chemical additives in the soup ration and starvation. Ladies who had been very fat on arrival at the camp, soon had breasts like long empty balloons drooping to their navels. Those that survived a few months found that their breasts shrivelled away to nothing.

'The SS were, for reasons I never established, especially brutal to pregnant women. They executed them at once, or sent them to the medical block where they underwent terrible, often fatal experiments. A friend, on a *Kapo*'s errand to the crematoria, observed a circle of male and female SS guards surrounding several dozen, naked and pregnant women. Dogs were loosed on these girls while whips lashed and boots kicked at their stomachs. Then the guards dragged them screaming to the furnace doors and flung them in alive.

'Block Eleven at Auschwitz was the torture block and because a prisoner's life was already so miserable, the SS needed to be especially imaginative to produce further prolonged agony worthy of the word "torture". They succeeded in this, but I will not describe the depraved depths to which they sank.

'Block Ten in the women's camp was used for medical experiments, and those selected were called "rabbits". Some were subjected to extreme radiation doses on their ovaries, which were then cut out without anaesthetic for further studies.

'Other "rabbits" were injected with various chemicals in the name of hormone research for the pharmaceutical company Bayer, which also sent the doctors various trial concoctions that were being developed to combat tuberculosis in the German armed forces. The doctors administered these drugs to the "rabbits", monitored the way they died and then sent their lungs back to Bayer.

'A number of the female patients were subjected to X-ray beams until they died, some had their genitals injected with acids of different strengths, and others had their uteruses cut out. Another group had their limbs amputated, infections induced and wartime wounds replicated on their flesh, so that the doctors could test surgical and medical remedies. Three hundred sick prisoners were pegged out in the sun without water, to see how long, on average, it would take them to die. This was described as a "scientific trial". A friend of mine working over at the Dachau camp later told me he had witnessed many hundreds of experiments on behalf of the armed forces into, for instance, how long it takes to die after scaldings at different temperatures, ice-water immersions, or after experiencing high-altitude pressure.

'Those awaiting their turn in Women's Block Ten could see the courtyard of Block Eleven, where a blood-soaked sandpit and a bullet-stopping wall were in daily use as torture victims were terminated.

'Block Twenty-Five was where the SS took women too sick or weak to work. In a few days this block would fill up, and those who had been there for three or four days would have died of thirst because nobody in Block Twenty-Five was ever given water or food. They knew they were there to be gassed. Convoys of trucks took them to the gas chamber in full view of our daily roll-calls. Sometimes, one of them would raise an arm and feebly wave at us.

'The Hamburg company, Tesch and Stabenow, supplied the camp with Zyklon B insecticide pellets. Four kilograms sufficed to kill a thousand humans through the release of hydrogen cyanide. The fumes paralysed the lungs and, depending on how close a prisoner was to the chamber's gas inlet, his or her suffocation would take between three and twenty minutes. There was always a good deal of struggling, screaming and fighting for air by the dying, which the guards observed through the chamber's peep-holes.

'The SS kept the gassings as economical as possible by cramming naked prisoners tightly into each chamber. I think seven hundred and eighty at one time was the record. Babies and small children were often among the last entrants and they would be tossed onto the heads of the assembled adults just before the doors were closed and sealed.

'Often a technical hitch or generator breakdown caused delays for the SS operators who carried out the gassing process. The awful crush and panic inside the chamber might then last for hours.'

'How do you know all this, Bippi?' Aunt Ruth whispered, so shocked she was hardly able to speak.

'Hundreds of prisoners were sent to join the *Sonderkommando*, the prisoner units who worked at the chambers and crematoria right beneath the chimneys. They were segregated from the rest of us to keep the killing system secret, but the information was leaked out by many different methods including written and smuggled testaments.

'In some ways, gassing was a comparatively humane way to go, for whenever the Zyklon supplies failed to keep up with the constant influx of Jews from all over the Reich, the SS turned to *direct* usage of the furnaces as a means of extermination. This entailed thousands of prisoners being burned alive. A living, thinking person was turned to ashes within twenty minutes.

'About half an hour after a gassing session ended, the chamber would be unsealed and *Sonderkommando* teams wearing gas masks would drag the bodies out. Many corpses were locked together in tight embraces. Due to the overcrowding, most were squatting or even standing, their skin pink with red or green spots. Many foamed at the mouth or bled from the ears. The teams had to work fast to clear, air and prepare the chamber for its next session, since the work went on round the clock. The bodies they threw out were wet with sweat and urine, their legs covered with excrement and blood. Babies and children were often found crushed beneath adult bodies. The work was not for the fainthearted or squeamish.

'Various teams then handled the "harvesting". Hair was cut from scalps and stored in bags, gold teeth were yanked out with pliers, often with the gums still attached, spectacles and artificial limbs were collected. In a separate room, specialists soaked the teeth in muriatic acid to remove muscle and bone fragments before the gold was melted and cast into one-kilogram ingots. Any bodies with tattoo numbers that denoted they had been "wealthy" Jews were set aside for dissection so that any concealed diamonds could be located.

'All the bodies were then burned either in open pits or in the furnaces. Pit burnings were often held when it was raining, and specialist teams mixed the fatter corpses of the newly arrived with those of starved veteran prisoners, since otherwise there would not be enough body fat for a thorough incineration.

'Another team collected the residue of bones and ash in sacks, and this was then spread as infill in bogs, fertiliser in fields, and in winter, as grit on icy camp paths used by the guards.

'The SS recognised the extreme effects of this work on the *Sonderkommando* prisoners and rewarded them with extra rations. Nonetheless, the job did not guarantee survival and, apart from a few oven specialists, all *Sonderkommando* were themselves periodically gassed in batches to keep the whole process confidential.'

'I don't think I can listen to any more,' Aunt Ruth said. 'Thank God you escaped, Bippi.'

'I didn't escape, Frau Jacobs. I was one of the lucky few to be sent to a labour camp in Germany. But Auschwitz is still at work and, according to rumours, Himmler is expanding it, because there are still millions of Jews in Europe to be exterminated.'

'How,' Aunt Ruth asked, 'does Himmler find individuals depraved enough to act as SS guards in such places?'

'I don't know.' Bippi shrugged. 'But he has certainly managed well enough so far. Most of the guards are German and, when they are out of uniform, they may well look like you and me. But that doesn't stop them torturing and killing other people. Their job is to terrorise and murder. It has become as natural to them as it did to Reinhardt.' Bippi nodded towards the house.

'The production of Jewish misery is a key part of

their daily work. Their toolkits consist of whip, truncheon and rifle. They kill with pleasure and laughter, and they seize every opportunity to be brutal. If they once possessed moral principles, they must have renounced them. There is no official check to the atrocities they inflict on their helpless victims. In all my months at Auschwitz, I never detected the slightest trace of human warmth on an SS face.'

'Surely,' Aunt Ruth remarked, 'you received better treatment as a German and not a foreign Jew?'

'If I did, I never noticed it. Not all the SS were from Germany. Some of the worst guards were ethnic Germans, Ukranians, Latvians, Lithuanians, Romanians and Poles, or pro-Nazi Russians. And, of course, there were *many* German prisoners among us. Not counting Jews, the Nazis had imprisoned over three hundred thousand German "wrong-thinkers" even before the war began.

'When my "posting" from Auschwitz to Flossenbürg Labour Camp in my native region of Germany came through, I was a happy man. I thought things could only get better if I was back in my own country. Perhaps if my sexual orientation had remained hidden, life would indeed have improved, but I was in for a nasty surprise.'

CHAPTER NINE

'Hundreds of thousands of German workers were conscripted into the armed forces, so prisoners had to fill the vacuum in the factories. Even Jews with the relevant skills were employed to help fill this drastic manpower shortage and my file disclosed my degree in engineering.

'In May 1943, I was sent to Flossenbürg, a concentration camp in the hills close to Weiden near the Czech border, and less than ninety kilometres south of Plauen. Civilian instructors taught and supervised us in the manufacture of wings for Messerschmitt planes. We worked in dank tunnels cut into quarries inside the camp perimeter.

'A few days after my arrival in Flossenbürg, somebody must have told the camp authorities that I was a homosexual for, without warning, an SS sergeant had me brought to him by my block *Kapo*. I was stripped naked, bent over a bed and held tight while, amidst much hilarity, four SS men thrust a broom handle up my anus. The pain was more excruciating than anything I had ever experienced and I fainted.' Remembering that he was talking to Aunt Ruth, Bippi reddened and apologised for talking of this. He continued nonetheless.

'I woke up back in my barrack block with another man holding my hand. Ben was a Polish Jew with a much sought after job in the camp stores. This gave him black market influence with *Kapos*, and his support over the next few days allowed me to survive long enough for my ruptured anal passage to heal. For two long days he covered my absence from the daily work sessions, but on the third morning he warned me I *must* return to work in the quarry workshop like everybody else, as he could protect me no longer.

'In agony, I staggered to the workbench and survived the day standing up, God knows how! When I recovered, Ben and I became lovers. In our dormitory, known throughout the camp as the "queers' block", the lights were kept on and we had to keep our hands outside our blankets all night whatever the temperature. These two measures were designed to prevent all sexual "misbehaviour" including masturbation; an activity considered normal elsewhere in the camp. We were forced to use the seldom patrolled latrine block for our trysts.

'I now had to wear a pink triangle beside my yellow one and suffered constant sneers from non-queer prisoners, in addition to beatings from the *Kapos* and guards. These same prisoners, *Kapos* and guards were themselves freely indulging in sex with young Polish prisoners known as "dolly boys" but passing it off with a knowing smile as "natural relief in the absence of women". These dolly boys were an emergency outlet for the sexual urges of "normal men", whereas we were referred to as filthy queers and considered the lowest form of humanity.

'I resolved to escape to Plauen. I knew the countryside between the two towns pretty well, and in May when the weather warmed up, luck came my way.

'A detachment from my block was sent to work in Würzberg, and I took over the work of a temporarily absent clerk. This involved liaison with a clerk who was selecting suitably skilled workers from the ten thousand Flossenbürg prisoners to work at the aerospace tool supplier Dr Th. Horn in Plauen. Taking my life in my hands, I offered the clerk the relatively substantial sum of money I had amassed, from black market activities with Ben, in exchange for one of the jobs at this Horn factory. He refused, but I did, in return for my entire black market fortune, buy help to escape as a "corpse" from the camp infirmary. In Flossenbürg there were SS officials just as corrupt as the *Kapos*.

'On 15 June, I began my cross-country escape to Plauen, moving only by night. Events I will not describe, lest I compromise the Bund's security, brought me to the Clinic. If only I had resisted the urge to see Richard I could have stayed here in safety.'

Bippi lapsed into silence.

Aunt Ruth stared at him making clucking noises with her tongue. 'You have been very stupid for sure, but you are young, oversexed and thoughtless.

Nobody could say you are unique in that. Listen, don't despair. I will talk to Ludwig. Maybe he will reconsider . . .'

Bippi dropped to his knees and kissed my aunt's hands. He said nothing but his wide brown eyes staring up at her spoke volumes. Within the hour, Aunt Ruth had repeated his story to Uncle Ludwig and a compromise had been reached. Bippi would do full-time kitchen duties for Maria, and was never to compromise our safety again in any way. In return, Ludwig would say nothing to the Bund. Bippi was deliriously happy. He kissed everybody except Reinhardt and his trademark smile returned.

Late in 1944, Bippi's firm resolve faltered and he began a relationship with a Hungarian *Schütze*, or rifleman: one of the three guards manning the Clinic's gate in a twenty-four-hour rota-system, with similar inclinations and frustrations to his own. Only months later did we discover what they were up to.

Thanks to Uncle Ludwig's wireless we were able to keep in touch with outside events through the long years of 1942–44. Sitting huddled around the squat black box, our little, mostly German, group would give heartfelt cheers as we learned from the BBC of yet another German disaster. In the autumn of 1942, British and Commonwealth forces had broken through Rommel's army in Egypt, the Allies had landed in French North Africa and Soviet armies had begun to show their teeth at Leningrad and Stalingrad.

Germany still dominated most of Western Europe however, and Hitler's ability to exterminate all Jews, including *Mischlinge*, had increased hugely when three specialist killing centres came into full operation in late 1942. These were Treblinka, Sobibor and Belzec; all designed for wholesale mass murder. The gas chambers at Auschwitz–Birkenau were also upgraded to kill 12,000 people every day. And their incineration facilities easily coped with the colossal output of corpses. Hitler must have known he was going to lose, and was racing to kill as many Jews as he could before he was ousted.

As the New Year of 1945 – our sixth at the Clinic – opened with an unusually cold winter, the Allied air forces began to bomb Plauen, Dresden, Weiden and Flossenbürg, all in our region of Germany, on a regular basis. The Clinic was sufficiently distant from Plauen city centre, railway and main war-factory sites to escape bombardment but we could never be sure that rogue bombs would not come our way.

When the sun shone, I learned to recognise the Allied bombers, the B-17s and the Lancasters; hundreds of them came in waves, glistening some 10,000 metres above us. Well before I could actually hear the bombers, the metal caps of Uncle Ludwig's walking sticks in the hallway umbrella stand would start to vibrate together like chattering teeth.

Then there was the scream of the Mosquito dive bombers targeting freight cars loaded with tanks from the VOMAG Panzer-factory not far from the Leuchtsmühlen Bridge over the Elster River, near our part of Plauen.

Apart from Uncle Ludwig and Rais, none of us knew the exact address of the Clinic, nor did we wish to, for if ever we were captured, we would prefer not to be able to betray the others. Even Bippi, who had found his way to and from Plauen, said he knew how to find the Clinic but had no idea of its postal address. The Nazis had apparently removed many road signs, and the bombing was daily transforming the city landscape.

On 26 March the factories of VOMAG, which produced more than 20 per cent of the Reich's entire tank force, were almost completely destroyed and the Clinic shook around us. The night sky was bright as day from the conflagrations, and we felt alternately fearful at the immense destruction and joyful at these signs that the previously all-powerful forces of the Reich were showing signs of vulnerability. German air defences had been visibly wilting as each week went by, so that by the time of the big raid on VOMAG, Plauen had virtually no defence at all against the Allied bombers.

On 11 April, Uncle Ludwig, looking even more serious than usual, summoned us all to a meeting in the kitchen. He went straight to the point.

'We are in serious danger, but thanks to Bippi here, we can at least try to find a way out of it. As you know, our very existence depends on my continuing work for the three senior Gestapo officers who established the Clinic without the knowledge or blessing of their superiors in order to protect their children from euthanasia. If their involvement here is discovered, they and their families will almost certainly face execution. Himmler does not like making exceptions to Hitler's rulings — when his own sister was caught with a Jewish lover, she was sent straight to a concentration camp.

'Bippi has been very honest. For some time he has . . . er . . . been seeing one of the three guards who take turns to man the Clinic gates. These men know nothing about the rest of you. They only know they have been specifically chosen and well paid to be guards here. They do not know that their senior officers are acting unofficially.

'They prize their job as it keeps them away from the Eastern Front, and they do not wish to rock the boat. One of them, Otto, and Bippi formed a liaison over a year ago and have been meeting up clandestinely ever since without the knowledge of the other guards or indeed any of us! Had I discovered this, as Bippi knows, I would have had to evict him at once as a threat to our security, but I have to say, his loose behaviour has proved to be helpful to us.

'About an hour ago Bippi learned from Otto that the recent bombing raids on Plauen, and the speed with which both the Soviets and the Anglo-American forces are closing in on the Nazi armies, have so alarmed the Gestapo owners of the Clinic that they have decided to remove their children and close us down immediately.'

'*Immediately?*' cried Aunt Ruth. My mother was aghast, and pulled me close to her.

'We must escape at once,' Reinhardt said to Uncle Ludwig.

Maria was wringing her hands, pale with fear. Rais

said nothing. She just sat watching Ludwig, her gentle face full of trust.

Bippi patted my head and whispered, 'Don't you worry, little Dieter, I'll see nothing bad happens to you.'

My grandmother and Liebchen worked on at their needles and wool, seemingly unfazed by Ludwig's announcement.

'What should we do?' Aunt Ruth asked.

'My first thought,' Uncle Ludwig went on, 'was for us to pack up a few things and walk tonight to an old doctor friend of mine in the city. But Otto told Bippi that Plauen has been reduced to rubble. Only a third of the city still stands, and ongoing raids threaten even those zones. All water and electricity supplies have been destroyed. People are filling buckets from streams or using the water that fills the huge bomb craters everywhere. Bread, milk and other such basic supplies are unobtainable.'

'American troops are only a day or two away, advancing down the main road from Syrau, so a major battle may well take place in the city. It seems that we have no choice but to stay here and hope that, when the Gestapo come to remove their children, they leave us alone. After all, we can do them no harm. They don't know of your presence here, and Rais and I are Aryans.'

Uncle Ludwig looked sternly at each of us in turn.

'Those are the facts. You should each decide for yourself on your preferred course of action, but my advice would be to wait and to hope. If for some reason, the Gestapo search this part of the house, there is room in the cellar for everyone to hide and I will place a carpet over the trapdoor once you are down there.'

'I don't trust the Gestapo,' Reinhardt's response was immediate. 'I would feel safer in the city. If the Allies are that close, it will just be a matter of living down in the main air-raid shelters.'

'That's okay for you,' Bippi said. 'You're not a Jew. We're not allowed into the shelters.'

'You don't have to wear your star. Everyone thinks that all Plauen Jews are already dead.'

'No, Reinhardt. Somebody would recognise me and denounce me. I would be shot at once.'

'You miss the point, both of you,' Uncle Ludwig said quietly. 'There are virtually no air-raid shelters left in the city. They have become mass graves. They were neither deep enough underground nor strong enough. Let me tell you what happened to Dresden, two months ago. Maybe I can make you realise that we are a lot safer here than in the city.

'Dresden was jam-packed the night of 13 February with refugees from other bombed cities. The bells began to ring and the sirens to howl and the shelters were soon full. After dark, the first wave of British and Canadian planes arrived and dropped incendiary bombs. Even before a second British attack a few hours later, the city's ancient buildings, which caught fire quickly, had become an all-consuming inferno that reached a temperature of over one thousand degrees Centigrade. Fire tornadoes of immense power hurled blazing items and bodies into the air like flaming meteors.

'Heinrich Meyburg says that one hundred and thirty thousand people died that night in Dresden. Others say only forty thousand dead have been identified. Twenty square kilometres of the city were reduced to an ashen wasteland. The tunnel escape systems filled with poisonous gases and hundreds died down there. The crowds of people packed into air-raid shelters were entombed, killed by asphyxiation, poison fumes, crushing or incineration. On the blazing streets, death was quicker, and the bodies of large men shrivelled in the searing heat to mere metre-high stumps.

'Survivors say the noise was terrifying. Especially the second attack. The stunning concussion of high-explosive bombs and the crash of falling buildings were secondary to the thunderous roar of the inferno. People rushed in droves to the city's water-storage tanks, but the water boiled them alive.

'Eighteen hours after the British bombers had gone, buildings were still collapsing and brick rubble was still too hot to handle. Rescuers found cellars full of people sitting down, looking as though they were alive and untouched, but all were dead. Army detachments and prisoners from Britain and America were brought in to dig below the ruins and bring up the thousands of bodies.

'They lined the corpses on the pavements for identification. Then they stacked them, using pitchforks, into mounds three metres high and six metres square. Anyone thought to be a deserter or a looter was shot on sight. American fighters flew low to machine gun relief-workers and refugees.

'That, Reinhardt,' Ludwig said slowly, 'is what you risk if you go to the city.' He and Rais left the room, and Bippi summed up all our thoughts.

'So! We either risk being fried alive in Plauen, or we stay here and hope the Gestapo take their children away and leave us alone. I think we stand a *far* better chance staying here.'

'When did Otto say they would come?' Reinhardt asked.

'He just said "immediately". That was an hour or so ago. What he actually told me was that he and the other two guards were ordered this morning to tidy their quarters in the old servants' block, pack up their gear and be ready to move straightaway. From this, Ludwig has deduced that the children are to be removed any time now.'

'Ah,' Aunt Ruth observed, 'so your Otto friend did not actually *say* that the children were the reason for the imminent departure of himself and his two colleagues.'

Bippi shrugged. 'It seems pretty likely to me that they *are* about to collect the children, and if they are in a rush to do so before the Allies get here, I would think they will just grab the kids and get going.'

'I wouldn't count on it.' Aunt Ruth turned to my mother. 'Anna, let's hide in the cellar, at least until after the Gestapo have come and gone. There's an ample supply of food, water, books and candles down there.' Bippi went off to bid a final covert farewell to Otto, then joined us in our comfortable hiding place.

Maria and Reinhardt decided to hide upstairs in

the house, believing that the Gestapo would not search it. My grandmother and Liebchen no longer seemed to know or care what was happening around them and refused to come down into the cellar, so we left them knitting in the kitchen.

'Good luck. See you all later!' Bippi shouted up the stone cellar steps as Uncle Ludwig closed the trapdoor. I had the impression from Aunt Ruth's memories that none of the household were particularly apprehensive that the Gestapo would do much other than remove the children and the guards, and warn Ludwig and Rais to say nothing to anyone.

The cellar was completely dark, apart from in one corner, where a small ventilator window high in the thick cellar wall allowed in a tiny amount of light. From outside, this ventilator was almost invisible, being at ground level and partly shielded by a clump of nettles. Every now and then, Bippi stood on a bench and peered through this peephole into the garden.

After about an hour, Bippi put his finger to his lips. '*They're here!*' he hissed. He stayed transfixed at the tiny window. We heard muted voices. The minutes passed and my aunt went across the room. She and Bippi conferred in whispers. When she returned to us she was pale and sweating. She hugged us to her. 'They've taken everyone out on to the lawn.'

'What will happen, Ruthie?' my mother asked.

'Only God can say.' Aunt Ruth crossed herself.

A few minutes later there was a burst of gunfire. Silence. Then muffled thuds upstairs. And after a while, the distant sound of vehicles starting up.

Bippi descended at last from his bench. His face looked haggard and drawn.

'This is difficult to say,' he addressed my aunt, 'but I must tell you what's happened. Should little Dieter listen?'

My mother sat me in the furthest corner of the cellar. I would learn soon enough, but not in detail, what Bippi had seen.

'I watched Otto and the other two guards,' he told my mother and aunt, 'pushing everybody into the centre of the lawn under the orders of some Gestapo officer. I don't think even Ludwig and Rais suspected the worst. They were chatting to Maria, Reinhardt was smoking a cigarette and the two ladies were still holding their knitting.

'Then, without warning, shots rang out, and I saw my poor Otto and the other two guards fall dead. Your family, Maria and Reinhardt were shot immediately afterwards. The officer must have used an automatic pistol. Deadly at short range. They all died instantly.'

Stunned, my mother and Aunt Ruth clasped each other in grief. Then Bippi went again to the window.

'We may be in trouble,' he said, no longer whispering. 'There is a lot of smoke outside. I think they have set fire to the house.'

'Will it be safe down here?' Aunt Ruth asked.

'I don't know.' Bippi was deep in thought. 'There's a lot of smoke outside already. It might be sucked in here. We may be safe from flames but not from lack of air.'

He looked around the room and his eyes settled on the long wooden bench below the window.

'If we are to escape, we have no time to lose. The trapdoor is only a few yards from the kitchen window above the sink. If I can open it, we must rush for that window however bad the state of the fire up there. One of you should keep hold of Dieter. Use the water from that jug and put wet cloth over your faces and hands. Make sure all your skin is covered. Wet all your clothes and shoes. Quickly! We must go at once.'

'Bippi tried to open the trapdoor by hand but the heavy carpet above made it impossible. He then used the bench as a lever from below and once the trapdoor was wedged partially open, he squeezed through and crawled out under the carpet. In minutes he was back having hauled the carpet off the trap. Black smoke stinking of kerosene descended in a billowing cloud and Bippi disappeared.

We stumbled up the cellar steps, our eyes smarting, and ran across to the kitchen sink. Bippi helped us climb into the sink and then out the window, lowering us, one by one, coughing our lungs out, on to the path outside. Smoke poured from windows all over the house.

Bippi ran off towards the old coach house shouting, 'Stay there. I'll be back.'

He returned a few moments later. 'The bodies have gone from the lawn. The Gestapo must have dragged them inside before setting fire to the place. We must get away at once before the neighbours and fire service arrive. I have borrowed a map from Ludwig's car.'

But there was no sign of neighbours or fire service.

Perhaps because nightly bombing raids on Plauen had recently reached a crescendo. Only the previous night, as we now know, over 400 British bombers had caused huge damage and fires in the city, killing nearly a thousand citizens. US fighters had also strafed it with bombs and guns, even targeting isolated houses and farms. The fire service was decimated and people no longer reacted to the glow of a single house on fire.

Keeping away from the main gate, Bippi led us through the hedge and over the wall. I had *never* been out of the Clinic grounds before. My mother and Aunt Ruth held my hand all the time. Bippi sometimes made us wait in hiding while he checked our route. He used to know the area but the war had brought changes in the last few years. And there might be Nazi roadblocks and patrols. For the first few hours, he led us generally to the south, keeping well clear of buildings and staying within the trees where possible.

Sporadic sounds of war, distant explosions and scattered shooting came from most directions. Many refugees, singly or in groups, were also moving at night. Some were heading towards Plauen and others away from it. But Bippi kept his nerve. When at last he called a halt in order for us to rest, he looked exhilarated.

'I think I know where we are,' he said, using his lighter under his jacket to view the map for the first time. 'We've just joined the Loichenweg close to the old windmill. Now we'll skirt to the east of Thiergarten village. Then our best chance will be to head south by night through the woods to the Czech border. That's about thirty or forty kilometres away. We could do it in three or four nights if we're careful. Very careful.'

We sat for a while in silence and soon began to feel cold.

'Where *was* the Clinic?' my mother asked. 'I ought to know where the others died and where my Dieter was born.'

Bippi smiled. 'That wasn't high on my priority list when we escaped, Frau Anna. I'm sorry but don't worry. We'll get together after the war and work out exactly where it was.'

Aunt Ruth, in her hospital bed in 1975, had laughed weakly at that memory. 'Of course Bippi was wrong. Your Uncle Pete and I did make enquiries about the Clinic a couple of years after we'd settled in Ottawa. But we got nowhere. In 1945 the city of Plauen had some one hundred and twenty thousand inhabitants, too many for one person to know all the others and, for a long while after the war few people knew what had happened even to their near neighbours. So many thousands of homes all over the city had been destroyed, including the courthouse and various police registration offices with their address records. On the city boundaries and in the outer suburbs, there was less bomb damage, but even there the previous inhabitants, mostly folk too old to fight, had unclear memories of those chaotic days.

'The German forces had fled before the Americans arrived, as did the city politicians like Mayor Woerner and the head Nazi, Alfons Hitzler, but not before they had set fire to the Braune Haus, their dreaded head-quarters, and all their records too.

'But going back to that first night of our escape, before things went so dreadfully wrong, I remember it started to rain and a strong cold wind blew south from the ruined city.' My aunt had gone on to tell me of our flight to the Czech border.

We moved on for we were beginning to shiver. When we had descended to the cellar earlier that day, we had not thought to dress for a long cross-country walk nor for cold, wet weather. Neither our clothes nor our shoes were suitable, but Bippi kept smiling and chivvying us along like chickens.

After a while, there were only a few scattered houses. No lights were visible anywhere now save when the sky lit up with some faraway explosion. No signs helped us at crossroads, for the Nazis had taken them away. At each stop Bippi showed us on his map how we were progressing. This was meant to encour-age us I think, but the Czech border seemed a very long way to the southeast.

For hours there were no signs of war and Bippi halted us only twice in the bushes by the roadside, to allow silent groups of civilians to pass by on their way north to Plauen. Towards dawn you, Derek, began to tire and shivered uncontrollably whenever we stopped to wait for Bippi's forays. So he found us a barn, and we slept close together high up on stacked hay. The temperature was much warmer when we woke towards midday. All of us were hungry and thirsty, but Bippi warned us not to move for there were farming folk about and we could trust no one. Better safe than sorry. After nightfall we could drink from a stream.

'Last night,' Bippi told us, 'we passed by Messbach and Taltitz villages. The hamlet immediately below us is Dobeneck, where we will have to cross the Weisse Elster river and the swampy ground beside it.'

During our second night's march the rain stayed away but the temperature dropped with the clear starry skies and Bippi kept us moving. We were lucky at Dobeneck for the Elster bridge there was unmanned, although Bippi warned us it was almost certain to be patrolled and we might have to wade across the river. He took us across a rail embankment and then over a patch of open country between the villages of Magwitz and Plauschwitz. Back on the road we passed through dark ravines with tall pine trees, hearing the gurgle of unseen streams.

At midnight, Bippi's extreme caution paid off, for he spotted movement ahead and hid us by the roadside as an army unit marched by, their equipment clanking rhythmically to the creak of their boots.

We waited in the cold wet undergrowth but there was seemingly no end to the column, so Bippi led us through a tangle of brush up a steep hill and away from the road. 'That was the northern end of Bösenbrunn,' he said. 'Quite a big village. Beyond it lies Bobennenkirchen, an even larger one, so from here we must keep away from the main road.'

We drank from streams but there was nothing to eat. You, Derek, began to hobble from blisters so Bippi carried you for much of the time. For the rest of that endless night and the following morning, we followed path after path, sometimes straight but usually winding through deep, dark forests with few clearings and no houses. Not even a farm. Bippi always took the southerly option when he could. He was tireless. Your mother and I somehow coped, but we were sore in every limb and our feet blistered badly.

The countryside was full of wildlife: deer, fox, wild pig, hares and many birds. Luckily the forest tracks we followed were unused. I suppose even the foresters had long since gone to war. By midday we reached a main road and a village.

'This must be Haselrain,' Bippi told us. 'We have come two-thirds of the way to the border but now the countryside opens up with many villages and farms. We will have to be more careful and there will be no more moving by day.'

'We *must* eat something,' I told Bippi. 'Dieter is very weak despite your kindness in carrying him.'

'I know.' Bippi shrugged his shoulders. 'But weakness is better than death. It is not far now. Maybe one more full night's march. We can survive a week without food. Until we reach the border we can trust nobody. If we run into a patrol, or if a farmer asks who we are and is suspicious, we may be handed over to the Gestapo. You might survive, but they will shoot me at once. I beg you to wait just a little longer. We are so close to freedom we must not risk everything for the chance of food. You think we are starving after two or three days. I assure you we could last much longer than you think. Remember I was in the camps. I have tasted *real* starvation.'

So all that night and the following day we limped on empty stomachs to the south, sometimes through open countryside between towns like Posseck, Nentshau and Prex, but mostly through dank, deep forests like the Kalte Bögen and Bloch-Wald. Rain clouds came and went, allowing enough sun to keep us from freezing. Late on the morning of 14 April, Bippi returned from one of his patrols. We were all asleep and he shook us awake. He was whispering again; a sign of danger.

'I have good and bad news.' He knelt beside us on the pine needle carpet of the forest. 'The good, is that we have reached the main road from Rehau to Neuhausen. The kilometre stone is marked eighteen, so it will take us only two or three hours to reach the Czech border at Neuhausen. Well done! All of you. Soon we will be with friends. No more Nazis.'

'What about something to eat?'

'Soon. Very soon,' Bippi assured us. 'The very first farm after the border. But just ahead of us there is a problem.'

He explained to us that on the road which ran from west to east in front of us – the border being some few miles to the east – a column of prisoners and guards had halted on the verge to allow an army convoy heading west to pass by.

Bippi's idea was that we should stay in the woods running parallel to the road. The only problem with this was that your feet were cut and swollen and you needed carrying. Bippi could not keep alert and react quickly with a child on his back, and though travelling on and near to the road was a great deal easier than in the deep forest, it was much more dangerous.

We compromised by staying within a hundred metres of the road with frequent stops to watch and listen. This was our undoing. A month earlier, to counter the demoralisation of the German population in the face of defeat, starvation and bombing, the Nazi government had issued a proclamation against *Wehrkraft-Zersetzung*, or demoralisation of the military. Anybody who showed any outward sign of defeatism or who disagreed with the view that the Reich would eventually win the war was to be executed immediately. Deserters and refugees were prime targets. Army and police patrols were despatched to enforce this measure and the Ministry of Justice was rigid in its execution. Over 10,000 German civilians and soldiers were hanged or shot in the last few days of the war as a result.

We came to a clearing and saw that on the other side of it, near the road, three bodies were swinging from ropes. One had a crude notice pinned to his chest inscibed with the word *Verräter*, traitor. The faces of the gibbeted men were bruised and bloody.

'Deserters,' Bippi whispered, 'no doubt caught trying to get away from the Soviets in civilian clothes.'

Bippi then made his first mistake, probably through extreme exhaustion, for he took us across the clearing rather than keeping within the cover of the forest. He moved some metres ahead of us with you on his back. He had all but reached the far side of the clearing when shots were fired and harsh voices sounded ahead of us.

We stood stock still expecting instant death as four men in mixed uniforms emerged from the trees. One had a rope coiled over his shoulder.

The leader, a tall man with a local accent, addressed Bippi with a sneer.

'Where do you think you are going with your two limping whores and the brat? Identity papers!'

Bippi stood his ground. 'We live in Plauen,' he said. 'Our home has been bombed and we are starving, so we are making our way to my uncle's place in Neuhausen.'

'And why, then, are you sneaking through the forest? Why not use the road? The last criminals to come this way' – he indicated the three hanging men – 'were deserters, and you see what we did to them. I repeat, your identity papers.'

'He is a Plauen Jew!' One of the men's voices was raised in recognition. 'I know his face.' He pulled up Bippi's left shirtsleeve and revealed the upside-down triangle and Auschwitz number on his forearm. 'You see,' he cried in triumph. 'They are Jews from Plauen. Shoot the filthy vermin. God knows how they are still around.' He brought his rifle up.

'Wait.' The leader raised his hand. 'I have seen uglier women.' He left Bippi with the others and came into the clearing. Your mother and I stared at the ground. I was sick with fear and loathing, for I had recognized the man, Karl Seidler, who, with his brother, had murdered my Uschi, raped your mother, killed your father and burned my grandparents to death almost seven years earlier in Jösnitz. I feared the worst.

A sharp pain seared my scalp as Seidler jerked my head up by my hair.

'A-ha.' He laughed with pleasure. 'You again. And your sister, no doubt? Life is full of surprises. So you have taken up with a Jew from the camps.' He looked at my arm. 'But *you*, where have you spent the war? I'll bet that's an interesting story. Perhaps you have been whores to Aryans who sheltered you in Plauen? Maybe someone I know? You have certainly kept your looks, even on the run. Heini! Lars! *Kommt her!*'

Two of his three subordinates held us while Seidler stripped us naked.

'Me first.' He smirked at the others.

'We can wait, *mein Führer*,' one joked.

Seidler unbuttoned his trousers and forced your mother to kneel before him. I had never seen such blind hatred in dear Anna's eyes as she faced that ultimate degradation in front of her young son.

'Go on,' Seidler rasped, 'what's the problem? You look hungry enough.' Grasping Anna's hair, he forced her to comply, but then he screamed in sudden agony and fury, thrusting your mother away from him. At that moment, I heard shots and cries from the edge of the wood. Everything happened at once. Anna lay stunned and naked on the ground. Seidler was doubled up, holding his private parts and blood streaming down his legs. Two SS guards with rifles appeared from behind us, and Bippi, with you, Derek, under one arm, disappeared into the trees dodging bullets from the fourth man of Seidler's patrol.

From that moment on, during the nightmare weeks that followed, I did not know whether you or Bippi had survived.

The SS guards were clearly superior to the deserter patrol, and Seidler, in extreme pain and embarrassment, spat out, 'Filthy Jew whores. We caught them trying to sneak to the border. Heini, Lars. Quick! Catch the Jew. He won't get far carrying the *Junge*.'

'Are you hurt bad?' one of the SS asked Seidler. 'We have no doctor with us. We are taking a thousand Jews to the south. Himmler's orders. But there was a hospital in the last town, Rehau. A few miles back west.'

'I know,' Seidler grunted. 'Don't you worry.'

'We will deal with the Jew women,' the SS man said. 'They can march with the rest.' He pulled Anna up by her hair and forced us to the road, which was narrow and straight, running eastwards through the forest.

We were taken to a crowd of some 300 emaciated women huddled together by the roadside. Even though the two of us were naked but for our shoes, dirty, scratched bloody by branches and hungry, we were nonetheless robust and healthy compared to even the strongest of these living wrecks. We had joined one of the Nazis' most infamous killing systems: a death march.

None of the women talked to us. They looked only at the ground and did not seem to notice us despite our nakedness. After two hours, of walking, we came to the Czech border at Neuhausen and were told to spend the night in an open field beside a farmhouse. Before we had arrived, I had heard the SS shoot four women who had lagged behind our group. I think there were three groups in all, spaced out, with about 700 women, maybe more, in total.

Two hours after dark, an open-backed truck stopped for a while. We heard that there were women aboard who were too sick or too lame to walk but who had had the luck not to be shot. Some died nonetheless. A guard I had not seen before, and who looked to be well into his sixties, approached us quietly and threw two long grey shirts on the ground between us. He said nothing. Stiff and blue with cold, we gratefully donned these stinking garments which had no doubt been removed from the dead bodies on the truck.

An elderly looking Polish woman introduced herself as Halina. She was in fact only 16, a survivor of Auschwitz and two long death marches prior to this one. Just hearing what she had already survived helped Anna and I realise that we were not as close to death as we had imagined.

Halina pointed out three of the SS male guards and one brutal-looking woman who, she warned, loved to kill at the least excuse. Pleased to have a friend in this new and utterly hostile environment, we fell asleep. But not for long. I awoke with a burning thirst and, seeing no guards close by, dragged myself downhill towards a puddle in the field.

Without warning, I felt the shock of a whiplash on my back.

'Where do you think you are going, Jew swine? Planning to escape? I will kill you now.'

I recognised one of the SS guards Halina had warned us about. His name, I discovered later, was Sebastian Kraschansky, an ethnic German from Romania and a sadistic killer. He began to beat me across the face and chest. I curled up but he straightened me out with a kick to my spine. The women all around us ignored my beating. They had become accustomed to violence. Only the arrival of a motorbike saved my life.

The rider was a senior adjutant, an *Untersturmführer* courier from SS High Command with a direct order to the death march commandant. His order was signed personally by Heinrich Himmler.

'When the Allies get too close to us,' Halina warned us, 'the guards will murder us all. This may be their orders. They will leave no witnesses to what they have done.'

The airline stewardess interrupted my memories of Aunt Ruth's story. I accepted the fresh white flannel she proffered and rubbed it over my neck and face.

By telling me about the humiliating assault on my mother in the forest – the assault that I had watched as a terrified five-year-old child – Aunt Ruth had answered my burning question. I now knew the identity of the man at Resolute Airport: Karl Seidler of Jösnitz.

In an hour or two, we would reach Paris and my past would begin to come together with the present.

CHAPTER TEN

The Secret Hunters have been successful for so long because of the dedication of their members. Each of us has our own personal reasons for bringing individual Nazi killers to justice, but many of us have had to give up looking for specific ones, so we help trace whoever the organisation has targeted.

I will not say where in Lyon I met my boss Laro, nor will I give away any details that might help the wrong person, or even an investigative journalist, identify him. Suffice it to say, he is a well-known businessman in the Part-Dieu district of Lyon.

My recruiter, Greg Wilson, first introduced me to Laro back in 1976. He, in turn, arranged my basic Hunter training in France and has since become my friend and confidant, in a way taking the place of the father I never knew. I told him now about Rwanda and Veronique and how much I loved her. Our dreadful shared experience had caused estrangement, I explained, but once this job was done, I intended to marry her if she would have me.

Laro shook my hand warmly, congratulated me with the words, 'Better late, than never,' and opened an expensive bottle of champagne.

I cannot use Laro's real name because, like the other Secret Hunters under his aegis, I do not know it. But I do know some of his history. He was born in the mountains of Alsace in 1925 to Jewish parents who died during a flu epidemic when he was six. Alsace had suffered alternate rule by French and German kings for 400 years but, after World War I, the French flag flew over the forests and hills of Alsace and Lorraine all the way to the Rhine.

In November 1938, when the Nazi terror of *Kristallnacht* destroyed my family in Plauen and forced them to sanctuary in the Clinic before I was born, Laro was a 13-year-old schoolboy in Saales studying to be an engineer.

Kristallnacht did not cause the French government to sympathise with the Jews. On the contrary, French Jews were in many cases classified as 'undesirable foreigners' and interned in camps. After Germany invaded France, the French police enthusiastically rounded up Jews everywhere and imprisoned them prior to despatch to camps in the east. Alsace was no different, so Laro left school to join the underground *Armée Juive* (AJ) as a runner. He worked between AJ units in Lyon, Nice and Paris and, in 1943, received training in radio communications at an AJ centre in the Montagne Noire.

Early in 1944, Laro began to assassinate informers in Nice, Lyon and Toulouse whose job was to locate hidden Jews for the Gestapo boss, Klaus Barbie.

Many of these informers were French, but some were Italian or exiled Russian Fascists. Laro and his unit killed their informer targets with quiet efficiency and successfully reduced the Jewish transports Barbie despatched via Paris to Auschwitz. Barbie managed to infiltrate the group Laro worked with and arrested their leader Ernest Lumbert. They overdid the torture procedures and killed him before he could be forced to name names.

Many of Laro's friends were tortured during the war and many of his relations were among the 75,000 French Jews sent to death camps. His hatred of the Nazis was implacable.

After D-Day, the German forces in the Vosges Mountains of Alsace, on the defensive, began a series of massacres in response to Resistance activities. Laro moved from Lyon back to the forested hills of his youth. He started a local partisan group to kill Germans and, in the summer of 1944, liaised with British SAS units operating in the Vosges forests.

When Prince Galitzine arrived in Alsáce in 1945 with his forward patrol from Supreme Allied Headquarters, Laro helped him locate the Nazi concentration camp at Struthof in the mountains. Naturally, when Galitzine's Secret Hunter group began their post-war search for the Nazis who had murdered SAS soldiers, Laro was closely involved with the head Secret Hunter, Major Bill Barkworth.

When the British disbanded the Secret Hunters in 1947, only 240 Nazis on their list had been executed. Laro was overjoyed when Galitzine approached him to join the unofficial re-birth of the Secret Hunters, and in the 1960s he took over the organisation of the group.

Laro had originally hoped to become a research scientist, but his wartime activities had sparked another interest, in radio communications. For a number of years, he was involved with highly successful, long-distance-communications research in Lyon and, like many of his Resistance colleagues, Jewish and non-Jewish, he became involved with the French equivalent of the CIA, the SDECE, advising them on clandestine communications from early post-war days and throughout the Cold War against the Soviets.

One of Laro's Resistance colleagues in Lyon in 1943 had previously worked on an Anglo-French cryptographic team decoding German messages. The German invasion of France forced this team to move to Britain's code centre at Bletchley Park. Laro met up with a number of these British and French decoders and maintained a mutually useful liaison with the electronic spy centre at Cheltenham which took over from Bletchley.

The end of the Cold War caused much heartache for both French and British spy snoopers who faced the spectre of unemployment. Fortunately new 'enemies' were soon found to replace the Marxists. In Britain, the IRA and drug criminals were upgraded in lieu of the lost Soviet business, while in France (as in Germany) new importance was attached to keeping tabs on the activities of the burgeoning right-wing parties of Le Pen and others. In the early 1990s, the French counter-intelligence arm, the DST, became alarmed at the increase in co-operation between their own extremists and senior figures in the German neo-nazi network. Laro naturally cross-fertilised information between his ongoing Nazi-hunting activities and his work against current 1990s neo-nazis in France.

In May 1993, his computerised files made the connection between the name Karl Bendl, a star player in a major neo-nazi convention recently held in Vienna, and a 1975 dossier from the Royal Canadian Mounted Police that described how the SDECE had been offered involvement in part-control of a Stasi spy, also named Karl Bendl, whom they had under observation. And thirdly, with the same name extracted from my own file.

The neo-nazi meeting in Vienna had been infiltrated by a Secret Hunter within the German governmental department, the *Verfassungschutz*, whose job was to observe that 20 per cent of the German population given to far right extremist views and activities. A full transcript of this meeting was circulated by our mole, and our relevant policy group, alarmed by the contents, decided to take action. Laro was tasked with some of the workload and, because he knew of my own long-term quest to locate Karl Bendl, he decided to involve me.

My reaction was extreme excitement. After all these years, the thought of meeting, denouncing and trapping Bendl was enormously satisfying. I had not been able to trace his whereabouts within the Stasi organisation after 1987 and could not even be sure that he was still alive in 1993. Now, suddenly, it appeared he was not just alive and kicking but at the forefront of neo-nazism in the 1990s. I was being given the chance to catch up with him.

I thanked Laro profusely for remembering my search for Bendl and for making the connection when it came up. He gave me a file on the 69-year-old Nazi.

'You'd think his capacity for evil would be diminishing by now,' he commented, 'but his evil genius lies in the ability to whip up hatred. He needs a world where extremism can flourish.'

'Not so easy these days in affluent Europe,' I mused.

'You are complacent, M'sieu Derek. You think our job is done?'

I laughed. 'Of course not, Laro. But you must admit the thought of genocide in Western Europe in the 1990s appears somewhat far-fetched.'

'So why are you still working with us? Just for your personal revenge? I don't think so. You know as well as I do that extremism can spring up anywhere, anytime, like some virus we think we have long ago vanquished. Of course the EU countries are cosy and civilised. Not like Yugoslavia or Rwanda. *Pas du tout!* But you make a big mistake if you think we can now go to sleep and stop watching the Devil, or think that he is beaten.'

'So what's the problem with Bendl?' I was impatient.

Laro tapped the file. 'Read it. Then we will talk. But let me say just this. Take France, Britain or Italy. Take *any* country you care to think of where there is a minority who pose a conceivable threat to the majority. You need only a small group of hate-mongers to sow the seeds of urban riot. Normally such sparks will blaze briefly, then go away or merely simmer a while. But, given special circumstances in any town, city or country, the spark can be turned by the Bendls of this world into an uncontrollable inferno.'

'And such circumstances are due in Western Europe?'

Laro nodded. 'In Germany over this next decade. Yes. Reunification is a witches' brew. It will take twenty years to equalise the living standards of the two Germanies and to satisfy the aspirations of the have-nots to the point where they no longer provide a perfect breeding ground from which to spread Europe-wide resentments.'

He left me alone to go over the documents. The Bendl report was concise. But, first, let me explain my previous work with the German neo-nazi movement of the early 1990s. Back in February 1991, Laro had passed me a similar file on a German living in exile in Canada, Ernst Zündel, author of *Did Six Million Really Die?*, which refuted the Holocaust, and which had landed him in court.

German neo-nazis concentrated on three main activities in the early 1990s; increasing membership in East Germany, terrorizing refugees and immigrants and, most importantly, gaining international publicity by denying that the Holocaust had ever taken place. The media loved the violent confrontations that such statements sparked off. Zündel had gained worldwide notoriety for his writings denying the Holocaust, as had a fellow German, Ewald Althans. My task was to find evidence that men such as these were involved with more extreme right-wing activities than just the dissemination of this sort of propaganda, for which they had already been convicted.

In April 1992, I had followed an ex-SS officer, Thies Christophersen, to a meeting in Toronto with, amongst others, convicted terrorist Manfred Roeder. This had led me to Madrid the following month, where I met up with Spanish counter-terrorist police. One of their plain clothes' police officers accompanied me to a meeting of Spanish neo-nazis at which Christophersen presided.

According to the Spanish police, at a coffee meeting immediately after the main Madrid conference, Christophersen and two Spaniards had arranged the murder of three prominent *antifas*, anti-fascists, in Berlin by a mercenary. My Spanish police friend had made contact with the *Verfassungschutz* in Berlin and, Laro advised me later that year, our evidence was sent to Chancellor Kohl as part of an attempt to persuade him to ban the main neo-nazi groups in Germany.

Laro had also been pleased with my work because any setback to these people helped to cut funds to the neo-nazi coffers. The one thing that could curb massive nazi-inspired trouble in the early 2000s, Laro assured me, was an inability to raise the very considerable funds they would need to fully utilize the vast increase in membership they were gaining through Germany's reunification. Such Holocaust denial campaigns were also beginning to prove extremely popular with the Arabs, including some very rich individuals in Saudi Arabia and the Gulf States.

Now, a year after completing that successful operation, I wondered if this new task, apart from my personal interest in Bendl, would prove as undemanding.

The Bendl report gave outline details of his background but missed the latter part of his Stasi career, for which no information was available. He had resurfaced at a key nazi meeting in Austria in 1990, and a Secret Hunter transcript quoted him, in conversation with neo-nazi leader Michael Kühnen, as promising huge funds for the post-reunification big push.

Then followed a Secret Hunter file note that Bendl had been heavily criticised at a conference at Rudolstadt in April 1992, for failing to produce the funds which he had previously guaranteed. This must have hurt his pride. Then, in May 1993, Laro's old SDECE friends, now working in DST counter-intelligence, reported that Bendl had been under observation in Paris at a meeting with former *Wehrmacht* officer Otto Ernst Remer. Bendl was recorded as saying he would shortly be in a position to produce 'unlimited funds' for the movement.

Laro, taking this seriously and remembering my own long search for Bendl, had asked the DST to discover his whereabouts. The answer, received the very day Laro had summoned me from Rwanda, was that Bendl had travelled from Paris to Bermuda where he had met up with the Belgian criminal Jan Meier who was known to Interpol. Bendl had then lost his DST tail and disappeared.

Laro suggested that I start my search in Bermuda.
My job was to locate Bendl, find out the source of his
'unlimited funds' and inform Laro accordingly. The
Bendl file included a faded photograph but I did not
recognise him. Then again, 18 long years had passed
since my last fleeting view of the man.

I discussed the report at length with Laro, and
stressed that although I would curb my inclinations
to do personal harm to the man behind my mother's
death, I *would* want to see him put behind bars
should my work manage to incriminate him.

'That is my intention,' Laro assured me, 'and I am
sure you will nail this bastard if anybody can. You
must appreciate that *my* main aim in all this, is to
prevent meaningful funds from reaching the nazis at
this dangerous time. But imprisoning Bendl would
of course be a great bonus.'

'How long have I got?'

'On expenses, a maximum of a month, unless you
uncover information on the source of their funds. If
there are no results after four weeks, you're on your
own financially, I'm afraid. *C'est la vie.*'

On 3 June, I took a British Airways flight direct from
London to Bermuda, and spent time en route learning a few facts about the sunny little island. Apart
from its tourist attractions and convenience as an offshore tax haven, it seemed to have little to offer. No
industry. No smuggling opportunities. No crime
scene. True, cocaine was more expensive in Bermuda
than anywhere else in the world, but that was due to
the highly efficient grip of the Excise on their isolated

islands. Why then, had Bendl and Meier met up there?

Before leaving France I had called Laro, but he had received no more news from his DST friends. Bendl had disappeared off the face of the earth and Meier, who had not returned to his Antwerp home, was assumed to be still in Bermuda and working there for Bendl. Otherwise, Laro had reiterated, why would Bendl have flown all the way from Europe to meet him on the island?

Armed with a file of 200 duplicate photos of Jan Meier and the knowledge that there was no other way of tracing Bendl, I had headed for the airport. Laro had delivered his usual lecture on staying only at the cheapest lodgings and counting every cent of my expenditure.

So what *did* Bermuda have that Bendl was after? According to the official tourist booklet the Bermuda islands, three hundred in all, consisted of a fish-hook-shaped coral archipelago perched at the summit of a long-extinct submarine volcano. It was first spotted in 1503 and avoided like the plague for a century. In 1609, a fleet of nine ships sailed from Plymouth in England to relieve an early American colony but their flagship foundered in a storm just off the eastern end of Bermuda. The entire crew survived and claimed the island for England.

The Bermuda Company was formed in 1612, and the new colonists built a fishing fleet, dived for pearls and grew tobacco using black slave labour. The great cedar forests of the island allowed for the building of speedy sloops, and for the next century or two, piracy became the financial mainstay of the islanders.

In 1941, the British Prime Minister, Winston Churchill, under pressure from an all-powerful Germany, had loaned part of Bermuda to the United States as a naval base in return for 50 US-built destroyers.

All of these facts gave me no clues at all as to any likely source of profit to be had in Bermuda from criminal activities. The hub of the island was its capital town of Hamilton, so I took a taxi there on arrival and signed in at a small guesthouse at a daily rate that Laro would appreciate. I hired a scooter which would mean that I could reach any point on the island in well under an hour, and then unpacked the box of tricks I had collected from my Paris safe deposit, consisting mostly of the electronic gadgets used by all of our field operators.

I placed four little satchels from the box into tailored compartments within my scruffy rucksack and pocketed a wad of travellers' cheques. The one thing Laro never stinted on financially was the bribing of worthwhile individuals. I changed 1000 dollars' worth of my cheques at the local bank and rode my scooter to Hamilton. The Customs and Immigration Office there was not exactly humming with activity and the officer on duty agreed to see me.

I showed him my passport and one of the photographs of Jan Meier.

'I work for a tracing agency in Europe,' I explained, handing him a phoney business card that Laro had provided. 'In this case we are representing lawyers in Brussels who need to make contact with Mr Meier. His mother has died and her will is involved. The lawyers know he is in Bermuda but they have no contact address. Can you help me trace him?'

The officer said he would see what he could do and I gave him my guesthouse address.

I called Laro to ask if he had a Bermudian police contact who might circulate photos of Meier to police officers all over the island. Laro was adamant that this was a bad idea, for the police might inadvertently alert Meier by heavy-handed tactics. He did however pass me the name of the venue where the DST had originally observed Meier meeting Bendl, the Elbow Beach Hotel, on the island's south coast.

I began to make a habit of spending an hour or two with a novel at the Elbow Beach Hotel's Café Lido, sipping cocktails on the beachside terrace and complimenting the barlady, Marion, on their construction. She seemed friendly, and accepted one of my Meier photographs along with my offer, on behalf of my imaginary lawyer clients, of a 500-dollar reward for informing me of any sighting of the man. I stressed that she should not approach Meier herself as he might be enormously upset to learn about his mother, and that she should instead call me at my guesthouse in Hamilton.

The days slipped by pleasantly enough and I wrote several letters to Veronique. My memories of Rwanda became less graphic and troubled me only rarely as I focused on my search for Meier. If he was still in Bermuda but using some other name, my use of his photograph should allow me to locate him.

I never varied my story, and I never had any problems with the people I approached. So long as I was patient, the work was easy. I ticked off the concierge or hotel manager at seven small guesthouses, four large ones, two dozen housekeeping cottages, six cottage colonies, two luxury clubs, eleven small hotels and five expensive resort hotels. I also visited ten estate agencies, fourteen petrol stations, four main car-rental offices and five yachting marinas.

My persistence eventually paid off. On 8 July, four days before I was due to give up and assume that Meier had left the island, a call came through from a petrol station near St George's, the island's second biggest town. The caller – a fuel attendant – gave me his address, the Blue Hole Hill Gas Station, and I drove there at once.

Jaybo – the only name he gave me – was a wiry, very black, Bermudian student of economics working part-time at the Blue Hole.

'This guy come here two hour ago maybe to fill up his machine.'

'A car?'

'No, man. A rented moped same as yours so I know he don't live here. His face look one hundred per cent like this.' He tapped the Jan Meier photo I had given him weeks earlier. 'So, anyhow, I do this for you . . . I jump straight onto *my* moped and, jus' like James Double O Seven, I follow the guy into St George's, and down to the boatyard where he gets on a boat . . . so how about the money? My Blue Hole boss don't like absentees, *and* this is all interruptin' my studies.'

'Sure, Jaybo. You'll get the money, just as soon as you show me the boat and I get to see it's the right man.'

We rode to St George's, the picturesque town on the eastern tip of the island and forked off onto the Wellington slip road to the harbour. Heading to the western end of the harbour, we came to St George's boatyard where we parked our scooters and sauntered like tourists between the lines of moored boats.

'Down there.' Jaybo pointed. 'Your man went aboard the grey yacht beside those crates.'

We found a boat with nobody on board and made ourselves at home on the rear deck. I took my Zeiss monocular from its sleeve and had a general look at the yachts being serviced all around the yard.

Nothing happened for an hour or two, but then two men appeared on the deck of the grey yacht. I trained the eyeglass on them from behind the mast of 'our' boat, and my heart beat wildly as I recognised the unmistakable features of Jan Meier.

I nodded at Jaybo and then motioned for us to leave the boat. We walked away from the quayside and I handed him five hundred dollars in cash which he counted meticulously before pocketing. He looked at me patiently like a dog waiting to be given a second biscuit.

'You need anything else, mister?'

'Like what?' I asked him.

'Like anything.'

'I thought you worked at the garage when in between studying for your degree?'

He grinned. 'I only work at the Blue Hole until somebody else pays me better. Right now, *you* that guy. I think also that I don't believe about his dead mammy's will! Okay?'

I tried to keep a straight face and ignored his implication.

'Could you find out where the man in the photo *lives*?' I asked him.

Jaybo didn't answer. He flashed me a wide smile and bounded away towards his scooter. 'I'll call you!' he shouted back.

Two days later he did just that. 'Your man,' he said, 'is at the Elbow Beach. Fine place indeed. Maybe one thousand folks stay there and your guy is by himself. I know Sam who works in Spazzizi's, the main hotel restaurant. You pay me more and I pay him. He can get you what you want there. Anything!'

I gave Jaybo another two hundred dollars.

'A pleasure to work with you, mister,' he told me. We agreed I would contact him via his apartment in Hamilton when I needed him.

Back in my room I called Laro with the news. Could I bend the privacy law a touch?

'If you do, *mon brave*, you know our policy. You act on your own. None of the equipment, if found, is traceable to here. But that's why you've got it . . . to use it, *non*?'

'One thing, Laro. Does Bendl have any past connection with yachts or yachting?'

'This boat you saw him on. Does it have a name? A port of registration?'

'No. The grey paint is new. The name has yet to be re-affixed.'

'I will look into it. For now, *bon chance*.'

He rang off, and I lay my bugging gear on the bed to check it out. In the morning, I would tell Jaybo, whom I now trusted instinctively, to come here during his lunch break for a basic lesson in 'buggery', the Ottawa RCMP terminology for domestic electronic snooping. The phone, the mini bar and the TV remote in my modest room would all be similar to their equivalents in Meier's doubtless more luxurious suite at Elbow Beach Hotel.

I doubted that Meier would leave his mobile lying around, but I would teach Jaybo how to bug one nonetheless. If he succeeded at Elbow Beach, I would reward him handsomely and maybe move him on to bugging the grey yacht. One of the Secret Hunters' policies was always to work at arm's length where feasible.

Jaybo proved smart and deft at basic bug-application. After a second tuition session I left him in my room and gave him 20 minutes to install the three bugs, then checked his work. I couldn't have done it better. He was extremely pleased with himself and, on his next day off, we waited separately at the Elbow Beach Hotel. As was my habit, learned from Laro, I made friends with the main hotel characters, Pogson in the lobby bar and the *maître d'*, Champagne Danny. You never knew when such relationships might prove useful.

Meier left his room at around 9am. I had lent Jaybo my standard mobile phone and retained my hi-tech military version. I followed Meier into town. He took a taxi to St George's and got out in front of the Tucker House, once the home of America's first black Senator and open to the public. I soon found that my basic training in tailing people (which had taken place in the old quarter of Lyon) was not up to keeping tabs on Meier. He was as slippery as an eel and lost me with ease in minutes, even though, I felt sure, he did not think anyone was following him. He was probably just using his standard procedure. Of course it did him no good, since I went straight to the boatyard and took up my previous position observing the grey yacht. He turned up there in a short while, and I called Jaybo to tell him he was clear at the Elbow Beach for at least 20 minutes.

A pock-faced man in his sixties and a muscular skinhead type in greasy overalls, carried a crate from the dockside onto Meier's yacht and began to break it open with crowbars.

I unpacked my camera from my rucksack and took photos of both men. A short while later, a middle-aged woman in a yellow tracksuit appeared, and I photographed her too. She resembled a squat and heavy jowled pugdog and her smile, as she spoke to the skipper, was more like a grimace.

Over the next three weeks, I learned nothing at all about Bendl but a great deal about the yacht and her motley crew. Jaybo's bugs had proved successful although less useful than my own electronic eaves-dropping on the chat between crew members. All my rucksack gadgetry was in use. I could hear conversations clearly from 50 metres' distance. I took more photographs of the woman, and of the silver-haired skipper, who spent a good deal of time talking to Meier. A third male crew member turned up, possibly in his late sixties but lean and sure-footed. I had not noticed him to begin with, for most of his work, on the boat's rigging, took place at Charlie Loader's Triangle Rigging Repairs in a different part of the yard. I posted the film of all five faces to Laro.

The three male crew members met most days at one or other of three local taverns, and it was then my listening device came into its own, allowing me to sit far enough away from their group not to be conspicuous and to tape their conversation without the use of bugs.

They spoke English well enough when ordering drinks but among themselves they preferred German. I learned that they had worked together many times for the man who had recently purchased the grey yacht, who they referred to as the *chef*, and that they thought Rischi was a lesbian; presumably a reference to the pug-like lady in the yellow tracksuit.

There was a good deal of idle speculation as to the destination of their pending voyage and who the passengers would be. They all hoped that a suitable cook would soon be found, since Rischi's cooking was, to translate their slang, 'garbage fit for pigs'. None of them liked Meier, their boss's admin man, and they wondered when the *chef* would turn up to explain what this 'operation' was all about.

Every morning Jaybo brought me a cassette, old-fashioned but unbeatably efficient, from Meier's room at the Elbow Beach. Meier's phone calls were mostly in-house calls to the hotel staff to fix escort girls, reservations at the Riddell's Bay golf club, dinners for two at the beachfront Surf Club and sundry other entertainments. I considered a favourite Secret Hunters' tactic of paying one of Meier's escort agency girls to divulge any useful gossip she might have picked up, but quickly dismissed the idea since he never used the same girl twice and I could not imagine him indulging in loose talk anyway.

My bugging equipment recorded the recipient's telephone number from every call that Meier made. I faxed these to Laro from my room. Several of the numbers had the dialling prefix for Germany; any one of them might help us locate Bendl.

In late July, by which time I was beginning to feel almost natural in my Bermuda shorts and flowery shirt, Laro phoned. His voice had a tight edge to it. One of the numbers that Meier had called several times during July, belonged to a luxury villa in Saalfeld, a town in Thüringen, in eastern Germany. The owner, well known to the *Verfassungschutz*, turned out to be Helmut Bayer, an ex-Nazi businessman turned active neo-nazi. Most of his time was spent outside Germany raising funds for the Fourth Reich, and his passion, outside politics, was ocean yachting.

'Well done, *mon brave*,' Laro said. 'I assume this has all been done economically?'

I told him how my finances were faring.

'*Pas de problème*. How much longer can you keep at it? We could replace you . . .'

'No, Laro,' I interrupted. 'I am happy with my

progress so far. However long it takes to trace Bendl, please let me stay with it. I have nothing pressing at home.'

'And the lovely Veronique?'

'She will wait.'

'You are confident.'

'I am hopeful.'

Laro laughed. He promised me somebody in Germany would follow up the Bayer link, hopefully leading us back to Bendl. Meanwhile information on the identities of the people in my photographs was on its way.

A courier package arrived that week, and I installed myself in a corner of The Frog and Onion pub at the western end of the island, with fish chowder in sherry-pepper sauce and black rum. My pleasant surroundings were in sharp contrast to the contents of Laro's dossier on Meier's crew, for each member had a violent history.

On 8 August, Laro called me with specific information. Bendl had been seen visiting Bayer's German villa and the crew members in my photos were all confirmed, apart from the woman Rischi, as past associates of Bayer. The yacht was obviously his, probably purchased locally by his emissary Meier. The yacht's impending voyage, Laro and his colleagues now believed, must be specifically involved with Bendl's 'huge funds'. If I could find no other way of establishing the exact source of these funds, or the nature of the criminality involved – since such funds were hardly likely to be legally gotten – I was to join the yacht's crew.

My desire to catch Bendl was all consuming, but the thought of close confinement for any length of time with Meier's crew was off-putting in the extreme. There was, however, clearly no alternative since I could not 'tail' the yacht, unseen, from another boat.

I remembered that the crew were keen for a change of cook but maybe the yacht had too few bunks. Jaybo made some enquiries at the boatyard with the rigger, Charlie Loader, who estimated that the grey yacht possessed either nine or ten bunks, quite enough to include a cook on the crew.

Jaybo advised me that August was a good time to apply for such a job. 'Now is big hurricane time, Mister Dee.' He would not follow up my invitation to call me Derek. 'Nobody sensible sails far from land at this time. So all the hippy boaties go away. In October, when all the Yankee yachts come back, *then* you'll get the pubs here full of boaties wanting crew-work. What you gotta do is put out the word now that you is a Number One cook, a chef maybe, and that you will go *anywhere* so long as the pay is up to scratch.'

'So how do we put this word around?'

'Mister Dee, you just leave it to me.' He paused for a while, a big theatrical frown on his brow. 'Only thing is, if I let you go on the yacht, how the hell am I goin' to make me a livin' on the scale I'm now accustomed to?'

Jaybo, true to his word, gave me a list of names and addresses. I placed adverts in the *Bermuda Sun*, the *Royal Gazette* and the *Mid-Ocean News*. I also spoke to the right folk at five local drinking holes, the Wharf Tavern, Freddie's, the White Horse, the Moonglow and St George's Dinghy Club.

Although I had spent time cooking for my aunt, various female partners and a goodly number of refugee centres worldwide, I took the precaution of buying a book on yachtboard cooking which was full of useful tips. Laro sent me a convincing-looking CV listing all the amazing voyages on which I had been ship's cook together with complimentary references from skippers. Then I sat back and waited.

Jaybo had tried to discover for me who the grey yacht belonged to. Friends at his university had enquired at the immigration centre in the harbour, known as the Yacht Reporting Centre, but the staff there said they could not identify a boat if we had no name for it and did not know when it had entered the harbour.

Bermuda Harbour Radio also kept a careful log of every boat visiting the harbour but they too needed a name with a port of registration or a radio call-sign to pinpoint the vessel's identity. They maintained a 24-hour radar watch so no boat could sneak past the harbour entrance unobserved even by night.

On a too hot day in mid-August, Jaybo, whose home address I had used for all my cook-job adverts, gave me a locally stamped envelope containing an unsigned note that gave no clue to its sender's address.

We are looking to hire experienced cook for voyage of four to five months leaving Bermuda mid-September.

*Needed on board for preparations as from 1
September. Come in working hours to the grey yacht
(name at present painted out) in St George's Yard
for interview.*

Before the interview, I moved in to Jaybo's apartment in Hamilton and paid him a healthy sum for
the tiny windowless room he normally rented to a
fellow student. Jaybo had paid the latter to move out
for a while with some of the money I had given him.
We stored my rucksack at the house of Jaybo's parents, which was also in Hamilton.

If, as I suspected, Meier had me checked out, he
would find nothing to indicate I was anything other
than a middle-aged hippy with a penchant for, but
insufficient funds to travel to, exotic spots.

Know your enemy. Another of Laro's oft-repeated
maxims. I re-read his report on the crew in the airless
confines of my new room.

Nothing at all was known of the woman who the
others called Rischi. The captain, Herbert Brandt,
was a dark horse previously hired by Bayer for long
deep-ocean voyages. The file on him gave no details
other than that he was 58 years old and an Austrian.

There was little to choose between the other
three – Habermalz, Grafmann and Krentz – in terms
of their unsavoury pasts. Franz Habermalz, at 32,
was a neo-nazi from Munich whose history of violent
racist activities, including murder, gave me the
impression he was trying to make up for lost time
having missed out on the war.

The two older men had both been SS camp guards

in Poland. Eugen Grafmann came from northern Germany and Machel Krentz from Warsaw. Krentz was as lean, shrewd and menacing as Grafmann was crude and bulky. In the 1960s the two men had finally been tried in Germany for their war crimes but, through insufficient evidence, they had not been imprisoned. Looking at their trial records I was amazed, and not for the first time, at how *any* known Nazi war criminals had ever been punished at all: the vast majority escaped their just desserts despite clear evidence of involvement in torture and mass murder.

I found myself imagining being on deck in rough seas with Grafmann or Krentz near the railings. It would be tempting.

Eugen Grafmann was born in Bremen and joined the Hitler Youth there aged 16. A year later, in 1943, he enrolled in the SS and was posted as a guard to Auschwitz where he supervised gypsy prisoners and the medical block. When Auschwitz was evacuated, he deserted, and made his way home to bombed-out Bremen to find his mother and brother dead and his home destroyed. He became a mechanic and got involved in the post-war black market. His file was littered with petty crime convictions and *Verfassungschutz* reports on his neo-nazi group activities. Over a period of 35 years, he had worked for Bayer on many occasions.

Machel Krentz, an ethnic German from Stettin in Poland, had enrolled with the SS in Warsaw aged 17. After two years spent policing the ghetto there, he was posted to Auschwitz where he met Grafmann. Keen to escape the Soviets in 1945, he deserted with

Grafmann to Bremen where, for a while, they worked
the black market together. But Krentz, more ambitious than Grafmann, became a successful salesman
specialising in boat chandlery doing business in
Bremen and Kiel. He met Helmut Bayer in 1965
when he sold him a yacht and subsequently bumped
into him at a Rudolph Hess commemoration event.
Krentz was soon participating in Bayer's neo-nazi
fundraising projects and crewing many of his ocean
jaunts. He probably introduced Bayer to his friend
Grafmann, who then became Bayer's part-time yacht
mechanic.

Jan Meier welcomed me aboard the grey yacht without ceremony. The sour-faced woman, Rischi,
brought me coffee and the other three crew members
ignored me. Captain Herbert Brandt was polite but
cold, and listened from the far end of the saloon as
Meier grilled me.

Meier made it clear that a number of prospective
cooks were under consideration. In turn I assured
him that there were other boats, soon to leave
Bermuda, who had offered me a place but that I was
attracted by the length of this yacht's prospective
voyage. Where did he intend to sail to?

He was expecting the question. 'We leave in a
month for Tierra del Fuego. We will then sail on at the
owner's discretion. He will join us in South America.'

My mind raced. The owner was Bayer not Bendl.
Nonetheless, if the two men were colluding in the
same operation, as Laro suspected, I could discover
what was involved whether Bendl appeared in person

or not. I hid my disappointment and told Meier that such a voyage sounded very attractive.

I was quizzed by Meier and the skipper on my cooking experience and ability. They seemed satisfied with my answers and my references, and showed me around the yacht which was crammed with miscellaneous equipment and unpacked stores. The galley was well laid out and the crew berths, though cramped, looked reasonable.

I noticed Rischi locking the door of the main cabin behind her. She did not converse with the rest of the crew.

'The owner, like many rich men,' Meier told me, 'has personal preferences when cruising. You, like the rest of us, must respect them. If you don't like it, you must tell me now and you can go on one of your other boat trips. Okay?'

I nodded.

'No photographs, except when you are ashore and then not of the boat or crew. Also, no mobile telephone or other communication with the outside world while you are with us.'

'May I ask why?'

'You may. The owner is a romantic. He enjoys the peace of his voyages and wants minimum contact with the outside world. He needs to know we are all cut off in a world of our own. As for photographs; he loathes the media who have plagued him for many years, and rightly, he is suspicious that people may try to sell photos of his voyages.'

Again I nodded. 'No problem, sir. *His* yacht – *he* sets the rules.'

Mr Meier told me the pay deal which, compared with average crew rates, was well above the norm. I was to be told Mr Meier's decision within the week by which time he would have seen 'all the applicants'.

That evening when Jaybo returned from work he asked me if my gear had been disturbed.

'Disturbed? How d'you mean?'

'Someone has been in here today. Someone who is good with locks but did not spot the tape markers you put on my door. Has your room been searched?'

'If it has, I can't see any sign of it.'

Jaybo shrugged. 'Well, man. So long as they took nothing and you ain't worried, everything's fine by me. How did it go on the yacht?'

I told him. He agreed I could stay at his place until I knew Meier's decision. He never queried my intentions; so long as I kept paying him well for his time, he was happy.

'What,' he asked me, 'are those bulky items on the yacht's deck? I took the bike down there in my break today, and from the quay, I saw they got padlocks on the tarps coverin' that stuff.'

'I didn't ask any questions,' I told Jaybo. 'No point in making them think I'm nosy.'

Two days after my interview, another note arrived at Jaybo's. I was to report for duty on the first of September with not more than two regulation-size matelot bags and my personal cooking kit. All foul weather clothing and boots would be provided.

When the day arrived, Jan Meier had disappeared and the skipper gave me my instructions. Everybody called him 'Kapitän', so I did likewise. He was meticulous in all things, handing me my preparation work details in a notebook including which local stores I should shop at. I must draw cash from him and account for even the smallest expenditure. Another Laro, I thought.

Jan Meier returned on the fourth day, but was as uncommunicative as the rest of the crew. A good sign, however, was that they all clearly appreciated my cooking.

I stacked a toolbox Jaybo had procured for me under my bunk. I kept it padlocked, and its upper two trays were stacked with a set of cooking implements. Almost undetectable to the eye, a third space existed at its base, in which I kept some of the Secret Hunter gadgets from my rucksack.

Only one event worried me, but not unduly. A shirt button-sized hole directly beneath the light switch above my bunk attracted my interest, trained as I was in surveillance gadgetry. That night, with the curtains drawn across my bunk compartment, I pressed a smidgeon of wet cotton wool on the lens hole, unscrewed the switch-plate and verified the presence of a video camera. Although not in operation, I was sure that it soon would be, and then I would be 'on show' 24 hours a day. Presumably, the video screen and sound playback were kept in the owner's cabin. No doubt other parts of the boat were also wired so I determined to be cautious. Fortunately, I had not yet opened my toolbox while on board.

All my life, I had slept naked and the presence of the video camera did not make me change this habit. This was to prove a bad mistake but I did not realize it at the time. As it was, I congratulated myself on successfully installing myself as Laro's cuckoo in Bayer's nest. I listened with care to everything that was said by my fellow crew members, but by the end of my second week on board, I had learned nothing of the yacht's mission nor its destination. I trod very lightly and asked no questions that might raise the slightest suspicion. Preparations and errands kept me busy and there was little chance for interaction with the crew.

Apart from the crew's bunks and the owner's state-room there were two other cabins, Rischi's minuscule nook and a cabin of moderate size with two bunks that I saw her making ready. This tallied with the number of eating places and food stores that the skipper had requested. But only roughly, since I had no idea how many days we were due to be at sea.

Adjacent to my galley was a bulkhead space with wide shelves containing radio equipment used by Krentz. In his absence, this was always covered by a locked metal blind.

When I took coffee to anyone working on the bridge, I tried to memorise the equipment without appearing overly curious. On a trip to Hamilton to buy in stores, I called Laro to describe the Satcom (satellite communications) equipment, Short Side Band (SSB) and Very High Frequency (VHF) radios, Global Positioning Satellite (GPS) system, log, depth sounder, wind instruments, rigging system, fuel dials and radar.

The day before we were due to set sail, the skipper asked me if every last galley item he had listed for me was on board and if I was ready to go. When I assured him that it was and I was, he held out his hand. 'Excellent,' he said. 'Your passport please. It is our custom that I hold all crew documents. This makes immigration checks so much easier.'

Rischi came aboard towards midnight accompanied by a beautiful Asian girl with a small suitcase. Her high-heeled shoes clicked incongruously across the saloon to the owner's cabin. I heard the door lock behind them. My mind was beginning to boggle.

CHAPTER ELEVEN

Late in the summer of 1993, Laro sent me a tape recording received from a contact in the *Bundesamt für Verfassungschutz* (BfV), Germany's internal secret service. The following is based on the contents of that tape.

On 14 August, a scorching hot day, over 500 neo-nazis met in the Palatinate of Fulda near Frankfurt to commemorate the death of Rudolph Hess, Hitler's deputy. Since such extremist events were banned in Germany, the organizers had played cat and mouse with the authorities, spreading many false rumours about the actual venue. As a result, police strength was stretched, and the illegal rally took place under police surveillance in Fulda's impressive cathedral square.

Nazi banners blew in the wind, and columns of mostly young men paraded to a drumbeat past an 18th Century palace and the magnificent baroque cathedral separated by an avenue bridged with a triumphal arch. Scuffles broke out and journalists' cameras were smashed. Some of the marchers were obese, others heavily muscled, and many were death's-head thin, shaven and tattooed. Camouflage jackets and trousers and Gestapo jackboots vied with T-shirts, jeans and Doc Martens.

Karl Bendl spotted the satisfied faces of known neo-nazi leaders at the front of the march. Christian Worch, the founder of the extreme *Nationale Liste* party, was there alongside convicted thug Norbert Weidner, known members of the British National Party, and nazi-group representatives from Sweden, Denmark and France. Beside them was the ruddy-faced figure of Friedhelm Busse, leader of the *Freiheitlische Deutsche Arbeiterpartei*.

After the street march and main rally, the leaders withdrew to a number of separate meetings. One group concentrated on a new Europe-wide operation to terrorize the opposition. The nazi magazine *Der Einblick* would be used to publish the names, addresses, telephone numbers and car registrations of prominent anti-fascists.

A number of violent nazi groups from various European centres had gathered now in Fulda to plan a campaign that would further their influence by any means. Part of this network was Christian Worch's illegal group, *Gesinnungsgemeinschaft der Neuen Front* (the GdNF), whose members had penetrated the German army and police force, and which could mobilise thousands for demonstrations and recruit hundreds of mainly young people into its front organisations. Worch had strong links with neo-nazis in Britain and America. It was reported that the current membership of the German active far right was 65,200 and that neo-nazi cells had been established in every main German town with sophisticated, centralised communication systems reliant on the Internet and fax. As soon as the Kohl government banned specific groups, they quickly changed their identities and used box numbers in Britain and Denmark to distribute banned racist material and details of venues for rallies. Progress was also being made in unearthing moles from the *Verfassungschutz* and dealing with them appropriately.

Foreign immigrants could no longer live anywhere in Germany without the constant fear of attack. Seventeen Turks had been burned alive in their homes over the past few months, and these murders had goaded young Turkish gangs into violent retaliation that had alienated hitherto neutral Germans. A new front had been formed to attack the handicapped and disabled, as these groups believed them to be sub-human and infecting their blood like viruses.

The details of the mounting political successes of the far right were illustrated by the recent election in Hesse: in Hanau, they had won 15 per cent of the suffrage; in Maintal 12 per cent, and so on. These results were pushing Chancellor Kohl towards the right to gain votes. It was pointed out that while the funeral of the Turks burned in Solingen was taking place, Kohl was at the re-opening of Berlin Cathedral, which the far right considered to be the symbol of imperial Germany.

One by one the local leaders reported their activities over the past year. Fire bombings were popular – targeting guest workers, asylum seekers, and Jews. Three young girls and two women had been burned alive in Solingen, and three Eritrean children in Heppenheim. A nazi sub-group in Wuppertal had achieved wide press coverage by beating up a butcher they assumed to be Jewish, soaking him in schnapps, then dumping his charred body just over the Dutch border.

A Bonn representative reported that infiltration of the German armed forces was progressing well despite the arrest the previous year of 53 soldiers – suspected of belonging to a nazi organisation – for the theft of large quantities of arms and ammunition. Earlier, three *Bundeswehr* officers had been suspended from duty in Kiel after a hand-grenade attack.

Others reported that many regional police forces, anti-fascist cells and even the *Verfassungschutz* itself had been successfully penetrated. Meanwhile, on the international front, immigrants were being terrorised or killed all over Europe. Jewish cemeteries were being desecrated and their shops daubed with swastikas, everywhere from Brittany to Copenhagen. Violent anti-Semitic or anti-immigrant outbreaks had rocked East Berlin, Puttern in Holland, Lund in Sweden, Lublin in Poland, Marseille, Naples, Leningrad, Budapest and 12 other major European cities.

In ex-Soviet territories, thriving new ultra-right-wing parties were gaining political influence, especially with ethnic German inhabitants in Polish Silesia, Czech Sudetenland and the Baltic States. A new liaison had been formed between the fascist *Deutsche Volksunion* and the Russian LDP led by Vladimir Zhirinovsky, who had won six million votes in the most recent Russian elections.

The next speaker was an active neo-nazi from Hamburg, Thomas Kunst, recently returned from Nice. Like Jan Meier, Kunst was a paid killer for right-wing groups and had recently placed explosives in the Nice Palais de Justice. A year earlier he had a hand in the murder of disgraced Nazi, Dieter Mason, who was about to reveal neo-nazi criminal activities to the police. Kunst gave an up-to-date report on the French fascist scene, focusing on Nice where Le Pen's *Front Nationale* was widely popular. The *Front*, Kunst said, was about to gain a staggering 15 per cent of the French national suffrage, and possibly as much as 25 per cent of the Marseille vote. He added that when individual anti-*Front* politicians became genuinely damaging to the cause, he would see that they were controlled.

Other representatives reported a whole series of terror actions that had been completed in the northern sector including the death of three Turks in a firebomb attack in Mölln the previous winter.

Helmut Kohl's Attorney General had announced in public that: 'the attackers want to re-establish a nazi dictatorship here in Germany'. This sort of free publicity was helping recruitment to snowball.

Karl Bendl attended some of these meetings, but he had come to Fulda to attend one specific meeting at the invitation of a Mainz-inspired initiative involving supporters of the HNG, an organization dedicated to helping Nazi prisoners in Europe and the USA. He had brought Helmut Bayer with him.

As instructed, they drove to a *Gasthaus* on the outskirts of Fulda and made their way to an upstairs room that was guarded by well-built thugs. Two senior nazis had been smuggled into the small hotel: German arrest warrants were out for both of them, so the organizers had taken great pains to hide their presence. Bendl was impressed by their efficiency. The sole purpose of this gathering, involving some 20 carefully selected individuals, was to discuss and launch a number of fund-raising projects including Bendl's. He was introduced to Wilhelm Hoettl, a onetime Stasi informer who, he knew, had worked for the CIA, MI6 and the KGB simultaneously.

The room had been carefully prepared with nazi posters and insignia on walls and tables. Two portly, bottle-blonde women in local costume served beer, spirits and delicacies, and then withdrew. Cigar smoke filled the air.

The four main sponsors of the meeting sat at a table on a raised platform facing the room. One, not named by the editors of the BfV tape, was a woman from the Mainz HNG. A second woman took notes, remained silent and showed marked deference to the two older men who together chaired the meeting.

Thies Christophersen, who was pursued by the German authorities and lived in Denmark, had served as an SS *Sonderführer* at the botanical institute in Rajsko near the Auschwitz death camp during the war. After three decades in various extremist parties, he founded the *Notgemeinschaft Deutscher Bauern* and published various fascist works, including the notorious *Die Auschwitz-Lüge*, or *The Auschwitz Lie*, in 1973, after which the European neo-nazi movement venerated him. In 1988, he had been a witness for the defence at Zündel's trial in Canada.

Sitting next to Christophersen was Otto Ernst Remer, also a legendary figure on the neo-nazi scene. He had served Germany as a professional soldier since 1933, and entered the history books as the commander of the Berlin Guard Battalion responsible for the vicious repression of the 20 July 1944 attempt to overthrow Adolf Hitler. Thanks to his role in these events, he was promoted by Hitler to Major General. Outlawed for extremist activities in Germany in the 1950s, he fled to Egypt where he was involved in various Arab anti-Israeli activities. Remer had long supported the revisionist campaigns and, in 1992, was convicted for Holocaust denial and incitement to racial hatred.

Christophersen and Remer needed substantial sums for their highly ambitious plans for the mid-1990s acceleration of East German nazism. The former chaired the meeting and showed keen interest in the Bendl plan by warmly welcoming the only other non-committee person present, Helmut Bayer, who was visibly impressed by his inclusion in this inner sanctum. Otto Remer, in particular, had long been a hero of his.

'Thanks to our initiatives,' Christophersen observed, 'there have been over two thousand attacks on immigrants by our groups in the last two months. Those are government statistics, not mine. However, we have a long way to go. Remember Germany is infested with nearly seven million foreigners and thirty thousand Jews.

'Two years ago,' he went on, 'one of our most controversial leaders, Michael Kühnen died. He was not loved by all of us, it must be said, but he was a brilliant strategist. You will all have read Kühnen's original paper *Arbeitsplan Ost* which, even in the late 1980s set out exactly how we should grasp and utilize the enormous potential that would result from political dislocation in post-Communist eastern Germany. Whatever his personal failings, Herr Kühnen had perspicacity and foresight. It is sad that since his death his successors have neglected to follow up his long-term plan, and have deflected the cadres in the pursuit of short-term activities like the race riots in Hoyerswerda and Rostock. Do you not agree, Herr Remer?'

Remer nodded and stood up. He struck the table for emphasis. 'Do you realise' – he glared at the audience – 'that over ten per cent of these new Germans in the key eighteen-to-twenty-four age group already vote for extreme right-wing parties? That is the opposite of here in the west where our voters are mostly over forty. Now, for the first time in fifty years, we can create a new Germany from scratch. We have the power to shape its destiny. The millions of ex-Communist easterners are in a political vacuum right now. They have been let down by Communism, but they have no built-in adherence to capitalism. We have the ability, judging by the polls alone, to mobilise as much as a third of all the youth in eastern Germany who have developed fascist attitudes, but who do not have viable political structures to join. This is a Nazi Party waiting to happen. We must weld this key cadre into a viable and professional organisational structure. Only then will we develop a reconstituted NSDAP ready for the twenty-first century – a truly frightening aspect for our enemies.

'But!' Remer shook a finger at his listeners. 'This marvellous opportunity will not last forever. The east will gradually catch up with the living standards of the west and the currently directionless anger of its youth will dissipate. It is imperative that we find funds immediately so that we can take action. The Kühnen plan must be revived and revitalised.'

Remer sat down, and Christophersen began to explain why large sums of money were needed. A vast propaganda machine must be funded, officials would need to be bribed, and others would need removing by costly professionals. The highly successful pogrom in Rostock the previous year had forced the Bonn government to ban many fascist parties: a number of key leaders had been jailed and their families needed support. Technical, printing and communications equipment had been seized by the police and must now be replaced, so that the effects of the clampdowns and bans could quickly be circumvented, and the cadres be kept intact and rebuilt.

Lastly, Christophersen added, they would need weapons, in order that the cadres feel confident. A hidden supply of arms always boosted morale, but some of the existing caches had been discovered and seized by the police over the past year.

Weapons practice with real arms and ammunition were a well-tested way of enticing violent activists to the cause, and would hopefully gain them new recruits from the east. Automatic pistols, grenades, machine-guns, and even rocket launchers were needed to replenish stock and to build up secret arsenals for the new cadres. Funds were also needed to send recruits to gain real military experience fighting for the Croatian HOS militia in the Yugoslav civil war.

'As Kühnen predicted,' Remer commented, 'our maximization of the eastern opportunity might take two decades to come to fruition, but now is the time to start, and seed money is the key factor.'

A number of ongoing Arab fund-raising projects were then discussed, as was the investment of the Rio Account, the growing fund from ex-Nazis domiciled all over South America. Then, turning to Bendl in the front row of the audience, Christophersen asked him to report on the state of his own plans.

Bendl was ushered to a lectern on the side of the raised platform. He, in turn, introduced Bayer. 'Herr Bayer first heard of the existence of a rare, open gold seam in Antarctica when on a cruise in the Pacific. We investigated the geologist who discovered the seam and he is genuine. He needs money, because his wife spends it like water, but he hasn't the drive to organise his own venture. So we pay him to act as our guide, but Herr Bayer will explain.'

Bayer joined Bendl at the lectern, eager to reveal his readiness to do anything and everything for the cause. He outlined his plan, and concluded, 'There is a risk attached, of course, in that any form of mining is illegal in Antarctica. But this risk is negligible since there is no police force down there and we will make sure nobody observes our passage south from Bermuda. We are talking of a vast area of hostile ocean with *very* few other humans sailing upon it. There is no visa requirement in those parts and we will not call in at any official port on our way down from Bermuda.'

'May I enquire,' Remer asked, 'what your arrangements are *in* Bermuda?'

'Ah! There is no possibility of a security breach there. Our captain and crew have all sailed with me previously on many voyages and are committed to our cause or, as in the case of our cook, are under twenty-four-hour surveillance.'

'And the other passengers?'

'As you know, Herr Bendl here is commanding the operation. My yacht is at his disposal for as long as it takes. My own health at present sadly precludes my participation. We are, as I said, checking out both the geologist, Mr Dean Witter, and his wife, who insists on accompanying him. Neither have any political or intelligence history. They are merely on the make to benefit from his discovery.'

'Will you go alone, Herr Bendl?' Remer asked.

Bendl hesitated momentarily. 'I will take only my

maidservant, Rischi. Her late husband was *Waffen-SS*. Need I say more?'

Remer persisted. 'And, when you quit Bermuda . . . there will be no passport awkward-nesses, no questions as to your destination?'

'My man in Bermuda,' Bayer replied, 'is very effi-cient and will ensure an undetected departure.'

'When and where will *you* go aboard, Herr Bendl?' Christophersen asked.

'At a later stage,' Bendl replied. 'I would prefer to say no more.'

'Of course,' said Remer. 'We all have friends in Argentina whose addresses must be treated with respect.'

There followed a discussion on how gold samples from the voyage would be treated and how initial mining operations would be funded the following year, and finally, how the profits would be realised without detection.

Bayer and Bendl were toasted and both men left Fulda pleased with themselves. The only irksome event in Bendl's day was a file handed him by Bayer as they parted.

'I am sure you will sort this out,' Bayer said, 'but if you need any help from me or action from Meier in Bermuda, just let me know.'

The file centred on a report from Jan Meier involving the cook he had hired in Bermuda. The crew were all pleased with the man's inoffensive manner and excellent cooking. There was no reason to suspect him but, as part of the normal check for old tattoos on anybody of a certain age, the negative of a frame from a video of him undressing by his bunk had been sent to Bayer. He in turn had passed it to an ex-Stasi friend who knew his way round the voluminous Stasi files, now the property of the Federal Republic.

Back in 1975, when Bendl had been attacked at Resolute Airport, he had not pressed charges but he had been given the name and address of Ottawa citizen Derek Jacobs by the Royal Canadian Mounted Police. Suspicious as to the motive behind the sudden assault, Bendl had asked his Stasi friends to have the assailant checked out. A Stasi sleeper in Ottawa had responded diligently by passing back everything known about the assailant and his family including his medical records from the local surgery.

The birthmark on Jacobs' upper leg was described and logged by his doctor as 'birdlike', so when Bayer's ex-Stasi friend entered the words 'birdlike' under the query *'Any Birthmarks or Other Idents?'* in 1993, the computer had quickly matched the phrase to the same description located in the many million personnel records once meticulously maintained by the Stasi.

So Bendl now knew that a man who had attacked him for no apparent reason 18 years ago, was currently on board the yacht due to sail at any moment from Bermuda. He did not believe in coincidences and immediately telephoned Jan Meier at the Elbow Beach Hotel. There was no reply so he left a message. He was not intending to join the yacht for a while so he called Helmut Bayer to check on the planned sailing schedule. His response was unhelpful: only Jan

Meier would know for sure, but the yacht *should* have left Bermuda already. Any communications with the yacht must go through Jan Meier.

The Witters came on board on 19 September, the evening before we sailed.

Meier must have paid a hefty sum to a local boat-man who lashed us alongside his craft and chugged out of the harbour after nightfall reporting his boat's presence to the Harbour Radio staff. Once hidden from their radar in The Cut, he sailed away from us and we motored up the buoy-marked Town Cut Channel, between the coral reef known as Sea Venture Shoals and Paget Island.

Jan Meier had been nowhere to be seen during our last day in the harbour and nobody new had come aboard. Goya, the Asian woman, appeared from the owner's cabin for the first time soon after we had left The Cut behind us and in choppy conditions, reached Five Fathom Hole. Vessels were not encouraged to enter St George's Harbour after dark and the Hole provided a safe anchorage outside Bermuda's Great Reef. Once in the open ocean, we headed east to clear all shoals before settling on a course to the south.

The skipper's aquiline features seemed to ease a touch when I brought him his grog. Perhaps he felt more at home on the open sea.

'Tell the others I will brief everyone in the saloon once we are well clear of St David's Head, say at 05:00 hours.'

'And the Asian lady?'

'I said everyone.'

'Of course, Kapitän.' I pictured myself clicking my heels but ignored the temptation and carried mugs of grog to the other crew members busy on deck. All but the skinhead Franz Habermalz grunted their thanks.

I had learned the basics of the *krav maga* combat technique from one of Laro's men back in the late 1970s but I was out of practice and out of condition and Habermalz was clearly a muscles fetishist. If and when I needed to confront him, I would do so from behind and fatally. I remember Laro himself stressing that such tactics are not cowardice but common sense.

Rischi took black tea, not grog, and when I told her the skipper's orders she complained, 'The girl is already asleep.'

'The captain said *everybody*.'

Rischi scowled. 'The girl does not need any briefing and she is my responsibility not the captain's.'

I shrugged. 'Up to you, but every person on the ship is the captain's responsibility now.'

I knocked on the Witters' cabin door and when I handed mugs to their outstretched hands, Mrs Witter sat up in her bunk and smiled warmly.

'Come in. Shut the door. Make yourself at home. I'm Jane, and this here man of mine is Dean.'

I introduced myself and we all shook hands.

Dean fumbled about for his spectacles and, finding them, peered closely at me before laughing aloud.

'Hell,' he said, 'you sure gave me a shock. I was dreaming of a gold heist. I was a bank clerk lying on a marble floor with gangsters treading all over me as they shot the chandeliers to pieces with their tommy guns . . . Here, take a seat on the end of my bunk. There's not too much space in this little cabin.'

I thanked him and told them about the skipper's briefing.

'You know where we're going?' Dean asked.

'No,' I replied. 'I'm just the cook. But the skipper did say we would round Cape Horn and then, maybe, head east to Cape Town. He said the owner would join us in Argentina and make up his mind on the destination then.'

Dean chuckled. 'So Mr Bayer keeps tight security then. Good for him. Are you German, by the way? Most of the crew seem to be from those parts.'

'No,' I assured him. 'I'm from Ottawa. I'm a professional ocean nomad and ship's cook. We also have an Asian lady on board. Maybe you've seen her. But you're right, the skipper and all his crew are German or Austrian. You sound like you're from Texas or thereabouts.'

'Yep. I'm a Texan geologist by trade and Jane here's the finest real estate agent in Manhattan.' They smiled lovingly at each other.

'So, if I may ask, are you guests of the owner along for a cruise?'

'Oh, no! We're being paid like you. We—'

'I think,' his wife interrupted, 'we'd better not be too specific about our work just yet, Deano.' She gave me an apologetic, loin-tingling smile and I could not help but notice her tan and a mole on one of her breasts as she turned sideways in her bunk to sip her coffee. I thought wistfully of Veronique.

It seemed that these were two nice people whatever their connection with Bayer, and I hoped we could get together sometime, maybe on deck, away from surveillance.

'Who is the Asian girl?' Dean asked.

'I haven't had a chance to speak with her yet. The other woman crew member, who everyone calls Rischi, is not very communicative. She brought the Asian aboard a few days ago, but they spend most of the time in the owner's cabin. Today is the first day the girl has ventured out. The skipper calls her Goya.'

I returned to the galley noting on the way that Machel Krentz, whose duties included the radio, had for the first time left it uncovered by its metal screen. He was at work setting the sails, helped by Grafmann. I felt a tingle of excitement. We were sailing for Antarctica.

At 05:00 hours to the minute, our captain descended to the galley and officially greeted everyone on board his yacht.

'We will call her the *Lorelei*,' he informed us, 'even though in the rush of our preparations the crew failed to paint the name back onto the stern. There are as many German boats on the seas called the *Lorelei* as there are Austrians on the streets of Vienna called Schmidt. Our owner is a very private person who hates exhibitionism in any shape or form. When we took over this boat in St George's, he told me to christen her with this name.

'So, welcome, my friends, to the *Lorelei*. She is very sturdy and you need have no fear of the big seas we will doubtless experience over the coming weeks. Today's picture is: Wind North 15 to 20 knots with higher gusts and Tropical Depression 9 in the Bermuda area.

'Now that we are away from land, the owner, who will join us in South America, has enjoined me to brief you all on our plans, the likely conditions and, of course, our safety concerns. But first, since you may not all have met, let me list who is on board.

'The master cabin belongs to the owner who will introduce himself when he boards in Argentina. His good friend, Nguyen Thuy, from Vietnam likes to be called Goya as she knows how difficult "Nguyen" is for non-Asians to pronounce.'

Goya shyly bowed her head at us all from her corner seat.

'Rischi, who has not sailed with the rest of us before, works for the owner.' The skipper seemed to feel he ought to say more but was clearly ignorant of anything to add about this grim-faced woman so he passed on to me.

'Derek is from Canada and he cooks well in port. We must hope his abilities are not impaired along with his balance when we hit the southern rollers.

'Mr Dean and Mrs Jane Witter are from New York. They are important guests of the owner and the rest of us are available to help them at any time.

'Up on watch at this moment is Franz Habermalz from Bayern – Bavaria that is – who is known as "Bonehead" to his friends and whose strength is apparently legendary in the *Schützenfest* competitions of Allgäu, his home district. Franz is officially our deckhand and carpenter.

'Machel Krentz likes to be called Mach, not Macho. He is both our rigging and our communications expert. Also, if we run into a problem that requires superior intelligence, Mach is our man. He is from Poland but lives in Bremen, as does his friend here, Eugen Grafmann. Eugen likes to be addressed as Grafmann, even by his wife we are told, and he is vital to our well-being for he can repair any mechanical problem that God or Fate may impose on us.

'My own name is Herbert Brandt, but people normally call me "Kapitän". Do not let the age of any of the crew fool you into worrying about their abilities. We have been together on many oceans, over many years and seen huge seas. This is a fine yacht fully capable of taking on anything the South Pacific can throw at us.

'Now, our route. Our owner wishes to visit the coastline of Antarctica for he has never been there before. From the tip of South America we should reach the coast of that frozen continent in only a week, ice conditions permitting. Every year over a thousand tourists visit Antarctica, most on cruise ships, but many in yachts far smaller than the *Lorelei*. Our owner would of course like to try for a landing, but ice floes may make this difficult. Certainly, before January, we would need inflatable boats and sledges to access any part of the land mass. Time will tell.

'If there is a warm winter down there, we would be

able to penetrate the sea-ice earlier than normal, in which case we would need to be ready to do so by the end of November.

'Because Bermuda is at thirty-two degrees north, and the most accessible point of Antarctica, for our purposes, is at sixty-five degrees south, we have some two and a half months to sail over seven thousand miles. En route we will stop for a day at an Argentinian port for supplies. You will all be able to stretch your legs and the owner will join us there.

'We need to progress at an average of one hundred nautical miles per day and we will, of course, sail through the night so long as conditions are favourable. I cannot predict the weather, but between here and Trinidad at this time of year there is a risk of tropical storms.'

'Do you mean hurricanes, Kapitän?' Jane giggled, one hand to her mouth, the other around Dean's waist.

'Mrs Witter—'

'Please, Kapitän, call us Dean and Jane. *Everybody* must call us Dean and Jane.'

'A storm, Mrs Jane, may not be a hurricane, and in an average September or October, we would expect only one or two real hurricanes on a journey such as ours, some years none at all. If we hit such weather we heave to. It will not be the first time for this crew and we have been working to prepare the *Lorelei* for this voyage since June.

'With luck, we will be through to Trinidad by early October. After our supply stop we will sail straight to Antarctica.

'Between Argentina and Antarctica we will pass east of the Falklands. We may see no shipping at all, and there probably won't be any other yachts off the Antarctic coastline until late December at the earliest.

'Tomorrow we will discuss the emergency lifeboat drill. As in any ocean, we could hit a semi-submerged metal container or some other floating hazard at any time. Off Antarctica, we may knock against ice floes. We have strengthened the *Lorelei's* steel hull but you must always be ready to react quickly. A life jacket is under each bunk and we have with us two specially designed inflatable neoprene craft. Nobody should go on deck, whatever the weather, without a safety harness clipped to the jackstay railing wire. Everybody but Frau Rischi and Goya will take a turn at watches. I understand, Mrs Jane, that you are keen to do this?'

Jane nodded with enthusiasm.

'I think then . . . that is all. Enjoy the voyage. *Gute Reise*, as we say in Vienna.'

For two weeks we headed south enjoying the fine weather, starry night skies, leaping dolphins and, though I say it myself, excellent fare. I did nothing that might arouse suspicion but I watched and I listened.

The crew, including Rischi, appeared to have received no instructions to keep Goya, the Witters and me apart. Although I suspected that all parts of the boat's interior were under surveillance, I could find no evidence of any device on the foredeck.

When not at work, I stayed on deck to enjoy the breeze, the sun, and the slap of the sea against the hull. I chatted whenever possible with the three passengers and gradually learned about their lives. Goya's had not been easy. She was a professional escort girl based in Miami and, after answering an advertisement in a marine magazine from which she had picked up previous seaborne escort work, she had been interviewed by Rischi and flown to Bermuda. Once there Rischi had forbidden her to leave the cabin until the yacht left port.

'Weren't you suspicious of being kidnapped for some pimp?' I asked her. I called her by her real name Thuy and told her of my own experiences in Cambodia. I think she enjoyed my company and my ready sympathy. Most men she met were probably only interested in her undeniably pretty face and shapely body.

Thuy had been brought up by a kindly small-time madam and part-time whore, Nguyen Thanh Phan, who worked the rooftop bar at the Rex Hotel and lived in an alley off Dong Khoi Street in Saigon's fashionable District One. Thuy's real mother, pregnant and penniless at 16, had given her up as a baby to the 30-year-old Phan, who was childless. Thuy's father, a Korean mercenary and regular client of her mother, had died in the war in 1971, the year of Thuy's birth. Phan brought up Thuy as her own, but in 1975, Saigon fell to the Communists and Phan's American clients disappeared back to the USA. The new regime sent Phan and Thuy – tainted as they were by contact with Americans – to a tough re-education camp north of Hanoi. Senior guards there used the pretty, six-year-old Thuy for their pleasure until 1977, when she and her adoptive mother were released back to Saigon. There, they made a living from Communist sex, which differed very little from capitalist sex, and they saved their money relentlessly. In July 1979, they used most of these savings as bribes to 'go West'.

Joining 90 other rag-tag refugees on an overloaded junk, they sailed away from their homeland by night and soon ran into Typhoon Hope. They were lucky not to drown, but ditched on Hainan Island in China, they nearly starved to death while waiting for repairs to be made to the junk. They managed to evade pirates, however, and five weeks after leaving Saigon, they reached Hong Kong where the British interned them in a refugee camp.

For three years, they survived rival gang hostilities within the camp and Thuy learned good English from the European volunteer ladies who visited regularly. One of these good souls eventually helped them secure visas and tickets to the United States, and in October 1982 they flew from Kai Tak Airport to San Francisco and the land of their dreams.

Impoverished, the two Vietnamese women once again plied the sex trade to make a living, but when Thuy was 19, Phan died of AIDS and a wealthy client from Miami flew the grieving girl back to his beach house overlooking the sea. By the time he tired of her, she knew how to work the Miami sex scene without falling into its many pimp traps. She had developed a hard carapace after such a difficult start in life, but she trusted me and, in her own words, soon began to treat me like big brother Derek.

We both found the Witters easy to get along with, although Dean was apt to blurt out whatever came to mind, and this did not always please Jane, who clearly wore the trousers. I felt that he was keen to tell us *why* they were on board beyond their professed friendship with the as yet unnamed owner who nobody, including themselves, would talk about, and who I continued to assume must be Helmut Bayer. Whenever the garrulous Dean seemed about to broach this forbidden topic, Jane would leap in to change the subject.

I pondered whether, when alone on deck with Dean, I should risk warning him of the criminal nature of the yacht's mission, but decided not to since he might just be a clever actor and deeply involved in Bayer's plans himself. If that was so, I could expect to find myself overboard without a paddle in no time at all.

The weather became noticeably cooler after we passed by the unseen jungles of Brazil and veered slightly west to shadow the coastline of Uruguay and Argentina. Our luck held weather-wise as we avoided nearby Hurricane Emily, which achieved wind speeds of 100 knots, and Hurricane Floyd, whose winds reached 130 knots.

The first minor depression which struck us somewhere off Mar Del Plata to the south of Buenos Aires, was preceded by a plummeting of the barometer and an order from the skipper to wear full foul-weather gear and life jackets on deck. In the yellow Goretex hooded suits, everyone looked alike.

The advent of bad weather seemed to cheer up the

crew. When together, they spoke only German and they rarely conversed with the rest of us. Krentz once growled at me when I served him baked beans on the late watch: '*Gibt's den, nichts anderes?*' 'Is there nothing else?'

I had prepared myself not to be caught out and stared at him blankly. 'What?' I asked. After that, the three of them would continue their German chatter in my presence, for they thought I could not understand them.

Until the first storm, I picked up nothing of value from eavesdropping on the crew's gossip. Feeling seasick on the first evening of the rough seas, I jammed myself into a space between two blocks of tarpaulined deck cargo and leaned back to relish the fresh air. I must have dozed off, for I woke to hear Grafmann and Krentz talking as they smoked their foul-smelling Dutch cheroots in the darkness of the foredeck. The wild sounds of the waves and the clatter of the skeleton rigging blurred some of their conversation, but I picked up the general sense.

After that, I made a habit of squeezing into my concealed nook when my galley work was done and my watch completed. One night, in rough seas east of the Rio Negro's estuary, I overheard the chilling words of Bonehead Habermalz, who was not five paces from my hide.

'I can't wait to ram it up that Thai bitch,' he rasped.

'Vietnamese.' I recognised Grafmann's softer tones.

'Whatever she is, I will have her.'

'Not a chance. The only woman you can hope for, Bonehead, is the old bag.'

'Rischi! You must be joking. I'd sooner have sex with a sow.'

'Well, the Boss's man will be on board in a couple of days and the Asian whore is clearly here to keep him happy. If you're caught touching her, or the American with the big breasts, the Kapitän will brain you.'

'What's she here for,' Bonehead mused. 'Her, and her rabbit of a husband?'

'You've asked me that before, and I told you . . . Wait till the Boss's friend comes on board then we'll hear what's up. But one thing I do know. The Kapitän is not expecting our four "guests" to be on the return journey.'

'You mean—?'

'I mean they are all four here for a purpose and that purpose ends when we reach wherever we're going. Bayer said as much to that bastard Meier who told the Kapitän. I heard him. So, if you want your way with either of the *Damen*, you'll need to get in there quick before they're corpses.'

Their talk moved on to food and the merits of various German beers. My mind whirled as I took in the implications of what I had heard.

The Witters could hardly be implicated with Bayer if they were to be murdered on his orders. I must speak to Dean as soon as the chance arose and warn him that danger was imminent. In return, he would have to tell me exactly why he and his wife were on board so that, once we reached our port of call, I could use my hi-tech mobile to call Laro and tell him everything. He would then surely agree that I must escape from the yacht along with Thuy and the Witters, and doubtless, also notify the Argentinian police that the crew should be arrested on some pretext.

At noon the next day, I followed Dean up to the foredeck for his watch and, without preamble, said that I was from the CIA – one of Laro's favourite lies since it is difficult to check – and that the crew were international criminals. I told him that, whatever he and Jane were thinking of doing, it was these criminals' intention to murder both of them as soon as they had fulfilled their purpose. I explained how I knew this and that the same fate was also in store for me and for Thuy.

Dean reacted with open shock and fear, and grasped my shoulder. 'Are you absolutely sure of this?'

'A hundred per cent certain. I speak German as well as you speak English.'

He went visibly pale. 'What can we do? Nothing must happen to my Jane. This is not her fault. I am to blame. It's my scam.'

I quietened him down. 'You must tell me exactly what is going on. Then I can decide what we can do. We may still have a chance if we think clearly.'

The words began to spill out of the poor, frightened man's mouth. The background of his geological scam. How he had badly needed funds for Jane's major real estate breakthrough in the Village. How Bayer had taken the bait in New York and paid up the first half of the fee.

'So, there is *no* gold seam in Antarctica? Is that what you're saying?'

'No, no. Of course there's gold. It's just that *I've* never seen it, and I am *not* a geologist. I'm a . . . a . . . salesman. But, yes, there's certainly gold and I know where it is. Get me the British Admiralty Hydrographic chart of the Graham Coast, the 1960 version. I'll show you where my geologist friend found the gold. *The fish next to 140*, he said, and I checked chart after chart until I discovered what he meant. 140 was a depth measurement marked next to the most southerly isle in the Fish Island group.'

As Dean's words sank in, I gave an inward sigh of relief. My mission was all but done. I now knew the precise source of the funds that Bendl and Bayer had promised their nazi friends. As soon as we reached Argentina I would call Laro – I didn't want to risk using my mobile on board unless there was no alternative.

I would warn Thuy straightaway too. All four of us should escape at the next port of call before Bayer arrived on board, since I could not be sure, even if I made immediate contact with Laro, that the Argentinian police would be prepared to raid the yacht. The only question that nagged at my mind was what to do about Bendl. This might be my only opportunity to nail him and, by fleeing, I would blow that chance and my successful cover as ship's cook. I would have to weigh this against my likely fate if I stayed on board. I needed time to think and to plan.

'I will tell Jane at once,' Dean said, his voice still edged with panic.

'No, not inside,' I warned. 'Be very, very careful what you say. The interior of the yacht is bugged and your every move down there is recorded on video. Do nothing unusual. Don't pack anything. The only place you can safely talk to Jane is up here when the crew are all below.'

I memorised Dean's address in New York and told him I would make contact after our escape, for we agreed we would make our moves separately once off the boat.

At four o'clock, I took a mug of tea and some biscuits to the bridge or, as I called it, the cockpit. Fat Grafmann was on watch and, when I put his tray down on the chart table, I glanced at the GPS that displayed our constantly updated location. The main co-ordinates were 41° south and 60° west. From the world atlas on the saloon bookshelf, I worked out our position as roughly 100 miles off the Gulf of San Matias.

We were approaching the Argentinian coast and, should we hold our current course, our landfall in the Gulf was likely to be the only marked port, Puerto Lobos. But I could not be sure, for the poor quality atlas gave only minimal information.

After supper, Thuy, as was her wont, helped me wash and dry the dishes. I whispered to her and, soon afterwards, she joined me on the foredeck. I warned her of what I had overheard, and told her that the Witters and I would leave the yacht separately when we made landfall. It would be natural and not suspicious for all of us to want to stretch our legs. I suggested that she did likewise within a few minutes

of my departure. I also warned her of the yacht's surveillance system.

'If I go, I lose the money.' Thuy looked up at me.
'This is big pay job for me. My best yet.'

'But if you stay, it may be your last.'

'How can you be so sure? I am no threat to these
men. Why should they want to kill me?'

'Whatever they do in Antarctica, where we are
going, they will want to keep secret. We will all be
witnesses if we stay on board.'

She stared at me. Then she nodded sadly.

'You are right, Derek. I must go. It is too bad. You
are good to warn me. May I come with you when you
escape, for I know nobody in South America and I
speak no Spanish?'

I thought for a minute. 'Okay, but we must leave
separately. The port may be a very small place with
no police and maybe not even a church. Once we can
see the place from on board then we can agree on a
meeting point, okay?' She agreed with this.

I slept badly that night, although the weather
improved and the seas calmed to a heavy swell.
Towards noon the next day we slowed down and I
watched Grafmann and Habermalz lower the anchor.
At 100 metres of cable it held firm, although we
appeared to be at least 20 miles offshore.

The Witters joined me on deck and I borrowed
Dean's binoculars. The distant coastline sloping
gradually to the shore was featureless, but the sea
between it and the yacht looked menacing, with
several boiling overfalls indicating submerged
shoals.

At lunch, the skipper spoke to us. I thought there was a degree of unease in his manner.

'We are anchored off Punta Delgada at the southern end of the Valdez Peninsula. At this time of year, many whales come here. You may see them blow. For twenty miles off the coast there are many rocks, so we will wait here until the owner comes out to us rather than risk a landing.'

'But,' Dean's voice was shrill, 'you *said* we would be landing. We *must* land. There are . . . medicines I need to purchase . . . and . . .' He looked desperately at me. 'The others also need things. We will *not* go any further south without stopping.'

'Please be calm, Mr Witter.' The skipper would have made a fine headmaster. 'I did not say we would not make port, merely that the owner has found it necessary to come aboard from the Valdez Peninsula. Once he is with us I am sure he will select somewhere more suitable to the south for us to visit and take on supplies. Somewhere like Ushuaia maybe.'

The mention of supplies seemed to quieten Dean. Probably because he realised the yacht would *have* to take on fuel and water, whether the owner wanted to or not. At any rate, he calmed down and no more was said. For my part, I resolved to await Bayer's arrival and then react as best I could.

Soon after dark, I hid in my deck cargo nook again and was soon rewarded by a conversation between the captain and Krentz. The latter was emphasising that Meier had instructed him under no circumstances whatsoever to use the radio prior to the owner's arrival. There must be absolute radio silence except in the unlikely case of imminent shipwreck.

'But,' the skipper's voice was harsh, 'we need to be sure the owner knows we are awaiting him here and now. I am not happy with this anchorage. The holding ground is shingle and not to be trusted. Even here, at twenty-two miles out, there are uncharted shoals all around us. We must collect the owner and weigh anchor as soon as possible or we *will* have an imminent shipwreck.'

Krentz shrugged. '*You* are the boss, Kapitän, but if the owner is angry, please remember that you *ordered* me to use the radio.'

Down below, I made the nightcaps as usual and then retired to my bunk. I slept fitfully until the early hours, when I felt the reverberation of a powerful diesel engine very different to our own. For half an hour I heard the sounds of cargo movement and smelled diesel. And, for the first time since Rwanda I felt the sharp acid of fear in my stomach. My throat went dry and sweat broke out in my hair. We were being refuelled and doubtless restocked with water and supplies from another vessel. We would *not* be stopping anywhere between here and Antarctica. The skipper had lied to us. *Nacht und Nebel*. Bayer would force Dean to reveal his gold seam and, as soon as he was finished with the four of us, we would be murdered. I longed to be with Veronique. Thoughts of my own survival took precedence over my desire for revenge.

Then suddenly, everything changed. Footsteps descended the companionway and the saloon lighting glowed. The owner had arrived. Except, it was not the owner I had expected, Helmut Bayer. I saw through the chink in my bunk curtains the face of the man from Resolute Airport, older and altered to be sure, but unmistakable. Karl Bendl stood but a few metres from me, and in that moment, I knew what had eluded me 18 years before. This was the man who had assaulted my mother in the forest of Rehau, as I watched from my perch on Bippi's back.

Karl Bendl was Karl Seidler, the killer of my father and my grandparents, and the curse of my beloved Aunt Ruth, who had died hating him to the last for the murder of her daughter. When she had finally finished telling me the story of her life, she had begged me to find the men who had ruined her life, especially Seidler, and to square the account.

My fear gave way to rage. I thought of the sharpened knives in the galley but Laro's words rang in my ears. 'Always think cool before you act, *mon brave*. Do nothing in anger for then you may act like a bull in the ring. And the bull always loses.'

I stayed in my bunk and time passed. Seidler and the captain conversed in low voices. At length, one of the crew reported that all was ready and the anchor was raised. I must have slept again, and I dreamed that the curtains of my bunk were drawn slightly apart and that somebody stared at me long and hard before the curtains were pulled together again.

I awoke with the certainty that bad times lay ahead. The returning realisation of my predicament brought back prickles of fear, but then I remembered

Seidler's face and a surge of anger shifted me from cringing passivity to positive aggression.

I would not wait for the worst, but plan to be cunning instead. Nothing would happen to us while we still served a purpose. At least we should be safe until we reached Antarctica and, by then, I would have tried to even the odds on board the *Lorelei*.

CHAPTER TWELVE

I washed and dressed, then started breakfast preparations in the kitchen. All the crew were asleep save Habermalz who accepted his coffee with a grunt. He looked smarter than usual and was clean-shaven.

Back at my bunk and behind drawn curtains, I hung up my towel as though to dry, and in doing so, covered the spy-camera lens in the switchplate. Then I unpacked my toolbox and removed a bug packet and sound-activated recorder not much larger than a credit card, and only marginally fatter than the small XB15 tape which it housed.

After replacing the toolbox, I removed the towel and, pretending to be dissatisfied with the drying process, re-hung it at the other end of the bunk. The recorder stayed in my pocket and I attached the magnetised bug on the underside of Krentz's radio table. This took me all of three seconds as I carelessly dropped a spoon close to the radio. I knew from the conversation I'd overheard between Krentz and the skipper, that the radio was usable by the two of them now that Seidler was aboard.

As I cooked breakfast, I prepared myself for the coming encounter with Seidler. I must not betray the slightest recognition, nor any hint of revulsion and loathing.

He took his breakfast in the cabin, and I noticed that Rischi, who came to collect it, had spent the night with him and Thuy, and not in her own bunk. She looked flushed and excited; a contrast to her normal sullen behaviour.

Thuy emerged soon afterwards, closing the cabin door softly behind her. She was red-eyed and moved awkwardly as though her back or thigh was injured. She sat in the furthest corner at the saloon table and did not respond to my breezy, 'Good morning, Thuy.'

When she stretched a hand out for the coffee pot, I saw that her wrist was purple and swollen. Her neck was also bruised. I took the milk jug to the table and, as I filled her mug, whispered, 'The deck, at dusk.'

I carried two trays to the Witters' cabin and left a note on Jane's bunk since Dean, without spectacles, would probably not see it. At 11am they joined me on deck, all of us wearing our storm jackets against the spray flying up from the churning sea.

'You don't look good,' I greeted them.

'What d'you expect?' Jane hissed at me. 'We didn't sleep at all. What on earth can we do now? That bastard Brandt must have known all along that we wouldn't be calling in anywhere, and that Bendl and the supplies were to come aboard offshore.'

'I agree. But there's nothing we can do about it now. We've missed the chance we planned for, but we *mustn't* give up hope. That way lies our worst fate. You must both pull yourselves together and do what I say. Okay?'

They looked at each other, then back at me. Dean's eyes were hardly visible behind his spray-flecked spectacles, but Jane gave a weak smile.

'Okay.' She nodded.

'How do you know,' I asked her, 'that the guy who came aboard last night is Bendl? Surely you were expecting Bayer, the yacht's owner?'

'It makes no difference,' she replied. 'They're in this together, and we met them both in New York. I saw Bendl as he crossed the saloon to his cabin early this morning. We kept our door ajar.'

'Good. So you're keeping alert. That's important if we're to come out of all this in one piece. You must be pretty sharp to survive in the world of Big Apple real-estate rats, and Dean, I can't believe that someone making a living from fraud and scams can be all that ready to throw in the towel at the first sign of trouble.'

Dean tried to look positive. 'Point taken. We'll be all right. Just tell us what you've got in mind.'

I shook my head. 'Nothing yet, but one thing is in our favour. They'll do nothing to you or Jane until they *know* where your gold seam is. They need me to keep the food factory going and Seidler, I mean Bendl, needs Thuy to keep his bed warm. So, I can't see harm coming our way until Antarctica.'

'That's not much comfort,' Jane said. 'You're

saying we'll be murdered in a month or two at best, or two weeks at worst.'

I put my arms around their shoulders. 'The time element is important because it gives us a chance to help ourselves. When the next bad storm comes our way I'll see what I can do up on deck to reduce the opposition.'

'They have guns,' Dean said.

'How do you know?' I snapped.

'The day we came aboard, Krentz was unpacking a long box labelled "Rigging Gear". I saw him take out four weapons, but there may have been more.'

'Never mind. It's the people, not the guns that count. There are three of us, four if we include Thuy, and only five of them if you forget Rischi. Before we reach Antarctica I intend to even things up a bit. Meantime, keep your eyes peeled and your brains sharp. We must be ready to seize any chance that comes along. Okay?'

They both nodded. Even Dean seemed less hang-dog than before as they returned to the warmth of the saloon.

Lunch was quite tricky to prepare as the boat was lurching all over the place. Seidler must have been short of sleep before he boarded, or maybe he had overdone his exertions with Thuy, for he still had not surfaced by tea time.

I passed the time scanning the boat's *Arctic Pilot* which contained general marine observations for the region. It made for sobering reading: *Any abnormal change of pressure should be heeded as it may indicate the proximity of a potentially dangerous storm.*

Pressure at the centre of a tropical storm is extremely low and such storms may intensify without warning into hurricane strength. In extreme cases, winds of over 100 knots per hour have been recorded with torrential rain, mountainous seas and abnormally high tides. Near the centre of such storms groups of large waves moving in different directions create very irregular wave heights and can combine together to give exceptionally high waves.

At dusk, Thuy clambered her way up on deck and I followed suit 10 minutes later. We sat together with our backs jammed against stacked cargo and our feet against a bulkhead. Only with my ear pressed to Thuy's mouth could I catch her words against the din of the wind and the rigging. She had been weeping and her voice was weak with misery.

'He is evil, evil man,' she cried, 'and the woman Rischi is witch. They put plaster on my mouth and made "X" of my body with handcuffs that she has. All clothes off, then she whip me while he come at me every way. Then they make me upside down "X" and do very filthy things. When they finish she show me whip again and say I tell nobody or I go in sea. I want to kill them.'

'Do you know how to use a gun?'

She nodded. 'My friend in Miami teach me guns.'

'And a knife?'

'No problem.'

I believed her.

'Listen, Thuy. Somehow you must put up with these bastards just a while longer if you want to live. If you stop pleasing them, they may kill you. The same is true for me and the Witters although, of course, *we* are still having it easy.'

I felt her nod her head. 'Okay, okay,' she said, 'I manage that. What *you* do?'

'I can't tell you yet. I have to do what I can when I can, as the chance occurs. But I mean to cut down their numbers before we reach the ice. If you see any weakness in them, if you think of any sensible plan, you must tell me.'

'I can use kitchen knife in bedroom, maybe. Kill him sudden.'

'No. If you do that the others will kill us all. And don't forget the video cameras down there.'

'Okay,' she agreed. 'I do what you say.'

'Good luck, Thuy.' I hugged her. 'You are very brave.'

I saw the glint of her smile as she left me. I had done all I could to give the others some hope and to stop them acting in haste.

At supper, Seidler emerged from his cabin. I was sitting with the Witters at the saloon table and he joined us there. If I was expecting brutal behaviour, arrogance, or mere bad manners, I was disappointed for he emanated charm and bonhomie.

He gave me not the least sign of recognition, and treated me as I would have expected a wealthy businessman to behave with the hired help. But my own reaction to his presence was that of controlled fury. The passage of time had not dulled my revulsion. This man had committed unspeakable acts against my family and nothing could alter the fact that, in a just world, he should have been hanged at the war's end. I vowed to myself as I watched him across the table, that if I could not be sure of his imprisonment through the courts, I would end his evil life myself.

His English was heavily Germanic but clear and concise. He assured us we would have a great time in Antarctica. It would be a real treat for us to see one of the world's great wonders close up. He was sorry we had been unable to stop at Valdez, but his tight personal schedule had changed at the last minute. However, after our short visit to Antarctica his intention was for us to come straight back to Argentina, where we could all stretch our legs and enjoy the luxuries of Ushuaia, the most southerly town of South America.

While he talked, Thuy kept her face down and studied her fingernails. The bruises on her neck served to remind me of Seidler's true nature, a parody of his current urbanity. I pictured the forest clearing, the gibbeted deserters and my mother's cries as he assaulted her. I remembered too what Aunt Ruth said my mother had done to him. She could not have been very thorough judging by his sexual behaviour with Thuy.

The weather improved temporarily and gave me no opportunity to act. We passed by the Falkland Islands on 9 November. Towards midnight, crouched in my deck hiding place, I smelled fragrant cigarette smoke. Peering over the tarpaulin, I saw that Rischi was holding court with two others and all were smoking marijuana. I had no experience of drugs, but I guessed by the contents of their conversation that the cannabis was removing their inhibitions. They were regaling each other by swapping gruesome exploits, and it was obvious that their pleasure came from sadism. Rischi was describing the kicks she was getting from her job as Bendl's sex-games assistant. I heard her giggle as she related to her audience the torments inflicted on poor Thuy.

'I hope your boss leaves us the scraps before he finishes her off,' said Krentz.

'Listen' – this was the more gutteral accent of Grafmann – 'three years ago in Berlin we had fun. The night we won the World Cup. I was with Bayer, as part of his protection squad, in East Berlin. We stayed at Weitlingstrasse 122, then the *Zentrale*, headquarters, for the *Nationale Alternative* (NA), which was still legal at the time.

'Four of us had the night off. Bayer was with the convicted terrorist and sabotage expert, Ekkehard Weil, who you may remember had tried unsuccessfully to blow up Simon Wiesenthal's Vienna office. Free for a while, we walked down to the arcades in Alexanderplatz. Hundreds of our lads were rioting down Unter den Linden with baseball bats and chains, beating the hell out of any blacks or other *Untermenschen* they found. So, the police were busy. We cornered a young Turkish couple, left him with his head smashed in and took his girl back to the *Zentrale*. Oh, man! It made Rischi's fun-time seem like a priest's birthday party. We took turns for the whole of that night. There was *nothing* we did not get up to.'

'What happened to her?'

'Oh! Somebody was experimenting with a blunt instrument and must have gone too far. She started to scream the place down and one of the boys put a cushion over her face.'

'The war was the time.' Krentz shook his head and drew deep on his cigarette. 'You can't do much these days without courting trouble, but during the Reich you could do *anything*. If, like us' – he clasped Grafmann's shoulder – 'you were SS, then you were gods. Even when I was just a Gestapo apprentice in the Warsaw ghetto, we had power like you can't even dream of today.'

I switched my recorder on in the hope Rischi might narrate some story legally incriminating to Seidler, but she listened with rapt attention, except for the occasional appreciative murmur at the two men's disjointed memories of pleasures past.

'In 1940,' Krentz continued, 'we put a three-metre wall round that Warsaw hell-hole with one hundred and thirty thousand Jews crammed inside. A year later there were nearly four hundred and fifty thousand of them in there. Every few days we'd go in and shake them up a bit from the back of prison vans. We had an interrogation centre in Szuch Alley, so we'd take suspects there – we knew they were planning a revolt – from the Pawiak prison. I once unloaded a vanload of prisoners after a session and some were still alive despite crushed kidneys, all their nails torn out, leg bones broken. Still alive . . . amazing! The main street, Karmelicka, was so crowded that the Jews could never get out of the way of our vans quick enough. They screamed and panicked and fought each other. We ran some over and beat others with truncheons embedded with nails or razor blades.

'There was this group of us, all Gestapo, and all in our late teens. On off-duty nights we'd have a few beers then head for the ghetto. Sometimes we had competitions for shooting the night brats, the smaller kids who the Jews used for smuggling jobs through the storm drains under the ghetto wall. They slept like rats in basements, alleys and on sewer ledges. Some would sing in weak, weasel-like voices hoping for bread. In the winter of 1941 the cold killed off hundreds of them. Survivors took the rags off the corpses for warmth. On other nights two or three of us would wait by the storm drains. You'd hear a rustling noise. Then you'd see bare feet appear as the brat pushed himself backwards under the ghetto wall to collect black market goods. We'd wait until the boy was almost clear then shout. He'd scream in terror and try to eel back into the drain. One of us would catch him by the leg while the other beat his back with a rifle butt. You could smash a spine with one blow when you knew how. We would leave them there squealing.

'You had to be careful not to touch the sick Jews. If they brushed against you in the street, you could die of typhus – about two hundred died each day in the ghetto from it. They counted out five and a half thousand corpses in a single month. In Karmelicka you couldn't avoid the infected Jew scum. They coughed tuberculosis-laden saliva at you, brushed their bare legs against you, all red from open sores. Their breath stank and they crawled with lice, typhus lice.'

'They were vermin,' Grafmann said. 'Death was the only answer.'

'Yes,' Krentz agreed, 'but they didn't see it that way. Do you remember, Grafmann, how they hid when we went to collect them in 1942 for the gassings in Treblinka? I hate to say a Jew was good at anything but, man, could they hide! Our boys missed quite a few in the early days, but we soon learned most of their tricks and fetched out two hundred and fifty thousand of them in just eight weeks. We tapped walls and if the sound was wrong a few bullets would often set them screaming. Cellars could be difficult when the Jews had prepared false lids on dugouts. Their terror when they realised we'd found them gave me a real buzz. We burned out the most difficult ones. I really enjoyed those hunts.

'Once we'd cleared every house in every street of the sector due to be gassed, we drove them down to the railway siding. Some were slow so we shot them. Others wanted to stay with their children so we separated them. That really made them troublesome, so we shot them too. One mother held onto her two-year-old just as I was trying to throw the girl into a loaded freight car, so I broke her back over my knee like firewood.

'If you did it right, you could fit over a hundred adults into one freight car and then toss in a few babies over their heads. The trains then took them to be gassed in Treblinka. If there was trouble on a line they waited in the freight vans. I know of one train that sat on a siding for five days and nights. Some of the Jews froze, but most died of thirst or no air. You could hear their moans and cries each time you did guard duty on the sidings.'

'I once did a spell of ramp duty at Auschwitz,' Grafmann told Rischi, 'supervising the Jews who unloaded the freight vans. The smell when they opened the doors was indescribable. Often there were more dead than living, but they were all still standing. In the winter many were as stiff as boards, much easier to drag.'

'If they knew what was in store, why did they not take the easy choice?' Rischi asked.

'You mean suicide?' Krentz said. 'Of course, some did, but they never knew about the gassing until after '43 or '44, so they always hoped. Also, poison or sleeping pills cost too much for most to buy. Even rat poison was at a premium. But, yes, many of the richer Jews took it or gave it to their kids as soon as we started a gassing raid on their sector.'

'Plenty got to Auschwitz,' Grafmann added, 'and then realised their mistake. They should have topped themselves earlier, poison or no. Some of them ran at the electric fence and fried. What a job that was, eh Mach! Do you remember scraping them off? Their flesh would stick to the wire like bacon to a pan.'

'I'll bet you two saw some sights in Auschwitz?' Rischi sounded excited.

'Eugen worked for the professors in Block Ten and with the gypsies,' Krentz said. 'He saw some strange things in there.'

Grafmann nodded. 'Yes, Block Ten was never short of surprises. The doctors were working to save the lives of German soldiers, so they had to experiment on the Jews and the gypsies, the *Zigeuner*. Nowadays you get these bastard liberals with their placards in Berlin complaining when the research professors cut up monkeys and mice. Yet how else will we find the answer to cancer?'

'And Block Ten?' prompted Rischi.

'Where do I start? It was mostly Jews, but in the *Zigeuner* camp close by we had some three thousand gypsies for two years until we gassed the lot in a single night. A shame really for they were a sparky crowd. No running water in their camp and not enough food. A lot died of starvation and disease. The kids got the cancer 'noma' and the ulcerated flesh fell off their faces. You could see the bones of their jaws and their cheekbones. Every week I escorted some to Block Ten. The professors sent them off to the SS Medical Academy in Graz, which sent back reports. I saw photographs of the noma kids' heads in jars.

'Those *Zigeuner* really were a merry lot. For some reason, the authorities let them stay in family groups. I used to enjoy their music in Block Twenty-two. Sometimes, when we were supervising the weekly collection, we'd sit and watch their little girls dance mazurkas while the men rocked and hummed. Whenever we needed to shoot, gas or hang *Zigeuner* you could count on a performance. Not like the Jews, who often took it quietly. Oh, no! These gypsies would scream and howl and wring their hands and jump all over the place.'

'What exactly was the professors' work?' Rischi was obviously keen to hear the details.

Grafmann shrugged. 'There were so many different doctors. Hard to say really, for there must have been well over seven thousand experiments on different Jews in different laboratories there. In Clauberg's block they concentrated on sexual parts. We'd strip the adult Jews for the doctors, and in the lab X-rays would be concentrated on their genitalia, which often burned them scarlet. Afterwards the professors cut off the parts for study, removed ovaries and collected sperm.'

'Collected it? How?' Rischi asked.

'They shoved bits of wood up their bums and massaged their prostates. Afterwards they cut off one testicle to accompany the sample, all neatly labelled. The patients would then be taken to the courtyard of Block Eleven where we shot them. There were also a few hundred children, mostly twins, in the *Zigeuner* block used by Dr Mengele. He was always kind to them before the tests, and gave them sweets and stuff.'

'I remember the twins' block,' Krentz said. 'There was a long table in the hall lab where they laid out bits and pieces ready to send off to medical institutes. My friend Heber saw rows and rows of eyeballs laid out on white paper. He said all of them were different colours.'

'Yes,' Grafmann agreed. 'Mengele was interested in eye colour. If a twin had brown eyes and blonde hair, for instance, he'd inject the eyes, or just one of them, with various chemicals or dyes. Many went blind, some even died. But other doctors weren't as kind as Mengele to the Jewish kids. No painkillers. One professor specialised in breaking, then mending, then re-breaking children's arm bones. He needed to know how good the bones were at repairing themselves when the tissue was still growing. How those Jew brats would yell . . . I could have killed them.

'We carted some of the patients out of the labs on big trays to a post-experiment observation room. Quite a few were sewn together. Their veins had been joined up or their spines interlocked. Those professors must have learned a hell of a lot, and I often wonder where all their reports are now. What a waste if today's researchers aren't using all the work that they did.'

'Life is full of waste,' Krentz mused. 'Let's roll another round of joints.'

'Not a good idea,' Grafmann warned. 'I get the idea this Bendl doesn't appreciate sub-standard performance. He's a lot sharper than Herr Bayer.'

'He's a good man.' Rischi sounded protective. 'I've worked with him for twenty years, starting in the Stasi. If Germany had more like him we wouldn't be in the mess we're in today. But you wait, if this project works and we get the funds, he will set great things in motion. Our country will work her way to the top again.'

They passed a tube of toothpaste around. I could smell the mint. They're like naughty children, these monsters, I thought, ducking low in my hideaway as they passed close by to return below.

In mid-November, at the tip of South America, we plunged into the wild seas of Drake's Passage. Conditions deteriorated significantly on the 19th and I decided to act as soon as a chance presented itself. I had listened daily to my bug-recorder, but as yet, had learned nothing of interest.

Years had passed since I had cause to put my *krav maga* techniques to the test and that had not been during work for Laro. A drunken football fan had taken a dislike to me on the Metro in Paris, so I had floored him. I remembered the event with satisfaction, but I knew I could not rely on long unused, combat moves, so I dried another towel on my bunk and raided my toolbox for a thin steel stiletto much favoured by Laro's people.

Laro had warned me in the early days never to commence any act of physical aggression without first thinking it through step by step, and then only if I was certain of a favourable outcome.

Some 200 miles south of Cape Horn a severe force nine gale churned the sea all about us into a maelstrom. I had experienced nothing like it and wondered if the *Lorelei* would break up under the tons of water crashing over the bows.

The boat's mast must have been some 60 feet high yet many of the waves' foaming crests curled higher than the mast top. We were forced to the south-east with, in Dean's words, 'the main and stay sail fully reefed'. He had sailed before, although never out of sight of land, and had talked to Krentz about the *Lorelei*. 'They've got her on a storm-gib alone,' he advised us. 'They did talk about heaving to, but

decided that might end with us being rolled in a beam
sea. Krentz told me the *Lorelei* is strong enough to
weather anything the southern ocean could fling at
us. The keel alone weighs seven tons,' Dean said reas-
suringly, 'and our draught is over twenty-nine feet so
we're not likely to go keel up and, if we do, she'll roll
back in no time at all.'

I was kept busy taking snacks and hot grog to the
successive watchkeepers, for even under the cover of
the steel cockpit, wind-driven sleet and crashing
spray soaked us within seconds. I took to wearing my
storm-suit and boots all the time, as did the crew.
Even down below, I held onto something firm or
wedged myself into a corner. Working in the galley
became a major headache as the yacht bucked, rolled
and reared like a maverick stallion.

I took to tying a small rucksack with mugs, biscuits and thermos to my belt, leaving both my hands
free. Even the act of opening the door to the cockpit
at the top of the cabin steps needed careful timing.
When the movement of the boat steadied briefly I
would open the door, slip out, then close it behind me
at once. My eyeballs were immediately stung by the
spray and the bitter wind-chill, as low as −5°
Centigrade, cut into my cheeks.

Great heaving seas advanced from the south-west
under an ink-black sky. The wind screamed and
waves broke against or over the boat in a confusion of
sound. I knew the darkness would only last from 9pm
to 2am, but for my plan to work, I needed everyone in
the right place at the right time. Fortunately, the
weather continued to worsen. The barometer

dropped to 950 millibars and the sleet turned to a curtain of lashing, blinding snow.

Massive hills of dark green water were rushing by with the power of express trains, some breakers over 50 feet in height. These curving crescents advanced at over 50 miles per hour and, every now and then amid the general tumult, rogue waves swept against the general motion and crashed in foaming fury onto the deck. These killer breakers were horribly steep and would accelerate with ominous intent towards the *Lorelei*. The whole experience was both horrifying and fascinating.

By midnight, the wind speed was gusting to 75 knots, a force 13 hurricane, and the sea everywhere was white from exploding crests. At times we were momentarily becalmed in deep troughs between waves then, picking up speed, we hurtled forwards into the next breaker. Dean, in between bouts of seasickness, informed me with his usual love of use-less facts, that an 88-foot wave had been measured in 1972 in the North Atlantic, a 111-foot wave in the Pacific by the US *Ramago* in 1933, and a 278-foot tidal wave off Japan in 1971. 'But,' he added on a cheerful note, 'tidal waves are unknown this far south.'

I was impressed by the Germanic efficiency with which the crew had prepared the *Lorelei*'s storage and stowage. Every item had its tailor-made space, on the assumption that the boat would sooner or later be tossed through 360° thereby subjecting the cargo to tumble-dryer treatment.

Jane gashed her forehead on her bunk lamp when

a particularly steep wave hit us, and it transpired
that the ship's cook was also expected to be medic.
Sure enough, I found a comprehensive first-aid box
clamped in one of the lockers. Jane made no fuss
at all and trivialised her injury. She was truly a
treasure and I could see why Dean was so protective
of her: he must have grown accustomed to preda-
tors.

Around 1am the *Lorelei* was flung on to her port
side by a huge wave and chaos reigned. The steering
gear became inoperable when it was most needed, and
the boom ties somehow loosened. All hands – except
Thuy and the Witters who had sensibly strapped
themselves into their bunks – were ordered by the
skipper to various tasks, mine being to help Krentz
secure the rigging. Safety harnesses were soon criss-
crossing each other on the wave-lashed deck and, in
the mêlée, my opportunity came.

Krentz was temporarily down below to fetch a new
shackle, and a single yellow-clad figure knelt at the
deck rails by the forward cockpit hatch; either
Habermalz or Grafmann. I unclipped the snap-link
of his safety harness, waited for the next wave impact,
then jumped with all my force at his back. My boots
struck his spine. If he screamed the noise was
instantly smothered by the banshee howl of the hurricane and his body somersaulted over the
two-foot-high jackstay line in an instant.

I edged my way back past the mast with an iron
grip on the handrails. As Krentz reappeared, I was
waiting by the cockpit door. He handed me a shackle
pin and together we completed the rigging work. I

marvelled at the strength of his hands working in cold conditions, as adept as any man half his age. I wondered if my victim, whether Habermalz or Grafmann, was even now trying to keep afloat in the roiling ocean or whether he was already in the next world reunited with all those souls he had tormented in Auschwitz.

I returned below deck, and to my horror, I found both Grafmann and Habermalz joking in the saloon about their prowess in the storm. Panicked, I rushed to the Witters' cabin and, to my enormous relief, found them both still on their bunks.

An hour later, Seidler asked the skipper if Rischi was still helping out on deck. A search ensued, which I joined, but no trace of her was found. Seidler appeared unconcerned and the general consensus was that Rischi had been swept overboard after failing to clip her harness to the rail. Foul play was not suspected.

I analysed my feelings. I had never killed a human being, except in self-defence, but then neither had I been threatened with my own imminent demise. I felt no guilt. Just regret that I had dealt only with the least threatening of the Nazis.

Thuy stayed in Seidler's cabin throughout the storm and ordered only drinks which Seidler took to her. The Witters clearly thought that Rischi's death was an accident, for they cast no knowing glances my way the next time they plucked up the courage to visit the saloon.

That evening, the storm began to die down, so I settled into my deck hideaway and listened to the recorder. Seidler must have used the radio while I was on deck and his call had been to the German friends he'd been staying with in Argentina. He thanked them for their hospitality and looked forward to joining them again in two or three months' time.

Apart from comments about family members, the mellow tones of Seidler's Argentina-based friend imparted the news that five yachts were expected at Ushuaia – one of the Argentine ports frequently used by crews prior to crossing Drake's Passage – including an international climbing party on the yacht *Pelagic*. This last vessel intended to sail the same Antarctic coastal region as the *Lorelei* and would arrive there in a month or two.

This was good news to my ears, because the presence of another yacht – and it sounded like there would be at least half a dozen from Ushuaia alone – on the coastline of the Antarctic Peninsula meant we would have a better chance of alerting somebody to our predicament.

But Seidler, Bayer and Meier obviously aimed to complete their project before the yachting season began. If the sea-ice conditions were mild, the *Lorelei* would be well clear of Antarctica before anybody else arrived on the scene.

Even before we reached 60° of southerly latitude, we began to see floating ice in all directions. Any hope I had of dispatching a male member of the crew dissipated with the calmer conditions that set in during the second half of November.

On 23 November at 63° south, we sighted the

extinct volcano which marked Deception Island, the guardian outpost of Antarctica. Time was running out.

CHAPTER THIRTEEN

Deception Island passed by to the east; a sombre volcanic cone enclosing a flooded caldera.

The Witters and I spent as much time on deck as the biting cold and my galley duties allowed. We were determined to memorise every feature we passed as such knowledge might prove useful later. Dean was already surprisingly knowledgeable, thanks to the considerable time he had spent studying the geography of the area.

'It's my homework,' he explained. 'You don't get away with any worthwhile scam without meticulous preparation and a good memory for detail. Once I had identified the island where my informant found the gold seam, I studied the maps and previous history of its immediate region. British, Argentinian and Chilean scientists have been active all round here for several decades. Their old huts are scattered along the coast, and most of them are still stocked with food and fuel.'

Dean pointed at the outline of Deception Island.

'In good weather you can sail right through Neptune's Bellows, a narrow cleft in the walls of the crater, and take shelter in a perfect harbour. The Brits and Argies built huts inside the crater in the 1960s but both were demolished by an eruption. Sometimes, in the summer, hundreds of thousands of birds and penguins line the crater shores to feast on shrimp-like krill warmed by volcanic sub-sea springs. You'd not starve on Deception.'

'I'm not worried about starving,' Jane said. 'We're going to be murdered by nazis long before we get a chance to starve, thanks to your stupid gold scam . . . and *don't* say, "I only did it for you, honey".'

'But I did.' Dean was indignant. 'And don't get so down, my sweet. We've plenty of time to think of something yet. Derek here will sort the nazis out. He works for the CIA and he's probably dealt with far worse *banditos* than this lot, haven't you, Derek?'

I nodded as convincingly as possible and changed the subject. The *Lorelei*'s course had become increasingly erratic as the duty helmsman was forced to steer a complex passage through a maze of floes and glacial fragments. 'Did you see that giant berg last night?' I asked the Witters. 'It must have been as big as the White House.'

'That was nothing,' Dean assured me. 'Icebergs over one hundred and eighty miles long and over a thousand feet thick have been sighted. One, measured from the air six years ago, covered an area of five thousand square miles. You'd need to be a dozy skipper to run into that one.'

At lunch, Thuy kept her head down, but one of

her eyes was almost closed by a purple swelling. Rischi's absence obviously hadn't curtailed Seidler's brutal bedroom sports.

I was clearing the saloon table when rifle shots cracked overhead. I ran up the gangway followed by the Witters and saw that a small ice floe some fifty-five yards away was crowded with penguins, calling *ark*, *ark*, and flapping their little wings.

All three crewmen on the foredeck were competing in a penguin shoot and, as we watched, two of the unfortunate birds were hit.

'Chinstrap penguins,' Dean said. 'Common at this season.'

'You ignorant bastards,' Jane screamed and, squeezing past the cockpit to the foredeck, struck the nearest crewman, Habermalz, across the cheek. 'What harm have those poor birds done to you? Stop it at once.'

Grafmann's belly laugh at Habermalz's discomfort coincided with another penguin, shot by Krentz, falling into the sea. The sharp slap and swirl of a killer whale surfacing sprayed the floe's edge with penguin blood, and Jane grabbed at the nearest rifle. One of Habermalz's powerful hands grasped her by the neck, almost lifting her off the ground. Her eyes and tongue protruded as she choked.

Moving onto the foredeck, I kicked at the German's testicles, which seemed a more appropriate action than one of the more subtle combat techniques I could have tried to execute. At any rate it worked, for Jane dropped to the deck holding her neck and Habermalz writhed about groaning.

'Go back inside, Mr Jacobs.'

I turned to see Seidler holding a handgun. His voice was ice-cold. 'Krentz, take the woman to her cabin and, you two, there is plenty to do without playing games with the penguins.'

No more was said that day, but the atmosphere remained tense as we dodged through the floes and entered the awe-inspiring passage of Gerlache Strait between the towering crags of the frozen continent's coastline and the wild peaks of Brabant Island to the west.

We returned to the deck when Seidler was back in his cabin, and watched spellbound as several humpback whales circled the *Lorelei*.

'They can weigh over fifty tons,' Dean told us.

The cold air crackled the skin on my nose despite the fur-rimmed hood of my anorak and no clouds were visible anywhere. Great 9,000-foot-high peaks glinted to the west on Anvers Island although they must have been 100 miles away.

Anvers filled much of the immediate horizon in front of us; a vast plateau formed by layer upon layer of snowfield, soaring to summits two miles high, and framed against a dark blue sky.

As we slid ever deeper through the magical channel, an army of icebergs floated past the *Lorelei* in every imaginable shape and size with attendant shoals of remnant ice, bergy bits and floes. All very similar to the summer sea-ice conditions off the Inuit settlements in the Canadian Arctic.

A brisk breeze stirred the strips of open water, rippling the mirror images of snow-clad peaks and preventing the surface from freezing. Shoals and rocky islets abounded. Ice fronts of glaciers and Stygian black cliff-faces dropped sheer from the heavens to the sea. And though the ice everywhere sparkled in the sunlight, a waning moon caressed the frozen horizon, silent mistress of the tides.

My blood froze as the distant strains of a marching song, a tune of war, came clear over the water. Strong voices expressing a yearning for times past rose to a united crescendo, then faded away as though from a departing army. I had heard the song before at a neo-nazi rally in Berlin – 'Red shines the sun' – the song of the *Wehrmacht* paratroopers; as redolent of German might as the '*Horst Wessel*' chant of the Nazis. The singing was coming, in fact, from the open portholes below me.

By midnight, the strait had narrowed to five miles or less and the *Lorelei*, under motor power, eased through loose ice into the closer confines of the Neumayer Channel. Now our passage lay between two islands, Anvers to the north and Wiencke to the south. On Wiencke, an apparently unbroken range of steep-cliffed, snow-topped mountains hid from our view the even higher mountains of the mainland.

Streamers of cloud rose above the southern skyline, slowly at first, then billowing as though from a forest fire.

'The weather alters quicker here than anywhere else in the world. Fine one moment, fog the next,' commented the all-knowing Dean.

I decided to fix our position and the layout of the

islands as clearly as possible in my mind in case
visibility became limited. But although the skipper
was on watch in the cockpit, the chart's cover was
closed and a cloth cap like a falcon's hood covered
the LED fascia of the GPS.

'Kapitän,' I asked politely, 'can I have a look at the
chart? I just wondered how high those mountains are.'

'No.' Seidler's cold voice came from right behind
me. 'Mr Jacobs may not look at the chart and,
Kapitän Brandt, I want everyone on board but the
watch to be present in the saloon in one hour.'

I returned to the Witters on the foredeck and,
trying not to alarm Jane, I explained the turn of
events. I told Dean I must know precisely what he
had revealed about the gold seam's location to Seidler.

'Not enough for him to find it without my showing
him,' Dean assured me. 'That would have been foolish even by my standards.' He grinned sheepishly at
Jane. 'He only knows that the gold is on one of the
Fish Islands immediately off the mainland coast, and
near a place called Prospect Point. I told him there is
an easily accessible hut there with provisions.'

'Is that true?'

'As far as I know.'

'Do you have the hut's exact position?'

'Of course. Sixty-five degrees, twenty-one minutes west, and sixty-six degrees south.'

'So presumably we are going there right now?'

'I don't think so. Most years, a yacht like the
Lorelei couldn't expect to get there until January
when the local coast-ice should have cleared.'

'So?'

'So, he's had a sledge-boat built' – Dean indicated part of the deck cargo – 'to complete the journey to Prospect Point when the ice gets too thick for the yacht. I told him that the best natural harbour in these parts, used by cruise ships and yachts every summer, is Port Lockroy Bay. He can get everything ready there before attempting the last ninety miles along the coast to the gold seam.'

'If January is likely to be ice-free compared with now, why are we here so early?'

Dean shrugged. 'He needs to complete his reconnaissance of the seam without the possibility of anybody asking awkward questions. Once the *Lorelei*'s been seen down here, all the other yachties will want to meet up with us and have a gossip about what we're up to. Why are we at Prospect Point? Why did somebody see us at the Fish Islands? And so on . . . Bendl decided we'd better come early, hope for easy conditions, complete the survey of the seam and escape back out to the wide open ocean, free of curious skippers, before the summer tourists start flocking down here.'

'When *do* the first visitors arrive?'

'Probably early in January, with the exception of the British survey vessels that come to re-supply their active bases. They could arrive at any time.'

'Is Port Lockroy what they call active?'

'It may be, although there's no permanent staff there as far as I could ascertain. Anyway, that's what I told Bendl back in New York.'

'So there's a chance, if the *Lorelei* calls in there, that we might find some British scientists *in situ*?'

'Possibly.' Dean nodded.

'Excellent. So we must be ready to take full advantage if they are. I can't see the Nazis gunning us down in front of a group of scientists with radios. Do you know the position of the Lockroy hut?'

'Easy. It's sixty-three degrees, thirty minutes west and sixty-four degrees, forty-nine minutes south.'

'Do you know the position of every hut in Antarctica?'

'No.' Dean grinned. 'Just the two most appropriate to my seam, Lockroy and Prospect. It's the same as knowing the names of the two nearest towns somewhere more civilised.'

I could see what he meant. We went below and found Krentz doling out sleeping bags, polar clothing and boots to everyone on board. High-quality stuff; from Canadian Army *mukluk* snowboots, which I recognised from Inuit camps back home, to Goretex duvet jackets and double-layer gauntlets. I was trying mine on for size when Seidler entered the saloon and the skipper called the meeting to order. Only Grafmann was absent at the helm, nosing the *Lorelei* through patchy ice as the Neumayer Channel curved round to the west.

'Ladies and gentlemen,' Seidler began, without evident sarcasm. 'In three and a half miles we will find an anchorage off Wiencke Island, you can see it to port, and the real reason for this voyage will begin. I have decided that it is time to speak frankly. Some of you already know more than others, and some of you may know more than I think you do. I have avoided disseminating information to anyone, even the crew, until, as it were, the last minute.

'All of us must now be sensible and lay our cards on the table. The Witters and I have a business arrangement. Mr Witter will show me the location of a mineral seam not far from here and, once he has done so, he will be paid well. He and I will then both be happy.

'Kapitän, you and all your crew, who have for so long worked together with my friend Herr Bayer, should know that I am liaising closely with him on this project. All funds that eventually result from this mission will go to our cause.

'We will divide ourselves into two groups as soon as possible. There are two scientific bases in separate bays just around the cliffs ahead of us. One, Port Lockroy, may be visited at any time by British survey ships, so we will stay out of sight in Dorian Bay, less than half a mile to the north of Lockroy. There are two huts there which we will use, but if our preparations are effective we should be able to sail north again in a week or two.

'I will stay with the *Lorelei*, as will Kapitän and the girl.' He waved at Thuy as though she was the ship's cat. 'We will keep in radio contact with you.'

He unrolled a chart. 'This is the eighty miles of coastline between Dorian Bay and the approximate location of the mineral seam, close to an abandoned base called Prospect Point to the south. We have designed a sledge-boat specifically for the journey on the assumption that ice conditions will be bad. She is light but strong, powered by two sixty-horsepower outboard engines. Because of the heavy load – fuel, food, spare propellers, etc – she needs a minimum of

four men to manhaul her over broken pack-ice where
open-water progress is impossible. She can move at
nearly twenty miles an hour where there is no ice.
The journey could be done in a day, but it may take a
week. All will depend on the ice. Herr Krentz will be
in command and his authority is absolute.

'May I ask if you, Mrs Witter, have had second
thoughts? I repeat that the journey will be uncomfortable in the extreme, even for a man with polar
experience. For a New York real-estate lady, it is
frankly most unwise. Since your husband has flatly
refused to go without you, entirely because you
have told him to take that position, I cannot force
you to stay with the *Lorelei*. But I recommend that
you do.'

Dean reached across for his wife's hand and looked
at her searchingly.

'No,' she said, on the edge of tears. 'We go
together or not at all. Nothing has changed.'

'So be it.' Seidler shrugged. 'And now I must
broach a slightly unpleasant topic. Our cook, Mr
Derek Jacobs, is not the innocent, ocean-going hippy
he would have us believe. I have of course already
alerted the crew to this, and now, since prevention is
better than cure, I am warning everybody aboard. By
so doing, I hope to pre-empt any foolish attempt by
Mr Jacobs, or anybody else, to make trouble.'

Seidler went quiet, staring hard at me. Did he
expect me to comment? All the others stared too. A
look of satisfaction settled on Habermalz's harsh features.

'I have no idea what you mean, Herr Bendl,' I said

quietly, holding his gaze. I felt my heart beat wildly against my ribcage.

'I will not bore you with the details,' Bendl addressed his silent audience, 'but our charming chef and I have met before. In 1975, at an airport in Canada, his homeland, he attacked me for no apparent reason. At the time I did not press charges, but I did institute certain enquiries in order to find out what had prompted his aggression.

'In the course of these enquiries, his medical records were examined and found to include a reference to a purple 'birdlike' birthmark, or to be precise a congenital *naevus spilus*, on his upper left leg.

'Early in this voyage, it was noted that Mr Jacobs has just such a unique marking, so naturally I wondered why a man who had attacked me for no known reason nearly twenty years ago, should come to be on the *Lorelei*. Was this merely an extraordinary coincidence? In any event, here he is, and we will keep an eye on him.

'I am not a believer in coincidences, so I have to ask myself why Mr Jacobs has an interest in me, almost certainly a hostile interest. Is this something personal or is he perhaps working for some organisation interested in my business operations? Either way – here he is again! What should I do with him?

'The number of physically strong men needed to operate the sledge-boat is critical, and on our return voyage we may need all hands should we run into more foul weather. So, if Mr Jacobs behaves impeccably and can give me a reasonable explanation for his flattering but irksome interest in my person over the past two decades, I intend to let him disembark in South America on our return there and to pay him fully for his excellent work in the galley. For the moment, that is how we shall leave the matter.

'The exact location of the seam will be known only to myself, Mr and Mrs Witter and Herr Krentz, who will hold the necessary navigation charts, GPS and compass.

'Obviously, we must keep our activities to ourselves, so the *Lorelei* will be hidden at all times from early visitors to these waters. Once the sledge-boat has left us, Kapitän Brandt and I will anchor the yacht as inconspicuously as possible. To date nobody knows of her existence. At no time in Bermuda did Herr Meier allow her to be openly named or officially registered as the *Lorelei*. She does not exist and we must keep things this way.

'Some of our preparations will be easier to complete on firm ground, so we will use the most suitable of the two huts in Dorian Bay. You must not utilise the stores that you will find there, and the place must be left as we find it. Since the Kapitän, the girl and I, may leave the *Lorelei* at anchor, and base ourselves in the hut, we will retain the lifeboat, together with a supply of food.

'We will make our landing over the next few hours and begin the preparations at once. I would like you, Herr Krentz, to be ready to depart with your group by the first of December and, all being well, the *Lorelei* will be clear of this coast, our work done, within a fortnight at the latest. Are there any questions?'

Seidler, Krentz and the skipper withdrew to join Habermalz on the bridge. Grafmann was stationed on the prow with binoculars, so I was unable to meet the Witters there to discuss our best reaction to the briefing. An hour later, Grafmann shouted that the marker was ahead; a rock called Casabianca.

The *Lorelei* slowed to a crawl. We had entered Dorian Bay. The view was majestic in every direction and two small wooden huts soon appeared on a slope partly covered in snow, a few yards above the rocky shore. Gentoo penguins patrolled the rocks and, to Seidler's obvious relief, there was no sign of other visitors.

Habermalz made the anchor fast in what appeared to be an alternately rocky and muddy seabed in the shallow inner bay, and the yacht's sturdy inflatable lifeboat was launched. Krentz went ashore and returned in 20 minutes having checked out both huts. About 600 feet separated the smaller Argentinian shack from the well-equipped British one, which was built on concrete blocks with a gap between its floor and the stony beach.

Habermalz confirmed to Seidler that both huts were uninhabited, but that the British must have used theirs within the last few weeks.

'That is not likely,' Seidler told him.

'My eyes and my nose tell me somebody was in that hut very recently.' Habermalz looked sullen.

'*Macht nichts*,' Seidler shrugged. 'There's nobody now. We will stay anchored here and use the hut until Krentz's group is ready to go. Grafmann, climb the slope above the hut and check out Port Lockroy Bay on the other side. Be careful. It is possible the British are there and they must not see you.'

Grafmann soon confirmed that he had spotted a hut less than half a mile away in the next-door bay, but there were no signs of boats or people. So the unloading began. Krentz proved an efficient taskmaster, adept at delegation.

The weather remained fine, unusual in late November when, according to Dean, cloud and blown snow was the norm. The background noise was in keeping with the savage scenery; an irregular crack and boom of unseen avalanches.

Krentz used the ship's lifeboat to haul all the necessary equipment to the beach. While Habermalz, Witter and I ferried camping and personal gear over to the hut, both Krentz and Grafmann inflated the sledge-boat they had helped design in Bremerhaven. Custom-built to carry up to six persons with food and fuel, for a 14-day, 250-mile round voyage through mixed sea-ice, it was made of extremely tough neoprene, unlikely to be punctured by ice and easily hauled over floes. Six haulage rings spaced around the bows and sides of the boat's hull allowed for up to six people to manhaul the boat, even fully laden, like a dog-team with a sledge.

Boat hooks, oars, a grapnel line and a bow-mounted, hand-operated winch were all slotted or bolted into place, and then Krentz gave his prospective crew a lecture on the boat's abilities.

'Using trial reports from the US ice-ship *Nathaniel B. Palmer* as well as Canadian Forces Arctic equipment tests, we designed this vessel specifically for this journey. We call her *Eisfresser* – Eater of Ice.' Krentz looked at Grafmann as he said this. They were clearly proud of their brainchild.

'With her two sixty-horsepower outboards and a correctly balanced load, she will plane or skim at almost thirty knots. Her propellers are protected by mesh cages, but ice damage will still occur so we carry' – Krentz pointed at the neatly laid out cargo lines – 'a number of spare propellers and shear pins.'

'We will wear Bayley immersion suits so that, whenever necessary, we can swim ahead with hauling lines and fix them to anchor points to allow winching over difficult broken ice. Any areas of two-inch-thick, soft grey ice will be easy to penetrate by engine power alone and anything thicker than six inches can be walked over. Conditions between these two thicknesses, such as light brash ice, which is loose fragmenting ice, small pancakes and heavy *shuga*, slush, will be crossed or detoured with the help of our grapnel and winch.

'At this time of year, we should mostly meet ice solid enough to pull the boat over, or water sufficiently open to motor through.

'The only design feature to be aware of is that, because we had to make the *Fresser* towable through broken ice, it is not as wide as we would like for big wave conditions. It is unlikely rough seas will occur on this specific journey so overturning is not a great worry. But, should this happen, the fuel tanks and cans are lashed in and re-righting hand-lines are positioned along both sides of the hull. If the *Fresser* overturns we will simply stand on the hull floor and haul on the opposite side's lines. She will then flip over. If we do this quickly, we will avoid water in the fuel.

'We have two polar tents, one for myself, Grafmann and Habermalz. You three will share the other. Before we depart we will practise in the *Fresser* in this bay. Also, we will all acquaint ourselves with the tents, cookers and ancillary gear here by the hut.'

Once the equipment was prepared and packed into containers, the sledge-boat trials took place, and I was again impressed by Krentz's methodical approach. With all fuel, food and gear aboard there was still enough room for the six of us in our Bayley survivor suits to perch along the rubber hull, three to each side, with the Germans closest to the stern by the steering and throttle control. Grafmann steered, Krentz navigated and Habermalz nursed his snub-nosed sub-machine-gun. Krentz kept the chart, GPS and compass in a waist-bag slung back to front for ease of access.

Seidler and the skipper inspected the *Fresser* and her cargo in detail on the night of 30 November, as the fine weather front dispersed and light snow began to fall. At no time was I able to set up my hi-tech mobile phone, which was able to transmit to anywhere in the world from anywhere, but I did manage to remove my radio bug from the table on the *Lorelei*.

Krentz sent Dean with me to fill a heavy steel urn with snow from the slope above the hut. Habermalz watched us, but we were able to converse quietly.

'Listen, Derek,' Dean whispered as we lifted the heavy urn. 'If I locate the seam, I'll make a song and dance of showing the Germans how to use the geological hammers to remove samples. They're all likely to be distracted, at least briefly. Gold has that effect on folk. That will be the last chance you'll have to grab one of their guns. I've told Jane too.'

'Good thinking,' I agreed. 'I'll be ready. But if I miss that chance what will their next move be?'

'Krentz will record the seam's exact location and photograph it from all angles. He'll also note the nearest sea anchorage, the best landing spots and the ease of overland travel to the site. He'll want to take away as much gold as we can feasibly remove. I imagine Bendl's plan will be to return next season with a larger vessel, possibly in the guise of a privately chartered cruise ship, bringing light extraction gear, including small caterpillar digger and dumper vehicles. But that's just a guess. My work really ends once I've shown them the site and that's what worries me most.'

'No, Dean,' I shovelled blocks of cut snow into the urn as he held it steady on the slope. 'They'll definitely need our strength to be sure of returning safely to the *Lorelei*. Only then will they get rid of us. We must act before that point.'

I cooked a big meal that last night. There was nothing on board, even in the medical pack, with which to lace the food. The Germans all ate well. The rest of us did not, for the threat to our lives tied our stomachs in knots.

Krentz woke us at 6am on 1 December and three

hours later the *Fresser*, fully laden, nosed out of Dorian Bay into the fast-moving current of the Neumayer Channel. Visibility was less than a thousand yards at best and Krentz spat his instructions to helmsman Grafmann in low, taut tones.

When the sea seemed mostly free of brash ice, Grafmann twisted the hand-throttle and the *Fresser* powered forwards, her bows lifting clear of the water until she surged into a smooth fast skim over the black waters of Bismarck Strait, leaving Wiencke Island and the *Lorelei* beyond our stern horizon.

For several hours the *Fresser* headed roughly southwest through ever-decreasing visibility and past numerous low-lying rocky islands. Shoals were frequent and Krentz constantly nagged Grafmann to keep the speed down. Twice the boat shuddered as submerged ice struck the shaft of one of our outboard engines, and both times we stopped whilst Grafmann changed the propeller's shear pin.

Krentz kept a plastic container between his legs and every hour or so passed a biscuit or chocolate bar from it to each passenger. Vacuum flasks of hot black coffee, which I had prepared that morning, were also passed around every so often and Habermalz filled the outboard fuel tanks from jerry cans while on the move. Everybody except Jane used Krentz's navigation pauses to urinate over the boat's side.

At 9pm we passed by a turbulent zone where confused waves burst over a submerged rock skerry. Krentz declared that we were 'between Huddle Rocks and Lippman Islands'. He looked satisfied as he tucked his GPS back into his waist-bag. 'More than halfway there,' he said.

Habermalz took over the outboard tiller from Grafmann, who propped his back against the jerry cans and let his legs rest on the inflated hull with his feet sticking out over the sea. We did likewise in the mid-section of the *Fresser* and I dozed fitfully, pressed against the Witters for warmth.

The trouble started at some point during the night when Krentz shook the three of us awake. Despite our survival suits we felt cold and damp. The Germans were all at their posts and the *Fresser* was surrounded by jostling brash ice.

'Soon we will need to work our way through this ice,' Krentz said. 'But first, we must eat.' He doled out self-heat tins of US Army baked beans, buttered biscuits and more hot coffee. Jane took her chance to squat at the bows. Dean and I faced away from her, Krentz and Grafmann ignored her and Habermalz stared lewdly over his coffee mug.

'Now is high tide,' Krentz told us, 'and many rocks are just submerged. Also, according to the Kapitän the last ten miles may be blocked solid. Either way it will be slow and hard.' He looked up at the three of us. 'You do what I say quickly, *ja*? There may be no time for questions.'

We nodded automatically and Habermalz sneered. He kept his sub-machine-gun slung over his chest, paratrooper style. The other two had brought Mauser rifles with sniper scopes – good for hunting game, but not for close-quarter action. When I make a move, I thought, it must be for the sub-machine-gun.

By 6am on the second day, after three hours of non-stop toil using boathooks to smash through crowded brash ice and four-inch sludge, we came to a bottleneck between islands where a labyrinth of floes had jammed together. This allowed us to haul the *Fresser* over mostly solid chunks but, time and again, spaces of weak porridge ice intervened and then we had to half swim our way forward, or tread on semi-buoyant ice pancakes like river-loggers back home balancing on submerged logs. This became easier with practice, and the Bayley survival suits gave our bodies plenty of buoyancy.

Krentz was tireless at scouting the best route and directing our progress. The other two Germans obeyed his every shout like sheepdogs and we did our best. Jane was fit from a regime of work outs and running, and at first managed very well.

At Krentz's midday GPS check, we were jammed in a region of dangerously revolving floes and small islets to the immediate south of Straggle Island. Krentz decided to head back the way we had come and by the time we were able to advance again to the south, we had lost three hours of previously hard gained progress.

Jane's morale sagged visibly. 'I need to rest,' she told Dean. 'Tell them I can't go on without resting. I'm dog-tired and my shoulder is real painful.'

Dean pleaded with Krentz, but the German just shouted. 'Wait a bit more. This is a very bad place. We can't stop. If the wind comes we must be away from here.'

So we struggled on, sometimes swimming then

line-hauling, sometimes push-pulling the *Fresser* over jumbled pressure ridges and between huge fractured blocks, only under power in rare, ice-free stretches of water.

Then, with all of us on our last legs, Grafmann, scouting ahead with a long line, yelled, 'Open water.' Sure enough, as far as the eye could see, which was a mile or more, black water stretched towards the south.

Krentz pointed into the western gloom. 'Tadpole Island.' He straightened the chart on his knee. 'Maybe another five miles now.' He passed around chocolate bars and the last of the hot drinks. 'You okay for another hour, Mrs Witter?'

Jane nodded. The open water ahead was good for morale.

Grafmann, now at the helm, nosed the *Fresser* forward with caution. A rising wind briefly cleared the visibility to the east and revealed an unbroken coastline of ice cliffs.

'Maybe only two miles now,' Krentz told us. 'Soon we will see the hut along the beachline.'

Minutes later, there it was; a rickety Tom Cobbley shack, more like a garden shed than a base for scientists, but inviting enough from our point of view. However, the worst ice conditions we had so far encountered blocked the last mile or so to the hut. Through Krentz's binoculars I could see that it was perched on a rocky beach, the coastal ice cliff behind it a fairly gentle but fractured slope, promising access to the high plateau of the Antarctic Peninsula.

'The problem,' Krentz said, 'is the hut's position

inside the curve of the bay and its proximity to an offshore island. The inshore ice is snagging there like on a hook, and creating much more difficult conditions than any we have met so far. You can see how, every so often, the blockage of floes unhooks and shifts violently. Very dangerous to take the *Fresser* in there.'

He tried every approach technique we had used so far, but to no avail. A flotilla of new ice floes closed in from the north, cutting us off from the open water. Krentz sent Habermalz overboard with a long line and the grapnel to wade or swim his way to a firm floe to find a winch point. Grafmann took over the sub-machine-gun.

I was watching Habermalz jump between two chunks of ice and then steady himself on a third when, from immediately beneath him, a long grey, shark-like shape exploded through the surface sludge. I heard Habermalz's shriek of alarm, and beside me Krentz yelled at Grafmann, 'The rifle. Get the rifle.'

'Leopard seal,' Dean commented. 'They grow to fourteen feet and weigh one thousand pounds. Jaws like alligators and similar habits.'

I watched in fascination as a screaming Habermalz hooked an edge of a semi-submerged piece of ice with the grapnel. The giant predator had one leg of his Bayley suit in its jaws and, sinking its weight back into the sea, began to drag him backwards and downwards.

Krentz and Grafmann, resting their rifles on the rubber hull, sighted the rapidly disappearing leopard seal through their scopes.

Dean punched my shoulder. 'Now!' he hissed. 'Let's go for them now.'

I hesitated for only a moment, but by then it was too late. Both rifles jerked, and out on the ice, Habermalz slowly pulled himself to a sitting position. His attacker had disappeared, presumably shot through the head.

Habermalz limped and waded his way back to the *Fresser*. The Bayley suit had been punctured in many places by the leopard seal's teeth, and Grafmann slit open the trouserleg. Habermalz was wearing thick woollen under-trousers and, although soaked with blood, they had helped to prevent the seal's jaws crushing his leg bones. Grafmann sprayed the puncture holes with plastic skin, bound the leg tightly, then repaired the torn sections of the Bayley suit with duct tape.

Krentz made a decision. 'We cannot reach the hut, but there are many rock beaches on the islands we have passed. The wind is rising and we need sleep. We will head for the north side of Perch Island, the nearest land, and camp where we can.'

Nobody objected. His suggestion was welcome for we clearly could not gain access to the hut.

'Mr Witter,' he said. 'Tomorrow you will take us to your gold seam. It is close now, *ja*? Very close to the hut, you told Herr Bayer. Now we depend on you. You will not let us down.'

CHAPTER FOURTEEN

I could have slept on for hours, but Krentz shook me awake after a mere six hours' rest. He wanted the vacuum flasks filled with coffee and passed me the cooker and equipment through the tent flap, followed by a polythene bag of snow he had scooped up. Much as I detested the man and all that he stood for, I could not help but admire his fitness and efficiency. He was tougher and more capable than most men half his age.

The Witters dozed on as the cooker's heat warmed the tent. I glanced outside and was not impressed by the weather; a stiff moaning breeze, wan sun and near white-out.

I woke the Witters and offered them coffee. They sat up in their bags, looking disorientated.

'Today looks like being crunch time.' I kept my voice low. 'I guess we'll be on your island of gold in a few hours depending on the sea-ice.'

Dean fumbled for his spectacles. 'Is it cold?'

'I don't know.' I shrugged. 'Just below freezing, I'd guess.'

For a while there was silence as the Witters cupped their hands about their coffee mugs and the grim reality of our situation sank in.

'How's your shoulder?' I asked Jane.

'Better,' she said. 'But I hope there's no more boat-hauling.'

I switched off the cooker once the flasks were all filled as Krentz had stressed that I must be economic with fuel. A sudden silence took the place of the roar of our cooker and we listened to the Germans chatting in their tent.

'Oh God!' Dean groaned. 'How did I ever get us into this mess? I just don't know what to do. Whatever happens, we're up against it, aren't we? Whether I locate the seam or not, they will kill us.'

Jane put her free arm around his shoulders and hugged him as she tried to sound encouraging. 'Don't be so gloomy, honey. We'll be okay.'

'That's right,' I added. 'There'll be some opportunity we can grab.'

Dean was not impressed. 'You say that, but something won't just turn up. You've got to make it happen. You're CIA for God's sake. You *must* do something before they force me to show them the seam.'

Before I could reply, Krentz came back to the tent to remove the flasks and cooking box. 'Mr Witter, you will please be ready to come with me in fifteen minutes. We are already behind schedule. You will tell me the exact location of the open mine and we will go there at once. I must know now to which of these Fish Islands we are going. They are all within three miles of us, but there is much ice about.'

Dean and Krentz conferred with the chart out of my hearing. Then we packed up the camp and slid the *Fresser* back down the rocks. Newly arrived icebergs ground and jostled where there had been open water. A good deal of hauling would be needed even to get clear of the island. Krentz was grim-faced whilst Dean remained unresponsive even to Jane's concerned queries. At length he muttered, 'I told Krentz which island and where to try to land, but I refused to give him the seam's location. Once I do that,' his voice trembled, 'we are done for. They won't need us anymore.' The grumble of the engines ensured that the Germans did not hear him.

The ice forced us away from the target islands and we had gone at least two miles west before Krentz spotted a likely route, which would mean approaching our goal from the south-west and into the southerly current.

The sun was sometimes visible, not as a delineated circle, but merely as a sharper source of light, and just enough for me to keep a check on the general direction of our progress.

Krentz constantly consulted his GPS and chart as we forayed towards the islands. None looked higher than 250 feet and in most places they appeared flat and low through the gloom. Some were a mere few hundred yards across and none more than half a mile in length.

Krentz took us ever closer to the most southwesterly of the group, zig-zagging past obstacles and often sending two or more of us overboard with lines. After nine hours we made a landfall by a low rock promontory –

nine hours to cover a distance of only four miles. The Germans were not in the best of moods, impatient even with each other. A bad sign.

We hauled the *Fresser* up the rocks, and pitched the tents close together where Krentz indicated. I shivered inside my underclothes, damp from the sweat caused by exertion in my Bayley suit. Krentz passed a flask, mugs and biscuits into our tent, but he summoned Dean back outside in minutes. Again they studied the chart together and Krentz made Dean draw a diagram for him, presumably of the island.

'You are saying we may take hours?' Krentz's voice was raised. 'But this Salmon Island is very small, maybe only six hundred square yards. We must be quicker. But, for safety, we take survival gear. Wait.'

Krentz packed two rucksacks at the boat and gave one to Dean. They then disappeared into the blowing snow, lost from our sight in less than a hundred yards. I secured the door flap when they had gone, as Jane and I were already shivering.

'Dean was leading,' I told her, 'following a compass bearing. They shouldn't be long.'

Although the ensuing wait seemed to last all afternoon, they were actually only gone for three hours, and I had dozed off when I heard Dean fumbling at our tent door. We let him in and gave him coffee. He acted strangely, appearing aggressively confident for the first time since I had met him. 'We will be okay,' he said to Jane, hugging her closely. 'We will be okay.'

I put my finger to my lips to hush him so that I could hear Krentz speaking to the others. He sounded coldly furious.

'What's he saying?' Jane whispered.

I translated for the Witters. The cooker was roaring away in the Germans' tent so that, although I could hear them, they could hear very little outside the confines of their tent. Such is the strange way of tent acoustics.

Krentz told his colleagues that Dean was a fraud. They had searched all over the little island and, despite the poor visibility, Krentz felt they had covered every inch of the place without finding a thing.

'This is a farce,' he said. 'The American has fooled both Herr Bayer and Herr Bendl. We should shoot the bastard and get out of here.'

'Hold it, Mach,' Grafmann urged. '*Sei geduldig.* Be patient. Herr Bendl won't thank us for giving up so easily and, remember, you could have walked right past the gold without recognising it, *nein?*'

'True, but Witter would surely know it when he saw it . . . if he is genuine.'

'*Ja*, but don't forget, Witter is fearful for his life. Maybe he did see it, but didn't show you because he's hoping he can strike some sort of bargain?'

Krentz sounded unconvinced. 'I don't think so, but it is a possibility. We will have to put the situation to Herr Bendl. It is for him to make a decision.'

The Germans set up their Spillsbury SBXII-a radio set with its dipole antenna and made immediate contact with the *Lorelei*. After a deferential greeting, Krentz told Seidler the current problem with Dean.

'I believe he is fooling us. I think it likely he does not know where the gold is. Maybe he never did know and it is all just a fraud, a lie . . .'

There was silence as Seidler's response, a long one, came through.

'I understand.' Krentz's voice was subdued. 'We will do as you suggest straightaway. Witter will be given the ultimatum. One more chance to show us the place or we will use pressure via his wife to force him . . . *Ausgezeichnet, mein Herr*, excellent. I am sure this will work. We will call you back as soon as we have a development.'

He signed off and I briskly translated what I'd heard to the Witters. My words had an immediate effect on Dean. He grasped Jane by the arms and spoke to her tenderly but with authority. He was to blame and he would not see her suffer more than she already was. Without him, they would not hurt her. There would be no point. When searching the island with Krentz, he said, the cloud had lifted briefly and he had seen to the northeast how the islands were ice-blocked all the way to Prospect Point Bay. Only four miles away at most. In his Bayley suit, and with his survival pack, he could make it easily and once he reached the hut there would be provisions.

'But—' Jane interrupted.

'No buts.' Dean kissed her. 'Listen, my love, for once I will not change my mind whatever you say. If we are to survive this, my way is the only way. And I may only have seconds to get going. Krentz will be coming for me any minute.'

As he spoke, Dean began to stuff his sleeping bag

into its container. He lashed it to his survival rucksack and then untied the tent flap. Looking back, he said, 'I know you will eventually get to the Prospect hut. Until then I will be safe there. The CIA is a better bet than the US Cavalry!'

Jane embraced Dean, and I looked the other way as they parted. He left noiselessly, but I was relieved to hear the low roar of the Germans' cooker which meant they would hear nothing outside.

A few minutes later Krentz called out, 'Mr Witter, we need to discuss our plans. Please come to this tent.'

I replied at once, 'Witter is relieving himself in the rocks.' Anything to give Dean time.

Five minutes later, I heard Grafmann's heavy breathing outside our tent.

'Where is he? Which rocks?' he demanded.

The game was soon up; the Germans shouting at one another and rushing to prepare their gear to search for Dean.

'Come outside, Mr Jacobs.' Krentz's voice was raw with anger.

I poked my head out of the tent flap and squinted up at him, the glare of daylight intense, refracted as it was by the falling snow.

'We will be gone for a short while. Mr Witter has been very stupid, for this is a small island and we will soon find him. You and Mrs Witter will stay in your tent. Do not attempt to move the boat . . . Grafmann has the chain-lock key. Any act of sabotage will hurt you as badly as us.'

Because of the glare, there was no shadow and no

perspective anywhere, and I could see no boot prints in the snow. The three Germans soon disappeared, all of them armed and Habermalz limping. For a while, I could hear them calling to each other as they searched.

Jane was sobbing silently, her hands hiding her face. I thought of comforting her in my arms, but decided against it. Better to try to take her mind off Dean's likely fate. 'We must make plans while they are away,' I said.

She sniffed and rubbed away her tears. She is practical, I thought. Just as well.

'What do you think we can do?' she asked.

We tried to think of some positive course of action, but concluded that it would be best to bide our time for the Germans were armed, alert and expecting us to cause trouble. We agreed at length that regardless of whether or not Dean was captured, the best place for us to attack the Germans was on the boat and not on land. I searched their tent, but the guns and radio were missing, presumably taken with them.

'Tell me one thing, Jane.' I watched her closely. 'Has Dean ever told *you* that he knows where the seam is?'

She sighed. 'We're very close and love each other dearly, but he is and always has been a Walter Mitty. He can make himself believe anything if he wants it badly enough. Then he will be overgenerous with the truth, even to me, and his ability to convince others of any particular scam depends upon first persuading himself to believe it.'

'So what are you saying?'

'I'm not.' Jane gave a half-smile. 'I'm not con-
firming anything, just that I couldn't swear that he
does know the location of this gold or that he does-
n't. He may think it exists or he may have invented
it. Equally, if his informer exists then that guy may
have invented it all and fooled my Dean . . . who
knows?'

'So, should he be threatened by the Germans, he
may not be able to tell them what they want to
hear . . . not even if they hurt you in front of him. So,
you will both be caught in the trap of his own
making.'

Jane was quick to defend her man. 'I'm involved
with this because I've always had my eyes wide open.
I wouldn't let him go ahead without my involvement
and I'm not going to desert him now. If they hurt or
threaten me in front of him, he will tell them what he
knows immediately. If he knows nothing, the
Germans ought to be intelligent enough to see that
he'd tell the truth to protect me. Whichever way I
look at it, he'll have a better chance if I'm still in the
picture.'

'You're very brave.'

She shook her head. 'What if we do something
now, before they come back?'

'We've been through all that. What could we do?
They have weapons, remember.'

We were going round in ever-decreasing circles.

'Even if we were able to push the *Fresser* out to sea
right now,' she mused, 'they'd call up Bendl and bring
in the *Lorelei*. But then perhaps the *Lorelei* couldn't
reach us?'

'In these conditions, probably not. But this ice is forever shifting and in a few weeks it could ease up a lot.'

'We would starve by then.'

'That depends. If the *Lorelei* was to start out at once they could be here in two or three weeks. There's enough food on the *Fresser* to keep us going.'

'Okay.' Jane was getting desperate. 'So we get rid of the food.'

'You're not making sense, now. Do something like that and we all die. Dean too, if they bring him back.'

We were still arguing when the Germans returned, red-eyed and foul-mouthed. To my surprise, they had not found Dean. Habermalz poked his head into our tent, presumably in case Dean had somehow managed to return, or one of us had fled. His expression was venomous.

I listened as Krentz again called up Seidler. Every inch of the island, he said slowly and deliberately, had been searched. Witter must have gone out over the moving sea-ice towards the mainland . . . No, they had not seen his footprints. They could not even see their own in the white-out.

A long silence ensued as Seidler reacted.

'Okay, Herr Bendl,' Krentz replied at length. 'Understood. We are to reach the hut at Prospect Point by whatever means and wait there. Witter can only survive by going there. When he arrives we pressure him. If he does not come in a week, we assume he is dead . . . Correct, so far?'

Another silence, then Krentz again, 'Okay, I repeat. If Witter fails to return we put maximum pressure on his wife in case she knows the seam's location. He may have told her. That is the last option. Only then will we return to the *Lorelei*. Meanwhile, we call you twice daily.'

I told Jane nothing of this for there was no point in worrying her further. I said only that we were to try again for the Prospect Point hut.

We packed the tents, threw the equipment and food-bags into the sledge-boat and left what I now thought of as Witter's Island.

Krentz found a way to escape the mass of ice around the islands with some ease. We took a long detour north, then headed east to approach the hut in Prospect Point Bay and discovered a channel fairly clear of ice, at least 100-yards wide, running between the sheer ice cliffs of the coast and the belt of floating ice floes on our seaward side.

'With luck,' Krentz told Grafmann, 'this will lead us close to the hut. If not we will drag the *Fresser* over any intervening ice. Either way we will be there in an hour or two, then we will wait for Witter.'

Perhaps he would have been right but for the nature of Antarctica's ice-bound coastline.

Habermalz was sitting on the hull slightly forward of the other two Germans. He stared at us from behind his sunglasses, his hands never leaving his gun. He saw me glance briefly at the two hunting rifles lying on the jerry cans beneath his legs. He shook his head and drew one of his hands in a slitting gesture across his throat.

I smiled to myself a short while later, when a sudden boiling of the water startled him from his studied air of macho imperturbability. The dorsal fin, three feet high, of an orca or killer whale had surfaced close to the boat.

I think I already knew what would happen, and what I must do, a millisecond before the explosion. Perhaps, without consciously noticing it, my peripheral vision had picked up some movement high on the ice cliff that soared above us. God alone knows what prompted this particular section of the ice cliff to fracture, but the process was common enough all round Antarctica's coastline – Dean had told me so – and Krentz was taking a risk in sailing so close to it. Perhaps the vibration emitted by our outboards was responsible. Who can say? Whatever the cause, the result was spectacular and effective.

We craned our necks upwards at the source of the rumbling roar that followed the initial explosive crack, and the sky seemed to darken as a huge block of ice plunged outwards from the cliff and then downwards.

I could not see Jane, but the Germans, as one, scrambled away from the cliff-side of the boat. The icefall crashed into the sea and a tidal wave rushed towards the *Fresser*.

I focused only on Habermalz, for his thoughts were centred on survival. As the wave struck, I leapt for the sub-machine-gun and, in the somersaulting chaos that followed, wrenched its strap from around his neck. Then, like the others, I was under water.

When I surfaced, I swam for the boat and clambered aboard its upturned hull.

Where was Habermalz? Wiping the salt-water from my eyes, I saw that all four orange-clad figures were within a few yards of the *Fresser*. Habermalz, unlike the others, was not swimming towards the boat but to Jane. He had seen me and the gun. A pocket knife was clasped in his teeth. He was yards away from her. He would use her as a shield while the others disarmed me. I aimed and pressed the trigger but nothing happened. The safety catch. Desperately I searched the sides of the gun until I spotted the small, black button above the trigger guard. I pushed it across from 'S' for Safe to 'A' for Automatic.

By some miracle, I missed Jane with the spray of bullets that erupted as I squeezed the trigger. Habermalz's face appeared to implode as he died.

Grafmann had begun to haul himself aboard. I fired a burst at the top of his head and he slid back into the water.

I pointed the gun at Krentz. He was treading water and holding onto the *Fresser*'s bow.

'Take off your waist-bag.' My voice was hoarse with tension. 'Throw it to me.' He did not argue and, clasping the gun in my crutch, I strapped the bag around my own waist.

In that moment, the primitive instinct for survival took control of my mind. Perhaps that is the sort of excuse many killers use, I do not know. But, whatever my thoughts, or my conscience – call it what you will – my finger again closed over the trigger, just the fraction that was needed, and a single bullet passed through Krentz's mouth. Soundlessly, his face expressionless, he slipped away and, kept buoyant by his Bayley suit and life jacket, floated face up like the other two Germans.

Slinging the gun around my neck, I hauled Jane onto the hull and hugged her to me. She was shivering and her lips were blue with cold. We must quickly right the *Fresser*.

Remembering Krentz's instructions, I located two of the coiled, four-foot-long re-righting lines and pulled them out of the bungee loops that housed them along the side of the starboard hull. I gave one to Jane and, with both of us standing on the outer rim of the port hull, we tugged with all our weight.

The *Fresser* responded slowly to our joint weight hauling on the lines. Our fulcrum was the hull ring under our feet and soon the opposite side of the hull rose out of the water until the boat stood up in the water at an angle of 45°. Then she fell back, still upside down.

'We should pull at the moment the next swell strikes,' I suggested. We did, and to our relief, the boat reared up to 90°. As we fell into the water still pulling at the lines, so the *Fresser* completed her 180° turn and landed with a splash the right way up. We quickly got back on board. I looked around for equipment to salvage but all I could see was a porridge of floating brash; the detritus from the big wave.

An ominous sound came across the water as another ice-fall collapsed into the sea.

'We must fix the outboards,' I told Jane, 'and get away from these cliffs.'

Like many Canadians who have lived and worked with the Inuit, I was no slouch at tinkering with two-stroke snowmobile engines in winter and riverboat outboards in summer. The *Fresser*'s sixty-horsepower engines had taken water into their carburettors and cut when inverted, but the system, including the five-gallon feeder fuel can, was lashed in place so repairs were simple using the spanner and screwdriver in the toolbag attached to the transom clamp. Once I'd drained all the water through the carburettors' drain-holes, and removed the spark plugs, I cleared the cylinder bores by operating the ignition switch. After replacing the drain plugs and spark plugs, a few pumps on the squeeze-primer bulb completed the work. After some initial coughing, both engines were purring smoothly and the *Fresser*, lightly laden now that her cargo was gone, sped back along the shore lead and away from Prospect Point.

Once clear of the cliffs, I took stock of our immediate risk from the cold. The sea water that had invaded the loose neck-seal of Jane's ill-fitting Bayley suit should be warming to her body temperature, and I gauged she would be better off keeping the suit on, than removing it to empty it out.

I looked about the boat but there was nothing at all we could use for warmth or shelter. Everything was gone except for the fuel cans, oars and boat hooks, all in their specific lashings, and the waist-bag and gun which I had taken from the Germans.

I shook the water from my hair and pulled the tight-fitting hood of the Bayley suit over my head for I had lost my fur-lined polar cap in the sea.

Then I opened the waist-bag. The GPS and compass were there but the chart was missing. Krentz must have had it in his hand when the boat overturned. I closed my eyes and desperately tried to recall the vital numbers; the grid co-ordinates of Dorian Bay. They returned to me at once along with the figures for Prospect Point, and I silently thanked Dean for his wisdom in memorising them.

'Jane!' I called to her twice before she responded. She had curled up in a foetal position on the *Fresser*'s floor. Out of the wind, I hoped, she should avoid hypothermia.

'This is what we're going to do. We must reach shelter quickly while our bodies are still able to pump out heat. Without food or warm drinks, our time is limited. The air is probably only a couple of degrees below freezing, but visibility is getting a lot better which means a cold front is on its way. The chances of our breaking through the ice to the hut at Prospect Bay aren't good, but that's where Dean must be.'

Jane was sitting up now, her eyes wide. 'What are you saying? *Of course* we can get to the Prospect Hut. We *must*. You can't even think of going back to the *Lorelei* without Dean.'

'But he—'

'Don't give me "but" anything. We're going to the hut right now. You must be mad to think I would desert my husband!'

I could see that common sense would not prevail and turned the *Fresser* back towards Prospect Point Bay once more.

After two futile and fairly lethal hours in volatile ice conditions, Jane at last realised that I was right. Only then did I gently explain the advantages of heading back for Dorian Bay 80 miles to our west, saying that it would be far more practical than rendering the *Fresser* and ourselves useless in further attempts at the inaccessible one or two miles stretching between us and the Prospect Hut.

'Jane, Dean will be all right,' I assured her. 'Once he gets to the hut by island hopping on the jammed ice, he will have shelter, food and warmth for *months*. But we don't know when the next boat will call here, so we must be sure of rescuing him. If we leave the *Fresser* out here and try to reach Dean by foot, we too risk being marooned with him. The *only* way we can save him, and ourselves, is to get back to the *Lorelei* and the radio as soon as we can, and while we are still strong enough. That means right now. Do you agree?'

'I don't know what to think.' Jane covered her face with her hands. 'But I can see the sense of what you're saying, so yes, I agree. I hate it but it seems like it will be the best option in the long run.' She let her hands drop and gave me a weak, brave smile. 'Okay, let's go.'

'This really is the right thing to do, Jane. You won't regret it and nor will Dean. By ourselves we will never be able to drag the *Fresser* over the floes. In another day the ice could be loose enough, but in our state, we don't have time to hang around. We must be sure of finding shelter quickly and the only safe hut I know we can reach is the British base, next door to Dorian Bay, but out of sight of Bendl's hut and the *Lorelei*. That's got to be our immediate goal.

'Using the GPS and compass, we can easily locate the base as we know its position. Assuming the coastal waters we followed to get here are still clear, we should be back there in a day or so. You may feel miserable but our situation isn't lethal yet. We just need luck, and we must stay level-headed. If you start to shiver, do some exercises.'

'You're a good man, Derek, and you did great back there. I'll be okay. Don't worry about me.'

'And don't you worry about Dean. He won't starve while we're away. And now we're armed. We'll get back to the *Lorelei* and call up help on the radio.'

The journey back was much easier, ice-wise, than the outward voyage had been. The boat was lighter without cargo, and I just kept her going roughly northwest whenever the way ahead was free. If ice obstacles appeared, I detoured around or meandered through them. The main improvement was the visibility. The snow and the low clouds dispersed, and navigation became a great deal easier especially when, after some ten hours of travel, I could make out the general lie of the coastline ahead. This gave me a good sense of general direction and less need to constantly check the GPS and the compass.

Successive stretches of open water brought me ever closer to the coastal cliffs and, for 20 miles or so, innumerable shoals and islets had me dodging more and more to the east until the cliffs were less than a mile to our starboard.

At length, we came to a reach of fast-running water, mostly clear of all but brash ice, with towering cliffs on both sides.

'I recognise this place,' Jane said. 'It looks different now with no fog, but I feel we are very close to Wiencke Island and the *Lorelei*.' Her teeth were chattering and she shivered convulsively.

'How are you feeling?' I asked her.

Focused on navigation, I had not been paying attention to Jane's well-being. We had gone without food or water for some 24 hours. My entire thoughts and energy had been devoted to reaching Wiencke Island, and the British base there, in minimal time. We had been incredibly lucky both with the ice and the weather this far, and the GPS showed that Dorian Bay's position was a mere 20 miles north-west of us. The sky was five-eighths clear of cloud and the temperature had probably dropped as a result.

As the spectacular canyon dropped away behind the *Fresser*, the view ahead widened and Jane sat up suddenly. 'That's it,' she cried. 'That's our island. I recognise the mountains.'

Some ten miles in front of us, a majestic range of rocky snow-capped mountains rose sheer and dark. I failed to recognise the feature but, in terms of distance, they should indeed belong to our target island.

'I really need to stop,' Jane sounded desperate. 'My stomach.'

'I'll go for the next possible landing,' I promised her.

As the tension of the journey lessened with the

realisation that, all things being equal, we would soon be warm and dry in the deserted British base, I began to feel my own exhaustion. I was cold and clammy, but mostly thirsty.

'There's a long, low island over there,' Jane pointed. 'I really can't wait much longer.'

Keeping off to the port for a mile or so, I slowed the *Fresser* down and nosed through brash ice to a rocky beach. Jane, stiff and sore, limped onto the rocks and clambered up them. I waded thigh deep to a single jagged rock and made the *Fresser*'s bowline fast.

Only three or four miles away the sheer cliffs of what must be Wiencke Island reared skywards. All at once I felt utterly spent. The thought of grabbing just an hour's sleep was overpowering. And why not? Things had turned out remarkably well and, with the gun and surprise on our side, I saw no reason why we should not easily deal with the remaining two Nazis. I could already envisage Seidler with his hands in the air . . . If he wanted mercy he should have thought of that back in 1939 and again in 1945 . . . I was starting to daydream, nodding off right there, up to the waist of my Bayley suit in sea water with the swell sometimes rising to my chest.

I shook my head violently and tied the stern rope to a second rock standing proud of the water some 12 feet from the shore. The *Fresser* rose and fell gently, her bows a few feet from the rocks. I hoisted the hinged outboards and locked them with their shafts clear of the sea. I shouted to warn Jane that I was coming but, just over the lip of the beach rocks, I found her curled up in a nook with the sun's rays on her face and fast asleep.

I collected a handful of snow and woke her.

'Here, Jane, you must drink a little before you sleep. It may not make you warm but you will slowly re-hydrate, which will make you feel less awful when you wake.'

'What a comforting thought.' She sucked at the ball of snow.

'I'm going to wedge myself in beside you for warmth as soon as I've slopped out my suit, so don't think I'm trying to get fresh.'

'That,' she murmured, 'would be difficult in a Bayley suit.' She fell asleep as she spoke and 10 minutes later, after a jog on the spot to regain some body heat having emptied the sea water from my suit, I joined her.

I woke with a start. A glance at my watch told me we had slept for six hours. The sun had gone behind a wide bank of cumulus and I felt dizzy, dry-mouthed and disorientated. A dull thudding sound kept recurring, perhaps the reason for my waking. I lay there, half asleep, and slowly realised that my arm was clasped across Jane's back, and that her face was against my chest.

The thudding noise continued. The boat! I sat bolt upright and crawled to the nearby rock-edge. The sea, ten or twelve feet below was at least six feet higher than when we had arrived. The seaward rope had lifted off its rock and the *Fresser*, fastened only by her bow, was swinging to and fro, her propellers battering against rocks every few moments in response to the rhythm of the swell.

I slid down the rocks into the sea shouting for Jane and re-fastened the stern-line. I switched the ignition on, but to my dismay, the hydraulic ram motor refused to trim the propeller shafts back down into the water. Something was jammed.

For half an hour, with Jane holding the boat as steady as possible, I tried to unlock the outboards and drop their shafts into the water, but nothing I did would work. The engine mounting brackets were bent and I had no heavy tools, let alone a crowbar or sledge hammer with which to re-align them. I tried to use the boat-hook but it snapped and eventually I gave up.

'Do you mean we're stuck here?' Jane's voice was faint.

'I mean there's no way I can bend these clamp-plates or any part of this damn contraption into line so the outboards are useless to us. The only way we can reach Wiencke now will be to row. The wind is from the southwest, but we've no sail. The southern point of Wiencke is probably only three or four miles away. You can see it from here.'

'So if we make it over there, then what?'

'We'll have to see when we get there, but the GPS distance from here to Dorian Bay is only nine miles and the British base is probably less than eight. Rowing will keep us warm.'

'What about the ice and the current?'

'Think back . . . As I recall there was very little ice about when we first left the *Lorelei*. The current seems to be southerly all round here but if we keep close to the coast we should manage.'

'Last time we kept in close, look what happened.'

'It brought us luck.'

'Don't let anyone ever tell you you're a pessimist.' Jane's humour was still intact, despite her extreme anxiety about Dean.

Together we managed to heave the heavy outboards, minus their plastic hoods, off the *Fresser*'s transom, but in lugging them up the rocks, Jane twice lost her grip and we were forced to leave one in the water. We hauled the six remaining jerry cans and the feeder fuel can up to the nook where we had slept, then launched the *Fresser* in her new capacity as a rowing boat. She was completely awash, however, so I blocked off the bilge outlets at the base of the transom and, using the plastic hoods of the abandoned outboards, Jane and I bailed out most of the water.

There was no sign of the rowlocks for the oars so we detached two of the re-righting lines to provide rope alternatives. These worked fine and, seated side by side, we propelled the *Fresser* forward at near walking pace.

One or two floating barrages of ice blocked our direct route to the southern tip of Wiencke Island and we both cursed the resulting detours – so easy with outboards but enormous extra effort with only our manpower. What strength we still possessed needed to be carefully shepherded.

The prevailing wind helped our progress, but the current hindered it. The result was a speed of about one nautical mile per hour towards our immediate goal.

Halfway across from our island starting point, Jane screamed suddenly, interrupting my rowing-inspired trance.

'My God! I must be dreaming.'

She was pointing to a black rock, the size of a Jeep, floating by not a hundred yards from the *Fresser*.

'A floating rock,' Jane breathed, 'and I've not had a whiskey in weeks.'

'Don't worry,' I reassured her. 'I can see it too. It must weigh several tons. Back home we call them rock floaters. They come from rock-falls off mountains that land on moving glaciers. They end up in the sea and the submerged icebergs they've bedded into slowly melt away. They can be bigger than houses.'

'Know-all,' Jane said. 'You're as bad as Dean.'

'One thing I do know' – I briefly stopped rowing to point at the cape, now only a mile to our north – 'the current is getting stronger and trying to take us east. We'll have to pull harder, I'm afraid, or we'll be pushed round the wrong side of Wiencke Island.'

'You're joking,' Jane's voice was weak. 'There's no way I can pull harder.'

'Listen. If we don't go up the west side of Wiencke, where the British base, Dorian Bay and the *Lorelei* are, we could be in deep trouble. If we get taken round the east side of the island there may be no landing place and even if there is, we'll have to cross the mountains that run down the ridge of the island in order to reach any of the huts.'

Jane said nothing. The thought of not reaching shelter, warmth and food in the immediate future was appalling. We heaved at the oars as hard as we could, our hands already blistered.

Slowly but surely our strength gave out, and half a mile or less from the tip of the island, with increasing signs of a tide race, rocks and hidden shoals, we knew that we were fighting a losing battle.

Exhausted and frightened, we gave up and yielded to the power of the current sweeping us east into unknown waters.

CHAPTER FIFTEEN

'There is no hope any more.' Jane's shoulders were slumped. She pulled her oar through its rope rowlock and into the boat until its blade jammed. 'What's the point in rowing? The current is too strong for us and there's nowhere to aim for. Just look at it.'

She stared up at the ice cliffs of Wiencke Island's southern coast, the *wrong* coast. No rocky bays, no gulleys nor ramps, just a sheer ice front of uniform hostility plunging 100 feet from crevassed snowfields directly into the sea.

'It will change,' I assured her. 'All these islands have breaks in their defences. You just have to look hard enough.' I consulted the GPS. 'Listen, we're better off in the boat than on the snowfields up there, at least while we're heading in the right direction. We need to keep going east, as we are now, for another five miles in order to reach the same longitudinal line as Dorian Bay.'

'But what happens when we get to that point if we still can't land?'

'As my aunt used to say, "Sufficient unto the day is the evil thereof."'

'Well, I've never seen an island as evil-looking as this one.'

'Jane,' I begged her. 'At least try to think positive. If you let yourself slide into hopelessness, you're done for. We *do* still have a good chance of making it providing we stay alert. In another five miles we must land somehow. Then, we just have to head north, over the ridge of this island and down the other side to the huts. It's less than a six-mile hike.'

'A *hike*!' Jane's voice was shrill. 'You call it a hike. Just look at that cliff and the scarred ice above, all the way up to the bottom of the rock walls. How the hell do you think we're going to hike across that lot?'

'Cool down, you're sounding hysterical. The coast is bound to get better in a while and there must be a pass somewhere through the mountains.'

'Why must there be? That ridge probably goes all the way along the entire spine of the island.'

'Think back to when we were unloading the *Lorelei* at the bay. Behind the huts . . . you could see two distinct mountain ranges with a definite gap between them. That must be a pass. It'll just be a question of finding it from this side of the island. And the snow slopes inland from the huts looked pretty gentle. So, chin up and keep rowing.'

My attempt to cheer Jane up did seem to arrest her plummeting morale and she started to row again if only to keep warm. We lapsed into silence. But for our predicament, we could have been experiencing the journey of a lifetime. The sun was often clear of the drifting cloud banks and the mainland scenery to our south, across the strait to the mainland, was breathtaking. But the absence of any human input or facility, the vast scale of the elements, the rocks and the sea, the ice and the sky, served only to diminish my self-confidence.

The boat bumped against a growler, a waterlogged, semi-submerged remnant of bottle-green ice, jogging me from my depressed thoughts, and I decided to occupy myself with scanning the coast for a suitable landing point.

An hour after we had passed the cape, we paused to rest and the sudden sound of thunder interrupted my appraisal of the coastline. Not more than a stone's throw behind the *Fresser* a water spout rose from the sea, immediately followed by many more closer in to the cliffs.

'Rocks,' said Jane, staring upwards. 'All the way from the ridge-line up there. Can't we get further out?'

'I don't think we ought to,' I told her. 'The currents are much stronger out there and could pull us away from the island altogether. Then we'd really be in trouble.'

'No more trouble than being hit by rocks or icefalls under the cliff here.'

I contemplated dying from the impact of some plunging rock and decided it would be a lot quicker and more preferable to a lingering death adrift in the polar sea.

Without the constant grumble of the *Fresser*'s

outboards, every ocean sound was clearly audible and
often laden with menace. Each time the ocean swell
surged into the wave-worn caverns along the base of
the ice cliffs, the roar of booming surf thundered out
over the water. And as we brushed through floating
islands of loose brash – the shapeless flotsam of once
spectacular ice forms – a sound of distant music
seemed to rise from below. This, Dean had once told
us, was the noise of air bubbles, trapped aeons ago in
mighty glaciers, and now being released as that same
ice melted away into the sea.

My heart leapt with hope as we rounded a blunt
promontory some three miles past the cape. About a
mile ahead, the coastline was clearly indented by several small bays within the curve of a peninsula that
jutted out to sea. Rocks were visible along the rim of
these bays, and the ice above the rocks rose towards
the heights of the island in a far more accessible
manner than anywhere I had seen so far, resembling
more a stepped pyramid than the roof of a
glasshouse.

I pointed this defile out to Jane whose downcast
features immediately brightened.

'Fantastic,' she cried. 'I would kiss you, Derek, but
I know my nose is running and your stubble looks
sharp.'

We agreed to prepare carefully for our landing and
the subsequent climb. The current was minimal now,
probably due to the dead-water zone created by the
peninsula ahead of us.

Jane kept rowing gently with both oars while I
sorted out our pitifully few belongings. We would

need the equivalent of crampons, ice axes and a rope to save us from plunging into crevasses.

I detached all six of the *Fresser*'s re-righting lines and, squatting in the bows, wound one tightly around one of my Bayley-suit boots, wrapping it around several times at different angles to form as good a rope crampon as possible. I then did likewise to the other boot. I had learned many years ago while tobogganing with the Inuit children, that it was easier to climb back uphill for another go, if you gave your *mukluks* a rope tread. When satisfied with both my boots, I doctored Jane's in a similar fashion as she rowed.

The broken shaft of the boat hook was less than three feet long, but its curved prong would serve as a reasonable ice axe. I knotted the two remaining lines into harnesses, fixed them around our waists and slung the gun over my shoulder. All my attempts to untie the bow and stern lines failed.

'Shoot a bullet through the rope,' Jane suggested.

'I only have seven bullets left – about enough for a single burst, I imagine. But don't worry, after we land I'll cut the ropes between two stones.'

We gazed long and hard at our prospective landing point, the chaos of ice in the defile above it, and the shining slopes, heavily scarred by crevasses, which soared upwards to the higher rock walls. I tried to memorise, from below, what looked like the least hazardous ascent route.

'We will have to take an oar each,' I warned Jane, 'lashed to our waist harnesses. I had a friend in Ottawa who solo-climbed Mount McKinley in

Alaska and he held a long bamboo pole, like a tightrope walker's stick, whenever he suspected he was in a crevasse zone. If you drop through a snow bridge, the pole will, in theory, arrest your fall.'

'Did he say it worked?'

'I can't remember.'

'What about the *Fresser*?'

'She'll have to look after herself. She's too heavy for us to haul up the beach rocks and we'll need all her ropes.'

'But,' Jane remonstrated, 'if we anchor her where we land, she'll act as a pointer if anybody comes looking for us.'

'Jane, face the facts. Nobody will ever come looking for us here and once we leave the boat, we *must* cross the ridge and reach the huts in the next day or two. Without food or shelter that will be our limit. It's only five miles to go and every step will take us closer. You've got to keep remembering that, however difficult the climb ahead. Are you ready?'

She nodded and smiled. Despite her pallor, the dark rings under her eyes and the wet strands of hair half hiding her face, I was struck by her simple beauty. I would definitely buy real estate from her.

I checked the strap and the zips on my waist-bag and together we rowed hard for the rocks. We timed the moment of our landing to coincide with the surge of the swell and the *Fresser* cleared several yards of semi-submerged rocks before the sea receded leaving her stranded high and, briefly, dry.

We hobbled over the beach rocks, each with an oar, until beyond the reach of the sea. Finding two suitable stones, I returned to the boat and managed to sever the bow rope. At eight yards long it would serve as a safety rope so I ignored the much shorter stern line and left the *Fresser* to her fate. Sad. She had done us proud.

I joined our two waist harnesses together with the bow rope, checked Jane was ready and began to seek a route through the jumble of ice blocks at the base of the defile.

'Keep the rope fairly taut between us,' I told Jane. 'If you slip, I should be able to use the boat hook to stop us sliding. Have you ever climbed before?'

She shook her head. 'Only up the steps of the Eiffel Tower in France and that nearly killed me.'

As she spoke, I heard a swishing sound as of a large bird plummeting down past my head, then the slapping impact of rock on water. It struck me that many of the slabs of ice and rock we were climbing over had at some point landed in the defile from the high cliffs above. An uncomfortable thought. But the crampons were working well and Jane was coping with the climb.

We climbed for three hours, often in shadow and always at a snail's pace, but the angle of ascent was never impossible, and the jumbled nature of the fallen ice fragments made the going easier as few of the obstacles were large enough to form sheer, blocking walls with no way round.

Sometimes the oars dangling from our waist-belt loops were a nuisance, but mostly they helped, on occasions even providing a key foot- or hand-hold as we could jam the downhill ends into nooks for purchase.

Luck stayed with us despite the intermittent bombardment from above and, periodically, the impressive boom of some major icefall above or below us.

Jane never complained and was clearly proud of her new-found proficiency as an ice-climber.

'Do you know,' she commented breathlessly as we paused atop a teetering column of blue-green blocks, 'we are probably the first humans ever to ascend this mountain. I'm going to call it Mount *Fresser*.'

'It isn't exactly a mountain,' I replied, 'but you could call it a wall . . . Witter Wall.'

At about 1,500 feet above sea level, I reckoned we had progressed over a mile to the north of our landing point. The slope then began to drop away to our right into a re-entrant that was too steep for our rope crampons and boat hook to cope with.

We were now not far below the base of the sheer rock wall and needed to head to the northeast in order to traverse the ice-face which ran below, and parallel with, the wall.

'This looks like the worst bit,' I told Jane. 'How are you feeling?'

'Not good.' She was breathing heavily. 'But I can keep going. I won't let you down.'

I noticed that one of her woollen mitts had worn away at the fingertips, which would be a problem if the temperature were to drop. I prayed that the weather would remain stable, with enough cloud to help the temperature stay steady but not enough to cause a white-out.

Somewhere between what I estimated was 1,500

and 2,000 feet, the traverse line across the ice-face looked less horrific than at any higher or lower altitude, and so I led Jane cautiously towards a hanging glacier which seemed to cascade down from the rock-belt in a series of ice chutes that were green, blue or dark with the shadows of fissures.

For the previous four hours our hearts had been in our mouths over many sagging snow bridges which, in a week or two more of the Antarctic summer sun, would no doubt fall away into the sheer voids that they spanned. We had crawled across these perilous causeways with the utmost caution, spreading our weight with the help of our oars.

By great good fortune, we had reached the hanging glacier without breaking through into a crevasse. If only Lady Luck had stayed with us.

The next three hours were memorable, especially because of the feeling of naked exposure created by the severe drop beneath us and the rockfalls from above. The scenery in every direction was magical, from the icy fjords below to the far horizon of countless mountain ranges that gleamed in the soft polar twilight.

We came to a huge, green ice block that we could not traverse. There was no way of skirting beneath it, for there the ice was far too smooth to allow any purchase with our makeshift crampons and rudimentary ice axe. So we agreed to ascend a pile of loose ice blocks that were stacked against the larger block's flank giving access to its top. Once there, hopefully, we could continue our attempt to traverse the rest of the glacial face.

Gingerly, I made my way up the loose block stair-
case, halting each time a rush of ice shale skeetered
down from above and shot into the void. At the top,
weak at the knees, I flung myself onto the lid of the
giant block and crossed myself like some devout wor-
shipper, out of sheer relief and gratitude to the
Creator.

'Okay, Jane,' I called downwards, my voice as low
as possible, after hoisting my dangling oar onto the
block beside me and out of her way. I felt her tug on
the safety line between us, so I hauled in the rope to
keep it taut as she climbed the loose blocks.

Only a few feet from the top and warned by sudden
vibrations in the ice, Jane flattened herself against
the side of the block. Several tons of rock and ice
from the mountain above us poured down from ledge
to ledge, passing just to one side of our hanging glacier. The accompanying shock wave rocked the giant
block on which I was perched.

The stairway of loose blocks collapsed from beneath
Jane leaving her kicking the air. The safety rope
around my waist went taut, and slowly I began to slide
on my backside towards the outer edge of the block.

I cursed myself for not having established a more
solid stance before Jane had begun her climb.
Nothing could stop my inevitable progress towards
the edge. My life did not exactly pass before my eyes,
but I was sure we were both about to plunge to our
deaths.

The oar saved our lives, jamming in a crevice
behind me and, being lashed to my waist harness by
its line, halting my slide to oblivion.

I hissed at Jane to stop her wild, mid-air kicking which was jolting my precarious anchor. Although she was probably only half my weight, it took every last vestige of my strength to haul her up onto the top of the giant block. We lay there for a while staring up at the sky.

'At least,' Jane breathed, 'we know that nothing worse can happen to us now.'

Looking down, I could see we were directly above a coastal inlet and a fairly large offshore island. Still shocked by our brush with death, we picked ourselves up and traversed past this point slowly. The severe gradient began to ease and we were able to descend to somewhat less than 1000 feet above sea level, while still keeping parallel to the mountainous spine of the island.

'Can I get rid of the oar now?' Jane asked. 'I really am exhausted. Every bone in my body aches, especially my shoulder, and having to tote this damn oar about is the last straw.'

I looked around. Fairly gentle snowfields lay ahead to the northeast and the mountain ridge continued, with no visible pass, along the spine of the island. I could see no sign of crevasses.

'I suppose so,' I told her, in no mood to argue. She untied the oar and I continued with both oars dragging from my waist and the broken boat hook in one hand. This slowed me down and Jane, who was getting cold again, detached herself from the safety rope.

'There's no cliff to fall down now,' she explained. 'I'll walk on ahead to keep warm.' I gave her the compass and showed her where to aim for. Slowly the distance between us increased. Twice, as I trudged along with the oars bouncing behind me over ridges of windblown snow, I fell asleep, and came to with a start.

Knowing that I must keep moving, I tried to keep myself awake as I walked, by remembering what Aunt Ruth had told me about the death march. I was ploughing through snow and ice in a warm Bayley suit, but Ruth and my mother had been forced to march for days in freezing weather, sometimes without shoes, and dressed in thin clothing that provided no barrier at all against the cold. It was a miracle that my aunt had survived.

In the end, two men had been responsible for my mother's death and neither had been hanged at Nuremburg. They had escaped retribution and were still enjoying the good life without remorse. But Seidler, at last, was mine. Or soon would be. After I had dealt with him, I would return to Europe to finish the hunt, and perhaps I would also be able to track down those responsible for the murder of my father and grandparents. *An eye for an eye.* My experiences in Rwanda and the killing of the Nazis on the *Fresser* had made me realise what I must now do. My mother's ghost would soon be able to rest in peace.

Aunt Ruth's words rang in my head, mingling with the words and images of my own research into the death marches, fuelling my hatred and temporarily staving off my desire for sleep.

You, Derek, were saved by Bippi. You owe him your life. When Seidler and his deserter patrol caught us in the forest, Bippi, under fire, carried you off into the bushes.

Your mother, Anna, and I were taken by passing SS guards to join a column of several hundred starving, lice-ridden Jewish women being forced to walk away from the advance of the Allied forces. The Americans were approaching fast from the west and the Soviets from the east. Literally hundreds of such inhuman death marches took place involving nearly a million prisoners from the camps during the closing months of the war. Over 600,000 were killed on them.

On our first day on the march, as you know, I was nearly beaten to death by a guard for trying to slake my thirst from a puddle. Strangely enough, I was saved by the timely arrival of an SS lieutenant on a motor bicycle. I later learned from the post-war trial that this officer ordered the march commandant, Alois Dörr, to cease all further killing and beating of prisoners, as Himmler had begun negotiations with the Allies. Also, if the Americans were to get within 10 kilometres of our march, Dörr was to set us free in a forest and not in a village where locals might attack us.

The SS man departed to give the same orders to other death march commanders, leaving Dörr in a panic. Apparently, he summoned all 40 of our guards and gave them a censored version of Himmler's orders leaving it to each guard as to whether he or she should beat or kill us. He said nothing at all about what action should be taken when the Allies caught up with us, thereby leaving open the option of mass shooting of all prisoners.

When the meeting ended, Dörr learned that American troops were only 15 kilometres away, so he decided to cross the Czech border by night. Our guards returned in a hurry to the muddy field where some 600 of us lay shivering. The thud of clubs and the crack of whips marked midnight.

Along one edge of our field, low scrub led to a forest on the Czech frontier. In the confusion caused by Dörr's orders, five of the female guards, far more apprehensive of the Russians than of the Americans, fled into the scrub and 50 of the prisoners under their immediate control followed suit.

The 16-year-old Polish girl, Halina Goldberg, who had been kind to us from the start, introduced Anna and I to three other Polish women who had been through hell together for many months and somehow survived. The eldest was Golda Nucher from Sosnowitz, who was over 50 and tough but kindly. The other two were Paula Feiner from Oberschlesien, a shy 19-year-old, and 23-year-old Lola Lehrer, who was still pretty despite the pallid looks she shared with all the others.

'Where are they taking us?' I asked Paula as I trudged beside her. She limped badly and I saw that she had no shoes other than strips of rags tied with string around her feet.

'Nobody knows,' she answered. 'Not even the guards. Dörr and the Godmother – the head female guard – go ahead on bicycles each day to scout the route and I've never seen even them with a map. We heard one guard tell another that we're headed for a Czech camp in Zwodau but nobody's sure of anything. They're just trying to keep away from the Americans and the Russians. Soon we will either be free or they will shoot us all.'

'When will they give us food and drink?'

'God knows.' Paula's voice sounded devoid of hope. 'Maybe they want us to starve to death. Since we left camp three days ago, we have had nothing to eat and they kill you if you try to eat snow slush or drink from puddles.'

'I know about the puddles,' I told her, and showed her the black bruises on my arm.

'Which guard?' Paula asked.

'Halina says he's Kraschansky.'

'One of the worst,' Paula affirmed. 'But the real killers are Kowalev and Weingärtner. Kowalev's lover is the worst of the women guards – Inge Schimmig, the killer bitch. We call Kowalev, *der Schiesser*, the Shooter. The two of them walk at the back of the last group. When she sees somebody stop she tells the Shooter. He drags them to the roadside and kills them there. *Never* fall back near the rear of the march. That's a rule that has helped keep Golda and me alive so far. And never look them in the eyes.'

Anna and I had agreed never to talk about our background, nor even say that we were sisters, for we feared we would be shot if the guards found out more about us. We did not know whether or not some prisoners would betray their fellows to gain favours, so it seemed better to keep quiet and mix in with the mass of the Jewish women, most of whom were German or Yiddish speakers and came from Poland or Hungary.

I was grateful that our new friends sensed our reluctance to talk about our past and did not press us for details. They knew we were not Poles, but there were Jews from many European countries scattered throughout the columns.

Many of the guards made us march in lines of five, but this was not always possible due to narrow routes and to the movement of German troops in all directions. Wherever possible, Dörr avoided the bigger towns and busier roads. Often I heard the distant sounds of war, not rifle fire but heavy guns and bombing raids.

'Yesterday,' Paula told me, 'Golda, who has diarrhoea like most of us, stopped beside a bush. A Hungarian girl was crouching by a nearby tree. Kowalev the Shooter appeared suddenly and saw the Hungarian squatting, her face screwed up with stomach pain. "*Los*!" he screamed, and pointed his rifle at her, but she could not move. She covered her face with her hands and Kowalev's bullet passed through her hand and entered her cheek. Somehow she survived and started to scream. Golda watched the Shooter smash in the girl's head with his rifle butt till her cheek and jaw were crushed and one eye fell out. Luckily, he did not spot Golda.'

That night, after marching for 25 kilometres, we came to a town called Hoeflas where the guards locked us into a local farmer's barn. For the first time we were given big churns of 'Jews' soup': warm water with cabbage leaves and a few bits of boiled cow's head. There were frantic fights for the bits and much of the soup was spoiled.

When the farmer came to the barn, some of the girls begged him on their knees to let them eat the animal fodder from his store. The feed proved to be rancid and gave many of us cramps in the night. So as not to risk execution by lagging behind, many of the girls suffering from diarrhoea never halted and therefore reeked of their own filth. Anna and I, sleeping among them, were soon soiled and also began to suffer from the lice with which they and their rags were infested. Many girls died every night. Pus oozed from great ulcers on their legs and feet, and also from the infected sores all over their bodies caused by club and whip blows.

The next morning, many lives were prolonged by the kindness of a Czech farmer, who brought us sacks of cooked potatoes while the worst guards were off duty. Three of our guards at that time were older Home Guard men, who never beat or killed any of the girls. They seemed fearful of their brutal, mostly younger colleagues.

That night in the Hoeflas barn, Paula tore the rags off one of her feet to air it overnight. I was horrified at the raw, gangrenous mess, all blackened and noxious so, in the morning, when she found someone had stolen her rags and string, I gave her my own shoes to wear. Paula stared at me with grateful eyes and pressed my hand against her cheek. 'Thank you, God bless you. You have saved my life.'

By the time the guards arrived to clear out the barn, Paula had managed to squeeze her gangrenous foot into my shoe and I helped her limp out to join that column of living dead. My gift was later to cost me my own toes.

At noon we were stopped in the village of Nonnengrün when one of Paula's Polish friends, a small, elfish-looking girl, tried to escape across the village stream. Kraschansky laid his tin mug on the ground, picked up his rifle and aimed with care. Hit in the leg, the girl fell into the stream but carried on crawling. Kraschansky's second shot, two minutes later, struck the girl's shoulder and stopped her progress. She leaned against the far bank looking back at us. In a while, Kraschansky fired again and the girl's body crumpled onto the bank. He picked up his mug. Nobody made any comment and soon the lead group were marshalled to move on. The shooting was watched by Dörr, who had received Himmler's personally relayed command to kill no more prisoners.

The next night was cold and wet; even so, Dörr had us lie down outside in a field. There was neither soup nor water but 50 loaves from a local baker were thrown at us. Six hundred starving human beings were supposed to share them.

I was already more famished than I had ever been in my entire life, and I was desperately thirsty. So was Anna. We marvelled at how our fellow prisoners were alive after months or even years of such deprivation. That night, unsatisfied by the scrap of bread, we copied Paula and Golda who plucked and chewed grass, sucking at the moisture before swallowing the mouthful of slime.

On 17 April, the fifth day of the march, we arrived at Zwodau concentration camp and Dörr became enraged. Apparently, he had thought that Zwodau was the end of the march and that he would be rid of us, but due to a sudden American advance his orders were changed.

Now, he was to leave behind all non-Jewish prisoners and add to the remaining Jews another 200 emaciated wrecks together with 20 non-Jewish German prisoners who were to become our assistant guards. Our new destination was Dachau concentration camp.

According to two unrelated bits of guard gossip obtained while we lingered in Zwodau camp, President F. D. Roosevelt had died and Dachau was in US hands. Of his own accord, Dörr decided to re-route the march to Austria. Rumour had it that Hitler had built an Alpine fortress there, from which he would continue to lead the Third Reich.

Since all SS and German forces' telephone and radio communications had apparently been destroyed, Dörr could not refer to his own commandant for orders. He was on his own with enemy forces closing in from the west and east. A narrow corridor along, and either side of, the Czech–German border was his only hope for moving south towards Austria. He commandeered half a dozen horse-drawn carts for the dying and those incapable of marching. One hundred and eighty Jews were crammed onto the carts and some 500 of us continued the long march south.

Dörr and his girlfriend, the chief female SS guard, Herta Breitmann, known as 'the Godmother', went ahead on a commandeered motorcycle to organise a suitable route. They still had no map of the region.

Our guards muttered morosely for they saw no end to the march. They ate and drank their fill every evening and wore warm uniforms and jackboots, but they knew the Americans were closing in from the west, and to our immediate east – according to retreating soldiers – the hitherto subordinate Czech population was becoming ever more threatening.

The more fearful our guards became, the more unpredictable their behaviour. Put a foot wrong and you were dead.

We reached the town of Lauterbach and Dörr was told by the mayor that a large group of expected army auxilliaries had not arrived so the main civic hall was available for his prisoners. Dörr gave over the hall to his guards instead and billeted us outside on the town's sports field. It was the coldest night of the month. We received no food or drink that night nor the following morning, and Anna and I suffered greatly although not as much as the others, as we still benefited from our remaining body fat: a key layer of insulation long ago vanished from the bodies of our fellow prisoners.

All through that long night the women moaned and wept; 500 of us watched over by only four guards. Twelve girls died of exposure, while the other guards toasted the death of President Roosevelt in the hall.

Soon after our arrival at the sports field, Paula had given us a strip of blanket from one of the sick wagons. 'Its owner died today,' she said. Anna and I crouched together, close to Halina and two other friends of hers, Lilli and Halinka. Golda and Paula huddled beside us. They had long since learned to avoid the powerful temptation of sleeping when wet and cold on those dreadful nights when no shelter was provided. Since most of them had been marching from camp to camp since January in the worst European winter for 20 years, they knew all there was to know about survival.

They talked about their experiences and drew comfort from sharing each other's distress; their conversation fighting off extreme weariness and a slumber from which they might never wake. On average, 10 women were dying every night. There was snow on the ground that April, and day by day we were marching ever higher into the Sudeten mountains. While our companions spoke in low voices, a constant sound of misery and torment came from the hundreds of other prisoners around us; the starved, the wounded, the frostbitten – whose limbs would have to be amputated if they lived – and the nearly dead. The cries, the groans and the tears, echoed the suffering already endured by millions of Jews at the hands of the Germans.

A girl called Gerda Weissmann, who wore tough ski-boots, joined our group. She was Polish like the others. Anna and I listened to her and these other veterans of German cruelty, and felt almost ashamed of having spent much of the war unscathed in the Clinic, although like these women, we too had lost our family.

Most of them had been forced into various ghettos when Poland was first invaded in 1939, and then in 1942 they were deported to labour camps. After a spell in Auschwitz, Lola had been sent to Gross-Rosen concentration camp to dig anti-tank ditches in the frozen ground. The women guards there had kept themselves warm by using their whips and many girls had died in the ditches. Lola and 900 other prisoners were then marched for eight days to another camp further away from the advancing Allies, called Grünberg. On this fairly short march, 20 girls died of starvation and 130 were shot by the roadside for lagging behind. Only two days after the survivors reached Grünberg, they were moved again with a new group of prisoners due to a sudden Red Army advance. On this second hellish march through winter blizzards, 300 were shot and 400 died. The rest reached Helmbrechts camp near Plauen in a terrible state of health.

Gerda, a strikingly attractive girl, related to us the words of a friend describing her village's destruction. 'Old and young people, even mere children, were all taken to the marketplace. They were ordered to undress and lie naked on the stones, face down. Then the murderers on horseback trampled on the screaming human pavement, crushing and shooting and whipping many to death. The survivors were marched naked to dig their own graves.'

She had other memories of her own too. 'On my first march I saw a girl spot a milk can by a tree. She ran to see if there was any milk in it but an SS man grabbed her by the neck and forced her to her knees. I saw her stare up at him petrified as he took the rifle from his shoulder. She pleaded for mercy and threw her arms up as he fired, maybe in prayer. He kicked her body aside like garbage.

'Everywhere we marched, we left our dead. Some we buried. Others were left in the snow. Hundreds of girls had frozen feet, bloody and full of pus: I saw one girl break off a toe like brittle wood.

'We marched into Dresden at nightfall and big trucks were constantly forcing us off the road. We heard air-raid sirens and then, overhead, there were hundreds of planes. We stood on a bridge over the Elbe and watched from the city outskirts. It was as if the world was ending. Heaven shook. Houses collapsed. People screamed and some jumped into the flames, some into the icy river. Germany was being destroyed and I felt triumphant.

'We marched through Zwickau and Plauen in the snow. When we reached Helmbrechts camp, I was relieved for there were no chimneys, no furnaces. It wasn't a death camp. Just a camp, as we soon learned, where you died.'

Halina then described how one night her march had arrived in a village hall after two days with no food. 'It was like heaven because there were loaves of fresh bread in that hall. We took what we could, but when the guards entered they told us to put it all back. Nobody did, so they said, "*Dezimieren*." Before that I never knew what decimate meant. They took every tenth one of the girls in that hall out to a wood and shot them.

'Before we even made it to Helmbrechts,' Golda added, 'most of us had dysentery and partial frostbite and quite a few would scream all night from noma pains. Starvation had rotted their skin clean away, revealing their gangrenous cheeks and jawbones.'

Paula had also been at Helmbrechts and described the camp to us. 'I was there only six weeks but all of them were hell. In my block we were either Poles or Magyars, but despite all the suffering we had been through together, our two groups still did not fraternise and petty hatreds often flared up, especially in the queues for the soup that we were given every other day.'

'The water in the soup gave a lot of us typhoid and the lice gave us typhus,' Golda interrupted. 'The worst punishments from the guards were for hiding things. On arrival they took all our clothes and any little thing we treasured. My friend was seen burying a photo of her mother behind our block. The guard, Inge Schimmig – the one who beat a Hungarian girl to death this morning by the bridge – made my friend stand naked in the yard for twenty-four hours, and every few hours one of the guards would come out and pour cold water over her. There was a wind, and snow was on the ground. She died too.'

'The female SS guards,' Paula added, 'beat us with rubber hoses if we were caught looking at them or talking as they passed by us outside the block. To intimidate us they would point to a dead girl's head sticking out from the snow or at a rotting body hanging from a tree.'

'They are not *real* SS,' another woman commented. 'If you'd been in Auschwitz you would know the difference. The guards on this march, all of whom were in Helmbrechts with us, are not SS. They're just working-class German women who became camp guards.'

'If Schimmig isn't SS, she certainly should be,' said Golda. 'The worst male guards are the ethnic Germans from Hungary and Romania. They're army sharpshooters who were ordered to transfer to the SS, and include the real killers here. Kowalev has killed over twenty girls this last week, and Kraschansky and Weingärtner are not far behind.

'The Godmother used to lock us into our blocks each evening with one metal bucket between sixty of us. Most of us had dysentery. The resulting stench was terrible and infectious diseases spread quickly. The guards beat and killed five sick women for dirtying the barracks. We slept on filthy straw on the stone floor, and sat there day after day picking lice from each other's hair like monkeys. Head lice are usually black, you know, but in your armpits they are white.'

'There was a Russian prisoner acting as camp doctor at Helmbrechts,' said Paula. 'She escaped but was soon found and beaten senseless by Kowalev, Kraschansky and Schimmig. They still boast to each other about it. They used rubber pipes, and when she lay in the yard they kicked her continuously in the stomach and threw water over her. They left her outside after shaving her hair off and removing her clothes and shoes. If she moved at all, they beat her head and kicked her stomach. She died in the snow the following day. Her frozen blood was still visible four weeks later.'

Anna asked Paula how long it was since they had left Helmbrechts.

'I don't know,' she replied. 'Maybe a week.

Kowalev shot nine of us during the first sixteen kilometres or so of the march. That sort of thing makes
you forget to mark time.'

The women talked on and somehow the night
passed by. In the morning, 12 frozen bodies did not
respond to the guards' whips.

Anna had been deeply traumatised by the loss of
most of our family at home and at the Clinic, and
then there had been the horror in the forest at Rehau.
Now, the fresh cruelties she was witnessing and the
stories she was hearing made her think that you,
Derek, the jewel of her life, must be dead. I had to
work hard to keep her going for, as her will to survive
disintegrated, her body began to weaken under the
stress of the march. For my part, I clung to the hope
that you and Bippi were still alive. It gave me the
courage to carry on.

A few days of cold, near starvation, constant fear
and dehydration can kill a strong man if he lacks the
will to survive, yet a frail girl determined to live can
endure a year of such hell. Anna had lost this fighting
spirit. Her soul had shut down, was already seeking a
better place. I tried desperately to coax her on, for I
loved her dearly and, apart from you, she was my
only family. At night though, I could hear her sobbing and moaning your name. Each morning, she
would be a little weaker.

On the evening of the tenth day of the march, in
the pretty village of Neuwirtshaus, they crammed us
into a barn. Two girls lying beside Anna and I had
been badly whipped that day by Inge Schimmig. Like
most Gestapo whips, the leather was braided with

wire so a single lash could flick away your eyeball or
cut away salami-sized slices of skin, exposing the
bone. Both girls died in agony during the night and,
with difficulty, I unpeeled the bloody, rain-soaked
skirt of the larger girl and laid it over Anna.

Two dozen German prisoners from Zwodau had
been told by Dörr to act as assistant guards over the
Jews. One of these, a woman called Schewa, was
squatting close by. For Anna's sake, I took a risk. 'My
friend,' I told her, 'has given up hope and I fear for
her. Can you tell me when this march will end? How
much further must we go?'

The guards were all outside the barn and Schewa
responded in a low voice. 'There is no telling. It
depends on the enemy. If they catch us up then who
knows what Dörr will decide. Perhaps all the prisoners will just be let free and the guards will run off to
save their skins. Perhaps not.'

'That could be tomorrow?'

'I don't think so.' Schewa looked doubtful. 'We
hear explosions to the west and sometimes to the east,
but not rifle fire. Soon we will cross into Czech lands
again, away from the Americans. Even the guards
have no idea of Dörr's plan. They just follow each
day's orders.'

I decided to try an appeal to Schewa's humanity.
'This girl and I, we are not Jews, we are just German
citizens like you. When our house was bombed in
Plauen, we fled south and they picked us up in error.
Do you think you could ask the guards to let us go? I
must get my friend to somewhere warm with food
and water.'

Schewa touched my hand. 'Every one of us here has problems. I can promise nothing, but if the chance arises, I will tell them that you say you are not Jews.'

Ten more girls died in the barn that night and they were lucky for the following day was a living hell.

Paula marched on one side of me. One of her legs leaked pus as she walked and she coughed blood whenever we stopped. We passed through a small hamlet where the villagers collected in groups to watch us pass by. A Hitler Youth spoke to three children who jeered and threw stones at us. I saw no signs of pity or warmth on the face of any person in any German town throughout our march. I wondered if *they* had ever felt cold or wet, even briefly; if they had ever experienced even for a single day or night the awfulness of prolonged thirst, the pain that followed a beating by clubs or whips, or the utter wretchedness of soaking wet clothing day after day, night after night – the stench of your own and your neighbours' faeces on your clothes and in your hair, untreated sores festering and the lice infestation causing a relentless itch. Surely, if any of these cold-eyed onlookers knew of these things they would have offered, as we dragged ourselves past them, at least a word of human sympathy if not some food or drink.

Throughout the day, the rain poured down and there was no shelter. If Dörr had kept us outside that night, we would all have died. As it was we were put into two barns and the farmers brought us a container of warm liquid. This was wolfed down by the strongest women who elbowed aside the weak. A guard prevented the farmers from bringing us any more sustenance, but in the morning they mixed cattle bran with water in the trough and most of us managed to gulp down a handful of this mixture.

On the twelfth day, the rain stopped and the sun appeared. Many girls were seriously dehydrated. One Hungarian woman near us stopped to drink from a roadside puddle, but the guard Weingärtner saw her and shot her from behind. The front of her skull burst open and parts of her brain spattered the branches of nearby trees.

A long column of German soldiers passed us, heading south to the town of Ronsperg and, shortly afterwards, an American warplane attacked both our columns.

Many of our sick and dying that day were travelling on four open, horse-drawn trailers, lying across planks in their own dirt like sardines. The warplane strafed some of these trailers. In the confusion that followed, a dozen prisoners who were still able to run, escaped into the woods. Others fought to eat the dead and wounded horses; using their bare hands, they tore fat from the horseflesh, pulling out the entrails and cramming them into their mouths. They greedily quenched their thirst with the fresh blood and smuggled chunks of liver down their dresses, or into their rag-shoes. Among the older prisoners like Golda, there were many professional people including university professors, nurses and musicians. They too made the most of this miraculous chance to slake hunger and thirst.

We spent that night in a barn in the town of Wilkenau, and there in a shallow grave, we buried 11 girls killed in the strafing, alongside nine more who died in the night.

Dörr discovered that a passing German army officer had taken two Jewish girls hurt in the air strike to the Wilkenau medical centre for treatment. Furious, he sent guards to drag back both injured girls to our barn.

Some prisoners found a midden where farmworkers had disposed of fodder too rotten to feed their cattle. Ravenous, they threw themselves at it, but the guards Jaritz, Weingärtner, Kowalev and Rastel ran up to the squirming mêlée and ordered the girls to leave at once. Three of them stayed clawing at the midden and two were shot instantly. Rastel shot the third through her knee and watched her crawl into the courtyard of the barn. She lay there bleeding for a while until Rastel, annoyed by her moans, shot her through the head.

On 25 April, we entered the Czech region of Bohemia-Moravia. In the village of Neugramatin, a close friend of Golda begged the Godmother to allow her daughter, Rita Abraham, to travel on the sick wagon as she could no longer walk. Inge Schimmig dragged Rita by her hair to the roadside where Kowalev shot her through the breast. They left her in the bushes.

We limped through the Czech city of Taus and, to my joy, hundreds of Czechs screamed abuse at our guards. In the main street many more, wearing colourful local costume, showered us with sausages,

fresh bread and delicacies. The guards fired their
rifles in the air but it was too late, and most girls managed to eat whole chunks of bread and fatty meat;
the first food in days.

I seized Anna and broke away from the column
into the doorway of a jeering Czech. Two locals
helped us into a backroom, and for one wonderful
moment I thought we were free. But a woman guard,
called Stummer by her colleagues, burst past the
Czechs and clubbed us to the floor with her rubber
hose. The Czechs seized her, but Weingärtner
appeared with his rifle and, holding me by the throat,
spat in my face. 'They say you want to leave us, bitch,
because you are not a Jew. Well, well. That's a new
one. Who do you think you're fooling? I should shoot
you now but I will wait. We don't want to upset these
Czech bastards, do we?'

Stummer struck Anna with her rifle butt and
broke her nose. Blood streamed down her face. The
joy of our momentary escape had vanished from her
face and been replaced by a grey, defeated pallor. We
were forced outside and back into the lines of prisoners.

Dörr, frightened of the Czechs, headed south to
the town of Maxberg which was settled by Germans,
and turning down offers of barns, had us penned for
the night in a fenced-off orchard. There was hoar
frost that night and our sleet-sodden clothes hard-
ened like cardboard. We were given no food or drink
and again Golda, Halina and others of the Polish
group advised us not to give in to sleep or we would
die of exposure. Anna was in great pain from her

broken nose, and I knew she could not survive much longer if these conditions continued.

Lola had kept a piece of raw horse liver which she shared with a starving friend, but many of the girls who had eaten the rich food thrown at us in Taus were violently sick, for their stomachs could only cope with the simplest of food.

Three days later, the march climbed into the high forested mountains south of Olchowitz, still in Czech Bohemia. There were frequent heavy downpours and driving sleet, and the wind cut into the thin bodies of the survivors. There were now eight horse-drawn trailers for the dying and one for the baggage of the guards. Those who died en route lay in the middle of each trailer among those about to die. The girls with frostbite and gangrene sat along the trailer sides, their useless rotting limbs dangling over the edge, while the others stood leaning against each other as best they could. On average, one died every hour.

We toiled up endless gradients and the temperature dropped further. After 20 kilometres, even the well-fed, well-clothed guards began to tire and Dörr stopped the column near Althuetten at almost a thousand kilometres above sea level. By then the march was progressing at only a snail's pace with increasingly frequent halts as more and more girls collapsed in the road. My toes had become gangrenous, so that night Paula obtained shoes for me from a corpse. Anna was blue with cold and bruising had spread across her face from her nose.

At some point in the mountains we crossed again

into German occupied territory close to the village of Plöss. By great good fortune, the barns in Althuetten were well insulated with plenty of hay and this saved many lives, including Anna's, for the time being.

Two days later, the incessant rainstorms abated and the minor roads we followed through the woods started to descend again. Halina, walking in the row just ahead of mine, whispered over her shoulder, 'This place is truly lovely!' Startled, I looked around me and I saw what she meant. The Czech countryside stretched away on all sides, bathed in spring sunlight; the trees in bud and the flowers in bloom. Deer grazed in glades and silver birch clumps were dotted around the streams meandering through the meadows.

Through this wondrous scene, our long procession limped in pain and misery and thirst, while overhead the Allied airforce, undisputed masters of the skies, harried the beaten remnants of the *Übermensch*, the German 'master race'.

What of our guards? Each one of them could easily have fled, rid himself or herself of the incriminating SS flashes and headed back west towards the Americans, thereby avoiding the dreaded clutches of the Red Army. Instead, they continued to follow the commands of this fairly junior officer, Lieutenant Dörr, and, on their own initiative, to beat and shoot their Jewish charges even as they heard the sounds of war closing in on them.

On the eighteenth day of the march, the last day of April, we reached Unterreichstein where the mayor

offered Dörr enough food and shelter for all of us.
Dörr knew that even the strongest of us were at our
limits. Snow had fallen that day. Two thirst-crazed
girls had been shot for scooping snow into their
mouths, and five others had been beaten and kicked
to death in the Otava River valley for lagging behind
or collapsing. Yet Dörr still refused the mayor's offer
of shelter and quartered us in an open meadow outside the Unterreichstein church.

That was the worst night of my life. Several cen-
timetres of snow fell on us and, at dawn, I was
detailed with a group including Jadzia, Paula and
Golda to help bury the 14 girls who had died that
night in a 20-centimetre-deep grave.

Halina whispered to me soon after the roll-call, 'I
heard the guards . . . Hitler is dead . . . Hitler is dead!'

'Are you sure?' I asked her, hardly daring to hope
for confirmation of such great news.

She nodded. 'The guards would not joke about
such a thing. They say a local man from
Unterreichstein heard it on the wireless.'

'The war *must* be over then?'

Halina shrugged, 'We'll see soon enough.'

But it seemed that nothing would change the way
Dörr and his guards behaved. Himmler's direct order
three weeks back had made no difference, and now
neither did Hitler's death. Although their side had
clearly lost, although the march was utterly pointless
and benefited neither Germany nor Dörr, these 36
German men and women, none of whom, I later
learned, were regular SS or Nazi Party members, all
continued to prolong our agony into that last week of

the war. On May Day 1945, our guards were almost the only soldiers left in Europe willing to maim and murder in the name of the Third Reich.

That day Dörr's locally conscripted drivers deserted with their horses, so he commandeered a dozen span of oxen from the nearest village to pull the sick wagons. He chose a winding route that ascended to more than a thousand metres. In the morning a girl on one of the carts caught her gangrenous foot in the spokes of a wagon wheel. Her leg was crushed and her screams of pain were piercing. Kraschansky slung the girl back on the wagon where, in a while, she died.

After 18 kilometres we came to Aussergefild, where Dörr had requisitioned a wooden shed close by the Strunz sawmill. Halina had lost a close friend of hers that day and was unusually silent. The wind whistled through the planks of the shed and through our threadbare clothes. Nineteen girls died in shivering misery that night. The rest of us greeted the new dawn by focusing only on the next few hours. One more lash of Schimmig's whip, one more bruising blow from Stummer's hosepipe, or one more rain shower, could spell the end. We were on the very brink of death and we were not to know that the war would end in three days' time.

I managed to force your mother to leave the shed, to stumble over the frozen corpses and line up for the roll-call in the snow, but only just. As we stood there, Schimmig selected a burial group from our ranks. I was once again chosen for, despite my limp, I was clearly one of the least sick. Dörr stood over us as we dragged the bodies into the pit that we had managed to dig in spite of the cold conditions.

One of the German prisoners acting as a guard, a woman called Gertrud Van Eyle, told Dörr, 'Look, four or five of the corpses are motioning with their mouths and fingers. They are definitely not dead.'

'*Halt die Fresse, du Schlampe!* Shut your gob!' Dörr barked. 'They'll be dead shortly.'

We shovelled earth over the 19 girls, living and dead. Not to have done so would of course have meant *our* immediate execution.

On 2 May a messenger told Dörr that the Americans were a mere eight kilometres away. Himmler's explicit orders had been the release of all prisoners once the Allies came within 10 kilometres of a death march, yet Dörr ordered us to march on towards the Czech border again and 'away from the enemy'.

So Anna and I dragged ourselves 14 kilometres to Fils where 13 more girls died, then on towards the larger town of Wallern on 3 May. Along the way, four girls tried to escape into the forest. Our guards diligently followed their tracks in the snow and executed each of them.

At Wallern, Dörr consulted with Kowalev and the Godmother. He had been told that the US Army would reach Wallern the next day, and was confused. I learned all this much later – at the time, we knew nothing except what we overheard from our guards. Dörr must finally have decided to concentrate on saving his own skin. He would set his surviving prisoners free before the Americans arrived, but not in

Wallern; better to release them away from any inhabited place. Of his original prisoners, 320 were still alive, and he decided to split these into groups. One hundred and seventy of the least lame survivors would be marched on some 15 kilometres to Prachatice in the Czech Protectorate, where he could disperse them out of the way of the Americans. He and his guards could more easily escape from there.

That night in Wallern, we were locked up in a deserted bicycle-chain factory where nine more girls died.

The Godmother roused us later than usual on 4 May, and selected the strongest of us for Dörr's marching group. Now desperately weak, Anna refused to go further so I took her to lie among the sickest women and sat beside her hoping for the best. Perhaps because of the imminent arrival of the Americans, the Godmother was not as observant as usual and failed to notice our absence from the marching group. Halina and her friend Lilli were marched away, but the rest of the Polish girls we had come to know stayed behind with our sick group.

The guards hustled about three dozen of us onto a long, open, military truck and trailer with enough seats for the very lame. Lola, Jadzia, Paula, Golda and another girl Marget were crammed together standing up. Ruth Schultz, the pregnant girlfriend of Weingärtner and other female guards watched over us with pistols from the front of the truck. Dörr might release us the next day but until that moment these German women would ensure we died rather than escaped.

Some six kilometres northeast of Wallern, our truck stopped to allow a German forces' convoy to pass. I could hear the thunder of artillery and air raids behind us, so close that the ground shook. Then we moved on and soon overtook the ragged column of women on foot.

A few hundred metres further down the road, I heard the scream of a diving fighter plane. Looking up, I saw the stabbing flames of the aircraft's machine-guns and heard the cries of the girls beside me. Our truck slewed to a halt as explosive bullets slammed into our trailer. Anna and I hugged each other close.

Charlotte Stummer, the guard who had broken Anna's nose, screamed as a bullet sliced through her hand ripping off her fingers. The Godmother collapsed with parts of her feet blown away and Weingärtner's girlfriend spat blood as she died.

The following day, the war ended in all Bohemia, but for your mother, the worst was still to come.

By some amazing fluke, not a single prisoner on our truck was even slightly injured in the air attack. A few prisoners escaped during the confusion that ensued but most were too lame and too close to death to run anywhere.

Dörr sent the wounded guards back to Wallern and had the damaged truck's passengers locked up in a nearby barn, leaving the guards Kowalev, Kraschansky and Weingärtner to bring us on to Prachatice the next day.

'What will happen to us now?' I asked Paula. 'Surely they will set us free for the Americans must be just up the road?'

'Don't count on it,' she replied. 'I heard Kowalev tell Kraschansky we are witnesses. That is a bad word for him to be using.'

'And Weingärtner is sick with rage,' Golda added. 'His dolly-girl Ruth who was carrying his baby was killed on the truck.'

'I don't trust those three at all,' Jadzia commented. 'We must try to get away if we can.'

'Kowalev told me they planned to take us back to Wallern as soon as they can find some transport,' said Paula. 'I don't think we need to worry. This stable is warm enough and the war may end tomorrow.'

During the night, we heard the guards shouting in anger outside the stable but they left us alone. We found some water but no food. Shortly before dawn, Kowalev arrived, cursing and screaming at us to get out of the barn.

'*Quick!*' he said. 'We have found food for you on the other side of the hill. There is a big farm there.' He pointed across a field at a wooded hill.

There was no reaction from inside the stable. Most of the girls were disabled with frostbite. The room reeked with the stench of gangrene. Then Weingärtner arrived, red-eyed and foul-mouthed. He and Kraschansky used their rifle butts and jackboots to force us outside. Kowalev joined in. Many of the girls could only crawl on their knees.

By a pile of rocks outside the farmer's house, the three guards methodically executed 11 girls, including Paula, who could not stand up.

'Now will you move?' Kowalev addressed the rest of us. He lined us up as if for the normal morning roll-call but found that he had no precise record of our number. He also failed to notice we had hidden one of the most badly crippled girls under planks in the stable. There must still have been about 20 of us left as we forced ourselves across the field towards the woods and the hill.

'There is no food in the wood,' Golda whispered to me. 'They will kill us in there.'

'They may not.' I was pulling poor Anna along by the hand as she could barely walk.

Inside the wood, the youngest of the Polish girls, 14-year-old Ivana, stumbled over a rock. Weingärtner shot her through the mouth.

'She came from Sosnowitz, like me,' Golda was crying. She left my side to go back. I heard another shot ring out. Then another. I saw Jadzia limping by, trying to help a Hungarian girl.

I was terrified, not knowing whether to run away or keep moving up the hill. Anna collapsed and I could not get her up again.

'Anna, dearest,' I pleaded with her. '*Please* keep going. Just to the hilltop. Only another few minutes. Please.'

But there was nothing in her eyes save utter help-lessness. The terrible march and the horrors that preceded it had been too much. A shadow fell over us. I looked up and saw Weingärtner. His face was a mask of hatred. He fired once and Anna died.

At that moment, two girls to the side of us made a break for some rocks and Weingärtner moved away from us to kill them. Marget ran to me and grabbed my shoulders. 'Move on,' she cried. 'You must move on. Your friend would not thank you for dying by her side.'

I looked at the pale, bruised face of my dead sister. We had come so far together but now I had lost her, and perhaps you, too.

The instinct to live was still strong in me, so I left Anna where she lay, finally at peace, and hauled myself up the hill with Marget. By then, I think, there were only a dozen of us left.

I remember hearing single shots. It was as though the guards had come to some agreement. They would let Weingärtner assuage his grief and anger at his girlfriend's death by killing us all.

Marget was next to go with a bullet through her brain. A second later, I tripped up and simultaneously felt a hammer blow in my shoulder. I lay still between some rocks and felt the warmth of my blood seeping over my neck. The sound of sporadic shooting lessened and soon there was silence.

I began to shiver. My face was lying in snow. I raised myself up on one arm and felt myself. A single bullet had entered my upper arm and passed through without striking the bone. I unwound one of the ragshoes from Lola's feet and wrapped it as best I could around the wound.

I went back and found my poor Anna. I closed her eyelids and kissed her.

'The Americans will come, my dear,' I told her, 'and give you a proper burial with all our friends here. I promise I will try to find your Dieter and, if I do, I will bring him up to be free. I must go now, you understand, for the killers may come back this way when all the girls are dead.' I kissed her cheek and said a last goodbye.

I left her there and headed away from the guards, back down to the farm by the road. I intended to return towards Wallern and the American front but, when I reached the farm, the owner came running out with a pistol and screamed at me to go away. So I crossed the road close to where our truck lay half in the ditch and entered the woods on the far side. For two hours, I followed minor paths away from any habitation and then, feeling utterly drained, I approached an old lady tending vegetables by a forest shack.

She smiled at me and took me inside. She never spoke to me and only shook her head when I tried to converse. I stayed two days with her, and managed to wash myself and the flesh wound in my shoulder. But my feet were in agony. I had only one thing in my mind then – to find you. I remembered that Bippi had told us the name of the town, Rehau, that was near to the place where Seidler had stopped us. Maybe some farmer there had rescued you. That was where I must search.

On the third day, I thanked the kind, old woman and limped down a track from her shack to a nearby town called Zbytiny. There, I learned that the war was over. At the mayor's office, pandemonium was raging, and I was told the only trucks going anywhere were those containing timber, so I cadged a lift with a Czech truck driver who was taking logs 30 kilometres south to Freyung.

In Freyung, I visited the police headquarters of

the Military Government set up by the US Fifth Infantry Division. They told me to report to the Displaced Persons (DP) camp, where I saw an over-worked medic in a crowded medical centre. He treated and bound my shoulder and feet as best he could. I was deloused, given clean clothes and told to report for documentation the following day.

That night in the camp, where over 500 other DPs were already housed, I learned that the Allies were setting up similar camps and Military Governments all over the occupied territory. In each area they were publishing lists of all their DPs.

The very next morning I begged another lift. This time I went to the Military Government in Cham. Later, I made several unsuccessful sorties into Hof, not far from Plauen and Rehau to look for you. While I was in Cham, I visited the temporary medical centre where a surgeon cut off my gangrenous toes and told me I was lucky to keep my feet. For a while I used crutches, but soon retrieved my balance and was given a job in a US canteen where, three weeks later, I met Pete. I did not fall in love with him straightaway, but he was generous, kind and loving. He agreed to help me try to trace you but, as a US Army staff driver, his spare time was limited.

In mid-July, Pete located you at a DP camp near Chemnitz having read the entry *Dieter Jacobs: German: Age five* on the United Nations Relief and Rehabilitation Administration (UNRRA) list of dis-placed persons.

We visited your camp as soon as we could and our reunion was one of the happiest times in my life. You knew me as if we had never been parted but you had no memories of the past, not even of Bippi, whom I also tried to trace but could not find.

Pete and I married in Germany that autumn. Although serving in the US Army, he was a Canadian citizen and when he received his discharge papers in July 1946, we sailed from Hamburg to Halifax in Nova Scotia. My English gradually improved under his patient tuition and, being young, you picked up the language with ease.

My hatred narrowed over the years to focus on your mother's killers, for I knew their names: Karl Seidler, without whose personal venom we would never have joined the death march; and Michael Weingärtner who murdered Anna on the day the war ended.

Snow whipped into my face, and I realised that I had been mumbling the words from Deuteronomy that Aunt Ruth had quoted to me when I had promised her I would track down my mother's murderers: *Take utmost care so that you do not forget the things that you saw with your own eyes. Nor let them fade from your mind so long as you live. And make them known to your children and children's children.*

I became aware that it was now quite some time since Jane and I had parted company. Her orange silhouette was nowhere to be seen.

I shook my head to clear it and shaded my eyes with both hands. I screamed her name and waited for an answer. My call echoed back and forth off the snowfields and the mountain walls but there was no reply. Only silence, riven by the thunder of ice-falls.

Grabbing the oars under one arm and gripped by a rising panic, I followed Jane's faint trail as best I could, for the criss-cross track of her roped soles had not always left their imprint on the harder patches of surface snow. Then, all of a sudden I saw it, a hole no bigger than the outline of two footballs side by side, marked by a thin streak of red at one edge.

I lay on my stomach and peered into the hole, calling her name. To my enormous relief, Jane's voice, weak but audible, rose up at once.

'Thank God,' she called. 'I thought you would never come. I can't hold on much longer. My hands are getting cold.'

'You'll be fine,' I shouted. 'Just hang on. I'll be as quick as I can. I need to get the ropes ready.'

As my eyes grew more accustomed to the dim light within the crevasse, I could just make out Jane's head and shoulders by a tiny jutting ledge. Her falling body must have struck the ledge, partially destroying it, but somehow she had managed to keep a precarious hold on the anchored remnants. Beyond the outline of her upper body, I could see only darkness making it impossible to gauge the depth of the fissure below her.

Desperate, I unknotted the *Fresser*'s bow rope and both the oar lines and tied them together. I cannot remember any worse time in my life than the moment when I realised the ropes were too short by several yards.

'Can you stand up on the ledge, Jane?' I called to her. 'Perhaps you could reach up for the rope end.'

'Use the *other* lines too,' she called back. 'I can't move an inch. I can only hold on for a few more seconds. All my strength has gone. Please, please help me.'

There was nothing I could do, nothing I could say. There were no more lines. I just kept repeating her name.

Her last words came up clearly. 'Tell Dean I loved him. I will always love him.'

A noise like falling gravel sounded briefly. Then nothing.

I called down to her to see if by some miracle she had survived the fall, but my echoing cries were met only with silence.

I had only known Jane for a few weeks and then not very well, but I felt her death more acutely than any since Aunt Ruth's passing. I knelt in the snow, my face on my knees, and heard my own dry sobbing, as though I was somewhere outside my body, floating on the wind.

I began to shiver and grow cold. A violent explosion from above made me stare upwards at the soaring rock walls, and suddenly I saw what hopefully Jane had seen before she died.

Since she and I had first landed on the island and abandoned the *Fresser*, our northern horizon had been, ever and always, the high ridge-line of the island's rocky spine. Now, all at once, that uncrossable barrier had disappeared. Further to the northeast, along our previous line of march, the ridge reappeared as imposing as ever. This gap must be the pass that I had promised Jane, the gateway we had prayed for. Hope surged in my heart and I leapt to my feet.

One foot plunged at once through the snow crust where I had been kneeling. The snow bridge was as feeble below me as it was a couple of feet away, where Jane had fallen through. I saw then that it was her blood that had marked the snow red. She had tried to fight for a hold with her oar-blistered fingers and worn mitts, even during the split second of her unexpected fall.

I must concentrate, I told myself. Jane was gone. I was on my own now. Think ahead.

Crawling on my elbows and knees to spread my weight, I reached the oars and again lashed them both to my waist. The bow rope I looped and coiled over my chest alongside the gun.

I checked the GPS. I was less than four miles from the Dorian Bay huts. I thought of Seidler.

The lie of the snow slopes and a rash of crevasses forced me for a while to a lower altitude, where for the first time since Jane's disappearance, I could move without my legs plunging into unseen holes; my life no longer dependent on the support of the oars.

In under an hour, I reached the floor of the pass and, veering through 90°, I trudged northwest into a corridor between the two mountainous sections of the island's spine, as though creeping through a gaping hole in a row of giant teeth.

In places, I skidded on patches of blue ice, while elsewhere the snow was soft and deep. I regretted not having skis or snowshoes, but at least there was continued good visibility. Less than two hours later, I found myself deep within the canyon of the pass and increasingly having to detour round ice blocks, some part-covered by rounded snowdrifts, others green and fresh as though newly implanted in the pass.

An impressive rock cliff rose skywards immediately above me, soaring some three or four thousand feet to an imposing summit.

I heard a distant crackle, as of a tall tree splitting, and watched as a spume of spray erupted from the skyline ridge above the pass. Many thousands of tons of ice hurtled down the cliff and I turned to run. Behind me one of the oars jammed against an ice block and I fell headlong into the snow. It seemed a shame to have survived this far only to be crushed flat by tons of ice, but I was too tired to move and so lay there awaiting death.

A noise, exactly like a passing express train and an attendant shock wave reached me first. Then came a massive and prolonged roar as the avalanche struck the pass and I was weighed down, buried alive, by a deluge of falling snow.

I tried to lift my head but could not. I tried to breathe but my nose and mouth were blocked with fine snow. Panic gripped me and I thrashed about violently. One arm worked itself free. Then, pushing down with that arm and both knees, I broke out of my burial mound and sucked in great gasps of sweet, life-giving air. By luck, the main impact of the fall had been behind me.

I brushed the snow off and pressed on at once with the gun, one oar and the boat hook. After plodding up a long steep slope and over a snowfield, I reached the apex of the pass, and a whole new world began to appear. First, the peaks of faraway mountains, then lofty snow plateaux, followed by whole islands and finally the shining ocean including, less than two miles ahead, the twin bays of Port Lockroy and Dorian.

Closing my eyes as I sucked at lumps of snow, I focused on trying to recall exactly what I had seen when scanning the mirror image of this same view from the deck of the *Lorelei*. I needed to picture the terrain between the huts and my present position.

The closest hut was the British base at Port Lockroy, but I remembered seeing sheer ice cliffs up to a 100 feet high immediately behind Port Lockroy, whereas behind the Dorian Bay huts a gentle-looking snowfield had led inland. I must therefore take the Dorian option, even though Seidler and Brandt were there.

I could see no sign of the huts nor of the *Lorelei*, but the bay's location was clear enough, as were the shadowed runnels of a wicked-looking crevasse field stretching from the coastal cliffs of Port Lockroy all the way across my front to the base of another mountain. I decided to head for the foot of this last feature which was a mile or so from the Dorian huts, and then find a vantage point from which to observe and approach the Germans. I marvelled at how necessity had forced me to find reserves of energy and drive far beyond my normal capacity.

My planned route worked well and as I crested the last hill behind the huts, I saw, at the far rim of Dorian Bay, the wake of a small boat heading north up the Neumayer Channel.

Surely neither German would risk boating in these waters by himself? The chances were that both men were returning to the *Lorelei* which they had doubtless anchored in some inlet further away from Port Lockroy. With relief, I realised I could go straight to the hut.

Unshouldering the sub-machine-gun, I checked its barrel and found it solidly blocked with snow. I must thaw it out in the hut, and eat and drink to restore my strength.

Twenty minutes later, I was climbing the hut's four wooden steps. A crude penguin-shaped weather-vane was attached to its roof.

I opened the door.

CHAPTER SIXTEEN

A piercing scream sounded from inside the hut as I entered, so I grabbed the barrel of the sub-machine-gun to use it as a weapon. But it was only Thuy, naked and wide-eyed with surprise.

'Oh, *very* good!' she cried. 'Very, very good! You come back. I think you are dead.'

Overjoyed, she hugged me tightly. Then, sensing my embarrassment at her nudity, she went to one of the bunks and slipped into her polar underwear. I saw that her back, buttocks and thighs were a mass of swollen bruises.

'They are gone away,' she explained, 'so I take warm bath. Most days only one is here and the other stay by radio on yacht. But this last two days they both back here to mend ship radio.'

'He has hurt you badly? Your back—?'

She looked down and muttered, 'He very cruel man.' Then she brightened. 'But now all okay for you come back. CIA. Now you kill them, please.'

'Maybe, Thuy.' I sat down thankfully on a bench.

'But first can I use your bath, eat an elephant and drink a gallon of tea?'

'Okay,' Thuy giggled. 'I cook elephant for cook.'

'How long before they get back?'

'Not far away, I think. Maybe back in three, four hours. Maybe only one come back, one stay by yacht radio, like before. Where our friends Jane and Dean?'

'I'm sorry, Thuy, but Jane died in the ice on our way back. She was very brave. Dean is at a place called Prospect Point and he should be okay. As soon as I can I must get to the *Lorelei*'s radio and call for help.'

'Oh dear. Poor Jane. Very nice woman. And Dean . . . He will die very fast by himself. Too cold.'

'No. The place has a hut with food. He should be alright if we can quickly contact somebody with an icebreaker and a helicopter. The Argentinians, the Chileans and the Brits all have huts down here and their ships are due any time now.'

'Why Dean stay there? Why not come back with you and—' She suddenly remembered. 'Where the Nasties now?'

'The Nazis are dead and Dean escaped by himself. When Jane and I tried to reach him, the ice made it impossible. The ice is constantly changing round there.'

'*You* kill them? Karate? CIA teaching?'

'No, Thuy.' I could see no benefit in deceiving her. 'I am not really CIA. I work for myself. A long time ago Bendl, whose real name is Seidler, murdered members of my family . . .'

'Sorry.' Thuy looked sad. 'Very sorry.' She filled a

large saucepan from the outsize British kettle and poured it into the tub she was using as a bath. 'Here. You wash now. I cook.'

Nakedness obviously meant nothing to Thuy, so I climbed out of my Bayley suit after cutting away the rope crampons. Thuy scooped up my sodden polar underwear and other clothes, wrung them out as best she could and hung them on lines by the crude Brit cooker.

'You want I massage?'

She soaped me all over and then dried me off. She was happy again, and I almost forgot about Seidler and Kapitän Brandt.

I wolfed down a plate of baked beans followed by muesli and chocolate bars. After two large mugs of sweet tea, my weariness returned with a vengeance. 'You sleeping.' Thuy was shaking me. I had fallen asleep on the bench and was beginning to sway. 'Bendl come back soon.'

I shook myself awake and checked the gun. The iced snow blocking the barrel had melted. I checked the magazine. Seven bullets.

'Do they carry guns?' I asked Thuy.

'They have rifle. Only one and keep with them.'

'When they are here, where do they put it?'

'Close by them. Not trusting me, I think. Also Bendl very angry. Very angry after radio talking. Later, when radio stop work, he beat me up real bad. Kapitän Brandt say he fix radio so bring it back here. I hear him tell Bendl, maybe circuit-board connection fault.'

'Did he fix it?'

'Maybe, but he not sure because no power here. They take back now to yacht to make check. Bendl want to speak quick with Krentz.'

'Of course he does. He must be wondering what Krentz and company are up to by now.'

'He write in here most days.' Thuy indicated towards an A4-sized notebook.

I opened it. On the inside of the cover Bendl or Brandt had written *Lorelei*, and started a basic diary in German. Folded up in the middle was a copy of the yacht's chart for the immediate coastal region with more detailed soundings than on Krentz's lost chart. I could easily trace the route Jane and I had taken. The island where we had left the *Fresser*'s outboards and fuel was called Wednesday Island, and Witter's Island, a tiny blob on the chart, was officially Salmon Island.

'Boat coming.' Thuy's voice was urgent. I joined her at the door. She had opened it no more than half an inch but the *Lorelei*'s black Zodiac painter was clearly visible across the far cove of Dorian Bay, which was littered with floes of all sizes floating in the wind.

'Quick, Thuy, we must get ready.' I put my wet clothes back on but not the Bayley suit, which I hid under the bed. Thuy dressed and put away all signs of my meal.

'What we do?' she asked.

'Do you know where the *Lorelei* is?'

'No, but not far along coast. Easy to find.'

'So we can do all we need without them. I will make them drop their gun and lie on the floor. You then use those drying lines to bind them. Once we have them secure we can use the Zodiac to reach the *Lorelei* and the radio . . . okay?'

Thuy nodded and glanced around the room to check that there were no signs of my presence. I slipped behind the bunks, switched the control button of the sub-machine-gun to Automatic and waited. We heard the sound of the outboard over the bay. Then voices. The engine cut and boots crunched along the rocky beach towards the hut. They climbed the four wooden steps and kicked the door open. Brandt was carrying the radio and Seidler the Zodiac's 25-horsepower engine.

'I'll go back for the gun and fuel can,' Seidler said. 'Get the girl to prepare coffee.'

I moved from my concealment in the bunk-room into the kitchen, pointing the sub-machine-gun between the two Germans

'Don't move.' I tried to keep my voice and my hands steady. 'Stand exactly where you are.'

They stood stock still, their eyes adjusting to the comparative gloom of the hut and the implications of my presence sinking in. For a moment there was silence. No doubt their minds were racing, weighing up their options.

'So, Mr Jacobs, you are back.' Seidler had found his voice. 'May I ask where is Herr Krentz and the others? I saw no sign of the *Fresser* and I cannot believe even a Canadian would swim here.' As Seidler spoke, Brandt slowly moved to my right.

'They are dead and if you do not keep still, Kapitän Brandt, you will also die. Why have you brought the radio back again?'

Seidler's voice was smooth and reassuring. 'Of course you are wanting to use the radio. So are we all. The Kapitän here very cleverly repaired it but it can only be used with a suitable power unit. Sadly, we have bad news for all of us. The *Lorelei* is not where we anchored her. Somehow, after we last left her two days ago to make the radio repairs, she must have been forced from her anchorage by floating ice. She could be anywhere now, maybe crushed even. We searched as far as our fuel would allow.'

This was devastating news. What about Dean? Perhaps Seidler was lying. I felt the fog of my exhaustion returning.

Seidler's eyes drilled into mine, holding me with his gaze as his reasonable, charming voice purred on. 'Sometime over the next few weeks, no doubt, scientists will return to Port Lockroy and then we can all return to South America. Let us do nothing hasty or regrettable in the meanwhile. We can work this all out to our mutual benefit, I am sure. We have no yacht and no use of a radio but we have ample food and fuel to keep warm. Of course, I know that you have been sent to find out my activities down here. Maybe you will tell me who you work for, indeed have been working for since at least 1975, when we last met? I admit I am most curious. Whoever is paying you . . . I will pay more . . . We can work together.'

Something snapped inside me. I felt the urge to squeeze the trigger. The gun seemed to twitch within my grip as a birch twig might in the hands of a water diviner, but sensing evil not water.

'Your name is Karl Seidler. Hitler Youth, Rehau

Region Frontier Patrol, Stasi, neo-nazi fund-raiser. I
have followed you, searched for you for years, not for
pay but for justice. You murdered my family in
Jösnitz, destroyed our home and then, in the forests,
you abused my mother and sent her to her death with
an SS march to hell . . . Now you know why I have
followed you here. You escaped the Nuremberg noose
as did Eichmann. But his time came, and now so has
yours.'

Seidler shook his head in disbelief.

'Jösnitz. The Jews on the hill. Pretty bitches. How
could I forget . . . She bit me—'

Brandt timed his move to perfection. Seeing that
my focus and the gun was on Seidler, he sprang forward. I swung round and squeezed the trigger but the
bullets struck the radio that he held. The magazine
emptied in a second. Brandt dropped the radio and
went for my throat.

From the corner of my eye, I saw Thuy move as I
struggled with Brandt. The radio had fallen into the
tub of water. Seidler put down the engine and picked
up a saucepan, swinging it at my skull. For a moment,
the blow paralysed me and I let go of Brandt's arm.
But Thuy was behind him, a kitchen knife in her
hand. She plunged the blade deep into Brandt's
throat, then sliced sideways, opening a wide deep
wound. Blood gushed from his jugular. Seidler
slipped from the hut as Brandt lay there dying.

'Quick,' Thuy screamed at me. 'He is gone for
rifle.'

In my stockinged feet, I dashed out of the door
and down the beach. I caught up with Seidler as he

climbed aboard the Zodiac, which was rocking in the shallows, and reached for the rifle. I cannoned into him with the full weight of my body and we fell together into the sea on the far side of the inflatable.

Seidler was strong and as desperate as any man facing death. As we struggled we moved into deeper water. He seized my hair and pulled my head below the water. I struck out for his eyes with an open fist. Then we were apart and among small floes. Simultaneously, we pulled ourselves onto the nearest. He kicked out and his boot caught my cheek. As he closed in on me, a bullet struck him in the thigh.

Looking back, I saw that we were floating out to sea and Thuy, in the Zodiac, had the rifle to her shoulder.

'Jump,' she screamed.

I rolled off the floe and, half-blind from my watering eyes, made it back to Thuy. She helped me haul myself up into the boat and handed me the rifle.

'Kill,' she said. 'He is monster, what he do to me.'

I wiped my eyes. By now, Seidler was over a hundred yards away clutching his wounded leg. All the floes were sailing north from the bay in response to strong winds off the high peaks of Wiencke Island.

I focused the sniper scope onto Seidler's chest. Then his face. I controlled my breathing and began to squeeze the trigger.

This is for my mother, for the family, for Aunt Ruth, I told myself. But, in the final second, I could not do it. Only then could I admit to myself what I had long suspected but never been able to accept; what I had grudgingly worked out as long ago as

1975, when Aunt Ruth had first told me of the terrible events of the torch-lit attack on our home, of my mother's rape and of my own birth in the Clinic nine months later.

Seidler was in all probability my father.

I laid the rifle down and found myself sobbing like a child. My thoughts were too confused then for me to attempt to analyse them, and they remain so now. I had probably sent my father off to a slow lingering death. But then, just perhaps, he was not my father, since my mother's husband, whom I had never met, had lived until the day of the rape. This possibility is my best emotional anchor.

If I felt regret, remorse or anxiety during the moments after the confrontation with Brandt and Seidler, it was not for them, but rather for Jane, and for the missing Dean. Thuy did not ask for any explanation then or later. She helped me back into the hut. For 20 hours I slept dreamlessly, and when I at last awoke, Thuy brought me coffee and, what luxury, buttered toast.

'I watch him,' she said in response to my unspoken question. 'He go out to sea.'

Despite her bruises, she had wrapped Brandt in polythene bags taken from the kitchen cupboard and dragged his body down the steps and onto the rocks, then swabbed down the floor and tidied the hut. Together we fixed the outboard and fuel tank back onto the Zodiac and dropped Brandt overboard among the floes at the mouth of Dorian Bay. For the killer whales.

Back in the hut, I told Thuy that I must honour

the promise I had made to Jane. Now that I could not radio for help, I must do all I could to fetch Dean back from Prospect Point, and the sooner the better. Certainly, I could not count on the arrival of anyone, even the British, in what remained of the Antarctic summer. Thuy did not argue but said firmly, 'I come too. You go – I go.'

'No,' I said firmly. 'It may be dangerous and I will only be away a week at the most.'

'I am strong,' she insisted. 'I big help to you. Also, I not stay here alone with spirit of man I kill.'

I could see she was determined.

We checked up on the stores. There was only the one 25-horsepower engine and six jerry cans of pre-mixed fuel. Enough to reach Prospect Point, but not necessarily to return.

'I left a big outboard and plenty of fuel on an island near here,' I told Thuy. 'We can take Brandt's toolbox and fix it. That will allow us to get to the Prospect hut, collect Dean and come back. I know the way even without a chart. We'll take warm water-proof gear, plenty of food, spare propellers and Seidler's chart.'

We looked carefully at the map. I measured the direct route as 71 nautical miles. Since in open water the boat would easily manage 15 knots, we could in theory reach Prospect Point in five hours, given good visibility. It would depend on the ice conditions.

'The problem,' I explained to Thuy, 'is that sea ice is constantly floating by the coast round here and often gets caught up in bays and round islands. The islands immediately off Prospect Point can cause a sort of icy log-jam which is what stopped the *Fresser* reaching the hut last time. You can get close enough to even see the hut, but the last bit can be lethally jammed one minute then rushing by the next.'

'Okay, okay.' Thuy didn't seem to have a care in the world. 'We go, get him, come back. Then wait for scientists.'

'That's right. But we can't be sure the scientists will come. You must realise that. Dean said that some years they don't put their people in some of these bases. So we may have a long wait.'

'No problem.' Thuy gave her special little giggle. 'I like your cooking.'

Brandt had been wearing wind-proofs when he died, but his Bayley suit, which Thuy retrieved from his bunk, was too big for her. Still, it was better than nothing so long as she stayed *in* the Zodiac.

I will not dwell on our journey to Wednesday Island, where I straightened out the bent 60-horse-power outboard clamp, nor on our voyage in fine weather and good time to the northern limits of Prospect Point Bay. With the detailed chart everything seemed a great deal easier, and along the way there was far less sea ice overall than the previous week.

Unfortunately for us, Prospect Bay itself was still choked up with floes. As we nudged the rim of the ice we saw the entire convergence, suddenly and without warning, respond to some powerful offshore current and rush by in turmoil, as though towards some giant and temporarily unjammed plug-hole. Then, just as suddenly, a further obstruction brought a halt to the moving mass, temporarily suspending it again around the bay and its flanking islands.

Half a mile north of Perch Island, we spotted a narrow lead heading southeast towards the hut already visible on the shoreline. The lead soon petered out, but I was able to hop out onto a low floe and haul the Zodiac, which was much lighter than the *Fresser*, some 40 yards into another lead.

'With luck,' I told Thuy, 'we can make it to the hut this way.'

But luck was in short supply that day, for a movement in the pack caught us between the overhanging edge of a floe and the smooth wall of a six-foot-high berg. Desperate, we both jumped onto the floe with only our kitbags and heaved at the bow line. But the boat was already jammed, like a sawblade in a log and as the pack consolidated with millions of tons of pressure, the little rubber boat disappeared altogether.

'What we do?' Thuy sounded more curious than alarmed.

'We do what I hope Dean did last week. Walk over the pack all the way to the hut.'

Thuy waddled penguin-like in her outsize Bayley suit, holding the excess folds against her waist.

Twice over the next three hours, we were forced to take long detours when confronted by belts of brash ice and once, when the pack broke loose, we found ourselves drawn away from the hut. It was easy to panic at the prospect of floating out to sea but a new blockage saved us, and soon the barrier of Perch Island was close enough to hold the offshore pack more firmly. With more than 300 yards to go we had to wade through pools of ice fragments and Thuy was often up to her neck, but we made the shore with ease. I shouted Dean's name but there was no reply.

The hut, built on a low gravel beach only a few yards from the sea, was uninhabited.

'Where Dean gone?' Thuy asked.

'Perhaps the people who built this hut had another one, or at least a shelter, on one of the smaller isles out there. They were geologists, Dean said, and there's a lot more exposed rock on the islands than here.'

'So you think he out there still?'

'Not on Perch Island. If he got that far, he'd have made it here, as we have. But we've seen how quickly the ice can break away further out. Maybe he saw the danger, spotted a hut on an outer islet and decided to stay there. He had some food with him . . .'

The more I thought about it, the more I feared that Dean had either drowned between the islands or, cut off by unstable ice conditions, had died of exposure on one of them. I kept such thoughts to myself, however. There was little we could do for him unless there was indeed another hut, unmarked on my chart.

We examined the Prospect Point hut. Dean had been right about the stores for there was plenty of food; dried vegetables and canned meats for the most part. We emptied the contents of our kitbags onto the kitchen table.

'Why did you bring that?' I asked Thuy. She had packed Brandt's logbook along with her clothes and the basic survival items we had both taken in case we were marooned somewhere.

'The Kapitän make notes every day in here.' She tapped the book importantly. 'All way from Bermuda. Maybe very useful for us, I think.'

'Not now we're stuck here!' I said.

'I not know this happen.' She shrugged.

We cleaned up the hut and with bits of wood and anything combustible, built a beacon on a high spot along the beach. We agreed to keep a watch every half hour in case a ship or yacht appeared on the horizon. Beyond that, there was little we could do.

Thuy was a delightful companion and a good listener. We had plenty of time to talk. She said my life was interesting, and also, that the spirits of my family would want their story told. I began to write in Kapitän Brandt's logbook in the third week of December. As my writing hours increased, Thuy took over the walks along the beach to check for ships.

Now, on the last day of January, I have recorded as much of my story as I can reasonably recall.

2 February 1994. The fog of the last two days has cleared and the visibility is wonderfully clear. Thuy is excited as she thinks she saw a dark patch, like a hut, along the shoreline of Flounder Island not more than two miles away, and the icepack sometimes looks pretty solid all the way from here to there. It is just possible that Dean could be there. Jane would never forgive me if I gave up on him. He might be there. Too weak to move and running out of food right now. I told Thuy we should give it a go with caution.

There is a chance we will run into problems but that possibility does not disturb me greatly now that my story, my family's story, is set down. Even if we run out of food before somebody rescues us, or if we die out on the ice searching for Dean, somebody is bound to come here sooner or later and find this book.

If this is what happens, I ask that you, the finder, publish what I have written across the world for whatever lessons it may contain, and so that the suffering of my family and so many others will not be forgotten.

EPILOGUE

I found the logbook in January 1995 but, completely ignorant of its contents, I did not start to cut open the solidified pulp of its pages until the spring of the year 2000, and then only out of mild curiosity. The contents began to interest me and I enlisted the help of Paul Cook, the head of the Paper Conservation Section at the National Maritime Museum in Greenwich. He was enormously helpful with advice and supplied the correct technical materials to facilitate the page-separation process.

Fascinating though the story was, I could not be 100 per cent certain that the logbook was not an elaborate hoax, so with the agreement of my publisher, I decided to present it as a work of fiction. I determined nonetheless to check every detail for historical accuracy for I could well remember the fraudulent *Hitler's Diaries*. And furthermore, as an erudite member of staff at my publisher pointed out, the name 'Jacobs' has its roots in the Hebrew word for *deceit*.

Whenever I came across gaps in the narrative, I filled them in by locating and interviewing the people mentioned, if I was able to gain access to them. To this end, I made contact with the civic authorities in Plauen and Ottawa as well as the relevant 1945 Jewish records of displaced persons in Germany. I checked with the harbour authorities in Bermuda, with the British Antarctic Survey and with the Antarctic yachting fraternity as to sightings in 1993/94 of the *Lorelei*, the *Fresser* or any unusual events on the Graham Coast that summer.

I visited Plauen and met with the local German experts on Jewish history. We could not trace anybody Jewish who could remember pre-war events or families in Jösnitz. All 900 Jews in the region had either been killed or, if they had survived and I traced them, they had been too young at the time and were now too old to remember.

As for the displaced persons' records, I soon discovered they were anything but exhaustive. In the immediate aftermath of VE Day, there were more than seven million displaced persons in Germany and Austria and still over one million by late 1945.

As for Ottawan and US Army records, my lack of a surname for Ruth Jacobs' second husband, Pete, meant that I was searching for a needle in a haystack. I also tried to search for evidence of Derek and Veronique's presence in Rwanda, but there were no records of charity staff there for pre-1994.

My Antarctic enquiries initially indicated that the logbook must be false, since it was not normally possible for small boats to reach the Prospect Point coastline in late November or early December, as it claimed. A contact at the British Antarctic Survey suggested I check with the UK expert on the history of Port Lockroy and Prospect Point, one Alan Carroll. He checked the US satellite sea-ice records of the relevant area for the austral summer of 1993/94 and summarised them as follows: 'Sea-ice was less than average for this period . . . If we take the Fish Island region, satellite data shows the same pattern which would justify claims that a small boat reached Prospect Point; something that could definitely not be claimed during many other summers.'

Another ex-British Antarctic Survey scientist, Dr Norman Cobley, made contact with me because he thought he remembered seeing the name *Lorelei*, in the late 1990s, in the Visitors' Book left at the Damoy Point hut for many years. But, when I asked if the date of this entry could be checked, I was told the book had been stolen in 2000.

I was unable to trace Aunt Ruth's brother, Kurt, or her cousin, Alma. The fate of the twin brothers, Tomi and Toni, is also unknown. I checked through the register of twins who had been under the 'care' of Dr Mengele but their names were not listed.

Next, I turned to the death march and quickly discovered, from the Wiener Library in London, that such an event had indeed taken place and records of survivors would be available from Germany, Israel or the US.

I fired off requests in all directions while continuing to try to access more pages of the logbook. When I read of Jacobs' determination to find Weingärtner,

I decided to try to trace the criminals of the death march as well as the survivors. I wrote to the German authorities in Bonn, Ludwigsburg and Hof asking for access to the relevant war criminal files. Over a period of eight months I came up against a blank wall, so I contacted Lord Janner in the British House of Lords, who served as War Crimes Investigator in the British Army of the Rhine. He, in turn, wrote to his old friend, the famous Nazi-hunter, Simon Wiesenthal.

Wiesenthal eventually faxed me in May 2001 saying: 'Regarding information about the SS men Sebastian Kraschansky and Michael Weingärtner, we must tell you that we have no records of these two men. From other sources we have learned that there were only preliminary proceedings taken against them and that these most likely never came to trial.'

If the meticulous files of the world's most successful Nazi-hunter could not locate Weingärtner, I was not surprised that Derek Jacobs and his Secret Hunter colleagues had been equally unsuccessful.

In June 2001, further enquiries I had made to the relevant Austrian authorities were met with an e-mail from the archivist Dr Schwarz saying, 'We are terribly sorry but have no further information than Mr Wiesenthal about the two SS men.'

I received confirmation from the Director of the Office of Special Investigations at the US Department of Justice, Eli Rosenbaum, that the relevant trial records were definitely held in Germany at Hof and Ludwigsburg. The latter's office put all the onus on Hof and eight months after my initial enquiries, I finally received an official response from a Dr Wabnitz telling me that Hof could not help my enquiries in any way.

I fared no better in the United States. The National Archives told me: 'We regret we are unable to locate depositions of prisoners and captured guards and have been unable to locate any reference to the liberation of the Jewish female prisoners at Wallern.'

I made contact with various historians of the US 5th Infantry Division, the unit that liberated the Wallern survivors and came up with no further information even after advertising in their old boys' newsletter, the 'Red Diamond'.

Little, Brown had recently published a book by US historian Daniel Goldhagen which referred to the death march, but my correspondence to his office went unanswered.

Out of the blue, a 22-year-old German, whom I had met the previous year when lecturing to the Frankfurt International School, made contact from Pennsylvania, where he was studying at the Carnegie Mellon University in Pittsburg. In the course of a conversation about his fledgling precision-watch company, which he wanted me to help promote, I mentioned my research problems in Germany. He agreed to help out and, since his family owned Kobold, a large Frankfurt engineering business with a branch in Austria, he had many more means of pursuing the various avenues of investigation than I had. He wanted nothing in return for his help.

Late in the summer of 2001, I finally received a

helpful response from a new contact at the US
National Archives, one Richard Boylan. 'The file we
have on this case,' he wrote, 'runs to about 400 pages.
Weingärtner is listed as being Hungarian and in the
SS. Everything else about him is listed as unknown.
The charge against the group of which he was a part
is, "Murder, torture, starvation and cruel inhuman
treatment."'

My new German friend, Mike Kobold, with a
good deal of persistence, and despite running into as
many brick walls and evasive tactics as I had with the
Ludwigsburg and Hof authorities, eventually
received permission to visit the relevant War
Criminal Records' archives. He was not allowed to
remove documents but he could order copies of anything. He did so from the thousands of available trial
records, then translated those relevant to Ruth
Jacobs' march and faxed them to me in England.

It seemed that none of the Wallern death march
guards had been punished at the time of the post-
war Nuremberg Trials. Like many hundreds of
thousands of other murderers and torturers from
Germany and her Axis allies, Dörr and his colleagues
went unpunished. But then so did many thousands of
the really big killers who murdered hundreds of
thousands of Jews and East Europeans. Others
received soft sentences, like the Nazi, Otto
Bradfisch – to give a random example – who was
judged worthy of 10 years' imprisonment for the
murder of 15,000 Jews.

According to the documents Mike sent me, the
Americans closed their perfunctory Wallern death

march investigations in 1947 without a single conviction.

By 1947, the Allies' policy on post-war Germany was already changing radically. Due to the rapidly developing Cold War and the looming Soviet threat to the West, they lost their will to pursue the Nazi butchers. The new enemy was Marxism. Hitler's evils had to be forgotten, and the post-1947 US foreign policy included joining forces with ex-Nazis, SS men and Gestapo agents against the USSR. In short, a reprieve for the perpetrators of the most evil regime the world has ever known. The Catholic Church also helped many war criminals escape to new lives.

A tiny body of men, like Wiesenthal, Galitzine and Laro in Europe, and two dedicated groups based in Israel, determined to continue the fight for justice and as a result a few hundreds of the worst Nazi butchers were traced to far-flung hiding places and dealt with summarily. In the 1960s, following the Eichmann trial disclosures, Germany was shamed into re-opening trials against war criminals, but only proven murderers. All other crimes, such as mass torture, had passed the closing date specified by the Statute of Limitations.

In July 1969, Alois Dörr was tried in the German town of Hof for the murders he had committed some 25 years before. He was imprisoned for 10 years until 1979, and died of natural causes in 1990.

Dörr's one-time lover and fellow chief guard of Helmbrechts camp, Herta 'the Godmother' Breitmann, had turned state witness against Dörr at his trial, so she was never sentenced. Nor were the other guards, who between them had murdered over 200 Jewish girls on the Wallern march.

Mike's documents mentioned the brief case-histories of just two of the German women guards. Herta Breitmann, the seventh child of a Chemnitz school janitor and 27 years old in 1945, had attended eight grades at a state school, trained as a sales agent at a gentlemen's clothes shop, married and had a son in 1938. She was divorced in 1941, became overseer of forced labour prisoners at Auto-Union or Audi cars in 1942, served as a camp guard from 1943 until the war's end, and then married again in 1949. An average German woman with no particular attachment to the Nazi Party nor with SS training, Breitmann was not dissimilar to her equally murderous colleague on the death march, Inge Schimmig.

Schimmig's file was especially interesting because Mike had traced her on the Internet via a news report in a Berlin newspaper, dated 9 August 1996:

When the Berlin Wall came down, old murder charges against Schimmig were restarted by the State Assembly. She was judged to be 'innocent' last month. I tried to interview this 72-year-old, ex-Stasi agent in her Berlin-Pankow flat. She told me she had never killed anybody.

But Death has now overtaken Justice for Schimmig has died alone in her apartment. Since her case was re-opened, this former camp guard made her flat into her prison. She did not go out, even staying away from her balcony. When journalists came she used filthy language and slammed the door. The only

*photograph that exists of her shows tight lips, cold
eyes and a thin face; an evil woman.*

That seemed to me a fitting epitaph.

Death marches occurred throughout the war and
the sight of columns of starving prisoners being murdered along the roads of Nazi Europe was a common
one. By the beginning of 1945, Hitler knew he was
losing the war and told Himmler that the concentration camp inmates should not live to enjoy liberation.
Twenty-five thousand guards were involved with the
shifting of prisoners from camps likely to be reached
by advancing Russian, British or American armies.
These guards, especially in the last chaotic months of
the war, were individually responsible for how prisoners were treated. The sad truth is that, more often
than not, they showed themselves to be brutal murderers.

The last surge of European death marches took
place between January 1945 and the end of the war
that May. About 700,000 prisoners, 250,000 of them
in the war's last months, were involved in these
marches and between one third and a half of them
were killed en route. Of the 66,000 survivors in
Auschwitz, 15,000 died on evacuation marches. Six
thousand Jewish women were marched from
Königsberg camp on 15 January under the SS lieutenant, Fritz Weber. By the time they reached the
Baltic coast 2,500 had died. On the night of 31
January, the remainder were herded down a slope
towards the sea and machine-gunned. A woman who
survived wrote, 'When I came to, I was lying

wounded on a heap of corpses. The whole bay was awash with bodies sinking slowly into the sea.' Nobody had ordered Fritz Weber to murder his prisoners.

In April 1945, 6000 prisoners were marched from the Hanover area and after a week or so reached the town of Gardelegen, where they were halted for the night. A survivor recorded that: 'Several of our guards spoke to local people and it was agreed we should be killed. A mob of local conscripts, Hitler Youth and police chased us into a great barn. The Germans poured petrol onto the walls and set the barn on fire. There were between five and six thousand of us crammed in there. A few of us escaped into a wood but when the American soldiers arrived the following morning the great mass of heaped bodies was still burning.'

Such evacuations, marches and massacres continued until the last day of the war. One march in Sudetenland *began* on the night of 7 May, less than 24 hours before the Nazi surrender.

The prisoners, in their prolonged misery, were marched through the towns and villages of a Germany already vanquished and in its death throes. Nonetheless, the German people were able to terrorise, torture and murder the hated Jew to the very last moment, and long after Hitler's death. German children delighted in throwing stones and jeering at the piteous, skeletal figures limping by and begging for bread or water. Those prisoners who did manage to escape were more often than not seized by civilians and promptly handed over to the local SS.

Any Jew who came out of hiding too soon was liable to regret it. In Düsseldorf the Home Guard found a 72-year-old Jew, Moritz Sommer, just two days before the city was liberated. They hanged him in the local marketplace.

Reading Derek Jacobs' account of his aunt's story and the trial records from Mike, I found myself wondering why so many of the death march guards stayed with Dörr all the way to Prachatice. Why not simply flee towards the West and the American sector rather than continue towards the reputedly vengeful Soviets?

The answer can only be that the safest option at the time appeared to be that of remaining as herders to at least a few genuine prisoners. The guards knew that any armed person found avoiding service would be hanged as a deserter or at best sent straight to the notorious Eastern Front. Guarding a column of docile Jews was a handy way of avoiding combat.

I am not a Jew, and have no Jewish connections. I have many German friends and used to stay with a German family during winter holidays from school. I find, as a nation, that they are very similar to the English. My father and my only uncle were both killed in the world wars, but I have never held that against the Germans, nor have I ever been interested in the Holocaust.

Derek Jacobs' story has made me ponder several key issues. Could we, the British, or indeed any nation, have behaved as the Germans did? How aware was the German population of the mass murders carried out by their countrymen? What was the motive behind the slaughter? Who should be held guilty, and when, if ever, should they be forgiven?

Of course, there have been other mass atrocities – take those in Cambodia, Rwanda, Turkey, Burundi, China and the Soviet Union, all genocides of the twentieth century – but none involving the systematic murder of millions by tens of thousands of uniformed killers under government orders and over a period of several years. This was only possible in a country with enormous military power, innate discipline and a deep reservoir of hatred.

The Nazi atrocities were carried out by ordinary people living in a modern society just like our own. It is arguable that a good many of the killings were the work of individuals with no special feelings of hatred but well trained to do *anything* they were ordered to do. Thus, the Germans murdered many millions of Soviets, Slavs and gypsies and, indeed, thousands of their own non-Jewish citizens, such as children with physical or mental defects. In doing so, they and Hitler perpetrated an eternal disgrace with which all humanity now has to live. One politician of those times, Winston Churchill, wrote that: 'This persecution . . . is probably the biggest and most horrible crime committed in the whole history of the world and has been done by scientific machinery by normally civilised men in the name of a great State and one of the leading races in Europe.'

Why would Germans wish to kill Jews? After all, their own Jews, most of whom had lived in their midst for centuries, only wanted to be good German citizens, and the Jews of Eastern Europe were, in the main, warmly Germanophile.

Hitler and his Nazi Party were voted for by up to 40 per cent of Germans over a number of elections in the 1930s without hiding their basic anti-Semitic intentions. Over 30 per cent of 80 million German voters either desired a violently anti-Semitic government or ignored this facet of Hitler's promised programme, and concentrated only on his commitments to fight Communism and to restore economic prosperity. Once this government of their choice was in place, and its murderous excesses were slowly but surely revealed to them, they merely acquiesced and allowed the Pandora's box which they had opened to unleash its evil.

Germans went along with the Nazis for many reasons: peer pressure; the habit of obedience no matter what; the ostrich syndrome of putting one's head in the sand, or because of hopes of career advancement. Others were happy to see Jewish competition disappear and to profit as a result. Many were mere fellow travellers and opportunists, or were simply too frightened to be seen to step out of line. Nobody wanted to lose their job, to be visited by the Gestapo or to frighten off friends and neighbours. Even if all these reasons are understandable, they fail to explain why so many Germans never even *tried* to lift a finger to help the Jews. After all, when they did complain about Hitler's assault on the Catholic Church and his euthanasia project, the Nazi government backed down in the face of such popular opposition. So German citizens could have done more to stop the killing of the Jews. They *chose* not to.

Some say they never knew that the killing was going on, yet many certainly observed the death marches and saw the trails of bodies along their local roads. Germans lived around and worked in labour camps and factories. Hundreds of thousands of these German people knew about the killings. Did they never pass on even rumours? How did they explain the stench of the crematoria over their countryside?

Thousands of soldiers who were involved in the countless human massacres of Eastern Europe returned home wounded or on leave, and told their relatives and friends what they had seen and done. There were many thousands of prisoner camps in Germany, Berlin alone hosting over 400 in its immediate region. Thousands of railway trains were loaded with Jews on their suffocating, parched journeys to hell. German citizens worked on the railways and saw what was happening. Crowded streets of voyeurs watched the Jew deportations throughout all Germany. So the excuse, 'I never knew it was happening', is in most cases just that, a lame excuse.

In the war's immediate aftermath, there was too much anguish being suffered by too many people around the world for the purely Jewish tragedy to be fully understood. True, six million Jews had been exterminated but then the war as a whole had killed over 50 million people. And what about all the victims of previous wars? The carnage of the Somme, for instance. Why should that be eclipsed or down-graded by too much focus on the Jews' particular suffering?

Rather than attempt to organise and present my own conclusions on guilt and blame, it is surely more appropriate to quote Mike, who helped me in my year-long struggle to obtain wartime records from the German authorities. He wrote:

It is important that we continue to discuss the Nazis and the Holocaust, and I am sad that so many people treat it as a taboo topic. This only helps those who claim it never happened.

Millions of people were slaughtered like animals by a movement, not of a representative group of German people, but of a few outsiders like Hitler who used the people's fears and frustrations in addition to their traditional anti-Semitism, to conquer and subdue a huge empire.

Who, besides the Nazi leaders, should carry responsibility for the rise of Nazi Germany? I believe the answer is very largely the Allies – for not recognising the Communist threat in pre-war Germany and not helping the pre-Hitler government to deal with that threat. So I am not ashamed of being a German from the perspective of who was responsible for the rise of Nazism. I believe it could have happened to any society under similar conditions.

As for taking on responsibility for individual crimes during that time, I cannot say that I am ashamed of being German either. I used to be, but that was before I actively thought about the topic in

*more detail. I am only responsible for my own actions,
and I never committed any crimes during the Nazi
time because I was not alive then.*

*The question of collective guilt, which has been a
moot point for Germans since the end of the war, can
only be one for Germans who lived during that time.
For all others, a feeling of guilt and responsibility
cannot apply since they did not perform those acts.*

*However, that does not mean that a birth date
after 1945 and the notion of guilt in regards to the
subject of Nazism are mutually exclusive. I strongly
believe that the post-war generations have representatives who are indeed guilty; not of committing crimes
during the Nazi era, but of making the subject of the
Holocaust taboo, of being ignorant about, or denying,
what really happened, and of committing neo-nazi
crimes in the present day.*

*I believe that I have done, and am doing, every-
thing that I can to further the understanding of those
times, the concepts involved, and the condemnation of
the terrible acts committed. As a result, I cannot feel
guilty, responsible, or even ashamed. However, I am
very sorry that it did happen.*

One of the death march survivors we interviewed
in the Czech Republic, Reyna Dindova, lived by herself in a tiny flat in a tower block and had never
received reparations from Germany despite the years
of pledges from Bonn that such compensations had
been agreed. Mike, much impressed by her, founded
a charity back in Frankfurt, the Kobold Foundation,
to help support survivors of the Wallern death

march. (See the website: *www.Kobold-Foundation.org* for details.)

As an indication of current German attitudes to the Holocaust, in May 2001 I was to read a 12-page article in *Stern* – one of Germany's most popular and serious news magazines with a circulation of more than a million copies a week – which described New Labour Britain as inherently racist, adding: 'The Tories also try to attract votes with xenophobic slogans. This appeals to Her Majesty's subjects. In Great Britain, racism and xenophobia are smouldering like the funeral pyres of foot and mouth.'

As for the death march girls mentioned by Ruth Jacobs, I made contact with six survivors now living in America, Israel and Canada.

Gerda Weissmann married Kurt Klein, one of the US officers who liberated the girls left behind in Wallern by Dörr as being too sick to march on to the border of the Czech Protectorate. Gerda sent me details of what happened after Dörr's departure. Twenty more girls died before the arrival of the US 5th Infantry Division and when their medical unit sergeant, Melvin Jackfert, discovered the shack where the Germans had left the girls, he described what he found there: 'A hundred pairs of eyes stared at us out of the darkness and in complete silence. I can still smell that awful stench. Excrement in their hair, eyelashes, everywhere – from diarrhoea. Their feet and legs were black from frostbite and gangrene. Grotesque.'

'When these poor women saw who we were,' a Military Government officer, Major Henry Hooper, remembered, 'they showed their emotion with animal sounds like dogs. A few were past all treatment. All were covered in lice, vermin and deep poisonous ulcers. Many needed limb amputations but some were too frail and weighed less than seventy pounds. I cannot understand how they were still technically alive. I judged their ages to range from fifty to sixty years but later learned that many were still in their teens.'

One of the other survivors, Halina Kleiner (then Halina Goldberg), escaped when Dörr's marching column halted for a rest just short of the Czech Protectorate border. She and her friend Lilli hid in the forest until the guards moved on. The remaining 120 marchers were left in a wood on the far side of the border, where the last of the guards removed their uniforms and fled from the American advance.

Another girl, only 21 years old, whom Major Hooper found at Wallern, was Chana Kotlizki now living in Israel. She told me that Dörr knocked her teeth out when she begged to be allowed to stay in Wallern that day. After the US Army arrived, Chana was treated and was soon able to move around the Wallern hospital where all the survivors were given beds. To her amazement she found two of the most hated female guards, including the Godmother, being treated for bullet wounds alongside their erstwhile victims. Chana identified both women to the US medics, but neither woman was ever sentenced for her crimes.

Chana met a group of liberated Polish Jews in Wallern who told her about a local Sudeten German factory owner who had saved them from the Nazis. His name was Oskar Schindler. Chana spoke to her American friends at the hospital and Schindler was brought under American protection, saving him from being shot by the Soviets.

After Ruth Jacobs' escape, Lola, Jadzia and a third Polish girl called Luba were forced to march on to the top of the hill by Michael Weingärtner, Sebastian Kraschansky and Walter 'the Shooter' Kowalev. By the time they reached the knoll, only a 20-minute walk from the stable where they had spent the previous night, the guards had shot all the other girls. I traced these three survivors in the summer of 2001, and none had an explanation as to why their lives had been spared on that final murderous day of the death march; the last day of the war in that region.

'They took the SS flashes off their uniforms,' Lola told me, 'threw their rifles away and disappeared. In a while we three returned downhill past the bodies and back to the stable. The farmer saw us, rushed out and started to shoot at us. Eventually we found the Americans in Wallern.' The surviving women's families had mostly been shot or gassed and they themselves could not safely return home to Poland, for as they explained: 'The Poles hated us Jews even before the war. Now their reaction was, "How are you still alive? I thought you were all dead." They had taken over our homes and belongings, and many a Jew, trying to reclaim property, was quietly murdered by the new owners. Anti-Semitic gangs roamed Polish cities stoning Jews and beating them to death. So we no longer had homes or families.' Currently,

Lola Lehrer (now Krispow) lives happily in Los Angeles, Jadzia Goldblum (now Kichler) in Toronto and Luba Federman (now Dzialowski) in Tel Aviv. Along with their luck, they were blessed with strong characters and robust beliefs. They refused to give in.

I contacted Mike and we drove together along the exact route of the death march. At the spot where Dörr's truck was strafed by the American warplane, between Wallern and Prachatice, we found the remains of the stable – it had been demolished in the Communist era – and we walked through the wood and up the hill where Weingärtner murdered Anna Jacobs, Paula, Golda and so many others on the last day of the war. We stopped on the knoll and casting my mind back in time, I wondered why the three Germans had decided not to kill the last three girls, any one of whom, if left alive, could have given evidence against them.

The kindly ex-mayor of Wallern and his son showed Mike and I the graveyard where all the girls killed near Wallern had been buried. One of the bodies found in the wood above the stable had not been identified, even though the Americans had obtained lists of all the prisoners from death march guards they had captured. One list was for the girls from Helmbrechts and another for those who joined the march at Zwodau. Only one of the bodies found in the wood was untraceable so she was buried simply as *Neznama*, 'Unknown', in the little graveyard at Wallern. I wondered if this was Anna's resting place.

Mike called me in June 2001 to tell me that he had

discovered that although Kowalev had managed to disappear from the face of the earth, both Weingärtner and Kraschansky had settled in Austria. In spite of the testimony accepted at Dörr's trial and witness statements taken by the American forces in 1945, the two men had never appeared in court.

Mike had also found out that Kraschansky had died in Austria in the 1980s but that Weingärtner still lived there. After a month of clever detective work, he obtained Weingärtner's address, collected me from Munich Airport and drove us to a quiet backstreet in the prosperous Austrian town of Wels. En route, Mike told me, 'We need to be cautious in Wels. I've done some research about the place. Only 60,000 people, but a lot of retired Nazis. There are even some in local government who are known for their neo-nazi views. There is a restaurant in Wels which they favour, and their table is known as the *brauner Stammtisch*, the table of the regular brownshirt fascists. Notorious neo-nazi leaders are often visitors.'

That sunny Sunday afternoon, all the townsfolk of Wels were indoors watching their hero, racing driver Michael Schumacher, winning yet another Grand Prix. We parked outside the well-kept garden of the Weingärtner home and knocked on their door. Frau Weingärtner, a small, well-preserved lady seemingly in her early seventies, greeted us on her veranda. Her married son towelled himself by the swimming pool beside the lawn and Michael Weingärtner stayed inside watching Schumacher.

Mike Kobold introduced us. I had flown from England, he explained, and he from the USA. I was writing a book about a death march and wanted to ask Herr Weingärtner about his memories of those times. The Weingärtners could not talk just then. They said we must come back at 5pm. We did so but the house was empty, so we waited by their pool for an hour until they returned. They seemed surprised at our persistence. Weingärtner refused point blank to answer any questions.

After listening to his protestations that he had never been involved with any death march, Mike mentioned that he had heard that the Weingärtner on the Wallern march had actually released three Jewish girls and was their saviour. 'Yes,' he told Mike, 'I did let them go.'

'Why?' I asked. 'You killed all the others. So why let those three live?'

Weingärtner ignored me. 'I killed nobody,' he repeated. Then he went into the house and slammed the door. His wife said goodbye and we left.

Derek Jacobs, like Simon Wiesenthal, had failed to locate Weingärtner. Thanks entirely to Mike's tenacity, I had eventually run the man to ground, but to what end? Mike described him as evil afterwards but, had I not known of his involvement nearly 60 years earlier with the death march, I would not have noticed anything out of the ordinary about him. Certainly, he showed no signs whatsoever of remorse.

If Derek Jacobs and the Secret Hunters had located Weingärtner, would they have seen to it that justice, so long overdue, was done? If they had been able to find no official authority willing or able to take on the task, would they have taken their own steps to achieve retribution?

For how long should justice be sought? Two years? Twenty? Sixty? For example, there should be no excuse for the planners of the World Trade Center atrocity if they escape justice for sixty years. To my mind there can be no date nor age beyond which a person guilty of murder or mass murder should become immune to justice.

The alternative to exercising justice where it is due, is to allow a culture of impunity with potentially lethal results. In 1992–93 in Rwanda, there were many mini-massacres like the one witnessed by Derek Jacobs. No legal steps were taken to punish those responsible. Indeed, many of the guilty parties were later promoted by the government. The published report of the UN investigation following the mass genocide in Rwanda of 1994 stated: 'If those responsible for the 1992 and 1993 massacres had been punished, I do not think what happened in 1994 would have been possible.'

It is not merely a question of punishing criminals, but of openly purging a nation's conscience. For the psychological health of all people, such crimes must be tackled. Justice must be done and be seen to be done. Sooner or later.

Six months after I found Derek Jacobs' logbook, a few hundred survivors of Auschwitz revisited that place of death to mark the fiftieth anniversary of their liberation. One of them, Eli Wiesel, a Nobel Prize laureate, uttered these words of prayer: 'Please God, do not have mercy on those who created this place. God of forgiveness, do not forgive these murderers.'

That same month, across the world in Bosnia, General Ratko Mladić explained to his Serb officers how best to eliminate some 7,000 adult male Muslims in the town of Srebrenica. After the murders, which took place on football fields and in woods, the bodies were dumped in mass graves. Mladić had nothing to fear thanks to the United Nations' ongoing culture of impunity. He also remembered that during World War II, the Bosnian Muslims had, again with impunity, murdered a great many Bosnian Serbs including the majority of his own immediate family.

As I write in the summer of 2001, the Hutu killers of a decade ago are planning new mass genocides of Tutsis in Zaire. Like Mladić, they believe they need fear no retribution.

Somewhere, sometime, the man named Laro may read this book and remember his friend Derek Jacobs. For the men and women of the Secret Hunters, forgiveness is never an option.

INDEX

UNHOLY TRINITY

Paul Adam

Death, politics and the eternal city.

The murder of the Red Priest seemed like the beginning . . . Rome foreign correspondent, Andy Chapman, investigates the brutal killing of a controversial left-wing priest and discovers evidence which appears to implicate the Vatican in the death. He turns his information over to the investigating magistrate, the beautiful Elena Fiorini, and together they begin a hunt for the killers. Probing deeper, they find themselves up against the might of the Catholic Church and a sinister network of neo-Facist fanatics. Their quest leads them to the very heart of the Vatican and back to the last days of Mussolini's dictatorship, when people changed their identities but not their allegiances.

The murder of the Red Priest was not the beginning. It was merely another link in a conspiracy which powerful, unseen forces will go to unimaginable lengths to conceal . . .

SHADOW CHASERS

Paul Adam

'Tough, worldly . . . highly effective,
undoubtedly authentic'
Literary Review

Four million cigarettes destined for the Italian black market intercepted in the Bay of Naples. A ship's captain taken at gunpoint from a prison van in England and murdered.

Is there a link between the two events? British customs officer, Rob Sullivan, seconded to UCLAF, the EU's elite multi-national fraud investigation unit, is charged with finding out. With his alluring Dutch colleague, Claire Colmar, Sullivan must track down and confront the organised crime cartels which control the international cigarette-smuggling business.

But the smugglers' tentacles reach across every frontier of Europe and they will stop at nothing to preserve their billion-pound racket. And as the two agents follow the bloody trail of the traffickers, their growing closeness also brings pressures that threaten to destroy Sullivan's marriage. Then his family are put at risk and he realises just how high the stakes really are . . .

GIDEON

Russell Andrews

When they asked him to be a ghost writer, he didn't
realise they wanted him dead.

Struggling writer Carl Granville is hired to turn an old
diary, articles and letters – in which all names and locations have been blanked out – into compelling fiction.
But Carl soon realises that the book is more than just a
potential bestseller. It is a revelation of chilling evil and a
decades-long cover-up by someone with far-reaching
power. He begins to wonder how his book will be used,
and just who is the true storyteller.

Then – suddenly, brutally – two people close to Carl are
murdered, his apartment is ransacked, his computer
stolen, and he himself is the chief suspect. With no alibi
and no proof of his shadowy assignment, Carl becomes a
man on the run. He knows too much – but not enough to
save himself . . .

'A fast-moving thriller in the Grisham genre'
Sunday Telegraph

POSTMORTEM

Patricia Cornwell

A serial killer is on the loose in Richmond, Virginia. Three women have died, brutalised and strangled in their own bedrooms. There is no pattern: the killer appears to strike at random – but always on Saturday mornings.

So when Dr Kay Scarpetta, chief medical examiner, is awakened at 2.33 am, she knows the news is bad: there is a fourth victim. And she fears now for those that will follow unless she can dig up new forensic evidence to aid the police.

But not everyone is pleased to see a woman in this powerful job. Someone may even want to ruin her career and reputation . . .

'Terrific first novel, full of suspense, in which even the scientific bits grip'
The Times

CONFLICT OF INTEREST

David Michie

When he was head-hunted he didn't realise
they wanted his life . . .

It's the job offer of a lifetime: £120,000 a year, a top-of-the-range BMW, and the chance to work with charismatic sportswear billionaire Nathan Strauss. But on the very day that Chris Treiger celebrates his new job with Britain's most powerful PR firm, Nathan Strauss stuns the corporate world by falling off the balcony of his ninth-floor hotel suite.

Chris now finds himself reporting to Nathan's brother, Jacob, and his sinister spin doctor – a man whose loyalty borders on the obsessive. Meanwhile, investigating the bizarre death of a leading financial analyst, Chris's former lover Judith Laing discovers he was on the point of revealing damaging evidence about Chris's new bosses. Chris refuses to believe her – until another death occurs . . .

'When it comes to writing about
the world of PR skulduggery, Michie is
an insider trading on his strengths'
The Times

HART'S WAR

John Katzenbach

Life isn't easy when you should have died . . .

Tommy Hart, whose B-25 was shot down over Germany, is burdened with guilt that he is the only surviving member of his crew. He is just another PoW at Stalag Luft 13 waiting for the war to end. But the tedium of the camp comes to a halt with the arrival of a new prisoner, Flight Lieutenant Lincoln Scott, a black pilot who instantly becomes the target of contempt from his fellow prisoners. His most vociferous adversary is Vincent Bedford, a decorated bomber captain, and the hatred between them is as volatile as a primed grenade.

When a prisoner is brutally murdered, all the evidence points to the killer being Scott, and Hart is 'volunteered' to defend him. While Scott steadfastly maintains his innocence, Hart senses that he has been chosen merely to make a show of defending the accused in what is presumed to be an open-and-shut case.

In a trial rife with racial tension and raw conflict, where the lines between ally and enemy blur, there are those with their own secret motives – and a burning passion for a rush to judgement, no matter the cost.

'Katzenbach's best book by far . . . a novel
about honour and heroism'
Philip Caputo

Other bestselling Time Warner Paperback titles available by mail:

☐ Unholy Trinity	Paul Adam	£5.99
☐ Shadow Chasers	Paul Adam	£5.99
☐ Gideon	Russell Andrews	£5.99
☐ Postmortem	Patricia Cornwell	£5.99
☐ Conflict of Interest	David Michie	£5.99
☐ Hart's War	John Katzenbach	£6.99

The prices shown above are correct at time of going to press. However, the publishers reserve the right to increase prices on covers from those previously advertised, without further notice.

timewarner
paperbacks

TIME WARNER PAPERBACKS
PO Box 121, Kettering, Northants NN14 4ZQ
Tel: 01832 737525, Fax: 01832 733076
Email: aspenhouse@FSBDial.co.uk

POST AND PACKING:
Payments can be made as follows: cheque, postal order (payable to Warner Books) or by credit cards. Do not send cash or currency.

All UK Orders	**FREE OF CHARGE**
EC & Overseas	25% of order value

Name (BLOCK LETTERS) . . . .

Address . . . .

. . . .

Post/zip code: . . . .

☐ Please keep me in touch with future Warner publications

☐ I enclose my remittance £ . . . .

☐ I wish to pay by Visa/Access/Mastercard/Eurocard

Card Expiry Date
